D0953731

"INTENSE!"

"This is Adams' most impressive novel to date. The genuine and moving feeling for animals that dominated in *Watership Down* emerges here in intense dramatic form. Adams engenders such compassion, such desperate, urgent sympathy for "the plague dogs," that the reader yearns for a happy ending . . ."

—*Publishers Weekly*

"POWERFUL!"

"Better and more powerful than *Watership Down,* it should solidly establish Adams as one of the major English novelists of our time."

—*Providence Journal*

"GREAT SCENES ABOUND"

"Adams takes us to places where no author has taken us."

—*Washington Post*

Richard Adams

The
PLAGUE DOGS

FAWCETT CREST • NEW YORK

THE PLAGUE DOGS

THIS BOOK CONTAINS THE COMPLETE TEXT OF
THE ORIGINAL HARDCOVER EDITION.

Published by Fawcett Crest Books, a unit of CBS Publications,
the Consumer Publishing Division of CBS Inc., by arrange-
ment with Alfred A. Knopf, Inc.

ISBN: 0-449-23904-7

Alternate Selection of the Literary Guild

Grateful acknowledgment is made to A & C Black Ltd, London, for permission to reprint a condensed extract from
Who's Who.

Printed in the United States of America

10 9 8 7 6 5 4 3 2 1

To Elizabeth,

with whom I first discovered the Lake District

τῆς τε γὰρ ὑπαρχούσης φύσεως μὴ χείροσι γενέσθαι ὑμῖν
μεγάλη ἡ δόξα καὶ ἧς ἂν ἐπ' ἐλάχιστον ἀρετῆς πέρι ἤ
ψόγον ἐν τοῖς ἄρσεσι κλέος ᾖ. —Thucydides, ii. 45, § 2

Striding Edge, Helvellyn

QUEEN: I will try the forces
        Of these thy compounds on such creatures as
        We count not worth the hanging, but none human ...
CORNELIUS: Your Highness
        Shall from this practice but make hard your heart.
                        —Shakespeare, *Cymbeline*

There is in this passage nothing that much requires a note, yet
I cannot forbear to push it forward into observation. The
thought would probably have been more amplified, had our
author lived to be shocked with such experiments as have
been published in later times, by a race of men that have practised tortures without pity, and related them without shame,
and are yet suffered to erect their heads among human beings.
                        —Dr. Johnson

Maps in the text

To My American Readers

In 1715, when the Scotch Jacobites rose against the newly crowned English King George I, the citizens of Newcastle-upon-Tyne, near the English-Scotch border, shut the city's gates against the southward-moving rebels, thus contributing to their defeat. The disgruntled rebels nicknamed them "Geordies" (the North Country pronunciation of "Georgie") and this became the term for any inhabitant of Tyneside, or of Northumberland and Durham generally, as well as for the dialect spoken there.

Of all dialects spoken in the British Isles, Geordie, to a foreign visitor, is the hardest to understand. Listen to Tyneside workingmen talking among themselves and in all probability you'll understand hardly a word. This is largely because, as recently as a thousand years ago, this area of England—the Scottish border—formed part of the Danish Viking realm. Many Geordie words (e.g., hyem, meaning *home*) are Scandinavian, and several are entirely different from their English counterparts. (E.g., *hoy = throw; clarts = mud, dirt; lum = chimney* etc.) It is almost another language.

In this book the "tod" (fox), who is a wanderer, speaks Upper Tyneside, a rural form of Geordie, in contradistinction to the farmers and other inhabitants of Dunnerdale and Coniston in the Lake District (where the story takes place), who speak North Lancashire (an easier dialect to understand). In view of the formidable problems, for Americans, of understanding Geordie, even on the printed page, the tod's speech has been a good deal simplified in this American edition. However, to alter it entirely would have been to take much of the salt out of the tod's talk and character. Several Geordie words have therefore been retained. The following is a list of those not likely to be readily comprehensible to American readers.

Assa!: A common exclamation of emphasis, roughly equivalent to "Oh, boy!" or "I'm here to tell you!"

By: Another common exclamation of emphasis. E.g., "By, I'll tell thee it were cold!" This is simply an oath with the oath left out, e.g., "By (God!)," much as Americans sometimes tone down "goddam" to, e.g., "golddurn."

Canny: A much-used adjective, with many meanings. Clever, courageous (e.g., "canny lad"). Useful, welcome, helpful (e.g., "a canny drop of rain"). Careful (e.g., "Ca' canny"—take care). Numerous (e.g., "a canny few sheep"), etc.

Clagged: Fastened.

Fash: Trouble, upset (verb), e.g., "Dinna fash yersel' " —don't upset yourself.

Femmer: Faint-hearted, lacking in energy, courage, or drive.

Fyeul: Fool.

Haddaway!: Go away! Get away! Equivalent to "Get the hell out of it!" but also used figuratively, as equivalent to "What rubbish!" E.g., "Haddaway, ye fond fyeul!"

Hause: The neck or dip of lower-lying land between two peaks in a range; the "band" (as they sometimes call it) connecting one hilltop and the next.

Hemmel: Shed.

Hinny (also *marrer*): Geordie contains several words meaning *mate* or *friend,* and these are used constantly in colloquial speech. In conversation, a Geordie continually addresses almost anyone (not only personal friends) as "lad," "hinny," or "marrer." E.g., "Why ay, hinny" = "Yes, of course, my friend." "What fettle the day, marrer?" = "How are you today, pal?" Interestingly, one of these many "pal" terms is "butty," which crossed the Atlantic and has become the American "buddy."

Hoo: How.

Howway!: A gentler form of *Haddaway! Haddaway!* is critical, even derisive. It means *"You* go away!" (not me). *Howway,* though it can certainly be used sharply, means no more than "Let's go!" (i.e., you and I). Also a jovial greeting. When President Carter landed at Newcastle-upon-Tyne in May 1977, his first words to the waiting Geordie crowd were "Howway, tha lads!" (i.e., "How are you, lads?"). Naturally, they were delighted.

Hyem: Home.

Lonnin (really *lonning,* but in Geordie ultimate *g*'s are elided): An unmade lane leading from a farm to the nearest road. A lonnin may be anything from a few yards to half a mile long, or more.

Lugs: Ears. (As in "Wind? By, sennuf te blaa yer lugs off!")

Marrer: See *Hinny,* above.

Mazer: One who amazes; a winner, a smasher. A common term of praise and commendation. E.g., "Yon Raquel Welch—by, mind, she's weel-stacked, a reet mazer!"

Neet: Night.

Noo: Now.

Reet: Right.

W' (sometimes *wuh*): We.

Weel: Well.

Whin: Gorse. A large, gold-flowering bush, growing wild and often profusely on waste land. It is covered with very sharp thorns, and a thicket of gorse is virtually impenetrable to humans and to larger animals. A fugitive fox, dog, cat, etc., may well leave traces "clagged to the whin."

Wor: Our.

Yow: Ewe, a female sheep.

Preface

The entry to the Seathwaite coppermine shaft was blocked up some years ago, though the cavern at Brown Haw is still open. Otherwise the topography of the story is, to the best of my knowledge, correct.

The place-names are those in use by local people, and in the few cases where these differ from the names printed on maps, I have preferred local use. Thus the story speaks of "Wreynus," not "Wrynose" Pass, of "Bootterilket" rather than "Brotherilkeld" and of "Low Door" rather than "Lodore." (The poet Southey romanticized the spelling of what is, surely, a local name in plain English.) Similarly, words like *lonnin* and *getherin* are spelt phonetically, since no Lakelander would speak of a "lonning" or of "gathering sheep." The old genitive *it* (see, e.g., *King Lear*, I, IV:216–17) is commonly used throughout the Lakeland, not having been superseded by the modern *its*.

In effect, nearly all the pleasant people in the book are real, while all the unpleasant people are not. For example, Dr. Boycott, Digby Driver, Ann Moss and the Under Secretary are fictitious and bear no resemblance to anyone known to me. But Dennis Williamson, Robert Lindsay, Jack and Mary Longmire, Phyllis and Vera Dawson and several other inhabitants of Seathwaite and the surrounding neighbourhood are as real as Scafell Pike, though fortunately neither Dennis nor Robert has ever had to contend in reality with the activities of Rowf, nor has Phyllis Dawson ever found him in her yard at dawn.

The story is in one respect idealized. Things change. Jack and Mary Longmire are no longer to be found at the Newfield. Tough old Bill Routledge of Long House is dead (a loss to the valley which recalled vividly Milton's lines on Hobson, the university carrier,

'Twas such a shifter, that if truth were known,
Death was half glad when he had got him down).

Gerald Gray has been gone some time now from Broughton, though the "Manor" is still there; and Roy Greenwood has moved on from the parsonage at Ulpha. John
Awdry was, indeed, a brave parachutist, but long ago, in
the Second World War. There never was, in fact, a time
when all these people were to be found doing their thing
simultaneously. I have simply included them in the story
as they are best remembered.

There is no such place in the Lake District as Animal
Research (Scientific and Experimental). In reality, no
single testing or experimental station would cover so wide
a range of work as Animal Research. However, every
"experiment" described is one which has actually been
carried out on animals somewhere. In this connection I
acknowledge in particular my debt to two books: *Victims
of Science* by Richard Ryder, and *Animal Liberation* by
Peter Singer.

With the tod's Upper Tyneside dialect, I received in-
valuable help from Mr. and Mrs. Scott Dobson.

The diagrams were drawn by Mr. A. Wainwright,
already well known for his fine series of pictorial guides
to the Lakeland Fells. I seriously doubt whether an author
can ever have received more generous help and co-operation from an illustrator.

Sir Peter Scott and Ronald Lockley are, of course, very
real indeed. I am most grateful for their good sportsman-
ship in allowing themselves to appear in the story. The
views attributed to them have their entire approval.

Finally, my thanks are due to Mrs. Margaret Apps and
Mrs. Janice Kneale, whose conscientious and painstaking
work in typing the manuscript was of the highest standard.

THE
PLAGUE DOGS

FIT 1

Friday the 15th October

The water in the metal tank slopped sideways and a treacly ripple ran along the edge, reached the corner and died away. Under the electric lights the broken surface was faceted as a cracked mirror, a watery harlequin's coat of tilting planes and lozenges in movement, one moment dull as stone and the next glittering like scalpels. Here and there, where during the past two hours the water had been fouled, gilded streaks of urine and floating, spawn-like bubbles of saliva rocked more turgidly, in a way suggestive—if anyone present had been receptive to such suggestion—of an illusion that this was not water, but perhaps some thicker fluid, such as those concoctions of jam and stale beer which are hung up in glass jars to drown wasps, or the dark puddles splashed through by hooves and gum-boots on the concrete floors of Lakeland cattle sheds.

Mr. Powell, his note-pad ready in hand, leant across the flanged and overhanging edge of the tank, wiped his glasses on his sleeve and looked down the two or three feet to the contents below.

"I think it's packing in, chief," he said. "Oh, no, wait a jiffy." He paused, drew back the cuff of his white coat to avoid another, though weak, splash and then bent over the water once more. "No, I was right first time—it *is* going. D'you want it out now?"

"When it definitely sinks and stops moving," answered Dr. Boycott, without looking up from the papers on the table. Although there was in the room no draught or air movement whatever, he had placed the two graphs and the log sheet on top of one another and was using the heavy stop-watch as a paperweight to ensure that they remained where he intended them to remain. "I thought I'd made it clear the other day," he added, in a level, polite tone, "what the precise moment of removal should be."

"But you don't want it to drown, do you?" asked Mr. Powell, a shade of anxiety creeping into his voice. "If it—"

"No!" interjected Dr. Boycott quickly, as though to check him before he could say more. "It's nothing to do with want," he went on after a moment. "It's not *intended* to drown—not this time anyway; and I think probably not the next time either—depending on results, of course."

There were further sounds of splashing from inside the tank, but faint, like metallic echoes, rather as though a ghost were trying, but failing, to come down and trouble the waters (and indeed, as far as the occupant was concerned, any sort of miracle, being unscientific, was entirely out of the question). Then a choking, bubbling sound was followed by silence, in which the rasping call of a carrion crow came clearly from the fell outside.

Mr. Powell stood up, walked across the concrete floor and took down a shepherd's crook which was hanging on a peg. Sitting down once more on the edge of the tank, he began unthinkingly to tap with the butt of the crook the rhythm of a current popular song.

"Er—please, Stephen," said Dr. Boycott, with a faint smile.

"Oh, sorry."

The large mongrel dog in the tank was continuing to struggle with its front paws, but so feebly now that its body, from neck to rump, hung almost vertically in the water. The spaniel-like ears were outspread, floating on either side of the head like wings, but the eyes were submerged and only the black, delicately lyrated nose broke the surface. As Mr. Powell watched, this too went under, rose again for an instant and then sank. The body, foreshortened by refraction as it descended, seemed to move sideways from its former floating position, finally appearing on the bottom of the tank as an almost flattened mass and disturbing round its sides, as it settled, little clouds of dirty silt. Dr. Boycott clicked the stopwatch. Mr. Powell, looking quickly back to see whether he had noticed the silt (for his chief was particular about the cleanliness of equipment), made a mental note to insist to Tyson, the caretaker and head-keeper, that the tank should be emptied and cleaned tomorrow. Then, allowing for the refraction with the skill of a certain amount of practice, he plunged in the crook, engaged the dog's collar and began to drag it to the surface. After a moment, however, he faltered, dropped the crook and stood up, wincing, while the body subsided once more to the floor of the tank.

"Christ, it's heavy," he said. "Oh, no, chief, I don't mean it's any heavier than usual, of course, only I pulled a muscle in my wrist last night and it's been giving me a spot of gyppo. Never mind, never say die, here goes."

"I'm sorry," said Dr. Boycott. "Let me help you. I wouldn't want you to suffer avoidably."

Together they pulled on the crook, raised the heavy, pelt-sodden body head-first, broke the surface tension with a concerted heave and laid the inert dog on a foam-rubber mattress beside the tank. Here it resembled an enormous, drowned fly—very black, with a compressed shape something like that of a raindrop; and smaller than life, on account of a kind of collapse of the limbs and other excrescences into the central mass of the trunk. Mr. Powell began resuscitation; and after a little the dog vomited water and commenced to gasp, though its eyes remained closed.

"Right, that'll do," said Dr. Boycott briskly. "Now the usual tests, please, Stephen—pulse, blood sample, body temperature, reflexes—the various things we've been working on—and then plot the graphs. I'll be back in about twenty minutes. I'm just going over to the Christiaan

Barnard block to learn what I can about this afternoon's brain surgery work. And please don't smoke while I'm gone," he added, mildly but firmly. "You'll appreciate that that could have an effect on results."

"All right to put its muzzle on, chief?" asked Mr. Powell. "Only this one, seven-three-two, 's been known to be a right sod at times and it might come round enough to start in on me—sudden-like, you know."

"Yes, there's no objection to that," replied Dr. Boycott, picking up the stop-watch.

"And the time, chief?" enquired Mr. Powell in a rather sycophantic tone, as though the time were likely to be something to Dr. Boycott's personal credit.

"Two hours, twenty minutes, fifty-three and two fifths seconds," answered Dr. Boycott. "Without looking at the papers, I think that's about six and a half minutes longer than Wednesday's test and about twelve minutes longer than the test before that. It's rather remarkable how regular the increase apears to be. At this rate the graph will work out as a straight incline, although obviously we must reach a diminution somewhere. There must come a point where the additional endurance induced by the dog's expectation of removal is counterbalanced by the limits of its physical capacity."

He paused for a moment and then said, "Now, there's another thing I'd like you to see to, please. I forgot to mention it this morning, but Cambridge are anxious for us to go ahead at once with the social deprivation experiment. We have a monkey set aside for that, haven't we?"

"Yeah, I'm pretty certain we have," replied Mr. Powell.

"I thought you told me we definitely had?" Dr. Boycott's voice was a shade sharper.

"Yes, that's right," said Mr. Powell hastily. "We have."

"Good. Well, it can go into the cylinder this evening. Now you're sure that that cylinder excludes all light?"

"Yep. No light, restricted movement, adequate ventilation, wire mesh floor, faeces and urine fall through. It's all checked."

"Right, well, start it off, keep it under twice daily observation and, of course, mark the particulars up in a log. The total number of days should be kept up to date day by day, on a slate beside the cylinder. That's a matter of courtesy to the Director. He'll probably want to see it."

"Where's it to be kept, chief?" asked Mr. Powell.

"It doesn't matter, as long as it's somewhere where you can readily keep an eye on it," answered Dr. Boycott. "I suggest, near where you normally work, as long as it's not anywhere near any other animals. There should be silence, as far as possible, and no organic smells, of course. That's part of the deprivation, you understand."

"How about the balance-cupboard in Lab. 4, chief?" asked Mr. Powell. "Plenty of space in there at the moment and quiet as the grave."

"Yes, that'll do," said Dr. Boycott. Don't forget to tell Tyson about feeding, and keep me informed how it goes on. We'll aim at—well, say—er—forty-five days."

"Is that the lot, chief?"

"Yes," said Dr. Boycott, with his hand on the door. "But since it seems necessary to mention it, you'd better see that this tank's cleaned out. There's silt on the bottom which shouldn't be there."

It was only after a considerable administrative and political battle that the site for Animal Research, Surgical and Experimental (A.R.S.E.), had been approved at Lawson Park, a former fell farm on the east side of Coniston Water. As a Departmental project the scheme had, of course, attracted deemed planning permission, but following Circular 100 consultation both the County Council and the Lakeland National Park Planning Board had objected to it so strongly that the responsible Under Secretary at the Department of the Environment (having, no doubt, a vivid mental picture of himself in the chair at any confrontation discussions that might be arranged to try to resolve the matter in Whitehall) had taken very little time to decide that in all the circumstances a public local inquiry would be the most appropriate course. The inquiry had lasted for two weeks and at various times during the proceedings the Inspector (who in his private hours indulged a taste for seventeenth-century English history)

Coniston Old Man

had found himself wishing that, like that Mr. Bradshaw who presided at the so-called trial of King Charles I, he had been provided with a bullet-proof hat. The deputy county clerk had cross-examined the Ministry experts with brilliant penetration on the precise extent of the urgency and need to site yet another Government project in a national park. The Secretary of the Countryside Commission, subpoenaed by the Planning Board, had been virtually compelled to give evidence against the Department into which he was hoping to be promoted to Under Secretary. The Council for the Protection of Rural England had greatly assisted the case in favour of the project by testifying with passionate emotion that nobody ought to be allowed to build anything anywhere any more. A Mr. Finward, a retired merchant naval officer, who occupied a cottage on the fell not far from the site, had threatened the Inspector with bodily injury unless he undertook to report against the proposal. And a Mr. Prancebody, who testified amongst other things that he had discovered the truth of the British Israelite theory while exploring the Derbyshire caves, had read in evidence most of a sixty-three-page submission, before the long-suffering Inspector had ruled it to be irrelevant and inadmissible and Mr. Prancebody, violently objecting, had been somewhat eponymously removed by the police. There was, in fact, scarcely a dull moment throughout the proceedings. Of particular interest had been the evidence of the R.S.P.C.A., who were emphatic that they favoured the scheme, on the grounds that the experiments and surgery would redound to the benefit of animals in general.

After the inquiry the Inspector, pressed by the Deputy Secretary of the Department to complete his publishable report as quickly as possible (regardless of whatever length of time he might need to make a good job of it), had recommended against planning approval for the site at Lawson Park and consequently against the compulsory purchase order on the property. The Secretary of State, the Right Hon. William Harbottle (known to his Departmental civil servants as "Hot Bottle Bill" on account of his chronically cold feet), had succeeded in getting the matter up to Cabinet Committee, following which a decision to approve against the Inspector's recommendation had been traded with the Home Secretary and the Minister of Labour, *sub rosa,* for agreement to a new open prison in Worcestershire, the head of the Chief Alkali Inspector on a charger and the tail of a young lady named Miss Mandy Pryce-Morgan, who was currently dispensing her favours to certain of the Front Bench.

Upon the announcement of the Secretary of State's decision, public reaction had been generally adverse. Under fire, Hot Bottle Bill had stood his ground like a good 'un, manfully ensuring that the Parliamentary attacks were invariably answered by one of his junior colleagues, Mr. Basil Forbes (otherwise known as Errol the Peril, on account of his unpredictable imprudence). Eventually brought to bay by Mr. Bernard Bugwash, Q.C., the Member for Lakeland Central, he had, on the night, brilliantly contrived to be unavoidably absent and Errol the Peril had spoken for six minutes flat. The next morning a much better stick with which to beat the Government had appeared in the form of the report of the Sablon Committee, which recommended that more public money ought to be spent on medical research. Since the Government, keen to reduce public expenditure, were reluctant to accept this recommendation, the Opposition had naturally supported it: and since support for Sablon was virtually incompatible with any further attack on the Lawson Park decision, it was generally conceded that Hot Bottle Bill had contrived to survive yet another cliff-hanging instalment of his career. Lawson Park passed into Government hands; and the celebrated firm of architects, Sir Conham Goode, Son and Howe, were commissioned to design the buildings.

It was generally agreed that these blended very well into their surroundings—the open hillside and oak copses, the darker patches of pine and larch, the dry stone walls, small green fields and knife-bright, cloud-reflecting lake below. Sir Conham had retained the old farmhouse and outbuildings, converting them into a luncheon room, common room and offices for the resident staff. Local stone and slate had been used to face and roof the laboratories, the Christiaan Barnard surgical wing and the stables, while for the livestock block Lord Plynlimmon, the well-known photographer and aviary expert, had been co-opted to design a single, large building, comprising under one roof more than twenty various sheds and rooms equipped with cages. The establishment had been opened on midsummer day, in pouring Lakeland rain, by Baroness Hilary Blunt, the former all-time high in Permanent Secretaries, and the flow of letters to *The Times* had trickled, faltered and finally ceased.

"And now," said the newly appointed Director to Dr. Boycott, as the first consignments of dogs, guinea-pigs, rats and rabbits came rolling up the smooth, steeply gradiented tarmac in the station's three distinctively painted blue vans, "now let's hope we'll be left in peace to get on with some useful work. There's been a lot too much emotion spent on this place so far, and not enough scientific detachment."

The black mongrel, its coat almost dried, the muzzle removed and a flexible rubber oxygen pipe fixed close to its half-open mouth, was lying on a pile of straw in one corner of a wire pen at the far end of the canine shed. A label on the pen door bore the same number—732—as that stamped on the dog's green plastic collar, while below this was typed: SURVIVAL EXPECTATION CONDITIONING: (WATER IMMERSION): DR. J. R. BOYCOTT.

The shed comprised, in all, forty pens, arranged in two double rows. Most of these contained dogs, though one or two were empty. With the majority of the pens, all four sides consisted of stout wire netting, so that for the occupants of these there were three party walls and three canine neighbours, except where an adjacent cage happened to be empty. The pen of seven-three-two, however, being at the end of Row 4 and also at the end of the block, had one brick wall, which was, in fact, part of the periphery wall of the building itself. Since the adjacent pen in Row 4 happened to be empty, seven-three-two had only one neighbour—the dog in the back-to-back cage in Row 3, also situated against the brick wall. This dog was not at the moment to be seen, and was evidently in its kennel (for each pen contained a kennel), though there were signs of occupation—a well-gnawed rubber ball in one corner, a yellowing blade-bone with no meat remaining on it, several fresh scratches along the brickwork, some ordure, a half-empty water-bowl and, of course, a label on the door: 815. BRAIN SURGERY, GROUP D. MR. S. W. C. FORTESCUE.

Over the whole interior of the shed lay a pervading smell of dog, together with the sharp smells of clean straw and of concrete brushed down with water and Jeyes fluid. Through the high-placed, bottom-hung hoppers, however, most of which were open, other smells came blowing, borne on a fresh wind—bracken and bog myrtle, sheep shit and cow dung, oak leaves, nettles and the lake at damp nightfall. The evening was growing dark and the few electric bulbs—one at each end of each row—seemed, as the twilight deepened, less to take the place of the declining day than to form isolated patches of yellow light, too hard to be melted by the gentle dusk, from which the nearest dogs turned their eyes away. It was surprisingly silent in the block. Here and there a dog scuffled in its straw. One, a brown retriever with a great scar across its throat, whined from time to time in sleep, while a mongrel whippet with three legs and a bandaged stump stumbled clumsily round and against the sides of its pen with a soft, wiry sound not unlike that produced by a jazz drummer with brushes. No dog, however, of the thirty-seven in the block, seemed lively enough or sufficiently disturbed or stimulated to give tongue, so that the quiet noises of evening flickered plainly in their ears, as sunlight twinkling through silver-birch leaves flickers back and forth in the eyes of a baby lying in its cot: the distant call of a shepherd, "Coom bye, coom bye 'ere!"; a passing cart down on the Coniston road; the lapping (just perceptible to dogs' hearing) of the lake water on the stones; the tug of the wind in rough grass tussocks; and the quick, croaking "Go back, go back, go back" of a grouse somewhere in the heather.

After a while, when the October night had almost completely fallen outside, there came a sharp clawing and scratching of straw from inside the kennel of eight-one-five. This continued for some time, with a sound rather as though the occupant, whoever he might be, were trying to burrow through his kennel floor. Finally, indeed, there were distinct noises of gnawing and splintering, followed by several minutes' silence. Then a smooth-haired, black-and-white head—the head of a fox terrier—emerged from the door of the kennel. The ears cocked, listening, the sniffing muzzle was raised for some moments, and finally the entire dog came out, shook itself, lapped a little water from its tin bowl, raised a leg against the brickwork, and then made its way across to the party wire separating it from the next pen.

The terrier certainly presented a strange appearance, for at first sight it seemed to be wearing a kind of black cap, causing it rather to resemble one of those animals in children's comic papers which, while the draughtsman may have given it the head of a cat, dog, bear, mouse or what you will, nevertheless wears clothes and may even go so far as to possess inappropriate anatomical features (elbow-joints, for instance, or hands). Indeed, to the extent that a cap is a head-covering, it *was* wearing a black cap, though this was in actual function a surgical dressing made of stout oilskin and fastened securely to the head with cross-bands of sticking-plaster in such a way as to prevent the dog from scratching and worrying at the antiseptic lint beneath. The whole appliance, lozenge-shaped, was tilted rakishly over the right eye, so that the terrier, in order to see straight in front, was obliged to incline its head to the right—a mannerism which gave it a rather knowing look. Having reached the wire, it rubbed one ear against it as though to try to loosen the dressing, but almost at once desisted, wincing, and crouched down close to where the large, black dog was lying on the other side.

"Rowf?" said the terrier. "Rowf? They've taken away all the rhododendrons and just left the maggots. O spin like a ball, isn't it dark? There's just this one star shining down my throat, that's all. You know, my master—"

The black dog sprang to its feet, and as it did so the flow of oxygen from the pipe cut out automatically. Teeth bared, eyes glaring, ears laid flat, it backed against its kennel, crouching into the straw and barking as though beset on every side.

"Rowf! Rowf! Grrrrrr-owf!"

As it barked, its head turned quickly this way and that, seeking an assailant.

"Grrrrr-owf! Rowf! Rowf!"

All over the block other dogs took up their cues.

"I'd fight you all right, if I could only get at you!"

"Why don't you shut up?"

"D'you think you're the only one who hates this damned place?"

"Why can't we have some peace?"

"Ow! Oow! That's the damned dog that wants to be a wolf!"

"Rowf!" said the terrier quickly. "Rowf, lie down before the lorry comes—I mean, before the leaves catch fire! I'm falling as fast as I can. Be quiet and I'll reach you."

Rowf barked once more, stared frenziedly round, then slowly lowered his head, came up to the wire and began to sniff at the other's black nose pressed between the mesh. A few moments more and he lay down, rubbing his big, rough-coated head backwards and forwards against one of the stanchions. Gradually the hubbub in the draughty block subsided.

"You smell of the metal water," said the terrier. "You've been in the metal water again, so I tell, so I smell, well well."

There was a long pause. At last Rowf said, "The water."

"You smell like the water in my drinking-bowl. Is it like that? The bottom's dirty, anyway. I can smell that, even if my head *is* done up in chicken-wire."

"What?"

"My head's done up in chicken-wire, I said. The white-coats fastened it all round."

"When did they? I can't see it."

"Oh, no," replied the terrier, as though brushing aside some quite unreasonable objection, "of course you can't *see* it!"

"The water," said Rowf again.

"How did you get out? Do you drink it or does the sun dry it up or what?"

"I can't remember," answered Rowf. "Get out—" He dropped his head into the straw and began biting and licking at the pad of one fore-foot. After some time he said, "Get out—I never remember getting out. They must pull me out, I suppose. Why can't you let me alone, Snitter?"

"Perhaps you're not out at all. You're drowned. We're dead. We haven't been born. There's a mouse—a mouse that sings—I'm bitten to the brains and it never stops raining—not in this eye anyway."

Rowf snarled at him. "Snitter, you're mad! Of course I'm alive! Leave your face there if you don't believe me—"

Snitter jerked his head back just in time.

"Yes, I'm mad, sure as a lorry, I'm terribly sorry. The road—where it happened—the road was black and white —that's me, you know—"

He stopped as Rowf rolled over in the straw and lay once more as though exhausted.

"The water, not the water again," muttered Rowf. "Not the water, not tomorrow—" He opened his eyes and leapt up as though stung, yelping, "The whitecoats! The whitecoats!"

This time there were no barks of protest, the cry being too frequent and common throughout the shed to attract remark.

Snitter returned to the wire and Rowf sat on his haunches and looked at him.

"When I lie down and shut my eyes the water comes suddenly. Then when I get up it isn't there."

"Like a rainbow," answered Snitter. "They melt—I watched one once. My master threw a stick and I ran after it, along the river bank. That was—Oh, dear!" After a few moments he went on, "Why don't *you* melt? They'd never be able to put you in the water then."

Rowf growled.

"You're always talking about your master. I never had a master, but I know what a dog's business is as well as you do."

"Rowf, listen, we *must* get across the road. Get across the road before—"

"A dog stands firm," said Rowf sharply. "A dog never refuses whatever a man requires of him. That's what a dog's for. So if they say the water—if they say go in the water, I'll—" He broke off, cowering. "I tell you, I can't stand that water any more—"

"Where's the gutter for that water, anyway?" asked Snitter. "That's what I can't understand. Bunged up with fallen leaves, I suppose. And the whippet's leg—they must have eaten that. I asked him the other day in the yard, but *he* didn't know. Said he was asleep when they took it away. Said he dreamt he was tied up to a stone wall and it fell on him."

"Dogs are meant to do what men want—I can smell that, without a master. The men must have some reason, mustn't they? It *must* do some sort of good. They *must* know best."

"It's a nuisance, but you can't bury bones here," said Snitter. "I've tried. The ground's too hard. My head still aches. No wonder—there's a garden in my ear, you know. I can hear the leaves rustling quite clearly."

"Only I can't bear the water again," said Rowf, "and you can't fight it, not water." He began pacing up and down the wire. "The smell of the iron pond."

"There's always a chance they might lose it. They lost a sky full of clouds one day, you know. They were all there in the morning, but they were gone by the afternoon. Blown away—blown away like sheep's wings."

"Look, the wire's loose here, along the bottom," said Rowf suddenly. "If you come and put your nose under it, you can lift it up from your side."

Snitter padded up to him on the other side of the wire. A length about eighteen inches long had pulled loose from the horizontal iron bar dividing the floor of the two pens.

"I must have done that," he said, "chasing a cat—no. There used to be a cat once but they switched it off, I think." He pushed at the wire for a few seconds, then raised his head with a cunning look. "Rowf, we'll leave it till after the tobacco man's been round. Otherwise he'll only see me on your side and put me back, and that'll be the end of that. Let it alone, old Rowf."

"You're sharp. Listen, Snitter, is that the tobacco man outside now?"

"I'm mad as a gutter in a thunderstorm," said Snitter. "I fall and fall—my head falls and I fall after it. Can you smell the falling leaves? It's going to rain. Remember rain?"

As the latch clicked on the green-painted door half-way down the block, Rowf went back to his kennel and lay still as frost. Most of the other dogs, however, reacted vigorously and volubly. From all over the shed sounded scurrying and yelps, quick whines of excitement and resonant, harp-like rataplans of claws along wire mesh. Snitter leapt three or four times in the air and ran towards the door of his pen, jaws full of slobbering tongue and breath steaming in the chilly air.

The green door, which opened inwards, tended to stick against the jamb. A shoulder-heave from outside, which succeeded only in bending the top of the door inwards, was followed by the clank of a pail being put down and then by two heavy, rubbery kicks just above the threshold. The door burst open and instantly every dog in the shed was aware of the night breeze filtered through a pungent reek of burning shag. In the doorway stood the tobacco man himself, pipe in mouth and a pail in each hand, odorous of tobacco as a pine tree of resin, redolent from cloth cap to gum-boots. The yapping increased, the movement, noise and tension throughout the block mounting in contrast with the silent deliberation with which the tobacco man carried in the two pails, set them down, returned for two more and then for a final two. This done, he went back to close the door and then, standing in the middle of the six, took out his matches, struck a light, cupped his hands round his pipe and re-lit it very thoroughly and carefully, taking no notice whatever of the barking and jumping around him.

Snitter, muttering "That pipe hasn't got a chance—not a chance," put his front paws on the wire and cocked his head sharply to the right in order to watch the tobacco man as he fetched a five-gallon watering-can from a corner and, with a slow, unhurried clumping of gum-boots, carried it over to the tap, placed it underneath, turned the tap on and stood beside it while it filled.

Old Tyson had once been a sailor, then a shepherd, then for several years a road man employed by the county council; but had taken the option of a job with Animal Research because, as he said, there were less weather wi't and aall in't woon plaace like. He was well regarded and indeed valued by the Director and senior staff, being reasonably respectful, if somewhat dour, in his behaviour, reliable, generally conscientious and no more given to sentimentality about animals than any other Lakelander. Also, being well on in middle age, he was steady and regular and not prone to ailments or to odd days off on account of family problems—which in his case had all been solved (or not solved) long ago. He understood dogs well enough, his attitude towards them being equally valid for the purposes of A.R.S.E. or for those of a Lakeland hill-farm—namely, that they were pieces of technological equipment which one needed to know how to maintain and use properly. Tourists' and holiday-makers' dogs annoyed him, being useless for any practical purpose, frequently disobedient and a potential danger to sheep.

In spite of what seemed to the dogs his maddening deliberation, Tyson was in fact anxious to be off as soon as he could this evening, for it was Friday, he had been paid and was due to keep an appointment in The Crown at Coniston with a friend from Torver, who had told him that he could put him in the way of a second-hand refrigerator in good condition and going cheap. He was, therefore, in as much of a hurry as was possible for him—the general effect rather resembling that produced in a tortoise when its lettuce is put down on the grass. This is not to suggest, however, that there was anything foolish or absurd in Tyson's demeanour as he went about his task. Tortoises are dignified and self-sufficient and, though admittedly slow, considerably more reliable than—well—than—what comes to mind?—than—er—well, than distracted princes, for example, who give wild assurances about sweeping to revenge on wings as swift as meditation or the thoughts of love.

Tyson entered each pen in turn, emptied the metal drinking-bowls down the gullies and re-filled them from his watering-can. Then he poured away what was left in the can, put it back in its place in the corner and returned to the pails. Four of these were filled with bloody messes of horse-meat and lights, appropriate portions of which (big or small according to the size of the dog) were doled out at Tyson's discretion to all those on "normal diet." As this part of his task progressed, the noise in the block gradually diminished. When it was complete, he set to work to distribute the contents of the other two pails. These contained a number of separate paper packages, marked individually with the numbers of those dogs for whom special rations had been prescribed on account of the experiments in which they were taking part. Tyson took his spectacle-case out of his pocket, opened it, took out the spectacles, held them up to the light, breathed on them, cleaned them on his sleeve, held them up to the light again, put them on, emptied the packets out on the concrete floor and laid them in two rows. This done, he picked up the first and held it, above his head, towards the nearest light-bulb. Once he had read the number he had no need to look about for the destination, since he knew the dogs and their pens as surely as a huntsman his hounds.

Who can describe what drugs, what charms, what conjuration and what mighty magic those packages contained? They were indeed miracles of rare device. Some included, infused with the liver and offal, stimulants able to banish sleep, or to cause the consumer to perform, on the morrow, prodigies of endurance—to fight, to fast, to tear himself, to drink up eisel, eat a crocodile. Others contained paralytics which suspended colour perception, hearing, taste, smell; analgesics destroying the power to feel pain, so that the subject stood wagging his tail while a hot iron was drawn along his ribs; hallucinogenics able to fill the eye of the beholder with more devils than vast hell can hold, to transform the strong to weaklings, the resolute to cowards, to plunge the intelligent and alert head over ears into idiocy. Some induced disease, madness, or mortification of specific parts of the body; others cured, alleviated, or failed either to cure or to alleviate, diseases already induced. Some destroyed the unborn foetus in the womb, others the power to ovulate, the power to beget, to conceive, to gestate. One might indeed believe that graves, at Dr. Boycott's command, would wake their sleepers, ope, and let 'em forth.

Actually that is pitching it a bit high—drawing the long bow, as they say—but at any rate no one could say of Dr. Boycott that he would not have attempted resurrection if he had thought there was a sporting chance. He was a qualified expert, initiative was expected of him, his subjects had no legal rights; and intellectual curiosity is, after all, a desire like any other. Besides, who in his senses could reasonably expect Dr. Boycott to ask himself, on behalf of the human race, not "How much knowledge can I discover?" but "How much knowledge am I justified in seeking?" Experimental science is the last flower of asceticism and Dr. Boycott was indeed an ascetic, an observer of events upon which he passed no value judgements. He represented, in fact, a most ingenious paradox, noble in reason, express and admirable in action, his undemonstrative heart committed with the utmost detachment to the benefit of humanity. Something too much of this.

As he worked, Tyson spoke a few words to each dog—"Well, that's for thee, then. Get yon down." "Hey oop, old lad. Layin' on straw'll get thee nowheer"—much unlike the common way of Lakelanders, who seldom or never speak to dogs except to summon them or to give them an order or reproof. More extraordinary still, he more than once patted a dog or actually stooped down for a moment to scratch its ears. Though he himself could not have said why he acted in this uncharacteristic way, and if asked would have shrugged his shoulders to indicate that the question was not worth serious consideration, it is, of course, beyond argument that he understood very well, on his own level, the work and general purpose of the research station and the kind of effects upon animals which that work commonly had. Not even Dr. Freud, however, armed with the longest and most symbolical shepherd's crook in all Vienna, could have dragged from the silt to the surface any guilt which Tyson may, as an individual, unconsciously have felt; for clearly the Director and his colleagues knew more than he, both about the world's needs and about animals' capacity for suffering, and his orders, like his wages, came from them. If each of us insisted on stopping to weigh in every case the relative pros and cons of distress to others, whether human or animal, brought about by obeying our instructions, the world could never be run at all. Life is, as they say, too short.

This ancient saw was, at any rate, certainly true this evening as far as number four-two-seven, a mongrel cairn, was concerned, for Tyson found him dead in his kennel. Four-two-seven had been one of three dogs taking part in an experiment commissioned by a firm of aerosol manufacturers, who were trying to develop a spray harmless to dogs but lethal to their fleas and other parasites. It had been obvious for some days past that the particular preparation at present being tested, known as Formula KG_2, had the undesirable property of penetrating the skin, with adverse effects on dogs' health, but the firm's laboratory, though informed of this, had been reluctant to accept the finding, particularly since the directors were afraid that certain of their competitors might be successful in introducing a rival product to the market ahead of them. Dr. Boycott had decided that the simplest retort to their time-wasting pertinacity would be to continue the applications to their foreseeable conclusion, and accordingly four-two-seven had been duly sprayed again on the previous day. He had certainly settled the hash of Formula KG_2 and its obstinate protagonists, and had released not only himself, but also valuable working time for the station's staff to devote to more profitable pursuits. Tyson, remarking "Ee, th'art poor lyle boogger," removed four-two-seven's body to the cold slab cupboard for examination by Mr. Powell in the morning and returned his food packet to the pail unopened. Before knocking off, he would be obliged to carry it back to the ration issuer and get it struck off his list—a further troublesome delay before he could be done.

He now believed himself to have only three packets left, and was so near the end of his evening chores that he actually began to whistle "The Quartermaster's Stores" through his teeth (and without removing his pipe) as he picked them up. These packets he had deliberately left until last. Each was wrapped in bright yellow paper marked with a black skull and cross bones, to indicate that the food within contained a poison, infection or virus capable of harming human beings. The contents of these he emptied, one by one, carefully and entirely, into the specially lidded, non-spill feeding-bowls of the eager recipients, took the wrappers outside to the incinerator and made sure they burned, washed his hands under the tap with carbolic soap; and then and only then noticed a fourth, not-yellow packet lying in shadow on the floor. This, held up to the light, proved to be marked 732. He had overlooked it.

Tyson felt irritated. The oversight was of no importance, but he was as close to being in a hurry as was possible for one of his temperament and besides, he did not like seven-three-two, which had more than once tried to attack him. He had in fact suggested that it ought to be chained to its kennel, but the matter had been forgotten by the staff member he had spoken to (who did not, of course, have to enter the dogs' pens and in any case had no direct concern with seven-three-two) and no chain had as yet been supplied. "Ah'm noan gettin' chain mesen, tha knaws," Tyson had said on the second occasion when he mentioned it; "any rooad, sooner they drown you bluidy thing t' better." And thereafter he had simply carried a stout stick whenever he had to enter seven-three-two's pen. Now, however, he could not be bothered to go and fetch the stick from over by the tap. Picking up the packet, he placed it flat on his hand, unwrapped it, strode down the cage-line to the far end, opened the pen door, and had just tossed the whole thing inside when a voice from outside called, " 'Arry?"

Tyson raised his head. "Ay?"

"Didst tha say tha wanted lift int' Coniston? Ah'm joost off."

"Ay, aw reet." He stepped back from the pen, turned and came to the side door of the block, wiping his hands on his trousers. "Packet 'ere t'and back in—dog were dead. Else for that Ah'm doon."

"Coom on then, owd lad. I'll roon thee round by issuer's place, and then we're off."

The voices receded, and then the sound of the car engine. The returning silence gleamed gently with noises, as a night sky with stars. A drop of water fell from the tap. An owl hooted once—twice, in the oak copse five hundred yards away. The clanging thud of a body against the side of a pen was followed by diminishing vibrations of the not-quite-taut wire. Straw rustled. A mouse scuttered along the concrete, in and out of the drainage gully, pausing and listening. The wind had veered into the west and there was a distant rustle of fine rain blowing in from the Irish Sea. The sick retriever, his food untouched, muttered and stirred in his sleep.

Snitter, alert and continually moving his head under its canvas cap, could discern other, still slighter sounds—the trickling of the beck, a larch cone falling branch by branch to the ground, movements in the fern and roosting birds stirring on their boughs. After some time the rising moon began to shine through the glass of the eastern hoppers, its beams slanting first upwards to the exposed king-post roof trusses and then, as they moved transversely downwards and across, falling at length upon the nearer pens. An Alsatian began to bay the moon. Perhaps it felt it had rather be a Roman and contaminate its paws with base bribes, than such a dog. Snitter, becoming more restless, began padding up and down his pen, agile and watchful as a trout in a pool. Intuitively, he had become aware of something out of the ordinary, something commonplace but full of import, some small alteration to the familiar as slight but disturbing as the discovery of a stranger's urine against one's own garden fence. But what exactly could it be?

As the first beams of moonlight touched his pen he stood on his hind legs, resting his paws on the wire separating him from Rowf. Suddenly he tensed, staring and sniffing, and so remained for perhaps thirty or forty heartbeats; but nostrils, ears and eyes all continued to affirm nothing but what they had originally conveyed. First, he had perceived that the source of the tobacco smell left by Tyson's fingers—that is to say, the door of Rowf's pen—was in slight but unmistakable movement—stealing and giving odour, as it were. Next, his ears had caught the well-nigh inaudible, higher-than-bat's-pitch squeaking of the concentric hinges as they pivoted a quarter of an inch back and forth in the draught. Lastly, he had made out the moonlight moving on the wire as it might on a spider's web—a kind of irregular, minute sliding back and forth limited by the frail force of the draught that was causing the door itself to oscillate.

Snitter dropped on all fours and, after a pause to smell and listen specifically for any signs of human proximity outside the block, began scrabbling at the length of loose wire between the two pens. Soon he had pushed it high enough to get his head underneath. Points protruding from the border of the mesh pricked his shoulders and then his back, piercing here and there; but he ignored them, continuing to whine and go round and round with his head in the hole like a gimlet. Finally he succeeded in forcing his way through into Rowf's pen with nothing worse to show than a thin but fairly deep scratch across his rump. Once inside, he pattered quickly across to the kennel.

"Rowf! Rowf, come back! The tobacco man's left my head open! Let me explain—"

The next moment he was knocked flying as Rowf bounded out of the kennel and leapt towards the pen door. His jaws snapped at the wire, biting and worrying, and the catch which Tyson, when interrupted by his friend, had omitted to fasten properly, clicked open off the jamb. After a few moments Rowf fell back, blinking and staring like a dog awakened from a bad dream.

"What?" said Rowf. "The tobacco man? Not the white-coats—it can't be the whitecoats—it's still dark, isn't it? It's not time for the tank yet! I'll fight—I'll tear them—" He stopped and looked at Snitter in surprise. "What are you doing here, Snitter?"

"Heave-ho, the loose wire. You know, there was an old lady two gardens away who had a trap-hole made for her cats at night. In and out they went, in and out; but if ever they came into *my* garden, what-ho!"

"You're bleeding!"

"Rowf, the moonlight, the door, I've come to tell you, it's come loose on my head. The tobacco man forgot that it's not. How can I explain? The door's not a wall any more! Oh, my head aches!" Snitter sat on his haunches and began scratching and grabbing with one paw at the canvas cap, which remained, as it was intended to, resistant to his claws. In the moonlight Rowf looked at him grimly, but said nothing.

"My head!" muttered Snitter. "The tobacco man lit it with his matches. Can you smell it burning?"

"When did he?"

"I was asleep. The whitecoats put me on a glass table and I went to sleep. How the flies go round today! It's so hot, even in the garden. I think I'll go to sleep. If the lorry comes, Rowf—" He yawned and lay down on the floor.

Rowf got up and began to sniff at Snitter and lick his face. The effect was apparently something like that of smelling salts, the odour of his friend recalling Snitter to reality.

"The wire swing!" said Snitter, sitting up suddenly. "The door, Rowf! That's why I came! The door of your pen's unfastened!"

The Alsatian had stopped howling and for some moments the only sound in the block was a sudden dripping from the tap, plangent on the convex edge of the overturned bucket beneath it.

"We can go through it, Rowf!"

"What for?"

"Rowf, we might be able to get out of here!"

"They'd only bring us back. Dogs are supposed to do what men want—I've never had a master, but I know that."

"The suffering, Rowf, the misery you've endured—"

"As dogs we're born to suffering. It's a bad world for animals—"

"Rowf, you owe them nothing—nothing—they're not masters—"

"Canine nature—the whole duty of Dog—"

"Oh shit in the sky, give me patience!" cried Snitter in agony. "There's a dog with a red-hot nose sniffing me over! The lorry's coming, the lorry's coming!" He staggered, and fell on the straw, but picked himself up at once. "Rowf, we're going to escape! Both of us—through that door—"

"There might be something worse through the door," said Rowf, peering into the dismal confines of the concrete *huis clos* surrounding them.

Snitter's jaws worked convulsively as with an effort he converted and brought his mutilated mind in frame.

"Rowf, the water—the metal water! What could be worse than the metal water? Hours and hours of struggling in the metal water, Rowf, and in the end they'll drown you! Think of the whitecoats, Rowf—what you told me—peering down into the tank and watching you. They aren't masters, believe me; I've had a master—I know. If we could only get out of here we might find a master—who can tell?—a proper pack leader. Isn't it worth a try?"

Rowf stood tense and hesitant in the straw. Suddenly, from somewhere up the fell outside, there came the faintest sound of rocky splashing as a yow, or Lakeland sheep, scrambled its way across a beck. Rowf gave a short, snapping bark and pushed his way through the door. Snitter followed and together, in silence save for their clicking claws, they trotted quickly down the line of pens to the swing doors separating the canine shed from the next.

It took Snitter some time to get the hang of the doors. They were light; indeed, they were portable, constructed of thick asbestos sheets on white-painted wooden frames, for Lord Plynlimmon had thought fit, when designing the block, to provide for flexibility in the subdivisioning by enabling the various sheds to be made larger or smaller at need; and accordingly not only the doors but also the preconstructed modules of the party walls were capable (with a little trouble) of being removed and re-fixed further up or down the building, to increase or diminish the various floor areas. The doors, however, were fitted with fairly strong return springs, of the kind that cause such doors to jump back and hit smartly on the knee or in the face a man following another who is not particularly heedful or considerate.

Rowf hurled himself at the right-hand door, which swung open about six inches, and then, the spring coming into its own, threw him back across the concrete floor. Growling, he went for it again, harder this time and higher up. Once more it gave and, as he dropped to the ground with his head through the narrow opening, closed upon his neck like a trap, pinning him between the two forward edges. He struggled back in silence and was about to try to seize the frame in his teeth when Snitter stopped him.

"It's not alive, Rowf! It's—it's—you scratch it to be let in; but there isn't a man on the other side, you see—"

"There's some creature on the other side pushing it back! We'll have to kill it—or chase it away, somehow—but I can't get at it."

"Wait, wait. Let's have a smell round."

Snitter pressed his wet nose to the narrow, vertical chink between the two doors. The draught coming through bore smells, certainly, but nothing more alarming than birds' droppings, feathers, grain and bran—all strong and at close quarters. He could hear, too, no more than a few yards away, the rustling and soft movements of roosting birds.

"Unless it's a creature that has no smell, Rowf, there's nothing but birds in there."

A sudden, high-pitched yapping sounded from behind them. Snitter turned to see the occupant of the nearest pen, a cross-bred Pekinese, standing wide awake in a patch of moonlight and looking at them with obvious surprise. He went quickly across to the wire.

"Don't make a row, Flatface," he said. "You might bring the tobacco man back here."

"What are you doing?" asked the Pekinese, nose pressed against the wire. "Why are you loose? What's that on your head? It smells of that stuff the whitecoats put over everything."

"It's to keep the frost out," answered Snitter. "My head's a bird-table, you know. The whitecoats cover it with bread every morning and then watch while the birds come and eat it."

"Oh, I see." The Pekinese looked sagacious. "But how do they keep you still?"

"With chicken-wire," said Snitter. "I dote on it, actually. My friend here dotes on it, too. He takes over when I need a rest. We're both bird-tables through and through. Do the whitecoats go through and through? Those doors there, I mean? How do they do it?"

The Pekinese was clearly puzzled. "They made me

better," he said. "First they made me ill and then they made me better. I've been ill, you know."

"I can smell that," said Snitter. "You smell like a dog-blanket left out in the rain. Flatface, listen—does the tobacco man ever go through that door?"

"Yes, to feed the birds. It's all birds in there. You can smell them. Besides, I've seen through when he opens it."

"Through and through," said Snitter. "How does he do it?"

"He's usually carrying things, and he pushes it with his shoulder or his foot and then edges through sideways. Let me tell you what happened when I was ill. First of all the whitecoats—"

Snitter went back to the doors and pressed the wedge of his muzzle gently into the central crack. The right-hand door, which had the weaker spring, gave slightly, and he slowly pushed through first his jaw and then his whole head, accustoming himself to the sensation of the counterpressure. As soon as his head was through he turned his body sideways and began to press with the weight of his flank against the flat of the door.

"Follow me right up close, old Rowf. There's a board loose in the fence, do you see? Don't jump at it, just push. Why, what a cloud of flies—no, it's birds—birds!"

He eased his entire body through the door. Rowf followed him, nose to tail, and the swing doors closed behind them, cutting off the familiar smells of dog, straw and meat and exposing them, with all the suddenness of an airliner from the north discharging passengers in the tropics, to the immediate impact of strange light, strange air and strange surroundings.

The place was full of birds. They could smell, all about them, the light, sharp odour of their droppings and hear, too, the sounds, so much quicker and softer than those made by dogs, of their stirrings in the dark. A pigeon nearby preened a wing, uttered a single, sleepy "Roo-too-roo; took!" and was silent. There must be many, many birds. Pausing and listening, both dogs had the impression of a forest in which the leaves were pigeons, spray upon spray, rustling leaves receding into an airy gloom. Here and there a wiry branch creaked; here and there a fragment from a seed-trough pattered, like a fir-cone or a beech-nut, to the floor.

They had entered the pigeon aviary, reservoir of one of the more eagerly watched, important and ambitious projects in which Animal Research was engaged. The object was nothing less than to discover how and by what means pigeons exercise their homing instinct—a Promethean undertaking indeed, since the birds themselves have always been content with ignorance in the matter. The thoroughness of the experiments, devised and conducted by Mr. Lubbock, a colleague and friend of Dr. Boycott, was impressive. Here, systematically divided into groups and caged in different compartments, lived hundreds of birds, each a grain of coral in that great reef of conscious knowledge to be built by Mr. Lubbock for the good, or the advancement, or the edification—or something or other, anyway—of the human race. Of those birds which had already been released to flight at greater or lesser distances from the station, some had had one eye or both eyes occluded by special appliances; some had been fitted with minute contact lenses, to distort their vision; others had had the sensitivity of feathers, feet, nostrils, beaks, mouths or lungs impaired or destroyed before setting out; others again had undergone carefully planned conditioning designed to confuse them when exposed to normal weather conditions. In Cage 19 it rained a continuous light drizzle twenty-four hours a day. In Cage 3, which was blacked out from the rest of the aviary, there was perpetual sunshine; in Cage 11, perpetual darkness. In Cage 8 the source of light (a simulated sun) moved anti-clockwise. Cage 21 was unusually hot, Cage 16A (so termed to differentiate it, for the avoidance of possible confusion, from Cage 16, in which all the inmates had died of cold one night, necessitating total replacement) unusually cold. In Cage 32 a light wind blew from one direction night and day. Birds born in these cages had never known any other weather conditions until their time came to be released to a homing flight. Cage 9 contained a special ceiling which reproduced the night sky, but with the various constellations disordered. At the far end of the aviary was a row of individual cages, containing birds into whose heads had been grafted magnetic particles, some attractive, others repellent. Finally, there were those pigeons who had been deafened, but left with other faculties intact.

The results of all the experiments so far had been most informative, yielding the basic information that while some of the birds succeeded in returning home, others did not. Many, in fact, in obedience to their defective stimuli, had flown straight out to sea until they perished; which was most interesting. One could draw the firm and valuable conclusions: first, that birds whose faculties had been impaired were less swift and competent in getting home than birds whose faculties had not; and secondly, that in any given group, some succeeded in returning while others, who did not, presumably died. Six months ago Mr. Lubbock had taken part in a television programme on the project, when he had explained the pattern of the experiments and the system by which various possibilities were being eliminated. Since then, important evidence had been obtained in support of the theory that the birds possessed an instinct not really explicable in scientific terms. This was humorously known at Lawson Park as the "R.N.K." theory, from a remark once made by Tyson to Mr. Lubbock—"Reckon nobody knaws."

Snitter and Rowf made their way cautiously forward between the cages, half-expecting to meet some kind of enemy in this strange place. Or perhaps one of the whitecoats, with brisk walk and purposeful tapping of heels, might suddenly open a door and, pausing just inside in the way they did, raise his soap-smelling hand to the wall in the gesture that created light. All remained quiet, however, and they pattered on, side by side, to the further end of the aviary. Here they were once more met by double doors leading into the next block. Snitter eased his way through and Rowf followed as before.

At once, though in a place similar in form to the last and constructed of the same materials, they encountered another change, arresting as that, to humans, of red limelight to green. All was the same, all was utterly different. An intense, slavering excitement shot through them. They stiffened, sniffed the air, whined, scratched and trembled.

Rowf leapt forward with two quick barks. The place was crowded with rats, rats scuttling and crouching in innumerable cages. There were dead rats, too—that was plain to be smelt; and some strange kind of rat, the smell of which seemed to come from one quarter in particular—a gritty, black smell. Filtering through all, posseting and curding the thin and wholesome odour of rats, was a vile and loathsome redolence, as of pestilence or death, so that Rowf, even as he barked about, was struck by an instant tetter of horror, and slunk back silently to where Snitter, with head uplifted and ears cocked, was standing on the shadowy floor beneath a steel table.

They were in the cancer research block, where rats, after being infected with cancer, were treated with various palliative drugs and preparations, being dissected after death so that the results of treatment could be observed and noted. There were in actual fact sixty-two separate cages, not counting the single large cage containing the control pool or reserve, from which healthy rats were taken as required for one experiment or another. Here were cancers of the ear, nose, throat, belly and bowels; malignant and less malignant cancers, sarcomata of many kinds, all living and growing, like submarine anemones, in pharyngeal, uterine or abdominal worlds of silence needing neither sun nor rain. Secret was the garden, set in the pathless awe now confronting the two bewildered dogs. The rats ran in, the rats ran out and never a rat to be seen, save for those stiff bodies lying on the glass table, the crop of the previous day's work, neatly split across from end to end to disclose, like walnuts, the white, ridged and crinkled, kernel-like growths within.

In one corner of the block, like a private ward in a hospital, stood a separate compartment with a locked door bearing the notice, DR. W. GOODNER. KEEP OUT. AUTHORISED PERSONNEL ONLY. This, too, contained rats—black rats of Norway—despite the fact that they were not personnel, this term being generally understood at Lawson Park (and indeed elsewhere) to connote only men and women (as in the Rights of Personnel, or the Prayer for All Sorts and Conditions of Personnel, or even

All Personnel
That on earth do dwell
Sing to the Lord with cheerful voice).

The exact nature of the project being pursued in this locked compartment was secret. Dr. Goodner never discussed it with anyone but the Director; others at the station, however (including Mr. Powell), had hazarded the surmise that it had probably, like most such work, been commissioned by the Ministry of Defence.

Rowf paused at the locked door, sniffing at the crack beneath and listening.

"What's the matter with this place? What is that smell?"

"The leaves are rotten," whispered Snitter. For some reason the smell made him afraid. "They fall in autumn, you know—fill the gutters. Maggots and flies, maggots and flies. Are you hungry?"

"Not yet."

"Then come on. We're trying to get out, Rowf. Even if we were to get in there and eat that smell, we'd be all whistle-belly-vengeance by sunrise, and the tobacco man would find us lying here sick, or worse. There's some terrible sort of disease in there—that's what that smell's about. Come on, quick, before there's time to change your nose."

With this Snitter turned, led the way down to the further end of the block and once more pushed through the doors.

Later, the wanderings of that night merged, for both of them, into a half-remembered confusion of formaldehyde and surgical spirit, fur, feather and hair; of paint, glass and disinfectant, hay, straw and cotton-wool; of all manner of excreta and glandular secretions; carbolic and rust, dried blood and wet mucus, dust, drains and sweat; quick, low alarm calls of beasts unknown and windy suspiration of forced breath in darkness. They came to the next block, the sparrow and finch aviary, where diseases of cage-birds were investigated, together with the effect of various preparations used for dressing seed-corn before sowing. These particular sparrows had cost rather more than two farthings for five, certainly in overheads if not in purchasing price. There was a special providence in their fall; but whether they fell to the ground with or without your heavenly Father, or mine, or Dr. Boycott's (for he had, albeit unacknowledged, the same One as you and I), there is no telling.

They ran swiftly through the small coati and mongoose block, with its rank, tropical smell of procyonidae and viverridae (Mr. Powell had been set to investigate the relatively mild effect upon these creatures of snake venom, and several were injected daily with doses of varying quantity and concentration), and so came to the pregnancy testing unit, where the urine of young women was injected into mice, so that they (the young women, not the mice) might learn (by the reactions of the mice), a little earlier than they would otherwise have learned, whether they had been impregnated as well as imprudent, and incautious as well as incontinent. The operation of a normal pregnancy-testing centre was not, of course, within the true ambit of Lawson Park, but the Director, who was a doctor of medicine and retained a certain interest in gynaecology, had recently accepted a remit for the examination of new and swifter methods of pregnancy-testing without animals—for which purpose a control group of animals was, of course, necessary, in order that the efficiency of new methods might be checked against that of the old. Here Rowf, clumsy with uneasiness and impatience, knocked over a small table and with it a box of mice, each confined in a separate, glass-fronted compartment. The glass shattered and those of the mice who were not already dead or close to death escaped, several finding their way out of the building by way of the drains. Rowf was still sniffing about the glassy floor when Snitter once more interrupted him.

"Leave it spilt, old Rowf! Let it trickle away! It's made the floor sharp and the blood will run out of your nose. Come and push at the next door. It's too much for me."

They thrust their way hesitantly into the air-freight testing centre, where various methods were being examined of packing and transporting live animals by air. This work had been commissioned jointly by several airline companies, largely in order that they could reply that they had done so when faced with criticism of the deaths of various animals (such as small monkeys, lorises and aye-ayes, captured and bound not for the Carolina plantations but for zoos) which, having begun by being created, had ended by being crated, and succumbing to over-crowding, fear, thirst, neglect or to all four of these together. It was not, of course, difficult to design humane and efficient travelling crates for animals provided that cost was no object and that one could count upon a reasonable measure of responsible human care during the journey. To do the thing cheaply, however, and counting upon the prevalance of ignorance, indifference and neglect, called not only for ingenuity but also for expert knowledge of what various animals could be relied upon to endure. A principal factor was the fear and strain brought about by engine noise, sudden dropping or striking of crates, proximity of humans and alarming smells such as combustion engine exhaust, tobacco smoke and human sweat; and to these, accordingly, the control groups of animals were regularly exposed for longer or shorter periods, the results being carefully noted by Dr. Boycott, who had, in as short a time as three months, made the remarkable discovery that over-crowding, rough handling and prolonged thirst were beyond doubt the major contributors to higher-than-average death rates occurring among small mammals transported by air.

They wandered up and down the lines of hutches in the rabbitry, where experiments were being conducted to try to develop a food, similar to rat poison, which rabbits immune to myxomatosis would be eager to eat, with fatal results. Again, cost had proved a difficulty. A palatable and caustic poison, which burned through the intestines in twenty-four hours, had been tested succcessfully, but unfortunately its mass-production was not practicable at anything like an economic figure. A second poison, harmless to humans and cheap enough to produce, had been demonstrated by Dr. Boycott on television. On that occasion he had injected first a colleague and then a rabbit, the latter successfully dying in convulsions in less than two minutes under the cameras and the interested eyes of thousands of viewers. This poison, however, Dr. Boycott had so far not succeeded in making reasonably palatable, so that to date, injection remained the only means of administration. Of the possibilities of a certain sterility drug, however, he was more hopeful, and this was now being administered, in various forms and strengths, to both bucks and does. Rowf, having made several attempts to break into one of the hutches by leaping at the wire, and been requested by the rabbit inside to be so good as to let him die in peace, rejoined Snitter in his search for some way out other than the swing doors. They found none, and down to the next circle they went.

They searched the cat block, where cats were kept permanently in hoods covering their eyes and ears (in order to discover the effect upon cats of being kept permanently in hoods covering their eyes and ears). Here there was little noise or movement. Rowf, however, became fascinated by a single voice which kept repeating, "Oh dear, oh dear oh dear," in a tone expressive rather of worry than of actual suffering, and spent some time trying to track it to its source before Snitter, who had again failed to find any way out of the block, could persuade him onward.

They made their way through the aquarium block, where octopi, with or without the benefit of brain surgery, received electric shocks when they approached offered food (the purpose being to examine their capacity for remembering previous shocks and therefore not responding to stimuli or inducements that would result in their receiving another). The electric plates were switched off, the tanks dark and their occupants somnolent or at least torpid; but nevertheless the low, watery sounds, the lappings and gurglings filling the room, drove Rowf almost hysterical, so that it was he who pushed on to the next pair of doors while Snitter was still searching in vain for a negotiable open window.

They came to a halt at last in the guinea-pig house, where all manner of guinea-pigs—ginger, black, white, black-and-white, ginger-and-black, long-haired, short-haired, tragical-pastoral, tragical-comical-historical-pastoral—were kept in reserve for the needs of the station.

A number had had one or more of their legs amputated—the interesting thing being that they possessed no power of adaptation, but continued to attempt to behave as though they had four legs. Here Snitter, having searched the entire room, at last stopped in the furthest corner, his nostrils pressed to the crack under the door. This was no swing door, but a heavier affair altogether, a door of the normal kind, painted green and shut as fast as the Arabian trees.

"Wet mud and rain," said Snitter. "Gutters and leaves! Smell."

Rowf put down his nose. Both could smell a steady rain falling in the darkness outside. Rowf pushed at the unyielding door.

"No good," said Snitter. "Postman's door—paper boy's door. Oh, never mind," he added, as Rowf remained silent and uncomprehending. "We've eaten down to the plate, that's all."

"No getting out? Can't we fight the postman?"

"Cats up a tree. Climb until the top branches bend. Then what? Hang yourself up on a cloud while you're thinking. Hang me up on another." As though to reassure himself, Snitter lifted his leg against the door, peed a moment and then sat back on his haunches, shivering in the damp draught and wisps of cloud-wrack blown in across the sill. "It's cold. My feet are cold."

"Burn," said Rowf suddenly.

"What?"

"Burn, over there. Smell of ashes. It'll be warmer. Come on."

There was indeed a perceptible source of heat—not much, but some—coming from the opposite side of the block, beyond the central mass of guinea-pig hutches piled in tiers. Turning his head in the direction towards which Rowf was looking, Snitter could not only smell the ashes but see, in the dim light, minute particles, dust and motes, swirling upwards in an air current that must be warmer than the rest of the room. Following Rowf round the hutches, he found him already sniffing at a square door of iron set in a frame of brickwork and projecting from the wall a little above the level of his head. It was ajar. Peering upwards, he could glimpse, within, the roof or upper side of a kind of metal cavern, which must be deep, for not only was a warm draught coming up it and a light drift of powdery ash, but also minute sounds, tinklings and crepitations, magnified as they echoed against the iron sides of the shaft.

"What is it?" asked Rowf, bristling as though for a fight.

"No animal; so put your teeth down. Swing thing—door of some kind. Get it a bit wider open."

Rowf made as if to push at it and Snitter quickly stopped him.

"No, no, you'll shut it that way. You have to nose them open, or else use your paws. Let me show you."

He stood up and rested his front paws on the projecting brickwork, thrust his muzzle into the crack of the opening and jerked his head sideways, levering the square of iron wide on its hinges. At once he backed nervously away, bristling as Rowf had done. The two dogs crouched together under the lowest tier of hutches facing the iron door.

"What is it?" repeated Rowf. "Something's been burning, some sort of death—bones—hair—"

"These creatures in here—whatever they are—the whitecoats must burn them. It's the same smell, you see, only burnt. Yes, of course," said Snitter. "Of course that's it. They burnt my head, you know, and the tobacco man keeps burning that thing he puts in his mouth. Obviously they burn these creatures in there."

"Why?"

"Don't be silly." Snitter went slowly back to the open door. "It's still warm in there. Dead things—but not cold. Hot bones, hot bones. I'll throw my head in." He put his paws up once more, peering into the mouth of the square, metal cavern. Suddenly he gave a whine of excitement.

"Fresh air," cried Snitter. "Sheep, rain! Smell underneath the ashes! I tell you—"

The brick-encased, iron chute, sloping downwards through the wall of the building, led directly into a small furnace, not unlike that of a greenhouse, sited just outside. This was used for burning not only rubbish, such as old surgical dressings, fouled straw and bedding from the hutches, but also the dead bodies of guinea-pigs and any other creatures small enough to be conveniently disposed of in this way. There had been a brisk fire that afternoon, which had included the truncated remains of some twenty guinea-pigs unable to be of further help to the station, as well as a couple of kittens and a mongoose. Tom, the lad who helped Tyson about the place, had been told to go and draw the furnace at about five o'clock but, knowing that Tyson was in a hurry to get away and was unlikely to come and see what sort of a job he had made of it, had merely raked quickly through the ashes and fragmentary remains of straw, bones and hair, and decided to leave the job of clearing out until Monday morning. Tyson had not specially told him to conclude by closing the doors both of the furnace and of the chute in Block 12, and he was certainly not the sort of lad to allow such a refinement to occur to his mind spontaneously—there being, as a matter of fact, little room to spare there, what with the heavy demands made upon it by the fortunes of Manchester United, the products of Messrs. Yamaha and the charms of Miss Nana Mouskouri. After he had gone, the fire had revived for a time in the strong through-draught, filling the guinea-pig block with a light smoke and the smell of burnt guinea-pig coming up the chute; but had then died out, the furnace gradually cooling as darkness fell and the wind sifted its way through the tinkling, clicking ashes.

"Fresh air," said Snitter again. "Yellow smell—prickles —bees—only faint—and somewhere there's wet rhododendrons, too. Rhododendrons, Rowf!"

"What?"

"Gorse, the yellow. We could fall there! We could! We could fall there!"

Snitter gaped, showing teeth brown about the gums, the teeth of a dog recovered from distemper. He began trying to pull himself up and into the square opening of the chute, thrusting in his head and front paws and hanging a moment on the lip before falling back to the concrete floor. Rowf watched him.

"Is it hot?"

"No hotter than your dam's belly in the basket. Remember? But I can't get at the teat."

"Get in there?"

"The rhododendrons, don't you see? Outside. Smell comes in, so dog can go out."

Rowf considered. "Smells come through cracks. So do mice. Dogs don't. Suppose there's nothing but a crack? You'll stick in there and die. Never get back."

"You damned flea-bitten street-corner bitch-jumper, why do you think I'm going on like this? Once you get your head in there, you can feel the wind, wide as your arse, and smell the rain." Snitter jumped up and again fell back, his wet muzzle grey with powdered ash. "Burn, little bones, burn! Like my head." He wiped at his nose with a forepaw.

Rowf, the bigger dog, stood on his hind legs, rested his front paws on the lip of the chute and looked in. For some little while he remained thus, peering and listening. Then, without a word, he hoisted his body up and into the opening. His hind paws left the floor and for some moments kicked and scrabbled in the air, trying in vain to get a purchase on the iron lip. As he jerked himself forward, inch by inch, pulling and scraping as best he could with front paws pressed against the smooth iron floor of the chute, his penis caught on the sill of the door and was forced painfully downwards. He rolled on one side and as he did so succeeded in getting the claws of one hind paw as far as the projecting hinges. Using this purchase, he thrust himself forward and slowly disappeared from Snitter's view, his hind legs, with tail between, stretching out backwards and dragging behind him in the tunnel.

Snitter, full of frustration, remained running backwards and forwards in front of the open door. Several times more he jumped up at the opening and fell back, until at length, giving up, he lay down, panting, on the floor.

"Rowf?"

There was no answer from the tunnel.

Snitter got up and backed slowly away from the door, as though trying to get a better view inside.

"Rowf?"

There was still no answer, and beyond the lip he could see nothing.

"Hoop-la sugar lump!" barked Snitter suddenly. Running forward, he took a flying leap at the opening, like a circus dog jumping through a hoop. He felt his hind legs strike hard against the metal lip and gave a single, quick yap of pain; then, realizing that his body was more than half into the hole, he rolled on his side as Rowf had done and, being smaller, drew his rump and hind paws in without difficulty. For a few moments he lay gasping as the pain in his legs subsided, then collected himself and smelt ahead.

Rowf's body was blocking the square tunnel in front of him. No draught was coming up it and no smell except the metal water dog-smell of Rowf. Snitter began to feel afraid. In this tunnel he could not turn round, evidently Rowf could not hear him and worst of all, Rowf's body seemed not to be moving.

He crept forward until his head was lying upon Rowf's trailing hind legs. Only now did he perceive that Rowf was in fact moving, but agonizingly slowly—more slowly, thought Snitter, than a slug on a wet gravel path. He could smell Rowf's urine smeared along the metal floor. It was full of fear. Snitter began to tremble and whimper where he lay in the close, ash-powdery, cast-iron passage.

Cramped in that funnelled hole, he found himself, as he tried to stand, forced into a curious posture, half-crouching, his rump pressed tightly against the roof of the chute. He could not maintain so unnatural a stance and after a few moments fell forward, so that his head butted sharply against Rowf's rump. At the impact he felt the body give and move the least fraction—no more, perhaps, than the length of a tooth or claw. In frenzy, he pushed again and again with his head at the black, shaggy rump, which at each impact slid almost imperceptibly forward.

He did not know whether it was possible for Rowf to force his way out of the far end of the chute. All he knew was that Rowf was still alive, for at each push he could feel his pulse and the spasmodic working of his muscles.

For how long he continued in his desperate pushing and thrusting he had no idea. The air in the tunnel grew foetid and his own breath lay condensed and humid on the iron walls. He wondered whether daylight might already have come. Slowly the length of tunnel behind him grew longer, but still there was no sign that Rowf was likely to get clear of it. At last, just as Snitter felt himself exhausted and unable to do more, Rowf's rump slid suddenly forward as smoothly as a turd from a healthy anus, and dropped out of sight. Snitter, drawing in a wonderful breath of cool air, found himself looking at a square of fragrant darkness speckled with rain—an opening in some sort of wall beyond the chute and framed in its mouth. A moment later he himself, dropping over the edge, fell two feet into a drift of powdery ash sprinkled with tiny, sharp bones on an iron grid. They had reached the furnace chamber.

Snitter scrambled up and began smelling about him. The place was scarcely bigger than a dog-kennel, so that he and Rowf, lying side by side, covered the entire area of the floor. Yet, despite the dust and powdery ash thrown up by their fall, the air seemed fresher than any he had breathed for days past. Cool currents, carrying more scents than he could recognise, were swirling all about them, not only from below but also from each side. From somewhere beneath him he could feel a draught, delightfully refreshing, flowing up and along his stomach. The sensation, after the cramped agony and fear of the chute, was so reassuring that Snitter, with closed eyes and lolling tongue, rolled over on his side, basking in the cool air stream.

The furnace box was, in fact, open on four sides. From below the griddled floor, air was flowing in through a vent which could be opened or closed from outside by means of a sliding iron cover; its function being, of course, to control the fire and make it draw more or less strongly. This vent Tom had left half-open, so that a steady stream of rainy night air was being drawn up through the grid and out through the flue above the dogs' heads. At the same time—since Tom had also left open the larger, stokehole door above—another air current was passing directly across the furnace chamber and out through the door of the chute into the guinea-pig block. Since the walls of the furnace had now cooled to approximately blood-heat it was, for the two dogs, as pleasant and restful a place as could well be imagined.

Snitter, raising his head, nudged Rowf's broad, unmoving back.

"Are you hurt, old Rowf?"

"I was afraid—never get out—until I fell down. All right now. Tired. Sleep."

Snitter could smell a long, bleeding scratch along Rowf's flank. He licked at it, tasting the iron and burnt-guinea-pig-flavoured soot of the hopper walls. Gradually Rowf's breathing became slower and easier. Snitter felt the muscles of the haunch relaxing under his tongue. Soon he himself, full of warmth and relief, grew as drowsy as Rowf. He ceased licking, dropped his head and stretched out his paws to touch the warm side of the furnace. In a few moments he too was asleep.

For more than three hours the two dogs lay sleeping in the fire-box, exhausted by the strain of their escape and the terror of their passage through the chute. Outside, the rain became heavier, falling steadily from a drift of clouds so low that the higher fells were blotted out beneath it. The moon was obscured and almost total darkness covered the miles of rock and bracken, heather, moss and bilberry bushes, rowan and peat bog—a fastness little changed since the days of the moss-raiders and the invading Scots —those armies which had marched to defeat and death at Flodden, at Solway Moss, at Preston, Worcester and Derby. A wild land, familiar with the passage of fugitives and the forlorn, the lost and desperate, the shelterless and outnumbered contending against hopeless odds. Yet tonight there was none to bide the pelting of the pitiless storm. From Blawith to Esthwaite Water, from Satterthwaite and Grizedale across to Coniston, not a soul was abroad, the dismal wastes were lonely as an ocean and not Thomas Rymer of Erceldoune himself, returning to earth from fair Elfland after not seven, but seven hundred years, could have discerned, from the aspect of that dark and lonely place, what century had arrived in his absence.

At length the furnace, the bricks round the outside of

which had streamed with rain half the night, cooled to the temperature of the surrounding darkness and soon afterwards the wind, veering round into the south-west and blowing up fresh rain from the Duddon estuary, began to drive keener gusts in at the stoke-hole and the control vent below. Snitter stirred in his sleep, feeling in his off-side haunch the pricking of a guinea-pig's splintered rib-cage. A sharp point pierced his skin and he woke with a start.

"Rowf! Come back!"

There was no reply and Snitter nuzzled him urgently.

"Come out of the leaves, Rowf, come out of the water! We've got to get on!"

Rowf raised his head drowsily.

"Don't want to go. Stay here."

"No! No! The wide place, the rain, outside!"

"Stay here—warm and dry."

"No, Rowf, no! The whitecoats, the metal water, the tobacco man! The lorry! We've got to get out!"

Rowf stood up and stretched as best he could in the confined space. "There isn't any out."

"Yes, there is. You can smell it." Snitter was quivering with urgency.

Rowf stood still, as though considering. At last he said, "There isn't any out—isn't any free. There's nothing, anywhere, except—well, it's a bad world for animals. I know that."

"Rowf, don't start smelling like that. I won't sniff it—vinegar, paraffin—worse. I've lived outside this place, I've *had* a master, I *know* you're wrong!"

"Makes no difference."

"Yes, it does. Out of that hole. You first."

Rowf, pushing the stoke-hole door wider, looked out into the rainy darkness.

"You'd better go alone. The opening's too small for me."

"Go on, Rowf, get on! I'll come behind you."

Rowf, black as the darkness, drew back his head from the stoke-hole, crouched on the floor and then, springing up, thrust head and front paws together through the opening, blocking it entirely. His claws scraped and scrabbled on the metal outside.

"Rowf, get on!"

Rowf's reply came back to Snitter grotesquely, through the control-vent, up from the grid beneath his paws.

"Too small!"

"Fight it, bite it!"

Rowf struggled helplessly, breaking wind as his belly squeezed against the iron. One hind leg, thrashing wildly, caught Snitter across the face.

"Get on, Rowf, damn you!"

Rowf began to pant and gasp. Snitter realized with horror that his struggles were becoming weaker. His body was no longer moving at all. The truth—which Snitter could not have grasped—was that, whereas at first Rowf's front paws had been able to push strongly against the vertical side of the furnace immediately below him, the further he forced his body through the door the less effectively he was able to thrust against the brickwork. Now, two thirds of the way through, he was helplessly and agonizingly stuck, without a purchase to drag or push himself forward. In the fire-box behind him Snitter, as his desperation mounted, felt a stabbing pain in his skull and a wolflike ferocity that seemed to consume him, throbbing in the surrounding iron, the ashes and bones.

"Damn the whitecoats!" cried Snitter, frothing at the mouth. "Damn Annie, damn the policeman and the white bell-car! Damn you all, damn you! You've killed my master!"

His teeth closed on Rowf's haunch. With a howl Rowf —by what means none can ever know—convulsed his body, the iron square of the opening compressing and excoriating his loins as he did so, and fell forward into the puddled mud below the stoke-hole. Almost before he had had time to draw one gasping breath and feel the pain in his ribs, Snitter was beside him, licking his face and panting while the rain ran in streams off his back.

"Are you all right?"

"You bit me, you damned cur."

Snitter's astonishment was plainly unfeigned. "*I* bit you? Of course not!"

With some difficulty Rowf stood up and sniffed at him.

"No, I can smell, it wasn't you. But something bit me." He paused, then lay down in the mud. "I'm hurt."

"Get up and come with me," replied the voice of Snitter, an invisible dog-smell ahead of him in the hissing darkness.

Rowf limped forward on three legs, feeling under his pads unfamiliar textures of gravel, sticks and mud. These by their very nature were reassuring, assuaging his pain with kindlier sensations of reality. He tried to limp faster and broke into a clumsy run, overtaking Snitter at the corner of the building.

"Which way?"

"Any," answered Snitter, "as long as we're well away from here by daylight."

A quick run past the rabbits' execution shed, a turn round the kittens' quicklime pit, a moment's hesitation beyond the monkeys' gas-chamber—and they are gone: ay, not so long ago these canines fled away into the storm. It would be pleasant to report that that night Dr. Boycott dreamt of many a woe, and all his whitecoat-men with shade and form of witch and demon and large coffin-worm were long be-nightmared. One might even have hoped to add that Tyson the old died palsy-twitched, with meagre face deform. But in fact—as will be seen—none of these things happened. Slowly the rain ceased, the grey rack blowing away and over Windermere as first light came creeping into the sky and the remaining inmates of Lawson Park awoke to another day in the care and service of humanity.

FIT 2

Saturday the 16th October

Freedom—that consuming goal above doubt or criticism, desired as moths desire the candle or emigrants the distant continent waiting to parch them in its deserts or drive them to madness in its bitter winters! Freedom, that land where rogues, at every corner, cozen with lies and promises the plucky sheep who judged it time to sack the shepherd! Unfurl your banner, Freedom, and call upon me with cornet, flute, harp, sackbut, psaltery, dulcimer and all kinds of music to fall down and worship you, and I will do so upon the instant, for who would wish to be cast into the fiery furnace of his neighbours' contempt? I will come to you as the male spider to the female, as the explorer to the upper reaches of the great river upon which he knows he will die before ever he wins through to the estuary. How should I dare refuse your beckoning, queen whose discarded lovers vanish by night, princess whose unsuccessful suitors die at sunset? Would to God we had never encountered you, goddess of thrombosis, insomnia, asthma, duodenal and migraine! For we are free—free to suffer every anguish of deliberation, of decisions which must be made upon suspect information and half-knowledge, every anguish of hindsight and regret, of failure, shame and responsibility for all that we have brought upon ourselves and others: free to struggle, to starve, to demand from all one last, supreme effort to reach where we long to be and, once there, to conclude that it is not, after all, the right place. For a great price obtained I this freedom, to wish to God I had died by the hand of the Lord in the land of Egypt, when I sat by the fleshpots and ate bread to the full. The tyrant wasn't such a bad old bugger, and even in his arbitrary rages never killed as many as died in yesterday's glorious battle for liberty. *Will you return to him, then?* Ah no, sweet Freedom, I will slave for you until I have forgotten the love that once consumed my being, until I am grown old and bitter and can no longer see the wood for the starved, dirty trees. Then I will curse you and die; and will you then concede that I may be accounted your loyal follower and a true creature of this Earth? And, Freedom, was I free?

Far away, east beyond Esthwaite Water, Sawrey and Windermere, the sun, from between low streaks of cloud, shone its first, pale rays across the woodland and bleak moor of Grizedale Forest. Already the buzzards were aloft, watching for prey, ready to tempest and tear any creature too slow or weak to escape or defend itself. Before their eyes opened, under the sunrise, the immense western prospect; the hyaline expanse of Coniston Water, five miles from School Beck to High Nibthwaite, lined along its western shore with caravans—orange, white and blue; and beyond, the little town of Coniston itself, grey against surrounding fields and autumn-leaved woods. Behind stretched the Coniston fells, over which, as the sun rose higher, the cloud shadows would flow with a pace smooth and unaltering, like that of ships upon a deep sea. More than four miles away, closing the horizon, rose the Coniston range—Caw, Torver High Common, Walna Scar, Dow Crag, Old Man, Brim Fell and Swirral; highest of all, the Old Man appeared from the east as a sharp peak tilted to the right, its eastern face streaked with the broken, white thread of a falling beck.

Half a mile north of Lawson Park, Monk Coniston Moor rises, hillocked and undulant, above the oak woods below. An old, dry-stone hoggus (or hog-house—a "hog" being, in the Lakeland, the ovine equivalent of a bullock) stands, half-ruined, beside a stream, and a rowan lays its pliant branches and thirteen-leafleted sprays across the roof-slates. To one walking over the Forest from Hawkshead to Nibthwaite, or from Satterthwaite to How Head, one lonely knoll surmounted discloses another, all the way up to the watershed, and little moves but the falling becks, and grey sheep that start in alarm out of the fern and go bucketing away from intruders, whether human or animal: the proper landscape to lie drenched beneath a silver dawn, low clouds and an east wind in October.

Here, among the dripping grasses and spongy, sodden mounds of moss, Rowf and Snitter lay gazing in astonishment and dismay as first light made plain the emptiness about them.

"It *can't* be the whitecoats," said Snitter desperately. "Not a house, not a lamp-post, not a fence—it's not natural! Not even the whitecoats could—" He broke off and once more raised his head to the wind. "Tar—there was—yes—for a moment—but faint. And the dustbins gone—every single one—it's not possible!"

A cock chaffinch, slate-blue-capped and rosy-breasted, fluttered across a wall with a flash of white wing feathers. Snitter turned his head for a moment, then let it fall once more upon his outstretched front paws. "And no men anywhere—so why make it?—and all that sky, how can it ever stop raining? Rowf? Rowf, come back!"

Rowf opened his eyes, his upper lip curling as though in anger. "What?"

"What's to be done?"

"How the death should I know?"

"They've taken everything away, Rowf—the houses, the roads, cars, pavements, dustbins, gutters—the lot. How on earth can they have done it? I tell you it's not possible! And where have they all gone? Why make all this—make it and then go away—why?"

"I told you," said Rowf.

"What did you tell me?"

"The world, I said. I told you it would be the same outside the pens. There isn't any outside. You say it's been altered, so the whitecoats—or some men, anyway—must have altered it so that they could do something or other to some animals. That's what animals are for, to

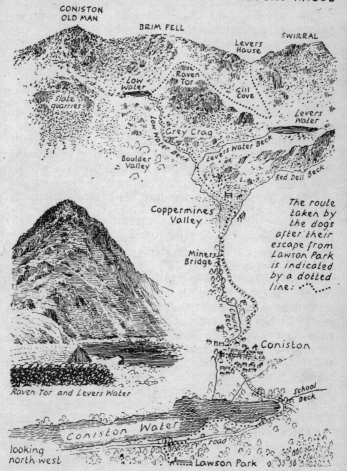

Friday and Saturday
15th and 16th October.

LAWSON PARK
TO
LEVERS HAUSE

CONISTON
OLD MAN

BRIM FELL

SWIRRAL

Levers
Hause

Low
Water

Raven
Tor

Gill
Cove

slate
quarries

Levers
Water

Low Water Beck

Grey Crag

Levers Water Beck

Boulder
Valley

Red Dell Beck

Coppermines
Valley

The route
taken by
the dogs
after their
escape from
Lawson Park
is indicated
by a dotted
line: ....

Miners
Bridge

Church Beck

Coniston

School
Beck

Raven Tor and Levers Water

Coniston Water

looking
north-west

road

Lawson Park

have things done to them by men. It's what men are for, too, come to that—to do the things, I mean."

"But Rowf, my master—my master never used to do anything to animals. When I was at home with my master—"

"He *must* have, else he couldn't have been a man."

"But how *could* they have taken away the streets and houses and made all this?"

"They can do anything. Look at the sun up there. Obviously some man must once have put up his hand to light it, same as the tobacco man does in the dog-shed. But you wouldn't believe it unless you'd actually seen the tobacco man do it, would you?"

Snitter was silent, shivering in the wind. The whole expanse of the fell was now light, heather and grass flashing with raindrops in the fitful sunlight breaking here and there through the clouds. The long call, like human laughter, of a green woodpecker sounded from the woodland below them.

"We've got to find some men," resumed Snitter at length.

"Why?"

"Dogs have to have men. We need masters. Food, shelter. Come on! We can't stay here. The whitecoats'll be looking for us."

He got up and began to pad away through the bracken, downhill towards the north-west. For some little time it seemed as though Rowf, still lying in the wet heather, would let him go alone, but at length, when Snitter had passed out of sight over the curve of the slope and reached the edge of the woodland two hundred yards away, he suddenly jumped up and ran after him at full speed, overtaking him under the trees.

"Do you think they've really gone, then?" asked Rowf. "I mean, suppose there aren't any men left, anywhere—if there was none at all—"

"There will be. Look—there are boot marks in the ground, and not more than a day old, either. No, there are men. What I can't understand is why they've changed everything. It's confused me—it's not what I was expecting. I was expecting streets and houses, naturally."

They had already pushed their way between the bars of the gate into the wood and were now following the path leading down to the road beside the lake. The air was full of the scents of autumn—acorns, wet fern and newly sprouted fungi. The rowan trees were glowing with brilliant orange berries, among which, here and there, robins perched to defy one another, twittering, listening and answering across their narrow territories. Despite the strange, lonely surroundings Snitter began to take heart—from the long-forgotten sensation of damp earth between his pads, from the twinkling light, moving branches and leaves, the coloured fragments all about him in the grass—harebell and lousewort, scabious and tormentil—and the smells and rustling sounds of other, unseen creatures. A rabbit crossed the track and he dashed after it, lost it, hunted back and forth and then forgot it as he stopped to sniff at a dor-beetle under a blue-and-green-banded fungus growing between two stones. At length he ran back to Rowf, who lay gnawing on a stick.

"There are cats here, anyway. Sort of cats. Long ears, but you can chase them."

The stick snapped and Rowf let the broken end fall from his mouth. "Nothing to eat."

"There will be. How the wind sends the leaves running across the trees! Then where do they go? Never mind, there are always more." Snitter raced away again. Rowf, hearing him crackling through the undergrowth on the other side of the brown, turbid beck, followed more slowly.

A mile below, they came out on the road skirting the east side of Coniston Water. The wind had died completely and all was lonely and deserted, with never a car on the road so early. The lake itself, where they glimpsed it between the trees, lay so clear and smooth that the stones, sunken leaves and brown weed within its shallow, inshore depths appeared like objects in a deserted room seen through the windows from outside. Yet at their next glimpse these had disappeared, their place being taken, under a burst of pale sunlight, by the reflections of moving clouds and autumn-coloured branches along the shore.

"Look, Rowf, look!" cried Snitter, running down towards the water. "Everything keeps still in there! I wouldn't be mad if I was in there—things would keep still —covered over—my head would be cool—"

Rowf hung back, growling. "Don't go down there, Snitter! Keep away if you've got any sense. You can't imagine what it's like. You couldn't get out."

Snitter, about to plunge, ran back up the bank but, still fascinated, went sniffing up and down along the edge, covering three times the distance of Rowf. Once the canvas dressing on his head caught in a long bramble and he wrenched himself free with a red blackberry leaf hooked into the black sticking-plaster. He ran along the shore with a shifting and rattling of loose pebbles, lapped thirstily, splashed in and out of a shallow place, shook himself and scampered back to the road, scrambling clumsily up and over the dry stone wall and dropping down into the wet grass along the verge.

"All the same, old Rowf, it's better out here than in the pens. I'm going to make the most of it. Only the flies in my head—they keep buzzing. And I feel like smoke. My feet are cold as a gate-latch."

Still surrounded on all sides by the early morning solitude, they came to the northern end of the lake, ran past the turning that leads to Hawkshead, crossed School Beck bridge and so on towards Coniston. Soon they found themselves approaching a little group of three houses, two on one side of the road and one on the other. The sun had risen clear of the clouds in the east and in the gardens, as they came to them, they could hear bees droning among the phlox and late-blooming antirrhinums. Rowf, coming upon an open gate, lifted a leg against the post, then made his way purposefully along the garden path and disappeared round the corner of the house.

The clang of the falling dustbin-lid and the overturning of the bin were followed by the sound of a first-floor window being flung open, then by threatening cries, the thudding of feet running downstairs and the sharp clack —one, two—of drawn bolts. Rowf's big shape reappeared, black and bristling, backing away from a man in a brown dressing-gown and felt slippers, his face bearded white with shaving-soap. As Rowf stood his ground the man stooped, picked up a stone from the flowerbed and flung it. Rowf ran back through the gate and rejoined Snitter in the road.

"I'd have fought him—I'd have bitten his ankle—"

"Oh, go and bite a policeman!" said Snitter. "Bite a postman, go on! You *would* spoil it, wouldn't you? It's not the right way, Rowf!"

"That bin—there was food wrapped up in paper packets, like the tobacco man's—"

"You should have put yourself in and shut the lid down. Why ever did I go to the trouble of getting you out? You've got treat men properly, Rowf, if you want— Did he hit you with that stone?"

"No, or I'd have gone for him. I tell you—"

"Oh my dam, this chicken-wire round my head!" cried Snitter suddenly. "I'm blind! I'm blind!" He flung himself down on the road, clawing and grabbing at his head, which jerked back and forth horribly, like that of a clockwork toy. "The flies—the flies are going to eat me! The road's black and white—the lorry's coming, the lorry's coming, Rowf!"

Rowf, pressed against the garden wall, watched helplessly as Snitter got up, staggered slowly to the other side of the road and once more fell down. He was about to follow him over when he heard the sound of an approaching car. As it came closer he slunk back into the gateway.

The car slowed down and stopped. The driver remained at the wheel while his passenger, a young man in fell boots, a blue rollnecked jersey, anorak and yellow woollen cap, got out and stood beside the car, looking down at Snitter in the road.

"Reckon it's took badly, Jack. Bin roon over, d'ye think?"

"Nay, not roon over, it's bin to't vet, look, has that. Yon dressing on it head. Oughter be kept close soomwheers, bi rights, ought that. Moosta got out."

The young man went up to Snitter who, with closed eyes, was lying limply on his side. Murmuring gently and reassuringly, he extended a closed fist towards his nose. Snitter half opened his eyes, sniffed at his knuckles and wagged his tail feebly.

"It's got this green collar, Jack, but nowt on it—

nobbut a noomber. It cann't have coom far, it's that bad. Let's joost put it int' back of car, like, to get it off rooad, and then I'll assk at woon of t'ouses. Happen soomun'll know whose 'tis."

He bent down and lifted Snitter in his arms. In the same moment Rowf hurled himself across the road and leapt for his throat. The driver gave a cry of warning and the young man, dropping Snitter just in time, flung up his left arm, which Rowf's teeth seized below the elbow of the anorak. As the young man staggered back, the driver leapt out of the car and began beating at Rowf's head with a pair of heavy driving-gloves. Snitter, yelping from his fall, was already twenty yards up the road when Rowf released his grip and dashed after him, leaving the driver rolling up his friend's sleeve and searching his pockets for an iodine pencil.

"I told you, Snitter, I told you! You think you know everything about men. I told you—"

"They were all right—they were masters. It was my head—all on fire—I couldn't see—"

"They were whitecoats—surely you know that? They were going to take you away, take you back—Snitter, are you all right?"

"I think—yes—I think so." Snitter sat down and looked doubtfully about him. "I wish the mouse would come back. I never know what to do without him."

"There are more houses further along this road—see them?" said Rowf. "That's one lot the men haven't taken away, anyhow—or not yet. Let's go down there—you'll feel better once we get among some houses."

"That cairn—Clusker—he was dead, you know," said Snitter. "I saw the tobacco man take his body out of the pen last night. He lay down, same as me—"

"When did he die?"

"You weren't there. I think it must have been yesterday afternoon, while you were in the metal water."

"What was wrong with what I did just now?"

"You mustn't rootle about in dustbins, however nice they smell. Not if masters are anywhere near. It makes them angry, for some reason. The proper thing, if you want to get food out of a man, is to go and make friends with him first, and then with any luck he gives you something. Mind you, I never had to do that with my master. I was always fed regularly. I knew where I was—in those days—oh, what's the use? But that's how you do it. You do the man *before* the food—not after. I'll show you, when we get to these houses."

At this moment, as they were entering Coniston, they both heard the sound of another car behind them, but still some way off. At once Rowf turned and slunk away down a nearby side-lane (or "lonnin," as the Lakelanders call them), between grey, lichened walls. After a moment Snitter followed him, in and out of the docks and goose-grass beside the track, disturbing clouds of blue-bottles and two or three tortoiseshell butterflies fluttering torpid in the autumn air. Around them grew, little by little, the smells and quiet sounds of a country town beginning the day—the soft, intermittent whirr of an electric milk-float, clinking bottles, a slammed door, a called greeting answered, smells of wood-smoke, of frying, of chickens released from the henhouse. Snitter, overtaking his friend, led the way by back gardens, yards and patches of waste land, always looking about him for some likely-looking man whom they could approach.

After some time spent in wandering, lurking, jumping garden walls unseen and dashing across open roads when there seemed no help for it, they found themselves near the left bank of Church Beck, not far from where it runs under the bridge in the centre of the town. The beck was loud, running strongly after the night's rain, carrying down its rocky bed a brown spate from the crags of Wetherlam, from Low Water, Levers Water and the eastern heights of Old Man. Rowf, giving it one look, slunk back towards the garden wall they had just scrambled over.

"Rowf, wait!"

"I'll be damned if I wait! That water—"

"Never mind the water. There's a shop full of food not far off. Can't you smell it?"

"What's a shop?"

"Oh, you know—a shop—a shop's a house, Rowf, where there's meat and biscuits and things and men who want them go and get them. Actually it's usually women, for some reason, but—oh, never mind. This one can't be far off. You're right, these houses are doing me a world of good. We'll find a master before long, you see."

Snitter, following his nose, led the way along the street and soon tracked down the shop which had wafted to him its tidings of cold meat, sausages, cheese and biscuits. It was an up-to-date grocer's, new and smart, its separate delicatessen and cheese counters conveniently arranged across the floor from the shelves of jam, shortbread, biscuits, potted meat, tins of soup, anchovies and teas in pretty packets and tins. It was not yet open, but the doors were standing ajar and a youth in a sacking apron was cleaning the tiled floor with a mop and pushing the water out on the pavement, while a young woman in a white overall was looking over the shelves and checking and rearranging some of the stock.

Snitter came to a stop on the opposite side of the road.

"Now watch me, Rowf, and remember—men first."

"Don't like men."

"Don't be silly. Of course we've got to find a man to look after us. A dog has to have a master if he's going to live properly. Poor old Rowf, you've just been badly treated by the wrong sort of men."

"It's a bad world—"

"Oh, try the other lamp-post for a change. Come on! This is going to teach you a thing or two. You'll like it."

Snitter ran across the road and put his head between the open doors. The young man in the sacking apron, looking up, saw his black cap, backed by the shaggy bulk of Rowf behind him. He stood staring a moment, then laid his mop aside and called over his shoulder into the recesses of the shop.

"Eh, Mr. T.!"

"What's oop?" replied a voice.

" 'Ave y'ever seen dog owt like this? It's got cap on! Theer's two on 'em tryin' to coom in, like. Seem to know wheer theer at an' all. Are they owt to do wi' thee?"

At talk of dogs on his premises the proprietor, a conscientious and fastidious man, who was washing his hands with disinfectant soap as part of his normal routine before opening shop, dried them and came hurrying forward between the shelves, buttoning his clean, white, knee-length shop coat as he went. Seeing, in passing, the ham knife lying where it should not have been on the cheese counter, he picked it up and took it with him, tapping the flat of the blade against his left hand in nervous haste.

"Where, Fred, where?" he said. "Where? Oh, I see. Good gracious, no, I've never seen them in me life. Have you, Mary? Mary? Are they anything to do with you?"

The young woman, carrying the stock sheets clipped to her fibreboard, also approached the door.

"Whatever's that on it head?" asked the proprietor, staring.

As he came into full view from behind the shelves and, hands on knees, bent down to look at Snitter, both dogs turned and pelted down the street like the hounds of spring on winter's traces. Round the nearest corner they went, past the Black Bull and up the lane beyond. After two hundred yards Snitter stopped and pressed himself against the wall, panting.

"Did you see, Rowf? Did you?"

"He was a whitecoat!"

"He had a knife!"

"He smelt of that stuff!"

"Scissors sticking out of his front pocket!"

"There was a woman whitecoat too, carrying paper, one of those flat board things they have when they come to take you away!"

"Oh Rowf, how dreadful! That must be another white-coats' place! Perhaps the town's all whitecoats, do you think? There seemed to be hardly anyone else about. A whole town of whitecoats!"

At the thought they began to run again.

"I'm not going back there! I bet they do throw dogs into that running water, whatever you say."

"That man must cut them up on those glass tables in there. It isn't a shop at all!"

"Let's get away! Come on, we'll go up here. It smells lonely."

"Yes, all right. Why, these are rhododendrons, Rowf! Rhododendrons!"

"Never mind."

"No, I mean it's all right. I tell you, we're bound to find some proper men some time today, before we're done."

"You'll kill us, Snitter—or worse. I'd rather keep away. I never got any good from a man yet."

They were making their way up a walled lane—almost a road—skirting the hillside above Coniston. Below them, at the foot of a steep slope covered with trees and undergrowth, they could hear the big beck shouting like a mountain torrent and from time to time caught sight of its white water foaming between the rocks of the ravine. So loud, indeed, was the noise that when a lorry came jolting towards them round a bend in the lonnin they were startled, having heard nothing.

Snitter, whining with terror, crept into the bracken and hid himself. Rowf, however, dashed at the wheels, and ran snapping for some distance behind the lorry before coming back to the place where they had first seen it. The back was open, with chains on its metal sides which clanked and slapped as it swayed along; and evidently loaded with wet gravel or stone spoil, for Rowf's black muzzle was daubed with a yellowish, ochreous sludge which had run out of the back. He sat on his haunches, wiping at his face with one front paw. Snitter emerged from his hiding-place and came back to him.

"What's the matter? I thought you said men—"

"A lorry, Rowf!—"

"*I* chased it away all right! Damned thing, it shat all over my nose—it must have been *terrified,* grrrrrr-owf!"

"Lorries—the—the blood!—they shut me up—don't do it any more, Rowf! You won't?"

"What a strange beast you are, Snitter! One moment you're—"

"I know what I'm talking about. Yes, I'm mad all right, but it's only the wind. It blows through my head, you know, where the brains used to be. Once the flies get in—"

"They won't. Let's get on. Wherever that lorry came from there might be some more men—better ones, you say. I doubt it myself, but if that's what you want to find so much—"

Soon they came to the heavy waterfall below Miners Bridge and now it was Rowf who sheered away at sight of the falling water.

"It's all right, Rowf. There aren't any whitecoats here—"

"How do you know?"

"Smell."

"I don't care—I'm not going down there."

From some distance beyond the fall they could now hear the grinding of a lorry in low gear and the intermittent rattling, sliding and hissing of stones being loaded. They went cautiously on. Stronger than the smells of diesel and of men, the very ground ahead of them seemed to be exuding a strange, disturbing scent; earthy, a smell of rain-washed stones bare of grass—a trampled, empty smell. Snitter seemed half-attracted and half a prey to misgiving. They came to a smaller beck running beside the track and he lapped doubtfully at it, licking his chops in distaste.

"I don't know—I can't make it out. Have they taken all the grass away? Something's tainted the water—can you taste it?"

"It's metal. I should know. You stay here, Snitter. I'll go and have a look round. If I come back running, don't hesitate—just follow me as fast as you can."

Rowf scrabbled up a nearby pile of stones and disappeared. A few moments later Snitter, hearing him bark, followed. Together they looked in astonishment across the wide hollow among the hills to which they had climbed.

The entire area ahead was void of vegetation, rocked and cratered as the moon. Across it stretched a track, where rainwater glistened in deep ruts, and beside this a cloudy stream ran in a kind of trough. Brown mud lay everywhere, and in the distance a pile of shale rose like a giant's unlighted bonfire. Far off, across the waste, a dirty lorry crept, rocking and splashing. As the two dogs watched, it backed slowly towards the pile, in obedience to a man in a yellow helmet who shouted, gesturing first with one hand and then the other. Somewhere out of sight the engine of a pump was put-putting steadily and they could see, dark against the tawny ground, the line of a thick, black hose, its spout discharging into the stream.

This was Coppermines Valley, once a mining site but now, its lodes long worked out, frequented only for small-scale winning of gravel and spoil by anyone who cared to bring a lorry; hence the activity on a Saturday morning. It was a scene of squalid desolation, of ragged spoil heaps and other debris of abandoned industry. In all directions across the disfigured landscape, channels, raw and man-made, ran like millraces, streaming down steep slopes or cutting unnaturally over patches of encroaching fell. A long way beyond, the hillsides resumed their crags and bracken, from which the breeze carried faint, mossy odours, partly occluded by the nearer smells of the workings.

The two dogs gazed for some time in silence.

"That explains it, of course," said Snitter at length.

Rowf scratched the back of one ear with a hind paw and scrabbled uneasily at the ground.

"That explains it, Rowf, don't you see? This is the part they're making now. They've just finished taking away all the streets and things and they're starting to put in the big stones and grass. When they've finished here I suppose they'll go lower down, to those houses we've come from; take them away and make that place into rocks too. But why? Especially if the houses belong to white-coats? I can't make it out at all. There's no sense in it, and you can't even get out of the wind." Snitter shivered and lay down.

"Out of the wind? It's the world we can't get out of."

"These may be the wrong sort of men too. They don't look much like masters to me, but all the same I'm going to try. What else can we do?"

Leaving Rowf sniffing the pungent, bitter scent of brown ants scurrying over their mound, Snitter ran quickly across the waste, splashed his way through half a dozen great puddles between the piles of shale and, wagging his tail, approached the driver of the lorry, who was kicking moodily at one of his front tyres. As the driver caught sight of him he stopped uncertainly, half-afraid and turning as though to make off. The driver, straightening his back, shouted over the bonnet to the man in the yellow helmet.

"Eh, Jack, 'ast seen yon afore? Whose is it, d'y know?"

"Nay. No dog 'ere. Nowt to do wi' place, like. What's yon on it head?"

"Dunno. Git away-aym! Goo on, get off, y' boogger!" shouted the driver, picking up a stone. Snitter turned and ran as he threw, missed and returned to his kicking of the tyre.

Rowf looked up from the anthill.

"What?"

"He was kicking the lorry—he was angry before I came; I could smell that."

"I suppose they must make the lorries run about in that place—tie wires on them, push glass things into them—all that. D'you remember Kiff told us they used to tie wires on him to make him jump?"

"They wound a cloth round his leg, he said, and pumped it tight with a rubber ball-thing. These *are* the wrong sort of men—"

"All men—"

"All right," said Snitter sulkily. "I admit I was wrong, but I haven't given up yet. We must go and look for some other men, that's all."

"Where?"

"I don't know. Let's go up that hill over there. It's in the opposite direction from the whitecoats' town, anyway."

They loped across the bare ground, past the old youth hostel hut and the millrace beyond, splashed through Levers Water beck and began to climb, on the line of Low Water beck, into the high wilderness on the eastern slopes of the Coniston range. The wind freshened, its sound in the heather rising at times to a shrill whistling, and carried the clouds continually across and away from the sun moving on towards noon, while their shadows, with never a sound, flowed down the slopes faster than swallows or drifting rain. Among the stones nothing moved. Further and higher into this solitude, with many halts and pauses, the dogs hesitantly ascended as the morning wore on. More than once, topping a slope or rounding a boulder, they came unexpectedly upon a grazing yow, and as she made off chased her, barking and snapping at her heels for forty or fifty yards until they lost interest or some other scent distracted them from pursuit. Once, not far away, a circling buzzard closed its wings and dropped into the grass. Some small creature squealed, but before they reached the place the buzzard rose again with no prey to be seen in beak or talons. Rowf watched it turn into the wind and slide away.

"Better not fall asleep here."

"Not in the open, no. Snippety-snap—don't bother to open your eyes—you haven't got any." Snitter's short legs were tiring. He lay panting on a patch of smooth turf littered with sheep's droppings while Rowf, in curiosity, cast unsuccessfully about for traces of the buzzard's victim.

Still climbing, they crossed a green path and above it the stream became yet more narrow, with many shallow falls into brown pools overhung by glistening patches of liverwort and tussocks of grass fine as horsehair. The ascent grew steeper until, reaching at last the lip of yet another hanging valley, they came all unawares upon Low Water, that still and secret tarn that lies enclosed under the precipices of Old Man and Brim Fell.

Rowf, leading the way past strange, pillar-like rocks canted upright as though set by human hands long ago, shrank back from the outfall, cowering at sight of the placid pool. In this seldom-visited place, windless and silent, the tarn and its surroundings lay as they must have lain for millennia past, unchanged by any accident or act of man. Through the limpid, grey-green water, perhaps a hundred and fifty yards across and nowhere more than a few feet in depth, could be seen clearly the stones of the bed, streaked here and there with a peaty silt. On the further side, the screes of Old Man fell sheer into the rippleless shadows, the mountain, rising nine hundred feet to its summit, shutting off half the sky above. In the unexpectedness of the tarn's disclosure, and the stillness of its stones and water, there seemed a kind of malignant vigilance—the cold assurance of one who, in silence, watches a fugitive or culprit unawares, waiting without haste for the moment when he will turn and look up, to learn from that impassive face that flight or concealment is useless and that all that he supposed secret has been observed and known from the first.

With a howl of dismay, Rowf fled up the slope towards Raven Tor. Snitter overtook him in a stony gully and he turned on him, panting and snarling.

"I told you, Snitter—I told you, didn't I? It doesn't matter where we go. The whitecoats—"

"Rowf, there's no one there—nothing—"

"You never saw the tank—it's just like that—in fact that *is* a tank, only a bigger one—the water doesn't move —you can see right down into it—then they pick you up—"

As some honest soldier might find his straightforward, workaday warmth and staunchness no match for the onset of shell-shock in a comrade, so Snitter, his desire to reassure overwhelmed by Rowf's vehemence, lay down without further talk, feeling against his own body his friend's tension and fear. After some time Rowf said, "I suppose they must be waiting somewhere—the whitecoats. Where do you think they're hiding?"

"It's not for us—not that water—it's too big—they must have made it for some bigger animal—" Snitter, unable to explain away the sudden and unforeseeable appearance of the tarn and almost convinced by Rowf's terrified certainty, was nevertheless still searching for some kind of reassurance.

"What animal, then? They obviously made it, didn't they—those men down there with the lorries—"

"For the sheep, of course," said Snitter, hoping desperately that it might be true. "Yes, that must be it. I tell you, we've escaped. They do it to other animals here— not to us. Look at the clouds—look at the beck—they only go one way—they never go backwards, do they? We shan't go back either."

"We can't stay here, though." With a down-pattering of stones, Rowf got up and padded over the shoulder of the tor.

The sight of Levers Water, a much larger tarn, with men's work clear to be seen in the concrete embankment and dam at the outfall, provoked in him, surprisingly, no further fear. As a stag or fox, having started up at the first scent of hounds or sound of the horn, will then collect its wits and begin in earnest to call upon its powers of cunning and endurance, so Rowf, having once come upon and accepted the evidence of what he had all along more than suspected—the ubiquity of the whitecoats—seemed now to have braced himself to contend with it as best he could. Within seconds of their first glimpse of the lake four or five hundred yards away at the foot of the slope, he had drawn back and crouched down behind a boulder. As soon as Snitter was in concealment beside him he wormed his way forward to a place from where, between two stones, he could look out over the water without exposing himself to view.

For nearly an hour the two dogs lay watching for any sign of human presence or approach. Once, almost a mile away, a man appeared over the shoulder of High Fell on the further side of the lake. For a few moments he remained within their view, waving one arm and shouting loudly to someone or something out of sight. His high-pitched, stylized cries carried clearly across the valley. Then he strode on and was lost to sight.

"He wasn't—well, he didn't look like a whitecoat," said Rowf uncertainly.

"No. But he looked like the tobacco man, and he sounded rather like him, too." Snitter had become devil's advocate. "All the same, that other water back there, where we've come from—it wasn't like anything you've ever told me about the tank—"

"It was—I tell you—just because it didn't smell of metal—"

"Smell's always the thing to go by, but I admit that doesn't necessarily mean it's all right. Lorries don't smell of anger, for the matter of that—no blood, no mouth-smell, nothing—but they come and kill—"

He broke off. Rowf made no reply and after a little Snitter went on, "But what's going to become of us? What are we going to do? They've taken away the whole natural world. There's nothing to eat. We'll *have* to go back."

For a long time Rowf made no reply. At last he said, "There's something—a smell in my mind—pitter-patter—very small—whiskers—"

A gust of wind came pushing round the shoulder, raced away down the fell and wrinkled, tugging, across the broken cloud reflections on the surface of the tarn. They could see the ripple pull up sharp and turn towards the outfall as it met and mingled with some other air current in the basin.

"A mouse—there was a mouse came into my pen—we talked—"

"They're bits of biscuit that get left over, you know. Make yourself a few teeth from bone splinters, pick up a tail and off you go. Well, it's a living. Sometimes they're fleas trying to better themselves. My dam told me. That must be why there's one in my head, I suppose. They get everywhere."

"This mouse said men never did anything to him—not like us—"

"Then they couldn't have given him food either."

"No, he had to find it. That was why he was there. We had food, you see. But he didn't have anything to do with men, this mouse. He just took what food he could get and lived that way."

"Well, but the whitecoats would kill him if they could, wouldn't they? I remember the tobacco man once running about, trying to stamp on one he saw."

"Ah, that's just it. What did the mouse do?"

"Got away down one of the gully-holes in the floor."

"Yes." Rowf looked up as a buzzard sailed into view, hovered a few moments, evidently decided to leave them alone and disappeared.

"The whitecoats *would* kill him if they could catch him," said Rowf. "But he took care they didn't, this mouse. That was how he lived, he told me. He only came out at night, slept down a hole—"

"Danced on his tail to save wearing out his paws. Wore a very small paper bag to keep off the rain—"

Rowf turned to snap, and Snitter jumped up and ran away a few yards among the loose stones. Rowf, about to follow, saw him check and remain staring.

"What?"

Snitter did not answer and Rowf joined him.

Far off, over the further brim of the valley, the man had returned. As the sound of his cries once more reached them, they saw the grey, pendent-coated shapes of two sheep appear, running hard over the brow higher up. Behind them, a black-and-white dog came racing out from among the crags, dodging in and out of the heather-clumps as it went. They watched it run in a wide half-circle before turning to descend towards the sheep, which thereupon changed direction and began to run downhill. Meanwhile the man, striding swiftly, had almost reached the edge of the tarn. At his further cry the dog stopped dead and lay down, while a moment later another dog came into view, chasing before it a third yow who ran to join the other two.

With a whine of delight, Snitter sprang to his feet.

"Rowf! Look! Take a good look! That, Rowf, is a master—a real master of dogs! We're home and dry, Rowf, and I was right and you were wrong! Oh, Snit's a good dog! Pass me a piece of that blue sky and I'll chew it up! Toss me a lamp-post and I'll carry it home! Come on, quick!"

"Where? What for? Snitter, wait—"

"We go and do what they're doing, don't you see, and then the man'll take us home with him! What luck! Come on!"

Snitter was off as fast as his short legs would carry him, scraping the pads of his paws on the rough stones, tumbling in and out of peaty rifts, thrusting breast-high through sheaves of wet heather. Rowf at first remained where he was, but when Snitter was well down the slope and showing no sign of hesitation or second thoughts, he too came out from their hiding-place and followed. He overtook him splashing through Cove Beck, above the steep crags north-west of the tarn.

"Snitter, wait, I tell you! I don't understand!"

"Neither do I, altogether. My master used to throw

sticks, but it's all the same. When you go out of doors with a master, he always likes you to run about and do things. This man must have sheep instead of sticks, that's all."

At this moment a yow which they had not seen got up a little distance ahead of them and began to trot quickly away. Instantly Snitter set off in pursuit, barking loudly, and after a few moments Rowf copied him. The yow broke into a sheep-gallop, covering the uneven ground with leaps and quick turns and leaving hanks of its un-clipped fleece trailing as it pushed through the patches of furze. Snitter, catching the coarse, warm smells of wool and sheep-dip, became even more excited, snapping and barking in the heat of pursuit. He put up another yow and as he overtook it found Rowf at his shoulder, charging into action like a hound in full cry. His voice rang over the fell.

"Rowf! Grrrrr-owf, rowf! We'll show 'em! We'll show 'em! Rowf, rowf!"

Both yows turned suddenly and ran back by the way they had come, blundering past the dogs with a quick clitter-clatter of narrow, agile hooves. Snitter was off again, this time biting at their very heels. Away below, on the nearer shore of the tarn now, but separated from them by the sheer crags, he caught a glimpse of the man, his cloth cap pushed back on his fell of hair, waving a long thumb-stick and apparently yelling encouragement. His teeth nipped the hindmost yow just above the hock and for a moment he tasted blood before she kicked backwards and her hoof took him in the muzzle. Dazed, he sat back on his haunches, panting.

"Hey! What th' 'ell doost think th'art playin' at? Art stark bluidy mad or what?"

Snitter looked up. Just above him, on a peat-bank, one of the black-and-white sheep-dogs was standing, glaring down with an expression of mingled bewilderment and blazing fury. It smelt as angry as any dog Snitter had ever encountered in his life. Frightened and confused, he said, "It's all right—we—er—we don't mean you any harm—you see, we need a master—we're straying—we were just joining in—"

Rowf was beside him now, silent and waiting.

"Art out of thy minds, chasing yows oop an' down fell, snappin' an' bitin'? Wheer's thy farm at? Wheer's thy masster? Tha's nipped yon yow, too, tha basstard—it's bleeding, is yon—"

The sheep-dog became inarticulate with rage and incomprehension. So overwhelming was his indignation that, like thunder or the smell of a bitch, it swept everything else from Snitter's mind. The excitement of the chase, his confidence in the friendliness of the man down by the tarn, his hopes of adoption—these vanished as he found himself confronting—as unexpectedly as Rowf had been confronted by Low Water—the outraged, incredulous anger of the sheep-dog. There could be no question of talk or argument. It was like a bad dream. Whatever innocent fault they had committed, it must be something worse than vomiting on a carpet or biting a child; and evidently the sheep-dog was merely the sharp end of a whole world's wedge of anger.

Snitter lay still as a stone while the dog came down and sniffed him over.

"I—I'm sorry—sir—you see—we—we didn't know—"

"Lay off!" cried Rowf angrily to the sheep-dog. "You let him alone! You don't own this place—"

"Doan't oan it? Then I'd like to know who bluidy dooz. Hey, Wag," cried the dog to his colleague, who now came running towards them, "it says we doan't oan this fell 'ere!"

"Bluidy cheek!" The second dog bristled. He looked, thought Snitter, a most ugly customer, smelling strongly of a more-or-less permanent disposition to attack. "What they reckon theer oop to, then?"

"Cheek yourself!" Rowf, the biggest dog of the four, was on his feet, hackles up and teeth bared. "What are *you* doing here, if it comes to that?"

"Getherin, ye dafft sod! Seekin' woolled sheep, a' course. An' then tha cooms down from top—like bluidy bulls on the loose—an' spoils hafe an hour's good work—"

"Ay—they'll be tourists' tykes, tha knaws," said the first dog. "Thee, with yon patch on thy head, wheer's thy

(84)

masster at?" he demanded for the second time. "Is he oop fell? Hast roon away, tha feckless gowks?"

"No, we haven't a master. We want to meet yours— we didn't mean any harm—"

"He'll fill thee wi' lead, joost," said the second dog, snapping quickly at a moth that came fluttering out of the underbrush. "Ay, he will that."

"He hasn't got a gun," said Snitter.

"Happen he has," returned the dog. "Thee bide around theer and thee'll soon find out. Hey, Wag, remember yon dog he shot last soommer, when it were chasin' doocks, tha knaws—"

"Ay. He were—" The first dog seemed about to enlarge on this pleasant recollection when a perfect fusillade of cries rose from somewhere out of sight beneath the sheer face below them.

"Don, lay down! Don, lay down! Wag, coom bye 'ere! Wag, coom bye 'ere! Yer Wag! Yer Wag!"

"Get off fell, tha booggers, that's all," said the second dog. "Goo on awaay!"

It raced off, responding, as it came into his view, to further instructions from the shepherd below. The first dog, Don, remained crouching tensely on the grass, tongue lolling and front paws outstretched, paying Snitter and Rowf no further attention whatever until, at a sudden cry of "Don, gow way! Don, gow way!" it leapt up, gave a single bark and tore uphill, climbing to get above and so turn two yows which were running before Wag.

Snitter and Rowf looked at each other.

"Thee'd best watch thesen," said Rowf bitterly. "Happen—"

"Oh, it isn't *funny.*" Snitter was distraught. "I don't understand. We were only doing the same as them—"

"They didn't want us to join their man. Jealous."

"Perhaps. I remember a cat that hid behind the door spit spit cuff scratch—just the same. No, but they were— oh, clouds in the sky, leaves on a tree, bark when you hear the key in the door—they belonged where they were, didn't they; they were at home? You could smell it. No whitecoat does anything to *them.* But what are we going to do, Rowf?"

"We've got to get out of here," said Rowf, "before they come back. Teeth rip it, yes and quick! My dam, the man's coming, look!"

Sure enough, the man with the thumb-stick had appeared round one end of the line of crags and was hurrying towards them in silence. They could see the teeth in his face and smell his meaty sweat and manure-mucky boots. Yet even as they made off up the fell, he too turned aside and disappeared, evidently satisfied to have seen the back of them and not wishing to leave his gethered sheep any longer in the sole care of his dogs.

Higher and higher. The wind had died altogether now and the heights ahead had become invisible under a sudden mist. It seemed the very manifestation of their hopelessness and bewilderment. There was no longer any trace of destination or purpose in their wandering. Upward they went in silence—for they did not know where else to go or what to do—close together, tails drooping, unresponding even when some creature—a rat or rabbit, half-concealed in the mirk—startled and ran across their front. The grass grew sparser and then was no more. They were in a barren land, a blotted-out place of loose stones and bare rocks, steep and high up. The mist swirled about them, thickening the higher they went and smelling of dampness, of wet lichen on the rocks, of a dead sheep somewhere and faintly, beneath all else, of the salt sea. They were climbing the 2,300-foot pitch of Levers Hause, the near-precipitous band between Brim Fell and Swirral; as wild, grim and lonely a place as any in the Lakeland. Night was falling and in all the waste about them they knew of no food, no shelter, no friend.

"I'm like an apple tree in autumn," said Snitter suddenly. "Tumbling down, full of wasps and maggots. And after that, you know, the leaves come down as well—the sooner you leave me the better for you."

"I won't leave you."

"Everything I've tried today has gone wrong. This isn't the world I left when I was sold to the whitecoats. It's all changed. Perhaps *I've* changed it. Perhaps I'm mad even at the times when I don't feel it. But surely all this smoke can't be coming out of my head?"

Brim Fell and Levers Hause

"It isn't smoke. There's no burning. You can smell. The whitecoats are mad themselves. That's why they cut you—to make you mad too."

The mist was close about them now and the slope very

steep. In the cold, the pockets and shallow pools of water among the rocks were already crizzling. Snitter could feel minute shards of ice splintering and vanishing under his pads. Presently he said, "Are you hungry?"

"I could eat my own paws. We'd have been fed by now, wouldn't we?"

"Yes, if you'd survived the metal water today. You always said you were sure they meant to kill you in the end."

The ground became level and now they could once more feel a light wind—or rather, a kind of draught—in their faces, causing the mist to stream past them, so that to themselves they seemed to be moving even when they stood still. Wet through and very cold, they lay down, both completely at a loss.

"We couldn't even find our way back to the whitecoats now," said Rowf at length. "I mean, supposing we wanted to."

"Why would we want to?"

"The tobacco man's got *our* food—the men we've seen today probably give food only to the lorries or to some other dogs—whatever animals it is that they have to hurt. Animals like us—if we're not the particular ones they hurt we don't get any food."

"Do you want to go back?"

"I don't know. We can't starve. Why did we come up here? I shouldn't think anyone has been up here since the men made it, whenever that was."

"The men with the lorries made it. No one dares to come up or down it now for fear of starving. Not even their tobacco man's used it. When he wants to come down he jumps off the top and lands in the water to keep his boots clean. He's really the wind, you know. He keeps *his* animals hung on his belt. He's dressed all in red leaves, and he gives them packets of maggots to eat. He lights his pipe with lightning and wears a cap made of cats' fur—"

"If he comes here I'll fight him—I'll tear him—"

"He won't come. He got lost in the garden and kicked my brains to bits trying to find the way out."

It was shut of eve now, dark and very silent. A sound of mallard's wings went whauping overhead, diminished and died, and in the cold a torpid beetle fell from a stone and lay on its back, apparently unable either to right itself or to crawl away. There was no sign of any other living creature.

After a long time Rowf rose slowly to his feet and stood with outthrust muzzle, staring ahead of him so fixedly that Snitter turned his head and followed his gaze, trying to perceive what new enemy might be approaching: but there was nothing to be seen. Just as he was about to speak to him Rowf, without looking round and as though to someone else, barked into the darkness, "I know I'm a coward and a runaway—a dog who can't do what men want, but I'm not going to die up here without making a fight for it. Help us! Help!"

Quickly, he turned and pressed his muzzle to Snitter's loins. "We've tried your way, Snitter. Now we'll try mine. That mouse isn't the only one who can do without men. We can *change* if we want to. Do you know that? *Change*—into wild animals!"

He flung up his head and howled to the blotted-out, invisible sky. "Damn men! Damn all men! Change! Change!"

Nothing moved in the silence, yet Snitter, nose lifted in fear and uncertainty, could now perceive, growing about them, a rank, feral scent. An old, wild scent it seemed, drawn up, one might imagine, from the depths of the ancient ground beneath their paws; an ugly scent, a snarling, bloody scent, far away, slavering, full of brutal appetite and savagery, of brief life and briefer death, of the weakest down and the desperate slayer torn to pieces at last, either by his enemies or his own pitiless kin. As it entered and overcame him, his head swam and in terror he sprang up, giddy as he was, and fled he knew not where across the cold stones. Rowf, stock-still and waiting, made no movement and seemed unaware of his flight; and after a little he returned, timidly wagging his tail and smelling at the black, shaggy body as though at a stranger's.

"Rowf?"

"Owl and rat, shrew and crow," muttered Rowf thickly. "Fiercer—older—fiercer—"

"Are you an owl, Rowf; a rat? I can't fall so far—"

Rowf lowered his muzzle to the ground.

"Long ago. Fierce sire; fierce dam. Fiercer than men. Kill or be killed—"

"Rowf—"

"Wolf and crow; penned in byre sheep and lamb. Smash the pen, belly filled. Jaws grip and teeth rip—"

He snarled, tearing at the ground with his claws. "Owls, yes but fiercer. Rats, but more cunning."

From the grinning jaws which he turned upon Snitter foam was dripping in viscous, sharp-smelling runnels. Snitter, belly pressed to the ground in subjection, felt rising from his own being the response of a tameless force, old, long-lost but now restored, innocent of mercy to any other creature, cunning and ruthless, living only to hunger, to smell out and pursue, to kill and devour. As he plunged to meet it, slobbering and urinating in the eagerness of surrender, it flowed over and engulfed him and he too tore and bit at the ground. The mist was changed to an intoxicant fume that was indeed pouring out of his own maimed head. Yet now he knew himself also the creature of the mist, that mist created by an all-wise providence expressly to conceal the hunter from the quarry; the hill-mist below which, in lonely valleys, men—not so long ago—had hidden, in their huts and caves, from the teeth of the prowling, four-footed enemy whom they could not even see before he fell upon their homes and cattle in the black night.

"Food, Rowf! Food, Rowf! Kill it! Kill it! Kill!"

"We're going to kill it now," answered the great, black hound, through bared teeth.

"Men? Men?"

"Men or their beasts."

"Which way? Which way, Rowf, which way?"

"The way I smell."

Running beside him, Snitter could wind at first only the emptiness of the high fell, the grass evenly wet as though a net of fine waterdrops had been cast over the whole mountain. Eyes and ears alike could tell him nothing more and his nose conveyed no sense of direction. Every smell—leaves, salt, rain, bracken, heather and rock —came from all directions and from none; was, in fact, the smell of the enveloping mist itself. If there was a beck trickling below, its sound did not penetrate the mist. If there were stars overhead, their light had no business here. This obscurity was more than darkness. It was void. Rowf, he understood dimly, had invoked to their aid a power which, although their own by ancient right, was also one of overwhelming ferocity, dreaded by men and animals from the beginning of time; cruel, furtive and slouching; a power whose servants were bound, in return for a thin measure of hazardous survival, to inflict the only law in the world, the law of Kill or Be Killed. Suddenly he understood why it was that, though he and Rowf were moving silently on, the stones, the wet grass and crags remained unchanged; why he could not tell up-wind from down-wind, mist from rain, starlight from darkness. For it was time through which they were moving; to a place where dogs knew of men only that they were enemies, to beware, to outwit, to rob and kill. Sharp flashes of pain came and went in his head. The watery air seemed to be choking him and now, as he peered about him, he perceived with fear that they were no longer two but many. Round them in the mist other animals were padding—shadowy animals with prick ears, lolling tongues and bushy tails—all silent, all voracious and intent, each knowing that his share would be nothing but what he could seize, tear, defend and devour for himself.

"Rowf," he whispered, "who are they? Where are we?"

Without answering Rowf bounded suddenly forward, leaping between two boulders and down into the rocky, sheltered space below. Snitter heard his high-pitched growling and the plunging and kicking of a heavy body. As he himself jumped through the cleft Rowf was thrown backwards on top of him. There followed a clicking of hooves and rattling of stones as the yow vanished into the darkness. Rowf, bleeding, picked himself up and spat out a mouthful of oily wool.

"It was too quick for me. I couldn't get it by the throat."

"To kill it? Is this—is this—where they kill?"

"And eat," said Rowf, "or starve. Come on."

Again he scented, tracked and found. Again the quarry eluded him as he sprang at it, and he pursued it down the almost sheer face of the fell, so that Snitter lost him and wandered, limping and yapping until, by chance rather than by scent or hearing, he came upon Rowf lying in a stony rift, panting as he licked at one bleeding forepaw.

"Don't leave me, Rowf! This place frightens me. I daren't be lost here—alone—"

"They're too quick," said Rowf again, "and very strong. They know their way about here, too."

"Those—those dogs this afternoon," said Snitter timidly. "Damn them!"

"Yes, but—wait—I'm trying to dig it up. If one dog goes alone after a sheep, the sheep runs away—more or less wherever it wants. Those two dogs went to different places—I was watching—so that they could drive the sheep down to the man. He kept calling out to them and they did what he said."

He could not tell whether Rowf had understood him or not. He waited in the empty darkness, rubbing his muzzle against Rowf's sodden, shaggy side. At length Rowf answered, "Well?"

"Two different places—dogs in two places—one runs while the other waits—There was a cat once," said Snitter, "in the street. I was chasing it and it ran round the corner straight into another dog."

"Well?" Rowf, a grim stranger, scratched impatiently at the stones. Snitter became confused.

"The cat floated down the gutter and I blew away with the leaves. The other dog was carrying his master's leg—that was before the lorry came—oh, my head!"

When he came to himself he was still in the remote, savage place, and Rowf was licking his face.

"Don't bite me, Rowf! Don't! I saw a sheep—a sheep like a cat. It turned the corner and you were there, waiting for it."

"I understand. Come on then."

They set off once more, at first climbing steeply and then, coming upon fresh sheep-dung on a narrow trod, creeping stealthily along it, one behind the other.

"There's two of them ahead of us," said Rowf suddenly. "Not too far, either." He sniffed the air again, then moved silently off the trod to one side. "I shall be waiting behind this rock."

There was no need for further talk. Snitter knew now what they would do and knew that Rowf knew also. Rowf had seen the cat turn the corner because they were no longer separate creatures. It was their nature, he now understood, to fuse as clouds fuse, to draw apart as the wind might impel them, to mingle again as waters mingle, obedient to the pull of the earth: to feel a single impulse, as a hundred pigeons turn together on the wing; to attack together, as common in purpose as bees driven to fury by a scent on the air; to retain nothing individual. He and Rowf were an animal—an animal that must eat, and had accordingly been given faculties to fulfil that need, including that of being in two places at once. It was this animal that he had left crouching behind the rock, this animal which was now slinking silently over the grass, climbing to get round the sheep on the trod below, creeping down beyond them, yes here was the line of the trod, turn back now in the direction from which he had come, sweet, rank smell of sheep's wet breath, bulky shapes in the mist—

Snitter, breaking into a fierce yapping, dashed forward. The yows fled from him immediately, one bleating and plunging away down the fell. The other ran back along the trod and even as he followed it a quick warning flashed into his nose, his feet and ears, uttered by the shadowy comrades hunting round him: "The first sheep went down the fell because you dashed in too fast and panicked it. Hold back and let this one keep on along the trod."

He stopped, uttering growls that ended in snapping barks. He heard hooves trotting, a shallow puddle stamped in, stones rattling and then, like an impact upon his own body, Rowf hurtling forward to bury his teeth in the sheep's throat. Dragging, battering, beating against the crags: kicking and plunging; and he was running after the sound in the dark. There was blood, steaming blood, sniff lick drooling on the ground, growling breath and a heavy body struggling, staggering forward, a clot of bloody wool, a choking, rattling noise somewhere ahead. Where? This was it, this was it, Rowf underneath, blood and shit and the smell of a sheep in agony and terror. He snapped and bit at the head, at the convulsed jaws and staring eyes, then found the edge of an open wound in the throat and ripped and tore. Suddenly, as he tugged, a great spurt of hot blood poured over his face. The wool and flesh gave way in his teeth and he fell backwards, recovered himself and leapt in again, this time to feel first an inert throbbing and then stillness. Rowf, a black, hairy bulk soaked in blood, was dragging himself out from under. Snitter, beginning to lick, could taste dog's blood mingled with sheep's. There was a jagged scratch along Rowf's left side and one of his fore-paws was oozing blood.

Rowf's weight thrust him aside, gasping with excitement.

"Tear it, tear it!"

When the stomach was ripped open they dragged the steaming entrails among the rocks, gnawed at the rib cage, fought over the liver, chewed the wet heart in pieces. Rowf tore at a haunch until he had it severed, sinew, ball-joint and skin, and lay crunching the red bone in his teeth. Warmth flowed through them, and confidence—in the dark night where others were afraid, and the cold retarding the alertness of their prey. Snitter pissed over one rock after another—"That'll show them who owns the place!"

Rowf, curled upon the bloody stones as though in a basket, opened one eye. "Show whom?"

"If those sheep-dogs came back here now, Rowf, we'd tear them, wouldn't we? Tear them—they'd break up like biscuit! 'What's this, what's this? Dear me, a piece of a dog, who can have been so careless?' I'm careless, Rowf, not a care, very fair, very far, ha ha!"

Incrimination and heady elation, cutting capers in the misty vapours, havoc and ravage hurrah for the savage life precarious, life so various, life nefarious and temerarious, pulling faces, fierce grimaces, leaving traces in rocky places, pieces and faeces all over the fleece is that a yow's shoulder they've left there to moulder stuck up on a boulder? Much to learn, Rowf, in the fern, of great concern, for this is the point of no return. Those who kill sheep should mind where they sleep, when there's nothing to hear the shot-gun is near, the curse of the farmer is likely to harm yer, a scent in the morning is sent for a warning, at a cloud on the sun a wise dog will run, it's the sharp and alert who avoid being hurt and a dog that's gone feral is living in peril. Those with blood on their paws and wool in their jaws should heed these old saws.

Rowf, as yet far from adept but uneasily aware that a great change had indeed come upon them, got up and began padding up and down, nosing about, listening and throwing up his head to smell the air.

Mist in the Lakeland can fall as swiftly as rooks fill the sky on a fine evening, almost faster than the fell-walker's hastily unlocked compass-needle can swing north to give a bearing: may swirl around the lost in icy folds until the very cairns themselves seem loosed and moving, weaving, deceiving, drifting landmarks in a muffled no-place where mountain gullies lead down into pits of air. And again, once fallen, the mist may break up as suddenly, opening as fast as a hastily ripped envelope full of bad news.

First Snitter saw the stars—bright Deneb in the zenith, Arcturus twinkling grim and very far. Through the fog they came and then, all on the instant as it seemed, the opaque, sound-muffling blanket vanished before a wind smelling of sea-weed and salt-drenched sand. Startled by the swiftness of the change, Rowf instinctively crept under a crag, as though knowing himself dangerously revealed beside their kill in the sudden clarity of moonlight.

It was a little below the high ridge of Levers Hause that they found themselves exposed—a watershed steep on both sides, so high and steep that yows seldom cross from one valley to the other—those that do being a mere handful, a half-dozen or so to be recognized at getherin by their marks and exchanged at shepherds' meet on Walna Scar. They had crossed the ridge to the Dunnerdale side. To the south hung the grim, eastern face of Dow Crag, that gully-riven precipice that has killed too many climbers, including a veteran of Kashmir. North-westward rose the flat top of Grey Friar and directly below lay the hanging valley known to Seathwaite shepherds as Rough Grund—the land above and draining into Seathwaite Tarn. A light wind was ruffling the surface of the tarn with a broken, maculate gleam, from the shallow, marshy infall down to the deep water round the convex curve of the dam. Thus seen from a mile away, the place looked, at this moment, peaceful even to Rowf—Charybdis asleep, as it were, or the clashing rocks of legend stilled in their noonday trance. In all the mile-wide valley they could see no movement save that of the becks and yet, watching from this high, bare shelf among the strewn remains of their kill, both dogs, hearkening unknowingly to the whispered warnings of that cunning, bloody power whose service they had entered, felt exposed, strayed beyond safety, out of shelter, dangerously in the open.

Snitter's high spirits flickered and died like a spent match. He sat clawing at his plastered head and looking down at the marshy floor below.

"We're birds on a lawn, Rowf, flies on a pane. The moon will come and run us over."

Rowf considered. "A man may come—we don't know. Those other sheep this afternoon belonged to a man; so this one must have too. He might have a gun, as those dogs said."

"The same man?"

"Or a different man. It doesn't matter. We must get away."

"But where?"

"I don't know. They've put tanks everywhere, you see—there's another one down there."

"But, Rowf, you know the whitecoats never come at night. We've got time to find somewhere to hide, somewhere to run before the sun, before the gun."

Rowf blew out warm, steaming breath. "Hide? They might be watching us now."

"How could they be?"

"Well, they might have something that makes things look close when they're far off. They might be watching from right away over there."

"Oh, that's silly, Rowf. I know they can disappear and breathe fire and create light and all sorts of things, but they couldn't possibly do that. You're letting your imagination run away with you."

Rowf yawned wide and licked his chops. Snitter could

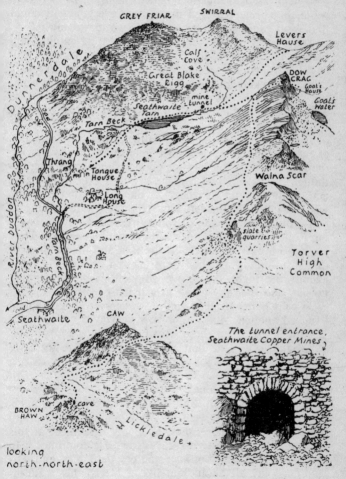

Saturday, 16th October
to
Thursday, 28th October

LEVERS HAUSE
TO
BROWN HAW

GREY FRIAR

SWIRRAL

Levers
Hause

Dunnerdale

Calf
Cove

Great Bloke
Rigg

DOW
CRAG

Goat's
House

mine
tunnel

Goat's
Water

Seathwaite
Tarn

Tarn Beck

Thrang

Tongue
House

Walna Scar

Long
House

River Duddon

Tarn Beck

slate
quarries

Torver
High
Common

Seathwaite

CAW

The tunnel entrance,
Seathwaite Copper Mines

BROWN
HAW

cave

Lickledale

looking
north·north·east

see fragments of sheep's flesh and sinew hanging between his teeth. "Anyway, we may as well go down into that valley as anywhere. If I can."

"If you can?"

"I'm bruised to pieces. I had to hang on by my teeth while that brute battered me against everything it could find. You can try it next time. I'll have to go slowly."

They set off down the hillside, Rowf scrambling and limping in and out of the rocks on three legs. Snitter, who could have gone twice as fast, kept running nervously from side to side, pushing his nose under stones and again turning to look out across the empty valley. The noise of the far becks came up with a wavering sound, receding and returning, and the outline of the distant, long shoulder of the Friar, too, seemed oscillating minutely to and fro, as though, poised yet not absolutely stable, it was sharing the movement of the air—or perhaps, thought Snitter, as though he himself had become a little giddy with gazing across the moonlit distance. As they came down on the wet moss the illusion left him. His paws were sinking in soft ground, boggy, full of watery rifts, and he was coaxing Rowf forward to no destination that he knew of. They could no longer see as far as the tarn and the outlines of the surrounding heights were altered, humped shapes against the night sky. Rowf stopped to drink, lapping noisily, and then lay down in a patch of rushes.

"You'd better go on, Snitter—wherever you're going. I've had enough—until tomorrow anyway."

"But if you sleep there, Rowf, in the open—"

"Might as well lie here as anywhere. Where were we going, anyway? I've got to rest, Snitter. My leg hurts."

"Caught stealing up on the table—"

"Snitter, let me alone!"

He bared his teeth. Snitter, catching the smell of his pain and exhaustion, went pattering quickly away, in and out of the bents and rushes. Suddenly it seemed, at this moment, a small matter to leave Rowf. He could not help him. Not his energy, but his resources were at an end. His ignorance lay all about him like a marsh, his madness within him like stagnant water. In this artificial, man-made wilderness he had no idea what might disclose itself, what might be lying just out of sight in any direction; nor, if granted the power to see, would he have been any wiser about what he ought to do. Once, there had been a master and a home: then, after the lorry—afterwards—the canine block, the tobacco man and the knives of the whitecoats. The escape from the whitecoats—all the cunning, courage and endurance—had proved useless because there was nowhere he and Rowf could go, no life which they could live. He remembered what Rowf had said in the pen—"There might be something worse through the door." True, there was no enemy present now, but since their escape they had not met with a single friend, animal or human, and though nothing had happened when they killed the sheep, he knew intuitively that they had committed a crime which was bound to come to light, a crime the perpetrators of which would not be forgiven. "He'll fill thee wi' lead, joost." Might it not be better to put an end now to the anxiety and fear, to accept that they had no alternative but to suffer as the whitecoats required of them? Rowf had said so from the outset; had joined him, against his own conviction that they had no chance, only because he could not face the metal tank again. Where could they go, what could they do, what plan could they make in such a place as this? They would simply wander about until a farmer shot them or took them back to the whitecoats.

Put an end, then. But how? Which way back to Animal Research? Please, sir, could you direct me to the nearest whitecoat? Do you happen to have seen a street lying about anywhere—a shop, a house, a dustbin? You see, I'm lost. My head was cut open and I fell in when I wasn't looking and now I seem to have kicked my brains to pieces trying to get out. There are leaves floating in black milk—I'm just looking for the way—no, not the way home, thought Snitter. I won't call it that.

The stream in the middle of the Moss was wide—a good five feet at the place where he came to it, and deep on the nearer side. As he stopped, peering down from the bank into the dark water, he suddenly saw, reflected over his shoulder, the figure of a man—grey-haired, dressed in an old brown overcoat and yellow scarf, carrying a walking stick, his lips pursed to whistle. As the man nodded and bent to pat him, Snitter leapt round and jumped up at his knees, barking for joy. There was no one there, and he fell forward on the squelching peat.

I wish it would stop. I thought it had. It always takes me unawares. I never remember. I always say next time I'll take no notice, but I never do. I mustn't sit here thinking about it; I must do something else at once.

He plunged into the beck, pulled himself out on the further side, scuttered up the bank and shook the water off. The wet ground was no different, but about two hundred yards away, at the foot of the hillside where it rose above the bog, he could now see a kind of platform of smooth grass, a square, flat-topped, steep-sided mound jutting out from the foot of the hill. It was so plainly artificial that at first he took it for another hallucination, and sat watching it to see whether the figure in the brown tweed coat would reappear. But all remained empty and quiet, and at length, half-hoping to find a whitecoat to whom he could give himself up, he ran across the intervening distance and up the steep bank.

On top was a levelled space of turf and small stones, perhaps half the size of a lawn tennis court. It was completely empty, but on the further side, where the foot of Great Blake Rigg, the south face of the Grey Friar, rose like a wall, was a symmetrical, dark opening lined and arched with stones—a doorway without a door—as wide as a man is tall and almost twice as high, apparently leading underground into the heart of the mountain.

Snitter sat staring in astonishment. There were no signs of human use or occupation, no sounds from inside the cavern, no man-smells that he could perceive. He went cautiously closer. He could hear currents of air whispering and echoing within. "There's a garden in its ear," thought Snitter, "but there's no one there, unless they're hiding or asleep. There's more in this than meets the nose, if I'm any judge." The only smells were those of clean stones and subterranean moisture. Keeping close to one wall and ready to run on the instant, he crept inside.

He found himself in an empty, spacious tunnel, more or less the size of the opening itself, its high, barrel vault smoothly and regularly arched with flat stones set close together, edge outwards, its floor a clean, dry shale of similar, loose stones. Some of these rocked slightly under his paws, but otherwise the ground was even and without faults. The tunnel ran back into the heart of the mountain and from the movement of air, as well as the tiny echoes he could hear, he realized that it must be very deep.

He moved forward, looking about him. As he went on, the dim light from the cave mouth receded, but otherwise there was no change. The tunnel remained level, arched above and shaled below. He came to the mouth of a drift running in from one side, and stopped to smell and listen. It was dry, chill but not cold, and apparently not very deep. As he turned to go back to the main shaft, he saw the opening to the fell as a distant semi-circle of dark blue, with one star twinkling in the middle.

Half an hour later, Snitter found Rowf where he had left him, asleep under a patch of bog myrtle. There was a light drizzle of rain, though the moon, setting in the west, was clear of cloud.

"Rowf, come back! Listen! Listen to me!"

"Why didn't you go? I thought you'd gone, I told you to go."

"I *have* gone. The mouse-hole, Rowf, the gully in the floor—it's real—we're mice—"

"Oh, let me alone, you brain-sick puppy!"

"The whitecoats can't catch the mice, Rowf! It's safe in the rhododendrons—I mean the hole in the floor—"

"It's a pity they didn't cut your head *off* while they were about it. You couldn't talk nonsense then. My leg feels like a door in the wind—"

Snitter made a great effort. "There's a place, Rowf, a place—secret, dry, out of the rain. I believe we couldn't be found there."

"Couldn't be *found* there?"

"By men—whitecoats or farmers—anyone."

"Why not? They must have made it."

"Yes, and come to that they made the gullies in the floor, where the mouse lived. Rowf, you're wet through—"

"It's clean water—"

"You'll get fever." Snitter nipped his fore-leg and dodged away as Rowf snarled and clambered shakily to his feet. "I'm sure I've found something good."

"How can there be anything good in a place like this?"

"Come and see."

When at last he had persuaded Rowf across the beck and up the steep bank to the grassy platform, the moon had set and they could barely make out the mouth of the cavern. Snitter led the way in, hearing behind him the clattering of the shale as Rowf limped on his painful leg. In the blackness of the first drift he lay down and waited for Rowf to join him.

For a long time they lay silently together on the dry stones. At last Snitter said, "Wouldn't there be a chance, do you think; if only we could go on killing food? It's deep—right down inside your head—and warm—out of the wind—and we could go a long way in if we had to—no one could find us—"

Rowf, lying stretched out on his side, raised his head sleepily. "Come over here; we might as well keep each other warm. Unless it's some sort of trap—you know, suppose a whitecoat suddenly comes in and makes light—"

"There's no smell of men at all."

"I know. They made it, but they've gone. Or else it's like the drains—"

"No, it isn't like the drains," answered Snitter. "We must always remember that, too. The whitecoats couldn't get down the drains; not even the tobacco man could. But they could come down here all right if they wanted to; perhaps while we were asleep. So they mustn't find out we're here at all."

"Unless they know now. Unless they can see us now."

"Yes—but somehow I feel they can't. How does it smell to you?"

Rowf made no answer for a long time. At last he said,

"I believe—I'm almost afraid to believe, but yes, I do believe you're right, Snitter. And if you are—"

"Yes?"

"It'll prove that we were right to escape after all; and *we'll* have a chance to prove—to ourselves anyway—that dogs can live without men. We'll be wild animals; and we'll be free."

FIT 3

Sunday the 17th October

It was not until some twelve hours later, on Sunday morning, that Tyson, his cap not actually removed (an action as unthinkable as for Santa Claus to shave his whiskers) but thrust vertically to the back of his head as a kind of cryptic token of a kind of cryptic respect, stood facing Mr. Powell outside the staff common room at Lawson Park.

"Ay, theer's the two on them gone," he said for the second time. "Ah thowt Ah'd better let thee knaw, like, first thing off. Theer noan anywheers int' block, but happen theer noan that far awaay."

"Are you sure they're not still in the block?" asked Mr. Powell. "I mean to say, there doesn't seem any way they could have got out, really. Are you sure they've not crept in behind something?"

"Theer noan int' block," repeated Tyson, "and Ah reckon theer nowheers about t' plaace at all. But happen they'll noan have gone far."

"It'd be much the best thing if we *could* find them today," said Mr. Powell. "You and me, I mean. Then there'd be no reason for either Dr. Boycott or Mr. Fortescue to know anything about it at all. They're both away till tomorrow morning, so that gives us twenty-four hours."

"Soombody moosta seen 'em, like," said Tyson. "Lasst time they were fed were Friday neet, so they'll 'ave had a go to get some groob out of soomwheers." He paused. "Happen they might a bin chasin' sheep ont' fell an' all. That'd be a reet do, that would. That's offence against law, tha knaws, bein' in possession of dog as woorries sheep."

"Oh, my God!" said Mr. Powell, appalled by the sudden thought that he might be held personally responsible. "Tell me again how you found they were gone."

"Well, like Ah toald thee, it were Sat'day evening when Ah coom in at usual time, to feed animals an' that," said Tyson. "An' Ah seen reet awaay that yon black dog, seven-three-two, were gone out of it caage. Door were oppen, see, an' spring o' catch were broaken. It moosta snapped some time affter Friday neet, for it were awreet then."

Tyson had, in fact, taken a screwdriver to the catch mechanism of the pen door. It was not that he was afraid of dismissal, or even that he cared particularly about reproof from the Director or from Dr. Boycott. It was, rather, that in some curious, scarcely conscious manner, he felt that by breaking the spring of the catch he was actually altering what had happened. After all, if the spring *had* snapped of its own accord, on account of metal fatigue or some fault in the steel, then that would have explained the dogs' escape. Now the spring *had* snapped, and therefore it *did* account for the escape—to himself as well as to others—and saved a lot of pointless speculation and inquiry. In Tyson's world, things that had happened had happened, and inquiry was a waste of time. If, for example, matters had so fallen out that it had been Tom who had reported the dogs' escape to himself, he would simply have cuffed his head and sworn at him, whether Tom were to blame or not (much as the Aztecs used to execute messengers who brought bad news) and then begun to try to put things right. The spring was now deemed to have snapped; a state of affairs not vastly different, come to that, from the building of Animal Research itself having attracted deemed planning permission from the Secretary of State.

"But the other dog," said **Mr. Powell**, "eight-one-five? What happened there?"

"It had pooshed oop wire along bottom with it noase," said Tyson. "Coople o' staples had pulled out, and it moosta scrambled oonder an' joined t' oother dog."

"That's not going to be so easy to explain," mused Mr. Powell. "That was an important dog, too, that eight-one-five. Adult domesticated dog—they're never easy to get hold of for this sort of work. It had had a tricky brain operation and was waiting for tests. There'll be hell to pay."

"Ay, well, Ah thowt thee'd want to knaw as soon as possible," said Tyson virtuously. "Theer were nobody here yesterday neet"—and here he contrived to suggest (not unsuccessfully, since Mr. Powell was almost young enough to be his grandson and unable—why did he try, one wonders?—to conceal the signs of his origin among people very much like Tyson) that he himself had been the only dutiful and conscientious employee of Lawson Park at his post on a Saturday evening—"but Ah coom oop first thing this morning to see if Dr. Boycott were here. Ah'll joost have to be shiftin' along now." For if a search there were going to be, Tyson had no intention of spending his Sunday in participation.

"You say they must have run right through the block?" asked Mr. Powell.

"Well, theer were box of mice knocked ont' floor like, in pregnancy unit. Dogs moosta doon it, noothin' else could 'uv."

"Oh, blast and damn!" cried Mr. Powell, visualizing the complaints from and correspondence with the general medical practitioners and other appointed representatives of the putatively pregnant young women. A sudden thought struck him. "Then they must have gone through the cancer unit, Tyson—the rat block?"

"Ay, they would that."

"I say, they didn't get into Dr. Goodner's place, did they?" asked Mr. Powell quickly.

"Nay, it were locked reet as ever. There's noon goes in theer but hisself."

"But you're absolutely *certain*—er, Mr. Tyson—that they didn't get in there?"

"Oh ay. He'll tell thee hisself."

"Well, thank the holies for that, anyway. That *would* have been the end, that would. Well, I suppose I'd better have a look round the place myself and then if they don't turn up I'll go out and see if I can find anyone who's seen them. I shan't tell the police—that'll be for the Director to decide. Dammit," said Mr. Powell, "someone *must* have seen 'em—they've got those green collars on, plain as day. Very likely someone'll ring up later. Well, thanks, Mr. Tyson. And if you hear anything yourself, ring up and leave a message for me, won't you?"

Some say that deep sleep is dreamless and that we dream only in the moments before awakening, experiencing during seconds the imagined occurrences of minutes or hours. Others have surmised that dreaming is continuous as long as we are asleep, just as sensation and experience must needs continue as long as we are awake; but that we recall—when we recall at all—only those margins and fragments which concluded the whole range of our imagining during sleep; as though one who at night was able to walk alive through the depths of the sea, upon his return could remember only those light-filtering, green-lit slopes up which he had clambered back at last to the sands of morning. Others again believe that in deep sleep, when the gaoler nods unawares and the doors fall open upon those age-old, mysterious caverns of the mind where none ever did anything so new-fangled as read a book or say a prayer, the obscure forces, sore labour's bath, that flow forth to cleanse and renew, are of their nature inexpressible—and invisible, therefore, to dreaming eyes—in any terms or symbols comprehensible to the mind of one alive, though we may know more when we are dead. Some of these, however (so runs the theory), floating upwards from psychic depths far below those of the individual mind, attract to themselves concordant splinters and sympathetic remnants from the individual dreamer's memory—much as, they say, the fairies, poor wisps of nothing, used to glean and deck themselves with such scraps and snippets of finery as humans might have discarded for their finding. Dreams, then, are bubbles, insubstantial globes of waking matter, by their nature rising buoyant through the enveloping element of sleep; and for all we know, too numerous to be marked and remembered by the sleeper, who upon his awakening catches only one here or there, as a child in autumn may catch a falling leaf out of all the myriads twirling past him.

Be this as it may, how terrible, to some, can be the return from those dark sea-caves! Ah, God! we stagger up through the surf and collapse upon the sand, behind us the memory of our visions and before us the prospect of a desert shore or a land peopled by savages. Or again, we are dragged by the waves over coral, our landfall a torment from which, if only it would harbour us, we would fly back into the ocean. For indeed, when asleep we are like amphibious creatures, breathing another element, which reciprocates our own final act of waking by itself casting us out and closing the door upon all hope of immediate return. The caddis larva crawls upon the bottom of the pond, secure within its house of fragments, until in due time there comes upon it, whether it will or no, that strange and fatal hour when it must leave its frail safety and begin to crawl, helpless and exposed, towards the surface. What dangers gather about it then, in this last hour of its water-life—rending, devouring, swallowing into the belly of the great fish! And this hazard it can by no means evade, but only trust to survive. What follows? Emergence into the no-less-terrible world of air, with the prospect of the mayfly's short life, defenceless among the rising trout and pouncing sparrows. We crawl upwards towards Monday morning; to the cheque book and the boss; to the dismal recollection of guilt, of advancing illness, of imminent death in battle or the onset of disgrace or ruin. "I must be up betimes," said King Charles, awakening for the last time upon that bitter dawn in January long ago, "for I have a great work to do today." A noble gentleman, he shed no tears for himself. Yet who would not weep for him, emerging courageous, obstinate and alone upon that desolate shore whither sleep had cast him up to confront his unjust death?

When Snitter woke in the near-darkness of the shaft, it was to the accustomed sense of loss and madness, to the dull ache in his head, the clammy sensation of the torn and sodden dressing above his eye and the recollection that he and Rowf were masterless fugitives, free to keep themselves alive for as long as they could in an unnatural, unfamiliar place, of the nature of which they knew practically nothing. He did not even know the way back to Animal Research or whether, if they did return, they would be taken in. Perhaps the whitecoats or the tobacco man had already decreed that they were to be killed. He had several times seen the latter remove sick dogs from their pens, but had never seen him bring one back. He remembered Brot, a dog who, like himself, had been put to sleep by the whitecoats, but had woken to find that he was blind. Brot had blundered about his pen for several hours before the tobacco man, coming in at his usual time in the evening, had taken him away. Snitter could recall clearly the desperate and hopeless tone of his yelping. He himself had no fear of going blind; but what if his fits and visions were to increase, perhaps to possess him altogether, so that— He started up from where he was lying on the dry shale.

"Rowf! Rowf, listen, you *will* kill me, won't you? You coud do it quite quickly. It wouldn't be difficult. Rowf?"

Rowf had woken in the instant that Snitter's body ceased to touch his own.

"What are you talking about, you crazy little duffer? *What* did you say?"

"Nothing," answered Snitter. "I meant if I ever change into wasps, you know—maggots—I mean, if I fall into the gutter—oh, never mind. Rowf, are you still broken?"

Rowf got up, put his injured front paw gingerly to the ground, winced and lay down again.

"I can't run on it. Anyway, I'm bruised and stiff all over. I shall go on lying here until I feel better."

"Just imagine, Rowf, if all these stones suddenly turned into meat—"

"If what?"

"Biscuits dropping out of the roof—"

"Lie down!"

"And an animal came in, without teeth or claws, all made of horse liver—"

"What do you mean? How could that happen?"

"Oh, I saw it rain from the ground to the clouds—black milk, you know—"

"You've made me feel hungry, damn you!"

"Are we going out, like—you know, like last night?"

"I can't do it now, Snitter. Not until I feel better. Another battering like that—we'll just have to wait a bit. Tomorrow—"

"Let's go back to where it's lying," said Snitter. "There'll be a good deal left."

He pattered quickly over the shale towards the vaulted opening, Rowf limping behind him. It was afternoon and the red October sun, already sinking, was shining straight up the length of Dunnerdale beneath. Far below the tawny, glowing bracken and the glittering stealth of the tarn, Snitter could see cows in green fields, grey stone walls, red-leaved trees and whitewashed houses, all clear and still as though enclosed in golden glass. Yet the sun itself, which imparted this stillness, did not share it, seeming rather to swim in the blue liquidity of the sky, wavering before the eyes, a molten mass floating, rocking, drifting westward in a fluid that slowly cooled but could not quench its heat. Snitter stood blinking on the warm turf near the entrance, scenting the dry bracken and bog myrtle in the autumn air. The dressing fell across his eye and he tossed up his head.

"Was there ever a dog that could fly?"

"Yes," replied Rowf promptly, "but the whitecoats cut off its wings to see what would happen."

"What did happen?"

"It couldn't fly."

"Then it's no worse off than we are. I'll go as slowly as you like."

Rowf stumbled stiffly forward and the pair set off towards the stream. In the windless warmth of the St. Martin's summer afternoon, Snitter's spirits began to rise and he pattered about the moss, splashing in and out of shallow pools and jumping in pursuit like a puppy whenever he put up a wheatear or whinchat in the bog.

They had no need to search for the carcase they had left. Even before they winded it they could hear the raucous squabbling of two buzzards, and a few moments later saw them hopping and fluttering about their rip-work. As the dogs approached, the big birds turned and stared at them angrily, but thought better of it and flapped slowly away, sailing down on brown wings towards the tarn.

"It's little enough they've left," said Rowf, thrusting his muzzle into the fly-buzzing, blood-glazed remains. Snitter hung back, looking about him.

"It's not only them. There's been some other creature—"

Rowf looked up sharply. "You're right. I can smell it. But what? The smell—makes me angry, somehow—"

He ran about the rocks. "I'll catch it. The smell—like a horse-mouse. What d'you make of it?" He was slavering as he spoke.

"Never mind," answered Snitter, pressing down with one paw upon the haunch he was tearing. "It's not here now."

"Yes, it is. Watching, I think. Lurking. Not far off."

"Let's not leave anything here if we can help it," said Snitter. "Eat all you can and we'll carry the rest back to the rhododendrons—a good chunk each, anyway."

They returned to the cave in the late afternoon, Snitter with a fore-leg, Rowf half-dragging the rank-smelling remains of the haunch. For some time they lay in the sun on the flat turf outside, retreating to the shaft only when the light was half-gone and a chilly breeze came rippling up the tarn from the west. Snitter scrabbled out a shallow recess in the shale to fit his body, lay down in it with a comfortable feeling of hunger satisfied and fell quickly asleep.

He woke suddenly, in pitch darkness, to realize that Rowf was creeping warily across the tunnel a few yards away. He was about to ask him what he was doing when something in Rowf's movement and breathing made him hold himself motionless, tensed and waiting. A moment later he became aware of the same strange reek that they had scented near the sheep's carcase. He lay still as a spider, letting the smell flow through him, seeking from it all that it could tell. It was not an angry smell, nor a dangerous smell: but none the less wild, yes and exciting, a sharp, killing smell, a furtive smell, trotting, preying, slinking through the darkness. And it was a quick-moving smell. Whatever the animal might be, it was on the move, it was alive here, now, in the cave with them. This, of course, was the reason for Rowf's caution and crafty alertness, which Snitter had already sensed in the moment of his own waking.

Why had the animal come? To kill them for food? No, this, he knew instinctively, it had not. Whatever it might be up to, it was trying to avoid them, although it smelt like an animal which could fight if it were forced to. Because this was its home? But its smell was very strong and distinctive, and there had been no trace of it here yesterday. Then it could have come only in order to try to steal their meat.

At this moment there was a sudden, momentary clattering of loose stones in the dark and immediately Rowf said, "Stay where you are. If you try to get past me I'll kill you."

There was no reply. Snitter, feeling himself trembling, got up and took a position a few feet away from Rowf, so that between them the way out was effectively blocked. "*I'll* kill you, too," he said, "and that'd be twice, so it wouldn't be worth it."

The next instant he jumped back with a sharp yap of astonishment, for the voice answering him was speaking, unmistakably, a sort—a very odd sort—of dog language. Barely understandable and like nothing he had ever heard, the voice, nevertheless, was undoubtedly that of an animal in some way akin to themselves.

"It'll de ye smaall gud killin' me, hinny. Ye'll not see three morns yersel'."

There was a kind of wheedling defiance in the voice, as though the owner had not yet decided whether to fight, to run or to cajole, but was trying the latter and putting an edge to it for good value.

"Who *are* you?" said Rowf. Snitter could sense his

uncertainty, and wondered whether the animal could also do so. "Are you a dog?"

"Why ay, Ah'm a derg. Watch ahint ye!" cried the voice in a sudden tone of urgent warning. Snitter leapt round. In the moment that he realized he had been tricked, Rowf blundered against him, dashing across the breadth of the tunnel to prevent the intruder's escape. Both were biting now and snapping, but as Snitter, picking himself up, jumped to Rowf's help, the scuffle broke off, the shale clicking once more as the animal ran back into the tunnel.

"Stay where you are!" said Rowf again. "If you run any further I'll follow you and break your back!"

"Howway noo, kidda," replied the animal, in the same strange dog-jargon. "Ne need fer ye an' me te start battlin'. Laa-laa-let, ma bonny pet."

Listening, Snitter felt his blood tingle, not with fear but with a kind of thrilled repulsion and attraction. The voice of the smell was obsequious, cunning, that of a thief, a liar, masterless, callous and untrustworthy. It was also full of sardonic humour, of courage and resource, and pitiless, most of all for itself. Its lilting rogue's jargon spoke to his own madness. Fascinated, he waited to hear it speak again.

"By three morns, the pair on yez'll bowth be deed. Forst ye bleed an' then yer deed," said the voice, in a kind of crooning spell. "Lie an' bleed, ye'll bowth be deed, crows hes been an' picked yer een."

Snitter found himself answering spontaneously, without thought.

"The sky opened, you know," said Snitter. "There was a thunderstorm and this lightning shot down into my head. Before that, it was black and white; I mean, the road was black and white; and then the lorry came and the tobacco man set my head on fire. I can bark and I can jump and I can catch a sugar lump." He threw back his head and barked.

"Shut up," said Rowf.

"De ye say so?" said the voice to Snitter. "Whey, mebbies. Howway wi' me, lad, tappy-lappy, aall tegither, an' Ah'll put yez on the reet road. Mind, thoo beats them aall fer a bonny mate, Ah warr'nd."

"Yes," said Snitter, "you understand a lot, don't you? I'll go along with you; you show me where." He began moving forward in the dark, towards the voice.

"By, mind, ye've been fair bashed, hinny," whispered the voice, close to him now. "Who gi' ye that slit o' th' heed? Who dun yon? Yer sore hurrt!"

"It was the whitecoats," answered Snitter.

The reek was all round him now, the pain in his head was gone and he and the voice were floating elegantly, effortlessly, towards the dark-blue, star-twinkling oval of the cave-mouth.

He did not realize that Rowf had knocked him down until he heard the strange animal once more run back down the tunnel. Then he smelt that Rowf was so angry that if he did not take care he was likely to be badly bitten. Lying quite still, he said, "Rowf, there's no point in killing him, whatever sort of animal he is. He'd fight and it'd be too much trouble."

"You didn't wake up soon enough," answered Rowf. "If I hadn't stopped him he'd have been off with that leg-bone you brought back."

"He says he's a dog. If your shadow could sing—"

"I don't care what he says he is, he's a thief. I'll make him sorry."

"Noo give ower," said the creature in the dark. "Go canny. Let's aall be pals, ne need fer brawlin'. Stick wi' me and we'll aall be champion. Else ye'll be deed soon, like Ah towld yez."

"Dead?" said Snitter.

"Ay, deed, an' ne argument aboot it, ne bother."

"Why should we be?"

"Whey, hinny, ne chance at aall, gannin' aboot th' fell killin' yows an' hollerin' yer heeds off," said the creature. "Ye gan on that style and ye'll have *me* kilt forbye. Ye should be neether seen nor hord, else yer deed dergs, Ah'm tellin' ye."

"What *are* you telling us, then?" asked Snitter, his fascination growing as he realized that, unlike Rowf, he could partly understand the creature's talk.

"Ye'll hunt an' ye'll kill weel, wi' me. Ye'll gan oot an' come back fed, wi' me. Ye'll run through th' neet an' foller me feet an' Ah'll keep ye reet. Ah'll keep ye reet, ye'll get yer meat." The voice had taken on a rhythmic hypnotic cadence, wheedling and sly, that made Snitter prick his ears and dilate his nostrils to the smell in the dark.

"Listen, Rowf, listen!"

"Whatever he is, he's not to be trusted," answered Rowf. "Anyway, I can't understand a word he says."

"I can," said Snitter. "I'll smell and I'll tell. I've listened to birds in the chimney and beetles under the door. My head feels better. It's open like a flower." He cut a caper on the shale.

Rowf growled and Snitter collected himself.

"He says we're strangers here and we're in danger because we don't know the place or how to look after ourselves, and for some reason that puts him in danger too. He's suggesting that we let him share what we kill and in return he'll give us advice and tell us what to do."

Rowf considered. "He'll only cheat us, and run away when it suits him. I tell you, he's not to be trusted."

"We've nothing to lose. He's a sharp one, Rowf— bright as the leaves on the trees." Snitter now felt that he would give anything to see the owner of the voice, or merely to keep him with them a little longer. The dreary cavern seemed crackling with his shifty vitality.

"Grab hold of your meat and lie on it," said Rowf. "I'm going to do the same. If you're still here when it's light," he said into the darkness, "we'll see what you are and whether you're worth feeding. What do you call yourself?"

The answer, taunting, mordant and inscrutable, came in a whisper from some further recess of the tunnel.

"Dry an' warrm's nivver harrm. Keep tight hold o' yer meat an' gud luck gan wi' ye. Noo yer taalkin' sense. Who am Ah? Ah'm tod, whey Ah'm tod, ye knaw. Canniest riever on moss and moor!"

"—so after we'd got out," said Rowf, "we didn't know where to go. We came to some houses, but I bit a man who was going to put Snitter in a car—he saw him lying by the road and picked him up—so we ran away. Then, later, a man with a lorry threw a stone at Snitter—"

"There was another man who was hunting sheep with his dogs," put in Snitter. "We went to help them, but the dogs drove us away."

The tod, lying on the shale at several yards' safe distance, head on sandy paws, listened intently as it continued gnawing on the remains of the fore-leg. Outside, the cloudy, grey light of morning showed a drizzling rain drifting across the mouth of the cavern.

"Snitter thought we ought to go on trying to find some man or other who'd take us to his house and look after us," said Rowf, "but I couldn't see the sense of that. To begin with, the men have taken away all the houses and streets and things—Snitter admits it himself—but apart from that, it's a silly thing to expect. Men are there to hurt animals, not to look after them."

"Noo yer reet, hinny. Guns an' dergs, an' trraps an' aall. Ye'd be a fond fyeul an' loose i' th' heed te seek oot th' likes o' them." The tod cracked a small bone and spat it out. "Crrunshin' bait's th' bonniest."

"I know where I ought to be," said Rowf. "Back with the whitecoats, like the other dogs. All right, I'm a deserter. I'd like to be a good dog, but I can't—I can't go near another tank."

"The whole place seems to be covered with these great tanks," said Snitter. "How often do the men put animals into them, and what sort of animals? They must be huge!"

The tod glanced shrewdly from one to the other, but answered nothing.

"*You*'re a wild animal, aren't you?" said Rowf. "You never have anything to do with men?"

"Ay, noo an' agyen." The tod showed its teeth. "Ducks an' new lambs." It rolled on one side, licking briefly at a long, white scar on its belly. "An' kittens i' th' barn, wad ye think it, noo?"

"Kittens?" asked Snitter, astonished.

"Th' aald cat come, so Ah teuk off wi' th' one."

"Teuk off with the one?" Snitter was at a loss.

"Ay, just th' one."

"*I* mean to live here as a wild animal, that's the long and short of it," said Rowf. "Snitter can go and look for men if he wants to. I'm a mouse and this is my drain."

"Wivoot me, bonny lad, Ah'll gi' ye ne mair than three morns."

"Go on," said Snitter, "why not?"

"Ah've seen nowt dafter, th' pair on yez, lyin' flat oot o' th' fell like wee piggies full o' grub, like there wez neether dergs nor shepherd aboot. Ye fells th' yow, bolts it doon ye, kips ye doon a spell an' comes back like a pair o' squallin' cubs. Ye took ne heed at aall o' shepherd's gun or dergs. Ah'd think shame o' ye, ye pair o' daft nowts."

Rowf's hackles rose at the sardonic mockery in the sharp, thin voice, and at once its tone changed to one of open, honest admiration.

"By, mind—ye pulled yon yow doon clever, though. By, hinny, yer a hard 'un. There's none like ye. Hard as th' hobs ye are—a fair mazer!"

"It knocked me about," said Rowf. "I'm bruised all over."

"Hinny, there's ways. Wi' me ye'll sharp knaw hoo te duck an' dodge. There's ways o' gettin' stuck in hard, an' ways o' duckin' oot. Wi' me aside ye, a greet, hard boogger like ye'll hev ne bother. Ye'll sharp larn th' ways, an' a sharp tod like me's th' one te larn ye hoo."

"Do *you* kill sheep, then?" asked Snitter in surprise, thinking that the tod was, if anything, smaller than himself.

"Whey, mebbies a bit young lamb i' th' spring if th' chances come. But yon derg's a mazer for th' yows," replied the tod, keeping its eyes on Rowf with a look of great respect. "Come te that, ye cud bowth be dab hands."

"Do you want to stay here with us—is that what you're saying?" asked Snitter, once more feeling, as he had felt in the night, a mysterious and exciting affinity with this devious, insinuating creature, whose every word and movement seemed part of the spinning of some invisible net of stratagem.

"Ah, whey, ye'll hev ne bother wi' me. Ah do nowt but pick at me meat," said the tod. It got up, slunk quickly to the cavern's opening, peered round one corner into the falling rain and returned. "Us tods, we nivver stop runnin', nivver till th' Dark cums doon. An' yon's a bonny way off yit—th' Dark—for Ah warr'nd they'll hev te move sharp te catch me."

"And that's what you're offering—you share what we kill and in return you'll teach us how to survive here and help us not to be seen or caught by men?"

"Ay. Noo yer taalkin'. Otherwise th' Dark'll be doon on ye, ne time at aall. Yon farmer'll hev yer hides full o' lead an' it'll be off an' away into th' Dark wi' yez."

The tod rolled on its back, tossed the knuckle-bone into the air, caught it and threw it towards Snitter, whose clumsy, late-starting grab missed it by inches. Annoyed, Snitter jumped across to where the bone had fallen, picked it up and looked around for the tod.

"Ahint ye!" It had passed him like a shadow and was hovering light-footed on the shale at his back. "Hill bide ye, an' fern hide ye, an' stream drown yer scent aside ye!"

"What's your name?" asked Snitter, having, as he spoke, a curious illusion that the tod was hanging poised on the stones as the buzzards on the wind-currents above the fell.

For the first time the tod seemed at a loss.

"Your name?" repeated Snitter. "What do we call you?"

"Why, ye knaw, ye knaw," answered the tod, with the hesitant lack of conviction of one unwilling to admit that he does not understand a question. "Mind, yer aye a canny 'un. Reet pair o' dazzlers."

There was a pause.

"He hasn't got a name," said Rowf suddenly. "Neither had the mouse."

"But how can he—"

"Dangerous thing, a name. Someone might catch hold of you by it, mightn't they? He can't afford a name—that's my guess. He hasn't got one. He's a wild animal."

Suddenly a great flame of abandonment crackled up in the thorny tangle of Snitter's mind. He could be done with care. He too could become burdened with no name, no past, no future; with no regret, no memory, no loss; no fear but caution, no longing but appetite, no misery but bodily pain. No part of his self need be exposed except his awareness of the present and that gone in an instant, like a fly snapped at and missed on a summer afternoon. He saw himself, bold and wary, floating on life, needing nothing, obedient only to cunning and instinct, creeping through the bracken upon the quarry, vanishing from pursuers like a shadow, sleeping secure in hiding, gambling again and again until at last he lost; and then departing, with a shrug and a grin, to make way for some other trickster nameless as himself.

"Stay!" he cried, jumping on Rowf like a puppy. "Let him stay! Wild animals! Wild animals!"

Frolicking, he rolled over, scratching his back on the shale, and began clawing and worrying in earnest at the tattered dressing on his head.

"It seems most unfortunate," said Dr. Boycott, looking up at Mr. Powell over his spectacles. "And I'm afraid I still can't make out, from what you've told me, how it came to occur."

Mr. Powell shifted his feet uneasily. "Well, I certainly don't want to put the blame on Tyson," he answered. "He's a good bloke as a rule. But as far as I can make out, he didn't notice on Friday evening that there was a length of wire netting loose along the bottom of eight-one-five's pen, and some time that night eight-one-five must have worried its way through to seven-three-two's side." He stopped, as though to suggest that there was no more to be said. Dr. Boycott continued to look at him as though there were, and after a pause Mr. Powell continued.

"Well, then the spring of the catch of seven-three-two's door happened to break and that's how they both got out."

"But if the door had been shut properly, it would stay shut, wouldn't it, even if the spring of the catch did break? It wouldn't move of its own accord."

Mr. Powell was undergoing the embarrassment and confusion not infrequently suffered by young officers who, having failed, through nervousness, inexperience and a certain misplaced respect, to press older (and gruffer) subordinates with awkward questions, later find themselves confronted with the same questions from their own seniors.

"Well, that occurred to me, too, actually; but the spring's broken all right—he showed it to me."

"You're sure he didn't break it himself?"

"I don't see why he'd do that, chief."

"Well, because he realized on Saturday that he hadn't shut the door properly on Friday, of course," said Dr. Boycott, allowing Mr. Powell to perceive his impatience at his subordinate's having failed to think of this for himself.

"We can't be sure of that, no," replied Mr. Powell. "But if he did, he'd never admit it, would he?" This answer, he felt, must surely end that particular line of inquiry.

"But did you ask him?" persisted Dr. Boycott, neatly reappearing, as it were out of the bracken, at a fresh point along the line.

"Well, no—not exactly."

"Well, either you did or you didn't."

Dr. Boycott stared over his glasses and under his raised eyebrows. The thought crossed Mr. Powell's mind that it was a pity that one could not, as in chess, resign, and thereupon at once resume a life in which the blunders leading to the resignation, however foolish, became mere fragments of a concluded parenthesis.

"Well, anyway," resumed Dr. Boycott at length, with the air of one obliged to struggle patiently on in a situation rendered virtually impossible by another's incompetence, "the two dogs got out of seven-three-two's pen. What happened then?"

"Well, then they must have run right through the block,

'cause they'd knocked over a box of mice in the pregnancy unit—"

"And you've told Walters about that, have you?" asked Dr. Boycott, with a sigh suggestive of a state of mind to which no further revelations of folly could come as any surprise.

"Oh, yes, first thing," answered Mr. Powell, catching at this straw for an opportunity to speak in a matter-of-course tone, as though it had never occurred to him that his efficiency or reliability could come under criticism.

"I'm glad to hear *that*, anyway," countered Dr. Boycott, suggesting, like an Impressionist painter, with one stroke, a host of things, unnecessary to define, which he had *not* been glad to hear. "How did they get out of the block and where?"

"Nobody knows," said Mr. Powell expansively, as though, having referred the matter in vain to New Scotland Yard, the Colditz Society and the staff of Old Moore's Almanack, he had been reluctantly compelled to abandon an enigma more baffling than that of the *Mary Celeste.*

Dr. Boycott clicked his tongue once, loudly, with the air of a super-camel which, while daily enduring the unendurable, can surely be excused if some momentary plaint involuntarily escapes its lips as the last straw is piled on.

"You mean you and Tyson don't know?"

"Well, yes," replied the toad beneath the harrow.

"You're sure they didn't get into Goodner's place?" asked Dr. Boycott, suddenly and sharply.

"Certain," replied Mr. Powell with equal promptitude.

"You're *absolutely* sure?"

"Yes, and so is he. I've already spoken to him. He says the cultures—"

"All right," said Dr. Boycott, raising one hand to stem the tedious flood of unnecessary and time-consuming detail, the purpose of which—his tone conveyed—he perceived to be nothing but a feeble attempt at ingratiation. "*He's* content, then. Thank goodness for that." He got up, put his hands in his pockets, walked across to the window and sat on the radiator. The actions suggested that Mr. Powell, while by no means off the carpet, was no longer, as it were, so completely on it—his superior now having need (*faute de mieux*, of course) of his advice.

"You've made quite certain, have you, that they're not hiding in the block or anywhere about the place?"

"As certain as we can be. Tyson and I have both been all over, independently. Of course, they might show up. I mean, they might come back—"

"Yes, they might," said Dr. Boycott reflectively, "and they might be *brought* back. It's a pity their collars don't carry the address of the station. Perhaps that ought to be changed. Still, it's too late in this case." He paused, and then, in a sharp tone, as though Mr. Powell had failed to reply to a question and already kept him waiting more than long enough, asked, "Well" (Mr. Powell started), "what do *you* think we ought to do?"

Mr. Powell had, as a matter of fact, got this bit fairly well stitched up. After all, he was required only to have thought of all the possibilities and to proceed to say what they were. He would also need to express some sort of preference, but once he had done this the decision (and the responsibility) would be someone else's.

"We could do nothing at all, or we could go out and search for the dogs ourselves, or we could give a description to all occupants of neighbouring dwellings and farms and ask them to keep a look-out, catch the dogs if they see them and then ring us up; or we could report the thing to the police. We could do all of the last three things," added Mr. Powell sagaciously. "They're not mutually exclusive, of course."

"And what would *you* do?" persisted Dr. Boycott.

"Well, quite honestly, chief, I think I'd be inclined to do nothing, for the time being. It's ten to one they'll either come back or else turn up somewhere where we can go and collect them; and if they don't, well, then we just have to write them off. The alternative's raising a hue-and-cry all round the neighbourhood, and then we've given ourselves a bad name, possibly all for nothing—I mean, they've been gone more than sixty hours, they may be miles away by now—halfway to Kendal—"

"Suppose they start worrying sheep?" asked Dr. Boycott.

"Then either some farmer shoots them and saves us

further trouble, or else he catches them, realizes where they're from and rings us up; in which case we only have to pacify one bloke instead of spilling the beans to the whole district," answered Mr. Powell.

"Well, perhaps that might be best," said Dr. Boycott reflectively. "I don't really want to bother the Director with a thing like this just now. I think it's more than likely either that they'll turn up of their own accord or that someone will bring them in. What did Fortescue say when you told him about eight-one-five?"

"Well, he said it was a nuisance and a lot of time and work down the drain."

"So it is. If they don't show up today," said Dr. Boycott, apparently unconscious that his decision not to sully the fair name of the station by publicizing the escape appeared, on the face of it, to be inconsistent with the high value he was ascribing to the missing subjects of experiment, "the work already done on them will probably be at least partly invalidated. It certainly will in the case of seven-three-two, since that's a conditioning experiment and the immersions were programmed for regular intervals. I don't know about eight-one-five, but I suppose Fortescue wanted to start it on tests today." A sudden thought struck him. "You don't think it's possible that Tyson might have stolen the dogs himself?"

"Well, it did cross my mind, actually, chief, but if he was going in for that sort of thing I don't think he'd start by picking on those two. I mean, he's no fool, and one's had brain surgery and the other's notoriously savage and bad-tempered."

"H'mmm. Well," said Dr. Boycott briskly, going back to his desk and picking up some papers, to mark his dismissal of the matter for the time being, "we'd better get on with something else. Is there anything besides that that you want to talk about?"

"Well, yes, two other things I think I ought to mention," said Mr. Powell, with some slight relaxation of manner. "The first one's that humane trap for grey squirrels that Ag. and Fish. sent us for trial."

"What about it?"

"Well, it's not turning out all that humane, really," said

Mr. Powell, with a giggle of embarrassment. "I mean, it's supposed to kill them outright, isn't it? Well, about four times out of ten, it's just sort of slicing—look, I'll try and draw it for you—"

"I'm not really interested in that, to be perfectly honest," replied Dr. Boycott. "It's not work involving any kind of scientific advance or fresh knowledge. Anyway, it'll be several weeks before Ag. and Fish. start asking us for anything. The squirrels won't be pressing them, you know," he added with a slight lightening of tone which drew a relieved smile from Mr. Powell. "You'd better try to work out some kind of modification yourself, to make it reliably lethal, but remember it's got to go on the market at an economic price. Anything else?"

"One other thing, yes, and this *will* be of interest to you," said Mr. Powell, with an air of "You want the best seats, we have them." "Those dogfish—the ones you wanted for experiments on how they're able to change their coloration to match their backgrounds, remember? Mitchell rang up about half an hour ago to say he's got them and should he deliver them today? I said I'd ask you and let him know later this morning."

"Can Fortescue spare someone this week to carry out the destruction of the selected areas of their brains and the removal of their eyes?" asked Dr. Boycott.

"Yes, he told me Prescott would be available to do it Wednesday."

"Fine. Well, get them sent along right away and see that the necessary tank-space is ready. Oh, and draw up a test programme."

"Right. Er—and about the other thing, chief," said Mr. Powell, hopeful of retrieving some part of his name at least by showing willing despite his lapse.

"Yes?" asked Dr. Boycott, without raising his eyes from his papers.

"Would you like me to let you have a written report? Only I do realize that there certainly are one or two questions outstanding—"

"Don't bother," said Dr. Boycott, maintaining his air of detachment. "I'll have a word with Tyson. What about that monkey, by the way?" he added, changing the subject

rapidly enough to suggest that even he felt this last remark to have been a little too insulting and painful to one
who could not answer back.

"Well, it went into the cylinder Friday evening, like
you said: so it's done two and a half days."

"How's it reacting?"

"It's been thrashing around a bit," replied Mr. Powell,
"and—and sort of crying from time to time. Well, making
noises, anyhow."

"Is it eating?"

"Tyson hasn't told me otherwise."

"I see," said Dr. Boycott, and returned to his papers.

Tuesday the 19th October

"How far away from them are we now?" whispered
Snitter.

"Aye creep an' peep, hinny, creep an' peep." The tod,
it seemed, had not spoken at all, but conveyed its reply
into Snitter's mind in a telepathic silence. They crawled
three feet closer to the edge of the chattering Tarnbeck.

"Are we to go upstream towards the farm now?"

"Na!" The tod, pressed to the ground under a rock,
appeared actually to have extended itself flat like a leech
and changed its colour to grey. "Heed doon!"

"What?"

"Bide there noo!"

Snitter understood that they were to remain completely
still and vigilant in cover. Upstream, in the Tarnbeck, he
could hear the Tongue House Farm ducks quacking and
blittering somewhere below the wooden footbridge leading
across to the meadow below Thrang. He felt acutely conscious of his black-and-white colouring, as conspicuous
as a pillar-box at the end of a street. There was a patch
of bracken to one side of him and he crawled silently beneath the brown, over-arching fronds.

After a few moments he turned his head towards the

crag where the tod had been lying. It was no longer there. Looking cautiously around, he caught sight of it ahead of him, inching forward, chin and belly pressed into the bed of the runlet that trickled down the meadow to drain into the Tarnbeck. Suddenly it stopped, and for a long time lay motionless in the cold water oozing round and under its body. The quacking sounded closer and a moment later Snitter's ears caught the paddling and splashing of the ducks as they drifted and steered in the swiftly flowing beck, thirty yards away at the bottom of the field. He realized that he was trembling. The tod was now closer to the beck by about three lengths of its own body, yet Snitter had not seen it move. He returned his gaze once more towards the tumbling patch of water visible between the alder bushes, where the runlet entered the beck.

Suddenly, floating down from upstream, a duck came into view, turned, steadied itself against the current and dived, the white wedge of its tail wagging from side to side as it searched below the surface. Snitter looked quickly at the place where the tod had been. It was gone. What ought he himself to be doing? He left the cover of the fronds and began to crawl forward as another duck appeared, followed by a brown drake, blue-wing-feathered like a mallard.

The drake and the duck began quarrelling over some fragment which the duck had found and, as they grabbed and quacked, floated three yards further downstream into shallow water. It was here that the tod came down upon them, silent as smoke. It did not seem to be moving particularly fast, but rather like some natural force borne upon the wind or the stream. Snitter dashed forward, but before—long before, it seemed to him—he could reach the beck, the tod had glided into the shallows, grabbed the drake by the neck and dragged it, struggling and clatter-winged, up the bank into the field. Behind rose a crescendo of splashing and the panic-stricken cries of the flock as they fled upstream.

Snitter, two yards up the bank, came face to face with the tod, its mask grotesquely obscured by the thrashing wings and feet of the drake clutched between its teeth.

Without relaxing its grip it coughed a shower of small, downy feathers into Snitter's face.

"What—what shall I do? D'you want me to—" Snitter, absurdly, was holding himself poised to rush into the now empty water. The tod lifted the corner of a lip and spoke indistinctly out of one side of its mouth.

"Haddaway hyem noo!"

Without waiting to see whether Snitter had understood, it trotted briskly—but still, as it seemed, without undue haste—downstream, quickly reaching the cover of a bank topped with ash and alder, along the further side of which they began to slink towards the open fell beyond. Once only it stopped, laid down for a moment the now-still quarry, and grinned at Snitter.

"Ye'll soon be waalkin' light as a linnet, lad. Th' next torn'll be yours. Mebbe ye'll get yersel' dosed wi' lead an' aall."

Snitter grinned back.

"Ye divven't say?"

The tod looked down at the carcase. "Can ye pull the feathers off a duck? There's a gey lot o' them. Ah'll hev t' larn ye."

Thursday the 21st October

Rowf lay crouched out of the wind, under a rock two hundred yards from the summit of Dow Crag. The moon was clouded and there was little light—barely enough by which to discern the mouth of the precipitous gully leading up from below. Snitter fidgeted impatiently. The tod was stretched at length, head on front paws.

"You say there's no need to come to grips?" asked Rowf.

"Ne need, hinny. Th' sharper it's runnin', th' sharper it'll go ower. Mind, ye'll be close behind, so ye'll hev te watch it. Tek care o' yersel' ye divven't go doon wi'd."

The tod paused and glanced at Snitter. "If th' wee fella there's sharp off his mark, there'll be ne bother."

Rowf looked down once more into the pitch-black depths below, then turned to Snitter.

"Now, look, it'll be coming up the fell as fast as the tod and I can drive it. It's got to be headed and forced down into the gully. It mustn't get past you, or turn back down the fell, d'you understand?"

"It won't," replied Snitter tensely.

"Assa, ye'll manage canny," said the tod, and thereupon set off with Rowf down the hillside.

Snitter took the place under the rock still warm from Rowf's body, and waited. The wind moaned in the funnel of the sheer gully below and blew a scatter of cold rain across his face, smelling of salt and sodden leaves. He stood up, listening intently, and began padding up and down across the gully's head. There were still no sounds of hunting to be heard from the western slope on his other side. He might have been the only living creature between Dow Crag and Seathwaite Tarn.

After a while he became agitated. Peering into the darkness and from time to time uttering low whines, he ran a little way towards the summit. Out beyond the foot of the precipice, far below, he could just glimpse the dull glimmering of Goat's Water—one more of the many tanks with which men had dotted this evil, unnatural country. Sniffing along the path, he came across a cigarette end and jumped back with a start as the image of the tobacco man leapt before his mind's nose. Confused, he lay down where he was and for the thousandth time raised one paw to scrabble at the canvas and plaster fixed to his head. His claws found a hold—some wrinkle that had not been there before—and as he tugged there came a sudden sliding movement, a giving way, followed at once by a sensation of cold and exposure across the top of his skull. Drawing back his paw, he found the entire plaster, sodden, black and torn, stuck across the pads. After a few moments he realized what it was and, capering with delight, gripped it in his teeth, chewed it, threw it into the air and caught it, threw it up again and was about to chase after it when suddenly a furious barking broke out on the fell below.

Snitter, jumping round at the noise, realized that he was uncertain of his way back to the mouth of the gully. As he hesitated in the dark, he heard the approaching sound of small hooves clattering over stones, and dashed along the ridge in the direction from which it came. Scarcely had he reached the rock where the tod had left him than the yow came racing uphill, with Rowf snapping at its hindquarters. Simultaneously, without a sound, the tod appeared from nowhere and lay with bared teeth, watching the yow as it turned towards Snitter, hesitated and stopped. Snitter leapt at it and all in a moment the yow plunged headlong into the blackness of the gully. Rowf, hard on its heels, disappeared also. There followed a rattling and falling of stones and gravel and then a single, terrified bleat which, even as it diminished, was cut suddenly short. Rowf, the whites of his eyes showing in the faint light, reappeared and flung himself down, panting, not a yard from the edge.

"I saw it fall. Liver and lights, I couldn't stop! I nearly went over myself. Well done, Snitter! You stopped it turning. Why—" He raised his head, staring at Snitter incredulously. "What on earth's happened to you?"

"Whatever do you mean?"

But Rowf, sniffing and licking at the great, stitched trench running clear across Snitter's skull, said nothing more. Snitter, too, lay instinctively silent, while Rowf, treating him as though he were a stranger, gradually brought himself to terms with this grim change in his friend's appearance. At last he said, "You say the tobacco man set it on fire?"

"I don't know—I was asleep when it happened. It often *feels* like that. And once I fell in, you know. If it wasn't for the chicken-wire—" Snitter got hesitantly to his feet. "It's not all that strange—not really. Holes—after all— I've seen holes in roofs. And cars—they sometimes open them, too. And there are pipes, did you know, running along under the roads? Outside our gate, men came once and dug down—you could see them. Of course, that was before the lorry came."

"Time w' wuh gettin' doon belaa! Ne doot ye'll be hunger'd like me." The tod ran a few yards, then turned and looked back at the two dogs lying on the stones.

"Which way?" asked Rowf. "How far down? That yow seemed to be falling for ever. I never even heard it hit. Is it a long way round to the bottom?"

"Nay, nay. Roond to the side an' doon. A canny bit of a way."

Yet even after they had gone down to the foot of Dow by way of Goat's Hause, it was nearly an hour before they found the body of the yow, which was lying on a narrow shelf near the foot of Great Gully.

Saturday the 23rd October

"Go on, kidda, bash it doon, then!"

Snitter hurled his compact weight again and again at the wire netting of the chicken run. When at last it gave way the tod was through in a streak and, before Snitter had picked himself up, had crept upwards into the closed henhouse through a crack between two floorboards which Snitter would not have thought wide enough for a rat. At once a squawking racket broke out within and a moment later a dog began barking inside the nearby barn. Lights came on in the farmhouse and an upstairs window was flung open. As Snitter, straining every nerve not to run, tried to cower out of sight behind one of the brick piers supporting the henhouse, the twitching bodies of two hens fell one after the other to the ground beside him. The tod, eel-like, followed instantly and Snitter leapt to his feet.

"Haddaway hyem?"

"Why ay! Go on, lad, divven't hang aboot!"

The bare, yellow legs were so hot that Snitter could hardly hold them in his mouth. From above, the beam of a powerful torch was darting here and there about the yard, and as they crept through the hedge into the lonnin a shot-gun went off behind them. The tod, putting down its hen to take a better grip, sniggered.

" 'Nother cat gone?"

Sunday the 24th October to
Monday the 25th October

In the grey twilight before dawn, Rowf sprang out of the moss and confronted the two returning raiders as they rounded the upper end of Seathwaite Tarn. From head to tail he was daubed with fresh blood. His bloody tracks had marked the stones. The body of the Swaledale sheep, ripped from throat to belly, lay beside the beck a little distance off.

"I knew I could do it," said Rowf, "as soon as I'd had a few days' rest. Nothing to it—I just ran it backwards and forwards over the beck a few times and then pulled it down with less trouble than the other. Well, come on if you want—"

He broke off short, for the tod, its eyes half-closed against the east wind, was staring at him with a look of mingled incredulity and shocked contempt. At length it began to speak in a kind of wail.

"Ye got ne brains i' yer heed! Ye greet nowt! Ne soon-er's me back turned than ye bloody up our ain place as red as a cock's comb wi' yer daft muckin'! Ye greet, fond nanny-hammer! Could ye not go canny till Ah tellt ye? Ye born, noddy-heeded boogger! Ah'm not bidin' wi' ye lot! Me, Ah'm away—"

"Wait!" cried Snitter. "Wait, tod!" For the tod, as it spoke, had turned and was making off in the direction of the dam. "What's the matter?"

"First ye kill on th' fell—reet o' th' shepherd's track, muckin' th' place up wi' blood like a knacker's yard. An' noo ye kill ootside our ain place! Yon farmer's nay blind! He'll be on it, sharp as a linnet. Ye're fer th' Dark, ne doot, hinny. Yer arse'll be inside oot b' th' morn."

Swirral and Carrs

"But, tod, where are you going?"

"Aarrgh! Haddaway doon te knock o' th' farmer's door! Mebbies Ah'll just shove me heed agin' his gun," replied the tod bitterly. "Save aall th' bother, that will."

Indeed, as the full light of day came into the sky from beyond the heights of Great Carrs and Swirral to the east, the cause of the tod's dismay became only too clear. The body of the dead yow lay on Tarn Head Moss like freedom's banner torn yet flying, a beacon, as it seemed, to every buzzard, crow and bluebottle in the Lakes. As the morning wore on Snitter, from the cave-mouth barely five hundred yards away, lay gloomily watching the pecking, squabbling, ripping and fluttering, which grew no less as rain began to drift up from Dunnerdale, blotting out the curve of the dam and the further end of the reservoir beyond. The tod had only with difficulty been persuaded to remain, and soon after mid-day had gone out to the western shoulder of Blake Rigg, whence it could see the trod leading up to the tarn from Tongue House Farm below.

By sunset, however, when the smaller becks were already coloured and chattering in spate, the reservoir valley remained unvisited by man or dog and the tod, pelt sodden and brush trailing, returned to the cave, muttering something about "a canny rain for them as desarved warse." There was no hunting expedition that night, enough being left of the sheep to satisfy all three.

Late the following morning, as Snitter was dozing in his snug, body-shaped concavity in the shale floor, he was roused by the tod who, without a word and with extreme caution, led him to the cave mouth. Down on the moss a man, smoking a cigarette and accompanied by two black-and-white Welsh collies, was prodding with his stick at the stripped backbone and bare rib-cage of the sheep.

Tuesday the 26th October

"—soom bluidy beeäst or oother livin' oop theer," said Dennis Williamson. "Theer is that." He walked round his van and kicked the off-side rear tyre.

"Git awaay!" replied Robert Lindsay. "D'ye think so?"

Dennis leant against the whitewashed wall of the Hall Dunnerdale farmhouse and lit a cigarette.

"Ah'm bluidy sure of it," he said. "Two sheep inside eight or nine days, and no snaw, tha knaws, Bob, an' the both lyin' in open places, like, nowt to fall off or break legs an' that."

"Wheer didst tha find them at?" asked Robert. "Wheer were they lyin' and how didst tha coom on them, like?"

"First woon were oop oonder Levers Hause, almost at top, tha knaws, joost this side, wheer it's real steep. It were lyin' joost this side of bit of a track—"

"That'd be *old* yow, then, Dennis. Ay, it would that."

"Nay, that's joost it, it were not. It were three-year-old, Bob, were that. I saw it bluidy teeth an' all."

"Oh, 'ell!"

Robert gnawed the top of his stick without further comment. An extremely shrewd man and older than Dennis, he had been the previous tenant farmer of Tongue House and knew—or had hitherto thought that he knew—everything that could possibly happen to sheep between the Grey Friar and Dow Crag. He never gave an opinion lightly or unless he was prepared to defend it; and if someone asked his advice he was accustomed to shoulder the problem and consider it as though it were his own.

Dennis was upset. Tenacious and energetic to the point of intensity, he had, a few years before and with virtually nothing behind him, taken the farming tenancy of Tongue House (or Tongue 'Us, as it is locally called), in the determination to live an independent life and make good on his own. It had been a hard grind at the outset—so hard that he might perhaps have given up altogether without the moral support and encouragement of his neighbour Bill Routledge, the ribald, tough old tenant-farmer of Long 'Us, the neighbouring farm across the fields. There had been weeks when the children had had no sweets, Dennis had had no cigarettes and meals had been what could be managed. Now, thanks partly to his own strength of character and partly to that of his courageous, competent wife, Gwen, their heads were well above water. The farm was prosperous, several consumer durables had been bought and installed and the girls were getting on well. If Dennis had an obsession, it was that he was damned if anyone was going to do him down financially or worst him in a bargain. The present nasty situation—which would have worried any hill farmer—reached him where he lived, as the Americans say. It raised the spectre of old, bad times and had about it also an unpleasant suggestion that something—some creature—up beyond the tarn was getting the better of him.

"Ay, an' t'oother, Bob, tha knaws," he went on, "that were ont' Moss, like, before tha cooms to Rough Grund, and joost a bit oop from top of tarn. They were both on 'em the bluidy saame—pulled to shreds an' pieces spread all o'er. An' I'll tell thee—theer were bones clean gone—bones an' quarters an' all—hafe bluidy sheep torn an' gone, one on 'em."

"That'll be dog then," said Robert emphatically, looking Dennis squarely in the eye.

"Ay, that's what Ah were thinkin'. But Bill's had no dogs awaay—had, he'd a' told me—"

"Dog could coom from anywheers, Dennis—could be out of Coniston or Langd'l. But that's what it is, old boöy, an' nowt else. So tha'd best joost get out thee gun an' have a run round int' early mornin'—"

"Bluidy 'ell!" said Dennis, treading out his cigarette on the road. "As if there wayn't enough to be doin'—"

"Ay, weel, tha canst joost fill boogger wi' lead first, an' then read it collar affter, if it's got one," said Robert.

"Has and Ah'll hev th' basstard in court," said Dennis. "Ah tell thee, Bob, Ah will that. There's been ducks an' hens gone too. Smashed henhouse wire reet in—no fox could a' doon it. Ah'll have soom boogger in court."

"Ay, so yer should," returned Robert, "so yer should." After a suitable pause he said, "Ah yer goin' in t'Oolverston?"

"Nay, joost as far as Broughton—pickin' oop coople of spare tyres, tha knaws. Is there owt tha wants?"

"Not joost now, old lad."

Dennis, still musing on his dead sheep, drove down the valley towards Ulpha.

"And the monkey's done ten days plus," concluded Mr. Powell. "I think that's the lot."

"The cylinder's being regularly cleaned out?" asked Dr. Boycott.

"Yes, it is. Oh, but what about the guinea-pigs, chief?" said Mr. Powell, returning his note-pad to the ready.

"The ones receiving tobacco tar condensates, you mean?" said Dr. Boycott. "What about them? I thought that was one thing that was proceeding quite straightforwardly?"

"Well, I mean, how long do we go on using the same guinea-pigs?"

"Use them up, of course," answered Dr. Boycott rather shortly. "They cost money, you know. Apart from that, it's only humane. The Littlewood Committee report had an entire chapter on wastage. We don't use two animals where one will do."

"Well, this lot have all had tar doses on both ears now, and the ears removed in just about every case—every case where there's a cancerous growth, that's to say."

"Well, you can go on and use their limbs for the same thing, you know."

"Oh, should we, chief? Righty-o. Only I haven't been in on one of these before. Do we ever use anaesthetics?"

"Good God, no," said Dr. Boycott. "D'you know what they cost?"

"Oh, I know—only Dr. Walters was saying—"

"I'm in charge of the tar condensates work, not Walters," said Dr. Boycott. Before Mr. Powell could get in even the most hurried of assents, he went on, "Did you ever hear any more about those two dogs—seven-three-two and eight-one-five?"

"Not a thing," said Mr. Powell. "I doubt we will now, you know. They've been gone—let's see—eleven days I make it. They could have been shot, or adopted, or just have run from here to Wales. But I shouldn't think we'll ever know."

"Touch wood," said Dr. Boycott with a faint smile.

Mr. Powell facetiously tapped his own head. Granted the faintest prescience of what the future held, he might well have broken his nails to claw the varnish off the top of Dr. Boycott's desk—for, unlike his own, it was wood and not plastic.

FIT 4

The tod had said never a word all day, even during the afternoon, when Rowf, surly at the anxiety of the other two and obstinately determined to eat the last of his kill, had gone down to the tarn in broad daylight, gnawed the remains in the open for half an hour and as darkness began to fall brought back the jawbone to chew and worry in the cave. At last it crept silently over the shale and picked up a fragment, remarking only, "Give us a bite noo, kidder. There'll be ne bait for us i' th' Dark, ye knaw."

"What in thunder d'you mean?" snarled Rowf, the reek of the tod seeming to tingle through his very entrails.

"Oh, let him have it, Rowf!" said Snitter quickly. "You know, that reminds me, I once saw a cat steal a whole fish and carry it up a tree. Oh, it grinned like a letter-box; it thought it was quite safe up there!"

"Well, wasn't it?" asked Rowf, curious in spite of himself.

"Hoo, hoo, hoo!" Snitter danced on the stones at his own recollection. "My master turned the garden hose on it. But even then the fish came down much faster than the cat." He became suddenly grave. "Rowf—the farmers, the whitecoats. Tod's right—we can't afford to be found. If they once discover we're here, they'll come and hose us out with our own blood."

"Eh, th' Dark'll pull ye doon soon eneuf," cried the tod suddenly, as though Snitter's words had driven it beyond further endurance, "an' weary ye'll be an' aall, but Ah'm not hangin' aboot. Ah'm away. Yon yow ye felled ootside'll be yer last, ne doot aboot yon."

All in a moment it had crept to the further side of the tunnel and, having thus put the breadth of the place between Rowf and itself, trotted quickly along the wall and out into the darkness.

Snitter ran after it, yapping, "Tod! Tod! Wait!" but when he reached the mouth of the cave there was nothing to be seen in the twilight. Only the rising wind, gathering itself high up in Calf Cove, moaned down the funnel of the valley and tugged at the bog myrtle and tufts of grass in the dreary, empty moss. There was a singing in his head, rapid and shrill, like a wren in a bush. Looking up at the last light in the pale sky, he perceived that the wind—and this, he now recalled, he had, indeed, always known—was in reality a gaunt giant, thin-faced, thin-lipped and tall, carrying a long knife and wearing a belt from which were dangling the bodies of dying animals— a cat whose protruding entrails dripped blood, a blinded monkey groping in the air with its paws, a guinea-pig lacking ears and limbs, its stumps tar-smeared; two rats grotesquely swollen, their stomachs about to burst. Striding over the moss, the giant returned Snitter's frightened gaze piercingly, without recognition. Snitter knew that he had become an object upon which the giant's thought was playing like the beam of a torch, the subject of the song— if song it were—now rising and falling either through his own split head, or perhaps—might it rather be?—through the solitude of this waste valley between the hills. Silently the giant threw his song a stick across the bog; and obediently Snitter retrieved and brought it back to him, carried in his own mouth.

> *"Across the darkness of the fell*
> *My head, enclosed with chicken wire,*
> *Seeks the far place where masters dwell,*

> *A stolen town removed entire.*
> *The lorry, churning through the mire,*
> *Foreknew and watched all ways I ran.*
> *With cloven headpiece all afire,*
> *A lost dog seeks a vanished man."*

Snitter whined and pressed himself to the ground at the wind's feet. The wind, taking the song from him, nodded unsmilingly and strode away down the length of the tarn, the jumbled, struggling bodies swinging at its back. Snitter understood that the seizure had passed; until next time he was free—to lie in the darkness and wonder what would become of Rowf and himself without the tod.

"What are you doing?" asked Rowf, looming blackly out of the scrub. His anger had gone and he lay down beside Snitter uneasy and subdued.

"Dancing like a piece of ice," said Snitter, "and singing like a bone. The mice do—it makes the sky blue. Where there were three there's only two."

"You look crazier than ever," said Rowf, "with that great hole in your head. I'm sorry, Snitter. Let's not quarrel—we can't afford to, you and I. Come in and go to sleep."

Once more Snitter woke to the smell of the tod and the sound of Rowf moving in the dark. Listening, uncertain what might have happened, he realized that it was now Rowf who was making towards the opening of the cave, while the tod was standing in his way. Just as he was about to ask what they were doing, Rowf said, "I can kill you. Get out of the way."

"Noo, take it easy, lad. Divven't be se huffy," replied the tod.

"Rowf," said Snitter, "where are you going?"

"Poor sowl, he's gone loose i' th' heed," answered the tod, in its sharp, fawning voice, "blatherin' like a bubbly-jock. Here's me comin' back te tell ye te lowp off sharp. Th' farmer's oot o' th' rampage—dergs an' gun; an' noo yer pal says he's off to gi' hissel' back to yon whitecoat fellers. Wad ye credit it?"

"Rowf, what does he mean?"

"I'm going to find the whitecoats and give myself up. Don't try to stop me, Snitter."

"It's you that's crazy, Rowf, not me. Whatever for?"

"Because I've come to see that all I've done is to run away from my duty, that's why. Dogs were meant to serve men—d'you think I don't know? I knew all the time, but I was too much of a coward to admit it. I should never have listened to you, Snitter. If they need me to drown for them—"

"Of course dogs were meant for men, Rowf, but not for that—not for the tank and the whitecoats."

"Who are we to judge—how do we know? I'm a good dog. I'm not the brute they all thought I was. The men know best—"

"Yes, masters, Rowf, but not whitecoats. They don't care what sort of dog you are."

"Yer nay a derg noo, yer a sheep-killer," whispered the tod. "They'll blow yer arse oot, hinny. Howway let's be off, or ye'll both be deed an' done inside haaf an hoor, ne bother."

"What end can there be to this?" said Rowf to Snitter. "To run about loose until they find us—how long?"

"You said we'd become wild animals. That's what *they* do—live till they die."

"Why ay. Run on till th' Dark comes doon. Are we goin' noo or div Ah go mesel'? Ah warr'nd ye'd best be sharp."

Suddenly Rowf, with a heavy, plunging rush, blundered past the tod and out through the cave-mouth. They could hear him howling as he leapt over the further edge of the grassy platform outside and down to the marsh. Snitter turned quickly to the tod.

"I'm going after him. Are you coming?" In the faint glimmer of light down the shaft he caught the tod's eye, wary and inscrutable, but it made no move. Snitter ran out alone.

Tarn Head beck is wide in places and Rowf, in his unthinking flight, had reached the nearer bank by the edge of a pool in which the dark water, reflecting the moonlight, gave no sign of its depth. He checked and turned downstream. Snitter caught up with him in the act of springing down to a bed of stones on the further side.

"Rowf—"

Rowf jumped across and at once struck out southwards. Snitter, following, set off once more in pursuit, from time to time drawing breath to yelp. Rowf took no notice but held on his way, up and across the western slope of Dow Crag fell. Snitter saw him halt and pause, looking about him as though intending to go down to the reservoir road, which showed clear and white in the moonlight nine hundred feet below. Making a great effort, he ran on as fast as he could and once more came up with Rowf before he realized that he was there.

"Rowf, listen—"

Rowf turned sharply away without answering. At that moment the fern parted and the tod put out its head and shoulders, breath steaming in the cold air, tongue thrusting between small, sharp teeth. Rowf started and pulled up.

"How did you get here?"

"Roondaboot."

"I said I could kill you."

"Killin'? Ye daft boogger, it's ye that varnigh got killed. There's none luckier than ye. Ye saved yersel' an' me an' yon bit fella an' aall."

"What do you mean?" asked Snitter quickly.

"Lukka doon there by yon gate," said the tod, itself neither moving nor turning its head.

Snitter looked down towards the high gate in the dry stone wall through which the reservoir road passed in descending to the lower fields and Long House Farm.

"Noo lukka bit back there."

"What d'you mean? I don't—" All of a sudden Snitter caught his breath and jumped quickly into the bracken. About a quarter of a mile above the gate, where the trod leading up from Tongue 'Us joins the reservoir road, a man, carrying a gun, was making towards the tarn. At his heels followed two black-and-white dogs.

"Yon's yer farmer, hinny," whispered the tod to Rowf. "What ye bidin' for, then? He'll shoot ye sharp eneuf if ye fancy it."

Rowf, motionless and in full view on the open hillside, stood watching as the man and his dogs, half a mile away, tramped steadily up the road towards the dam.

"There aren't any men you can go back to, Rowf," said Snitter at length. "The tod's right—they'd only kill us now. We're wild animals."

"By, mind, lucky ye moved se sharp. Ye just got oot in time."

"Do you think the man knows we were living in the cave?" asked Snitter.

"Mebbies. Ne tellin' what th' booggers knaws—but Ah'm keepin' aheed o' them. Ah saw him lowpin' up from doon belaa, so Ah comes back to tell ye. Yon fyeul" (it looked quickly at Rowf) "wez yammerin' on a gey lot o' daft taalk afore ye come oot o' yer bit sleep. Mebbies noo he'll do it ne mair." It turned to Rowf. "Ye best stick te killin' yows wi' me, hinny. Thoo's a grand chep for yon, an' Ah'll bide wi' ye an' aall. But howway wivvus noo, an' us hangin' aboot here, plain as yon moon i' th' sky!"

Rowf followed the tod in a mazed silence, like a creature barely recovered from a trance. Snitter, for his part, was plunged in that strange state of mind which from time to time visits all creatures (but perhaps more frequently in childhood or puppyhood) when our immediate surroundings take on the aspect of a distant fantasy, we wonder who we are, the very sounds about us seem unreal and for a time, until the fit passes, it appears strange and arbitrary to find ourselves in this physical body, in this particular place, under this singular sky. The black peat, the heather, the crags, the glittering droplets, each a minute moon, bending the grasses through which Rowf was shouldering his way—these seemed, as he followed the tod, to be unfamiliar things he had never hitherto smelt— things which might even, perhaps, dissolve and vanish in an instant. Mournful they seemed, scentless; and the white moonlight, draining from them the colours of the day, made of them a residue, an empty world, where nothing could be certain and upon whose smells and other properties no more reliance could be placed than upon the figments of his own castaway, wounded brain.

It was during this night that Snitter came to be possessed

Dow Crag

even more deeply by the delusion that the world where they now wandered—or at least the light in which it appeared to him—was both a product and the equivalent of his own mutilated mind.

He was recalled to some sort of reality by stumbling over a piece of sharp-edged slate. Piles of dark slate were lying all about them and beneath his pads he could feel the tilting, sliding and pricking of the flat splinters.

"Where are we?"

"Walna Scar," replied the tod briefly.

"Is this the Scar?" asked Snitter, thinking how odd it would be to find himself walking across his own head.

"Why nair—th' Scar's up ahight, on th' top there. These ower here's slate quarries—but they've been idle mony a year noo. Ne men come nigh, 'cept only th' time o' th' shepherds' meet."

"Where are we going?" asked Rowf, looking up, as they left the slate quarries and came out once more upon the open hillside, at the steep bluff of Torver High Common above them.

The tod dropped its head quickly, snapped up a great stag-beetle under a clump of heather, and padded on, spitting out the fragments of the carapace.

"There's mair than one place, ye knaw."

"Well?"

"Nearby an' a canny bit scramble."

"Oh, he knows where he's going all right," said Snitter, anxious as always for the precarious relationship between Rowf and the tod. "He won't tell you where—he's too sharp for that—but if you go on asking he'll only think you don't trust him."

"I trust him just as long as he goes on feeling I can fill his belly," said Rowf. "But if I broke my leg in a chicken-run—"

"We're wild animals," answered Snitter. "What could he do for you then—die with you? You tell him what sense there'd be in that."

For some time they had been trotting up a long, gradual slope, crossing one narrow rill after another and here and there startling a sheep under a crag. Suddenly, without another word, the tod lay down on a patch of smooth grass so unobtrusively that the two dogs had already gone a dozen yards before becoming aware that it was no longer with them. When they turned back it was watching Rowf expressionlessly, head on front paws and eyes unblinking.

"Yer doin' canny, hinny." There was a hint of derision, barely masked. "Ah warr'nd ye'll be hunger'd b' now?"

Snitter realized that the tod was covertly manipulating Rowf. If Rowf admitted that he was hungry, as he must be, the tod would then be able to seem to accede to a wish expressed by Rowf that they should stop, hunt and kill. Rowf would apparently have initiated the idea, and if anything went wrong with it the blame would lie with him and not with the tod. He forestalled Rowf's reply.

"We're not particularly hungry," he answered. "If *you* are, why don't you say so?"

"Mind, yon's bonny yows. D'ye see th' mark o' them?"

You can't win, thought Snitter wearily. Anyway, why bother? Let's get on with it.

"What mark?"

"Sheep mark—shepherd's mark, hinny. Yon's hoo they tell th' yin from t'other. Did ye not knaw? Yon mark's nowt like t'other shepherd's yonder doon be Blake Rigg. D'ye twig on?"

"He means we can kill more safely here because we haven't killed here before," said Snitter. "I don't know why he can't say so and be done with it."

"By, yer a grrand bit feller," said the tod. "So Ah'll tell ye what Ah'll do. Ah'll just go halfers wi' ye ower th' fellin' of yonder yow."

The kill took them over half an hour, the chosen Herdwick proving strong, cunning and finally courageous. When they had run it to a standstill it turned at bay under a crag, and the end proved a bitter business of flying hooves and snapping teeth. Snitter, first kicked in the shoulder and then painfully crushed when the sheep rolled on him, was glad enough to lie panting in the shallow bed of a nearby beck, lapping copiously and ripping at the woolly haunch which Rowf severed and brought to him. It was excellent meat, the best they had yet killed, tender, bloody and well flavoured. It restored his spirits and confidence. Later he slept; and woke to see a red, windy dawn in the sky, the tod beside him and Rowf drinking downstream.

"Where are we?" he asked, shivering and looking up at the black top outlined against the flying, eastern clouds.

"Under Caw. Yer not feelin' femmer? Think nowt on't. There's not se far to go noo."

"I'm not femmer," answered Snitter, "unless it means mad."

In the next mile they climbed and crossed a broad ridge, but had hardly begun to descend the other side when the tod stopped, casting one way and another over the short turf. Finally it turned to Snitter.

"This is Broon Haw. Yon's Lickledale, doon yonder. There's th' shaft straight afore ye. Mind, it's gey deep. We can bide safe there, se lang as th' big feller doesn't gi' us away wi' mair o' his fond tricks."

Snitter, more than ever puzzled at the vast extent of the land which the men, for some inscrutable reason, had desolated and refashioned with rocks, ling and thorn, felt no surprise to find himself once more at the mouth of a deep cavern. It was similar to that which they had left, but less imposing and lofty. Tired now, despite his chilly sleep on the fell, he followed his companions into the dry, windless depths, found a comfortable spot and soon slept again.

Friday the 29th October

"Th' very saame," said Robert Lindsay. "Th' very saame way as thine, Dennis, and joost way you told it me an' all. Joost."

"It moost be dog," said Dennis. "Cann't be nowt else."

"Oh, ay. Bound to be. *Bound* to be, Dennis. Noo doubt about it whatever. An' Ah'll tell thee, Ah'm not so sure as there weren't two o' th' booggers. That were yoong sheep, real strong— a *good* 'un, ay—an' it had put oop real bluidy fight, like—theer were blood all ower, an'

(146)

boanes dragged down int' beck, strewed all about, joost like yours. Ah doan't believe woon dog could a' doon it."

"Basstard things," said Dennis. "Ah were oop Tarn neet before lasst, int' moonlight, tha knaws, Bob, took dogs an' gun an' hoonted all about t' plaace, like, an' on to Blaake Rigg, but Ah nivver saw noothing—not a bluidy thing." He trod out his cigarette and lit another.

"Ay, weel, they'll have shifted, joost, Dennis. That'll be it. They've coom down valley. They have that."

"But wheer d' y' reckon they started out from?" persisted Dennis. "Pratt, Routledge, Boow—an' Birkett over to Torver, Ah roong him oop—no woon's lost dog."

"Ay, weel, Ah joost had ideea, Dennis. An' it *is* only ideea, but Ah were thinkin'. Doost tha mind old 'Arry Tyson—him as used to do rooads for Council a year or two back?"

"He's over't Coniston, isn't he? With Research Station at Lawson Park?"

"Ay, that's right, he is. Well, he were down int' bar at Manor Hotel i' Broughton a few days back, and seems he were sayin' as they'd lost two dogs out of Research Station. Cut an' run, ay. Gerald Gray—him as keeps Manor, tha knaws—told chap int' bank, an' this chap were sayin' soomthing about it this morning when Ah were in theer."

"Did ye' assk him about it?"

"Noo, Ah nivver did, Dennis. Ah were in reet hoorry, that's why, an' Ah nivver thowt about it at all until Ah were outside. But then it joost stroock me—"

"It's not like finding th' boogger, though, an' killing it, is it?" said Dennis. "Ah mean, even if we assked Research Station an' they said they'd lost dog, likely they'd not do owt to get bluidy thing off fell. They'd say it couldn't be saame dog—all that caper—"

"Well, happen they'd *have* to take notice, tha knaws," returned Robert, his blue eyes regarding Dennis intently over the knob of his stick. "Ay, they might that. That's Goov'ment Department-controlled, old booy, oop at Lawson Park, an' if they had t' admit they'd let dogs goo, like, an' couldn't tell wheer they're at, we could put Member o' Parliament on to them—"

"An' have doozen an' hafe more bluidy sheep go while

they're arguing!" Dennis detested Government Departments in general and the Ministry of Agriculture in particular, and the very thought of them provided a vicarious object for his anger over the slaughtered sheep.

"It's serious matter, though, to be in possession of dog that kills sheep, Dennis. Legal offence. And if that were Goov'ment Department as doon it, that'd be real embarrassing. They'd not like it at all. Even the possibility—"

Robert, who read the papers attentively and had both an extremely wide outlook and also a natural gift for seeing things as they were likely to appear to other people, was already letting his mind run on the potential for embarrassment that the sheep-killings represented—always provided that what he had overheard in the bank proved to be true. The more he thought about it, the more it seemed to him that they might very well have in their hands a really stout stick for beating people who, collectively, usually did the beating themselves as far as hill-farmers were concerned—that was to say, Government chaps and officialdom in general. Harry Tyson, whom he had known off and on for years, was neither unreliable nor foolish. It would certainly be worth finding out from him what, if anything, had really happened at the Research Station. Robert was of a circumspect and deliberate nature, and not given to seeking straight rows unless heavily provoked. It had not occurred to him that he might actually telephone the Research Station and ask them point-blank about the dogs.

Dennis, on the other hand, was a great man for direct rows, especially where his own financial interests were concerned. He was, in fact, fearless, with a long string of victories to his credit. The idea of telephoning the Research Station had already occurred to him.

Mr. Powell, having seen to the monkey isolated in the cylinder and, as instructed, chalked up on the slate its current score—thirteen days plus—was looking over the interim reports on the smoking beagles and considering the terms of a draft letter to I.C.I. The search for a safe cigarette, an enterprise of great scientific interest and potential benefit to the human race, was, he felt, entirely worthy of British scientific endeavour, and possibly also of the glory that was Greece and the grandeur that was Rome. (For example, the Emperor Nero had, for his own purposes, after compelling slaves to eat large quantities of food and then to act in various ways, e.g., lie down, walk gently about, run fast and so on, cut them open to examine the effects on their digestive organs; but the results, unfortunately, had not survived in any detail.) Of course, it was open to people to give up smoking, but this would plainly be an intolerable demand to make, as long as experiments on living and sentient animals held out a chance of something better. The experiments had, in fact, been described by I.C.I. themselves as "the ultimate safeguard" for humans—which proved that they were a much better safeguard than not smoking.

The dogs, trussed and masked, were ingeniously compelled to inhale the smoke from up to thirty cigarettes a day. (Mr. Powell had once shown his wit at a conference by remarking, "They're lucky—more than I can afford.") The plan was that after about three years they were to be killed for dissection and examination. At the moment, fortunately, I.C.I. were holding a firm line against the sentimental nonsense put about by Miss Brigid Brophy and the Anti-Vivisection Society. Only the other day I.C.I. had been reported as saying, "Smoking is a fact of life in present-day society. It is also acknowledged by the Government to be damaging to health. In recognition of this fact research is endeavouring to produce smoking materials that will demonstrably reduce the risk to health. The use of animals for experiments is always going to be a moral problem, but within the realms of our present knowledge it is impossible to ensure that chemicals and drugs are safe unless they are tested on animals." This was so well expressed that it had escaped Mr. Powell (until the maddening Miss Brophy had fastened on it) that tobacco smoke could scarcely be held to lie within the definition of "chemicals and drugs." Every care was taken, went on I.C.I., to ensure that the animals did not suffer unnecessarily and lower species, such as rats, were used whenever possible.

"That's clever," murmured Mr. Powell to himself as he

glanced through the papers on the file. " 'Course, rats are actually very intelligent and sensitive, only nobody likes rats. Pity we can't import some smoking jackals or hyenas or something; we'd be all right then—no one'd mind."

The trouble was, everything you said in this field was explosive. You could never feel sure that a letter might not, somehow or other, leak into quarters where parts of it were likely to be twisted against you. On full consideration, it might be more prudent to suggest to Dr. Boycott that they should arrange a meeting with I.C.I. to talk over results—especially as the last batch of dogs dissected had—

At this moment the telephone rang. Mr. Powell had never been able to overcome his dislike of the telephone. If there was one thing, as he put it, that really bugged him about the job at Animal Research, it was being on the end of somebody else's line and liable to be summoned to go and see one or another of his superiors at a moment's notice. The present probability was that Dr. Boycott wanted to talk to him about the smoking beagles before he himself was ready to do so. Trying to console himself, as was his wont, with the thought that after a lot more experiments he would be a Boycott himself, he picked up the receiver.

"Powell here."

"Mr. Powell?" said the voice of the switchboard girl.

"Yes, Dolly. Is it an incoming call?"

"Yes, it is, Mr. Powell. I have th' gentleman on the line." (This was, as Mr. Powell at once understood, a covert warning to watch what he said. Everyone at Animal Research watched what he said, and never more closely than on outside lines.) "He's assking for the Information Officer, but I have no one listed under such an appointment." (Too right you haven't, thought Mr. Powell.) "I didn't know whether you'd wish to take th' call, Th' gentleman says he wants to talk to someone about dogs."

"Well, what about dogs? Who is the gentleman and where's the call from?"

"I think he's a *local* enquirer, Mr. Powell. A private person. Will you speak?"

Whoever he is, she's evidently very anxious to pass him on, thought Mr. Powell. He pondered quickly. Better the devil you know than the devil you don't know. If he did not take the call, it would look evasive and the caller would be referred to someone else. Also, if he did not take it and it turned out to be a matter within his responsibility, it would only come back to him in the end; whereas if it were not within his responsibility, he would have found out someone else's business without being any the worse off himself.

"All right, Dolly. I'll be glad to help the gentleman if I can. Please put him through."

"*Thank* you, Mr. Powell!" (Quite a ruddy lilt in the voice! thought Mr. Powell.) Click. "Putting you through to Mr. Powell, sir." Click. "*You're* through!" (Wish we were!)

"Good morning, sir. My name's Powell. Can I help you?"

"Have ye lost any dogs?"

"Er—who is that speaking, please?"

"My name's Williamson. Ah'm sheep-farmer at Seath't, Doonnerd'l. Ah'm assking have ye lost any dogs?"

"Er—could you tell me a little more about your problem, Mr. Williamson? I mean, how you come to be asking us and so on?"

"Ay, Ah will that. Theer's sheep been killed in Doonnerd'l, three or four o' 'em, an' Ah'm not th' only farmer as reckons it's stray dogs. Ah'm joost assking for a straight annser to a straight question—have ye lost any dogs?"

"I'm sorry I can't tell you the straight answer just off the cuff, Mr. Williamson, but I—"

"Well, can Ah speak to th' chap who can? Soomone moost know how many dogs ye've got and whether owt's missing."

"Yes, that's quite right, but he's not here just at the moment. Mr. Williamson, may I ring you back quite soon? I assure you I will, so don't worry."

"Well, Ah hope it *is* soon. Theer's chaps here as has to *work* for *their* living, and sheep's money, tha knaws—"

Mr. Powell, despite his bleak misgivings, decided to try a counterattack.

"Mr. Williamson, have you or anyone actually seen these dogs?"

"If Ah had they'd not be alive now, Ah'll tell thee. Do your dogs wear collars?"

"Yes, they do—green plastic ones with numbers on."

"Ay, well, then you'll joost know if there's any missing, wayn't ye?"

Dennis gave his own number, reiterated his hope for an early reply and rang off. Mr. Powell, with a sinking heart, went to seek audience of Dr. Boycott.

"—Assa, what a sad carry-on an' aall, mind," said the tod. "Rakin' aboot aal ower th' place, bidin' oot o' neets from here to yon. But mark ma words, ye *must* kill away from hyem, aye kill away from hyem, else it's th' Dark for ye, ne doot at aall. Nivver muck up yer aan byre, like ye did back yonder." It became expansive. "Lukka me now. There's none se sharp. Ah wez littered a lang step from here, far ahint th' Cross Fell. Ah've waalked aall ower, an' Ah'm as canny off as th' next, fer aall th' chasin'."

"Ay, yer canny, ne doot," said Snitter, rolling comfortably on the shale to scratch his back. "I'd never say you're—er—wrang."

"Nivver kill twice ower i' th' same place, and nivver kill inside o' two mile o' yer aan byre. An' nivver bring nowt back wi' ye. There's mony a tod has gone to th' Dark wi' chuckin' guts an' feathers aboot ootside its aan byre."

"Hitty-missy faffin'," murmured Snitter lazily. "I say, tod, I'm getting rather good, don't you think?"

"Mebbies we'll kill ower b' Ash Gill beck or some sich place th' neet," went on the tod, ignoring Snitter's sally. "But farmers is sharp te find bodies an' it's us that's got ter be sharpest. So eftor that it'll be Langdale—or Eskdale—ten mile's not ower far. Aye roam te th' kill, an' ye'll see hyem still."

"I'm game," said Rowf. "I'll go as far as you like, as long as we *do* kill."

"If ony boogger says Ah's not clivver, whey Ah's still here an' that's eneuf to prove it."

"You can join the club," said Snitter. "The Old Survivors—very exclusive—only three members, counting you. And one of *them*'s mad."

"That was Kiff's joke—he knew what it meant—I never did," said Rowf. "What *is* a club?"

"It's when dogs get together—run through the streets and piss on the walls; chase the bitches, scuffle about and pretend to fight each other—you know."

"No," said Rowf sorrowfully. "I've never done that—it sounds good."

"D'you remember when they took Kiff away, and we all barked the place down singing his song?"

"Yes, I do. Taboo, tabye—that one?"

"That's it—d'you remember it? Come on, then!"

There and then, in the darkness of the shaft, the two dogs lifted up their muzzles in Kiff's song, which that gay and ribald tyke, before his death by cumulative electrocution, had left behind him in the pens of Animal Research as his gesture of defiance, none the less valid for remaining uncomprehended by Dr. Boycott, by old Tyson, or even, come to that, by I.C.I. After a little, the tod's sharp, reedy voice could be heard in the burden.

> "There happened a dog come into our shed.
>   (Taboo, taboo)
> He hadn't a name and he's sure to be dead.
>   (Taboo, taboo, taboo)
> He wagged his tail and nothing he knew
> Of the wonderful things that the whitecoats do.
>   (Taboo, tabye, ta-bollocky-ay, we're
>   all for up the chimney.)
>
> "I heard the head of the whitecoats say,
>   (Taboo, taboo)
> 'We're getting another one in today.'
>   (Taboo, taboo, taboo)
> 'The tobacco man needn't waste his grub,
> We'll sling him into the pickling tub.'
>   (Taboo, tabye, ta-bollocky-ay, we're
>   all for up the chimney.)
>
> "So they laid him out on a nice glass bench.
>   (Taboo, taboo)

His entrails made a horrible stench.
*   (Taboo, taboo, taboo)*
And this next bit will make you roar—
His shit fell out all over the floor.
*   (Taboo, tabye, ta-bollocky-ay, we're*
*   all for up the chimney.)*

"O who's going to stick him together again?
*   (Taboo, taboo)*
His ear's in a bottle, his eye's in the drain,
*   (Taboo, taboo, taboo)*
His cock's gone down to the lecture hall,
And I rather think he's missing a ball.
*   (Taboo, tabye, ta-bollocky-ay, we're*
*   all for up the chimney.)*

"When I've gone up in smoke don't grieve for me,
*   (Taboo, taboo)*
For a little pink cloud I'm going to be.
*   (Taboo, taboo, taboo)*
I'll lift my leg as I'm drifting by
And pee right into a whitecoat's eye.
*   (Taboo, tabye, ta-bollocky-ay, we're*
*   all for up the chimney.)*

"If you want to know who made up this song—
*   (Taboo, taboo)*
'Twas a rollicking dog who didn't live long.
*   (Taboo, taboo, taboo)*
His name was Kiff, he was black and white,
He was burned to cinders—serve him right.
*   (Taboo, tabye, ta-bollocky-ay, we're*
*   all for up the chimney.)"*

"Good old Kiff—he was a hard case. If he were here now—"

"Wish he was," growled Rowf.

"If he were here now, I know what he'd say. He'd ask what we meant to do in the long run."

"Long run?" asked Rowf. "Hasn't it been long enough for you?"

"How long do you suppose we can keep it up—running

about in this empty, man-made place, killing fowls and animals and dodging guns? I mean, where's it going to end—where's it going to get us?"

"Where it gets the tod—"

"Why ay, hinny—let's be happy through th' neet—"

"But they're *bound* to get us in the end, Rowf. We ought to be planning some way out. And you know very well there's only one way—we've got to find some men and—and—what was I saying?" Snitter scratched at his split head. "Milkman, rhododendrons, newspapers—linoleum smells nice too—and sort of tinkling, windy noises came out of a box—used to make me howl, then rush out of the garden door—cats cats quick quick wuff wuff!"

"What on earth are you talking about?"

There was a pause.

"I can't remember," said Snitter miserably. "Rowf, we've got to find some sort of men. It's our only chance."

"You wouldn't let me when I wanted to, the other night."

"Well, you weren't going about it the right way. That would have finished us all."

"You're a good little chap, Snitter, and you've had a bad time. I'm not going to quarrel with you—but no more men for me; that's flat. I wasn't myself that night."

"There *was* a good man, once." Snitter was whining.

"Haddaway, ye fond fyeul! Giv ower! A gud *man?* Ay, an' soft stones an' dry watter—"

"I know there was one *once,* long ago," said Rowf. "My mother told me that story in the basket—it was about all she had time to tell me, actually. But he went to the bad; and there'll never be one again—you must know that."

"What story, Rowf—what do you mean?"

"She said all dogs know the story. Do you mean to say I know something you don't?"

The shale rattled as Snitter turned over.

"Do *you* know it, tod?"

"Nay—but Ah warr'nd it'll be a mazer. Let's hev yer wee tale then, hinny."

"She said—" Rowf was pondering. "She used to say—well, there's a great dog up in the sky—he's all made of stars. She said you can see him; but I never know where to look, and you certainly can't *smell* him; but sometimes you can hear him barking and growling, up in the clouds, so he must be there. Anyway, it seems that it was he, this dog, long ago, who had a great idea of creating all the animals and birds—all the different kinds. He must have had a lot of fun inventing them, I suppose.

"Well, anyway, when he'd invented them all—so she said—he needed somewhere to put them, so he created the earth—trees for the birds, and pavements and gardens and posts and parks for the dogs, and holes underground for rats and mice, and houses for cats; and he put the fish in the water and insects into the flowers and grass, and all the rest of it. Very neat job—in fact you'd wonder, really, wouldn't you, how it was all managed? Still, I suppose a star dog—"

"Listen!" said Snitter, leaping nervously to his feet. "What's that?"

"Haald yer gobs an' bide still!"

They all three listened. Footsteps and human voices approached the mouth of the shaft across the turf outside. They stopped a moment, their owners evidently looking in, and voices boomed in the mouth of the cavern. Then they passed on, in the direction of Lickledale.

Snitter lay down again. The tod had not moved a paw. Rowf was evidently warming to his tale and no one had to ask him to go on.

"Well, the star dog needed someone to look after the place and see that all the animals and birds got their food and so on, so he decided to create a really intelligent creature who could take the job right off his back. And after a bit of reflection he created Man, and told him what he wanted him to do.

"The man—and he was a splendid specimen: well, perfect, really, because in those days he couldn't be anything else—he considered it for a bit, and then he said, 'Well, sir' (he called the star dog 'Sir,' you know), 'Well, sir, it's going to be a big job and there'll be a lot to do—a hard day's work every day—and the only thing I'm wondering is what *I* stand to get out of it?'

"The star dog thought about that and in the end he said, 'This is how we'll fix it. You shall have plenty of intelligence—almost as much as I have, and as well as that I'll give you hands, with fingers and thumbs, and that's more than I've got myself. And of course you shall have a mate, like all the other animals. Now, look, you can make reasonable use of the animals, and part of your job will be to control them as well. I mean, if one kind starts getting to be too many and harming or hindering the others by eating all the food or hunting them down beyond what's reasonable, you must thin that kind out until there's the right number again. And you can kill what animals you need—not too many—for food and clothing and so on. But I want you to remember all the time that if I've made you the most powerful animal it's so that you can look after the others—help them to do the best they can for themselves, see they're not wasted and so on. You're in charge of the world. You must try to act with dignity, like me. Don't go doing anything mean or senseless. And for a start,' he said, 'you can sit down and give names to the whole lot, so that you and I will know what we're talking about for the future.'

"Well, the man did this naming and a nice, long job it proved to be, what with all the cows and rats and cats and blackbirds and spiders and things. Of course, most of them—like tod here—hardly had any idea that they had names—but anyway the man did. And in the end he got it done, and settled down to look after the world, as the star dog had told him to. And after a time the animals had young and the man and his mate had children and the world began to be quite full up, so that the man had to do some of the thinning out that the star dog had said would be all right.

"Now it seems that about this time the star dog had to go away on a journey—I suppose to see to some other world or something: but apparently it was a great distance and he must have been gone a long time, because while he was away some of the man's children grew up, and with them that always takes years and years, you know. Anyway, when the star dog got back, he thought he'd go and see how the man and all the animals were getting on. He was looking forward to a visit to the earth, because he'd always felt that that was rather a good job he'd done—better than some others, I dare say.

"When he got down to the earth, he couldn't find anyone at all for a long time. He wandered about the streets and parks and places, and at last, in a wood, he caught a glimpse of a young badger, who was hiding under the branches of a fallen tree. After a lot of trouble he persuaded him to come out and asked him what was the matter.

" 'Why,' said the badger, 'some men came this morning and dug up our sett and smashed it all to pieces, and they pulled my father and mother out with a long pair of tongs with sharp teeth on the ends. They hurt my father badly and now they've put them both in a sack and taken them away—I don't know where.'

" 'Are there too many badgers round here, then?' asked the star dog.

" 'No, there are hardly any left,' said the young badger. 'There used to be quite a lot, but the men have killed nearly all of us. That's why I was hiding—I thought you were the men coming back.'

"The star dog moved the badgers who were left to a safe place and then he went to look for the man. After walking about for quite a long time, he heard a confused noise in the distance—shouting and barking and people running about, so he went in that direction and after a bit he came to a kind of big yard, and he found the man there and some of his grown-up children. They'd made a kind of ring at one end of the yard, out of sheets of corrugated iron, and they'd put the mother and father badger in there and were throwing stones at them to make them more fierce and trying to make some dogs attack them. The dogs weren't very keen, because, although the male badger had a broken paw and was badly wounded in the face, he was fighting like the devil and his mate was just as brave as he was. But the dogs had been kept very hungry on purpose and anyway they supposed the men must know best, especially as there were about twelve dogs to two badgers.

"The star dog put a stop to what was going on and sent the two badgers off to be looked after by their family until they were better, and then he told the man that it had come to his nose that things weren't as they should be and asked him what he thought he was doing.

" 'Oh,' says the man, 'you said I was to keep the numbers of the animals down and some of them had to be killed if necessary. You said we could make use of the animals, so we were just having a bit of sport. After all, animals are given us for our amusement, aren't they?'

"The star dog felt angry, but he thought that perhaps he ought to have made clearer to the man in the first place what he'd meant, so he explained again that he regarded him as responsible for seeing that the animals weren't killed without good reason, and that their lives weren't wasted or thrown away for nothing. 'If you're the cleverest,' he said, 'that means, first of all, that you're supposed to care for the others and consider them as creatures you've got to look after. Just think about that, and make sure you get it right.'

"Well, anyway, after a long time the star dog decided to come back to the earth again and this time he chose the middle of the summer, because he thought it would be nice to roll about on the grass and have a run through the parks, and the gardens of the houses, when all the leaves and flowers were out and smelling so nice. When he arrived it was a hot day and he went down to the nearest river to have a drink. But he found he could smell it from half a mile away and it was awful. When he got up close he found it was full of human shit and crammed with floating, dead fish. There was a wretched water rat making off as fast as he could along the bank and the star dog asked him what had gone wrong, but he only said he didn't know.

"After some time the star dog came upon a crowd of men who were all shouting at each other and holding some sort of meeting, so he asked them if they knew what had happened in the river, and how all the fish had come to die in poisoned water.

" 'We're the sewage workers,' said one of them, 'and we're not going to do any more work until our demands are met. It's a very serious business, too—do you realise we're so short of money that we haven't got any for gambling or smoking or getting drunk?'

" 'My fish are all dead,' said the star dog.

" 'What the hell's it matter about a lot of bloody fish?' said one of the men. 'We know our rights and we mean to have them.'

"This time the star dog told all the men he met that if he found them once more wilfully misunderstanding or taking no notice of what he'd said, he wouldn't warn them again."

Rowf paused.

"Noo what wez at th' bottom o' thet, then?" asked the tod.

"Well, of course, it *did* go wrong," said Rowf morosely. "I'm not telling it very well, but he came back again. Kiff knew this story, and he said the star dog found the men sticking iron, pointed things into a wretched bull and making it rip the stomachs out of a lot of poor old broken-down horses, and they were laughing at them and pelting them with orange peel while they went limping about. But I think my mother said he found some birds in cages which the men had blinded to make them sing. They sing to assert themselves, of course, and keep other cock birds away, so as they were blind they kept singing as long as they had any strength, because they couldn't tell whether there were any rival birds about or not. Anyway, whatever it was, the star dog said to the man, 'Because thou hast done this thing, thou art cursed above every beast of the field. *They* will continue to live their lives as before, without reflection or regret, and I will speak to them in their hearts, in hearing and in scent and instinct and in the bright light of their perception of the moment. But from you I shall turn away for ever, and you will spend the rest of your days wondering what is right and looking for the truth that I shall conceal from you and infuse instead into the lion's leap and the assurance of the rose. You are no longer fit to look after the animals. Henceforth you shall be subject to injustice, murder and death, like them; and unlike them, you shall be so full of confusion that you shall loathe even your brother's and sister's bodily fluids and excretions. Now get out of my sight.'

"So the man and his mate, with faltering steps and slow, took their solitary way. And ever since that day all the birds and animals have feared man and fled from him; and he exploits them and torments them, and some of them he has actually destroyed for ever from the face of the earth. He bruises us, and those of us who can bruise him. It's a bad world for animals now. They live out of his way, as best they're able. I believe, myself, that the star dog's given it all up as a bad job. He must have, for what good are men to animals?"

"Yon's a fine tale noo," said the tod. "Ay, a reet dazzler, an' yer a grrand hand at tellin' it."

"Yes," said Snitter, "you told it well, Rowf. And you're quite right—I *have* heard it before. Only you left out one very important bit, which they told me. When the man was disgraced and told to go away, he was allowed to ask all the animals whether any of them would come with him and share his fortunes and his life. There were only two who agreed to come entirely of their own accord, and they were the dog and the cat. And ever since then, those two have been jealous of each other, and each is for ever trying to make man choose which one he likes best. Every man prefers one or the other."

"Well," said Rowf, "if that *is* the moral—and I don't believe it is—then I've just had my trouble for nothing. I suppose you can twist a story to mean anything you like. But all I can say again is, no more men for me—"

"If you did find a master, Rowf—I mean, just suppose you did—what would he be like? What would he do?"

"It's a stupid idea."

"Well, but go on—just for fun—just suppose! I mean, suppose you found yourself sort of forced to be with a man who turned out to be—well, you know, decent and good and honest—what would he be like?"

"Well, first of all, he'd have to leave me alone until I was ready—and take no notice even if I barked the place down. If he tried to force himself on me or started messing me about, I'd bite his hand off. And I'd judge him on his voice as well as his smell. He'd have to let me take

my own time about smelling him—his hands and his shoes
and all that. And if he was any good, he'd be able to tell
when I'd begun to feel all right about him and then he'd
say, 'Hullo, Rowf, have a bone,' or something like that;
and then he'd give me a good one and let me alone to
gnaw it while he went on with whatever he was doing.
And then I'd lie down on the floor and—oh, what's the
use? Snitter, you're just tricking me into making up a lot
of rubbish!"

"I'm not—but it only shows you've got *some* sort of
idea at the back of your mind—"

"Isn't it time to go out and hunt yet?" interrupted
Rowf. "I'm hungry."

"Why, let's away noo. Yer in gud fettle then? Ducks
an' gimmers'll sharp put ye reet, Ah warr'nd."

Monday the 1st November

"Well, Stephen, you'll be delighted to know that your
ideas were entirely the right ones." Dr. Boycott seemed
positively jovial.

"Sorry, chief, which ones were those?"

"About the dogs."

"The smoking autopsies? Well, if we—"

"No, no, no—the dogs that got out. Seven-three-two
and that other one of Fortescue's."

"Oh, those, chief. But as far as I remember the only
idea I had was that we should say nothing at all about
them."

"Yes, and you stuck to it very sensibly. And the—"

"But—excuse me, chief—what do I say to this Mr.
Williamson when we ring him back?"

"I'm coming to that. I was saying, the Director thinks
yours is entirely the right line. So all you have to do now
is telephone Mr. Williamson and tell him."

"What, tell him the dogs are ours and we're not going
to do anything?"

"Good gracious, no! After all, how do we know that the dogs *are* ours? You don't know, and neither do I: it's only a guess. And from what you tell me, there may not even be any dogs at all. No one seems actually to have seen them. No, you simply tell Williamson that we have nothing to say in reply to his question."

"But—but I mean, won't he think that's very suspicious?"

"He may, but he's just as likely to be wrong as right. The sheep-killings may stop of their own accord. If they *are* in fact due to a dog or dogs, they may get themselves shot and turn out not to be ours. Even if they *are* ours, they may not be traceable to us, if Tyson's got any sense. They may have worried their collars off by now. The Director thinks it's unlikely that anything embarrassing could be laid at our door, and more than unlikely that any of these farmers could or would sue us. They're much more likely to claim their insurance and let it go at that. Whereas if we stand in a white sheet, start admitting liability and try to take some sort of step towards helping in a search, we shall only attract adverse publicity and put Animal Research in the wrong when it may be nothing of the kind. Besides, if we were to incur any expenditure in that way, how would we justify it at audit?"

"But what *about* Tyson, chief? He may already have spilled too many beans outside for us to be able to take the line that we haven't lost any dogs."

"We're not taking that line, Mr. Stephen, my good sir. We're simply saying we've nothing to say. Let them take it from there. I've already had a word with Tyson—pointed out to him that the most he can truthfully say if he's asked is that two pens were found empty. I stressed that it would be quite unjustified on his part to put two and two together and make five, and that the Director would be most upset to think that anything of the kind was being said. *Most* upset, I said. I think he got *that* message all right."

"Nudge nudge wink wink say no more, eh? But is that quite fair to Williamson?"

"My dear chap, we're under no more obligation to stand and answer Williamson's questions than any private person would be. If he thinks evil, let him *prove* evil—if he can. I repeat, it's all very unlikely to come to anything."

"I just don't particularly fancy ringing him back, that's all."

"Well, in this place we all have to do things we don't like sometimes, don't we? Even the animals, ha ha. Anyway, cheer up. You'll be pleased to hear about the dogfish. The colour-plate tests on the eyeless ones show—"

"Williamson sounded hellish angry," said Mr. Furse, the assistant editor of the *Lakeland News,* downing the last of his second pint. "In fact, I couldn't really get an awful lot of sense out of him, for that reason."

"Well, wouldn't *you* be?" replied Mr. Weldyke, the editor. "What's his damage—three sheep, did you tell me, and a chicken pen smashed in or something? Oh, nice of you to come over, Jane. Two pints as before, please."

"Ay, but I mean he doosn't have to take it out on me, now, dooz he?"

"Y' shouldn't be standing in the road, should you?" said the editor. "Anyway, what's your notion—are you going to do a piece on it?"

"Short piece, ay, might as well. 'Mysterious sheep losses in Dunnerd'l'—you know the sort of thing. Thanks, Jane. Cheers, Mike! But it'll all blow over. Happen fella whose dog it is knows very well already; and he's keeping his mouth shut. If it goes on, he'll maybe go out himself one night by moonlight, find it and get rid of it—shoot it himself, as like as not, and no one the wiser."

"But you said Williamson was accusing the Animal Research place at Coniston. Did you ask them about it?"

"Oh, ay—rang 'em up. They'd nothing to say at all. 'No comment.' Just what I'd say in their position. I can't see much point in pushing any harder where they're concerned, can you? I mean, God knows what they have to do to all those poor brutes up there. I know it's in a good cause; you've got to have science and progress; but I mean they very probably don't know from day to day what's dead and what's dying and just how many they *have* got. You can bet your boots the N.F.U. wouldn't want them pushed around—they must be far too useful to farmers in general. So it follows that *we* don't, doesn't it? Ours is a farming area and our readers are farmers."

"Ee—yes, I can see that," replied the editor reflectively, looking out at the men striding like scissors down Market Street to get out of the rain. "So we cover it without mentioning the research station, right? N.F.U. or no N.F.U., farmers are entitled to expect this sort of thing to be covered in their local paper. If there *is* a dog gone feral, playing merry hell in Dunnerd'l or Lickledale or somewhere, we ought to find out as much as we can and print it, if only so that local chaps can get together and organize a hunt with guns if they think it's worth while."

"Good afternoon, gentlemen. Nice to see you. How are you?"

Mr. Weldyke and Mr. Furse looked up to encounter the smile of a dark, very much dressed man of about forty-five, who affably waved a hand beringed with two large stones set in gold. (His other was holding a double whisky.)

"I couldn't help hearing what you were saying," said this gentleman ingratiatingly. "We haven't actually met, but you'll remember my my name, business-wise—it's Ephraim, manager of the Kendal branch of Suitable Suits. You've kindly printed a lot of our advertising, of course, as you'll recall."

"Oh, yes, of course, Mr. Ephraim," said Mr. Weldyke, his gaze, as it returned for a few moments to his pint, encountering *en passant* a dove-grey waistcoat adorned with mother-of-pearl buttons and a thin, long-and-short-linked gold watch-chain. "Nice to meet you. Are you going to join us?"

He drew back a chair and as he did so his eye caught Mr. Furse's for the briefest of moments. That eye said, "I don't have to tell you that local newspapers never disoblige their regular advertisers."

"Well, thanks, if I may. Only for a moment."

"We've just slipped out for a jar and a snack. It's my round—that's whisky you're drinking, isn't it? Good. And can I get you a pork—" (Mr. Furse kicked him under the table.) "I mean, they have some good chicken sandwiches, or there's hot Scotch eggs in that glass thing there, if you prefer."

"No, no, thanks, I've had lunch. I'll only stay for a quick one with you." As Mr. Furse departed from the bay-window table to attract Jane's attention once more, Mr. Ephraim went on, "It was just an idea that occurred to me, Mr. Weldyke, for a little stroke of business— business with benefit to the community, one hopes, and perhaps a bit of sport as well. As I said, I couldn't help hearing what you were saying about the wild dog down Dunnerdale way and how the farmers might be wanting to organize a hunt. Now my idea is this. By the way, is it quite convenient to put this before you now? Have you time?"

"Oh, yes, certainly, Mr. Ephraim. We should be most interested to hear your idea."

"Ah, you're back quickly, Mr. Furse. Easy to see you're a favoured customer, eh?"

"Oh, me and Mike here practically support th' place. Cheers!"

"Good health! Success to journalism! Well, now, we're anxious to expand business a bit in that western area— you know, get some fresh custom, let the locals know who we are and all that. Of course, I know hill-farmers aren't millionaires, but even they're spending a good deal more on clothes than they used to and we feel there's a potential. Affluent society, you know, and all that. What I feel we've got to do is meet the country farmer half-way— show him we're offering value for money and nothing up our sleeves—let him see we're human, you know. So—tell you what I'll do! Suppose *we* were to organize this dog hunt—with your help on the publicity side, of course. Just thinking aloud, we'd provide six—well, say five cartridges for every man taking part, and offer each gun, up to twenty, his choice of either two hard-wearing shirts or a pair of good, serviceable trousers. And then for the one who actually kills the dog—have to think how we're going to be sure he's killed the right one, of course—a ready-made two-piece suit, with a free fitting thrown in. You do the photographs—the lucky farmer shaking hands with me over the body and all that, eh? What you're thinking, eh?"

"Well, I should think it's worth it from your point of view, Mr. Ephraim. From ours, it's a whale of an idea. There's one or two details we'd have to work out, of course—"

"Of course, of course. But we're wanting to move fast, eh? The dog might stop raiding or maybe someone else shoots it before we do—you know?" (Mr. Ephraim waved his hands expressively.) "You get something in the paper Wednesday, our Mr. Emmer goes round the farms Thursday, gets it all set up for Saturday—I'll be out there myself, of course—"

"Fine, Mr. Ephraim, fine. Now look, can you just come back for a minute to the office? Then we can get the thing roughed out, and young Bob Castlerigg can get to work on a piece—you'll see it before publication, of course—"

Friday the 5th November

"Where did you say we were going, tod?" Snitter shivered in the chilly evening rain and sniffed at the sheep-rank turf, where even now a few late tormentils and louseworts were in bloom. They were crossing Dunnerdale.

"Ower to Eshd'l. Bootterilket groond—ay. Noo whisht a bit! Haald on!" The tod looked one way and the other, north to the Leeds mountain hut at Dale Head and south to Hinnin House and the dark, coniferous plantation rising up the fell behind it. Other than cows, no living creature was in sight. The tod slipped across the road in front of the gate and cattle-grid and Rowf and Snitter followed him along the line of a dry stone wall which led them across the pasture and down to Duddon tumbling noisily over its stones among the ash trees. On the bank, Rowf checked.

"Water? Look, I told you—"

"Haddaway! There's mair stones than watter. In w' goin' fer a duck!"

The tod slid almost daintily into the edge of the main channel, swam the few yards across and ran over white stones to the peaty bank on the farther side.

"Oh, look!" said Snitter suddenly, "a fish—a big one!"

"Ay, sea troot. It's upstream they go about noo."

Snitter, fascinated, watched the iridescent trout as it almost broke surface in a shallow place before vanishing into deeper water.

"D'you ever eat fish, tod?"

"Ay, Ah've had a few deed 'uns as th' folks has thrown oot."

"Dead? Where d'you find them?"

"Middens—dustbins. Are ye comin'?"

Rowf set his teeth, hit the water with a splash and was out on the further bank. Snitter followed.

"My head's an umbrella, you know," said Snitter. "It opens and shuts all right—it's open now, actually—er—forbye there's a rib broken. The water runs from front to back and trickles down inside the crack."

"Mind yer a fond boogger, ye, an' not ower strang neether, but yer ne fyeul."

"Thanks, tod," said Snitter. "I really appreciate that."

They skirted the edge of the plantation along the foot of Castle How and turned westward again, leaving Black Hall to the north.

"I'm sorry," said Snitter three quarters of a mile later, as they reached the crest of the steep slope. "I'm not built for this, you know. The dilapidation—no, the degradation—I mean the destination—oh, dear." He sat down and looked about him in the failing light. "Wherever have we got to?"

"Hard Knott. Bootterilket's doon bye. Yon's Eshd'l, ye knaw."

"What happens now?" asked Rowf.

"Hang on a bit till neet-time, then we can run doon th' fell an' take th' forst yow ye fancies. By, yer a grrand provider." The tod looked at Rowf admiringly. "Ah've getten a full belly runnin' wi' thoo."

"Going to make us wait, are you?" said Snitter, sitting

Thursday, 28th October
to
Friday, 12th November

WANDERINGS
IN
DUNNERDALE

Eskdale · HARD KNOTT · CRINKLE CRAGS
CARRS
SWIRRAL
Cockley Beck · Levers House
HARTER FELL · GREY FRIAR
Dale Head · DOW CRAG
Castle How
Hinning House · Seathwaite Tarn
Tarn Beck
Grassguards · Thrang · Walna Scar · Levers House
Tongue House
Long House
Torver High Common
High Wallowbarrow
Hall Dunnerdale · Seathwaite · CAW
High Kiln Bank · BROWN HAW
River Duddon
Ulpha
route of return to Levers House
Dunnerdale

looking
north·north·east
River Lickle · Lickledale
Broughton Mills

Routes taken
by both dogs
travelling
together

Snitter's route
when alone

Rowf's route
in search of
Snitter

Routes taken
by Rowf and
the tod,
travelling
together

back on his haunches in a wet brush of ling. "You'd better sing us a song, tod, to pass the time. Do tods have songs?"

"Ay, we do, noo an' agen. Ay, Ah mind our aald wife made up a bonny 'un, lang time back."

"Your dam? Did she? What's it called?"

The tod made no reply. Snitter recalled its confusion when he had asked its name and hastily went on, "A bonny 'un?"

"Ay, it wez a canny bit song. She wad sing it on shiny neets."

"Well, never mind shiny neet," said Snitter. "Can ye not remember noo? Come on, Rowf, you ask him."

"Oh, may as well," said Rowf. "Can you smell that yow down there? I'll tear it, you see if I don't."

"Ay, it'll be varry soon felled an' fettled when us gets at it. Just tappy lappy doon th' bankside an' grab it b' th' slack o' th' neck."

"Well, sing up, then, tod," said Rowf. "If it's going to be that easy, you've got something to sing about."

The tod paused a while, rolling on its back and scratching on a patch of stones. Snitter waited patiently, the rain running down his nose from the trenched gash in his head. He could be no wetter. A car churned slowly up the pass and as its sidelights topped Fat Betty Stone and it started to creep away downhill in low gear, the tod began.

> *"A hill tod it wor layin'*
> *Atop a roondy crag.*
> *An' niff o' powltry doon belaa*
> *Fair made its whiskers wag.*
> *Th' farmer's canny lad, ye ken;*
> *Geese fast i' th' hemmel, ducks i' th' pen.*
> *Then fyeul shuts henhoose less one hen!*
> *Begox, yon tod wez jumpin'!"*

"Terrific!" said Rowf. "Go on!" The tod obliged.

> *"Next neet th' farmer's woman,*
> *By, ye shud hear hor bubble!*
> *'Ah'll skite th' lugs off yonder tod*

> That's puttin' us te trouble!'
> She's roond th' stackyard i' th' rain,
> She looks i' th' barn an' looks again.
> She nivver stopped th' back-end drain!
> Hey-up, yon tod wez jumpin'!"

Snitter yapped happily and after a few moments the tod launched into the final spasm.

> "Th' light's gan oot i' th' farmhoose.
> It's gey an' quiet it seems.
> The aald chep's flat-oot snotterin'
> An' dreamin' bonny dreams.
> An' when yon sun comes up agin,
> There's hank o' feathers clagged to th' whin,
> But nowt to show where tod got in!
> By, mind, th' gaffer's jumpin'!

> "There's mist o' th' tops te hide ye.
> There's bracken thick o' th' fell.
> Streams where th' hoonds won't track ye.
> Ye've lugs, me tod, an' smell.
> There's shiny neets ye'll lowp and lark
> And randy run te th' vixen's bark.
> Ca' canny, else yer fer th' Dark—
> Yon fettles aall yer jumpin'!"

"What became of your mother, tod?" asked Snitter.

"Hoonds," replied the tod indifferently, and began licking one paw.

As night shut down the rain slackened, though the salty wind persisted, carrying their scent away eastward. From far out at sea, beyond Eskdale, the west yet glimmered with some streaks of day. Nothing could now be seen in the deep cleft below, but from the sharp-eared and keen-scented three the blackness concealed no movement of the Bootterilket Herdwicks among the rustling bracken below. Two yows together were moving slowly down into the bottom, while a third lagged further and further behind. At a final glance from the tod the hunting pack spread out and, with practised smoothness, began their encircling descent.

(171)

"—playin' bluidy 'ell," said Robert Lindsay firmly, while carefully keeping his voice below the level of the conversation in the bar. "They are that—and theer's not a doubt they're dogs, 'Arry—cann't be nowt else. Livin' systematically off o' sheep."

"Oh, ay?" Old Tyson drew on his pipe and looked down, swilling the remaining third of his pint round and round the pot.

In response to all hints and leads he had so far remained uncommunicative. Robert, with reluctance, decided that, much as he disliked asking direct questions, there was evidently going to be no alternative to taking the bull by the horns.

"Weel, 'Arry, it were joost as bank chap i' Broughton were sayin' as tha'd told Gerald Gray at Manor soomthing about dogs gettin' out o' research place, like."

"Oh, ay?"

"Well, it's serious matter, 'Arry, tha knaws, is sheep-killing, an' a bluidy lot o' woorry for thim as has sheep ont' fell. It is that. Happen Gerald were wrong—"

Tyson re-lit his pipe, took a pull at his pint and again gazed reflectively into the almost empty pot. Robert, whose sympathetic imagination knew intuitively just how far to push his man, waited in silence, eyes fixed on the tiled floor. Among his many gifts was that of sitting still and saying nothing without seeming in the least put out or causing any embarrassment.

"Theer's plenty Ah could saay gin Ah were stoock int' box," said Tyson at last. "Ah'm noan dodgin' owt, Bob, tha knaws. But Director oop at Lawson says to saay nowt, an' Ah divven't want to lose job, tha knaws. It's reet enoof job, is that, an' suits me joost now."

"Ay, it's reet *good* job, 'Arry; it is that. Ye'd not be wanting any trooble."

There was another pause.

"Theer's organized hunt tomorrow, tha knaws," said Robert. "Got oop by tailor chap in Kendal, for advertisement like. Ah'll be gooin' along, joost for a bit o' sport."

"Oh, ay?" said Tyson.

Silence returned. Robert finished his light ale.

"Well, this wayn't do, bidin' sooppin' ale, Ah'll joost have to be gettin' along now," he said, rising briskly to his feet with a clatter of nailed boots on the tiles. "Ah've still a bit to do milkin' cows, owd lad. 'Appen if tha *had* lost dog out o' yon plaace, tha'd knaw it'd not be woon to be chasin' sheep; so no bother, like."

He nodded and made to move towards the door, from beyond which sounded an intermittent popping and banging as the young of Coniston celebrated the debacle of Guy Fawkes. At the last moment Tyson touched his sleeve.

"Woon on 'em were fair devil of a beeäst," he murmured into his beer, and immediately, without putting on his glasses, began studying the evening paper upside down.

Saturday the 6th November

"It's too much for me," said Snitter. "Haddaway hyem, tod. And you, Rowf. I'll have to follow you back later."

It was perhaps an hour before first light. The night's hunt along the steep, western slopes of Hard Knott had proved the longest and most exhausting they had yet undertaken. Without the tod's uncanny ability to tell which way the quarry was likely to have fled, they would certainly have lost it in the dark and been obliged to begin the whole hard task once more. Rowf, kicked and battered yet again before the death, had broken up the kill ferociously, his own blood mingling with the sheep's as he gnawed hoof, gristle, bone and sinew in his ravenous hunger. The splinters of broken bone, pricking Snitter's belly as he lay down to sleep, recalled to him the guinea-pigs' tiny remains in the ashes of the furnace-chamber.

Waking in the night with a vague sense of menace and danger, he had found himself so chilled, stiff and lame that he began to doubt whether he would be able to manage the return to Brown Haw with the others. He felt strange.

His head was full of a far-off ringing sound that seemed to come between his hearing and the wind and he had, looking about him, a renewed sense of detachment and unreality—symptoms which he had come to know all too well. For a time he limped up and down while the others slept on, then lay down again and dreamed of an enormous, explosive crash, of disintegration and terror and of falling endlessly between the sheer walls of a putrescent cleft smelling of disinfectant and tobacco. Starting up, he felt his ear nipped between pointed teeth and found the tod beside him.

"Yer weel woke up oot of that, kidder."

"Oh—a dream! You didn't hear—no, of course not." Snitter struggled up. "Was I making a noise?"

"Ne kiddin'. Ye wor rollin' about an' shootin' yer heed off. Fit te be heard a mile, hinny."

"I'm sorry. I'll have to get some feathers for my head, won't I? It's ringing like a white bell-car; no wonder it feels noisy." Confused, he hopped a few yards on three legs, peed against a stunted rowan and came back. The tod lay watching him with an air of detached appraisal.

"Hoo ye goin' on? Ye heven't tuk bad?" Before Snitter could reply it added, "Ah'll caall up th' big feller noo. We'll hev te be goin'."

"Already?"

"Ay, time w' wor away hyem."

"Which way?"

"Up ower th' top of th' clough there."

"I hope I can do it."

"Ye'll hev te tek it canny, lad. Yer far ower tired fer runnin' aboot, so th' sharper we're off, th' forther we can get afore th' leet comes."

The rain had ceased. Rowf, still half-asleep, dragged the sheep's fore-leg out of the sticky welter and carried it as they set off, climbing steeply up the bed of the gill and so out on to Harter Fell's north shoulder. It was here that Snitter began to fall behind and finally lay down. The others came back to him.

"It's too much for me," gasped Snitter. "I'll have to follow you home later. I feel so strange, Rowf. My feet are cold."

Rowf put down the fore-leg and sniffed him over. "You're all right—it's only in your head, you know."

"I know that—it's looking out of it that's so difficult. I'm not at all sure it's me inside, either." Snitter kicked gingerly, testing one back leg. "Is it—is it—glass or what?" He stood up and immediately fell down again. "My leg's over on the other side of—of the—"

Rowf sniffed again. "Your leg's all right—"

"I know it is, but it's over there."

"That's the sheep's leg, you fool."

"That's not what I mean," said Snitter miserably. "I can't—what is it? Talk—to my leg."

"Let's away, an' give ower yammerin'! If wor still on th' fell when th' sun's up, wor knacked. Them farmers— if they clap their eyes on us—"

"Oh, *do* leave me and get on!" cried Snitter desperately. "Let me alone! I'll be back before mid-day. No one's going to see me—"

"See ye a haff-mile off in a mist, hinny—ye an' yer magpie's jacket—"

Enveloped in the mist pouring from his own head, clung to by impalpable flies, enclosed within a jolting, invisible helmet of chickenwire, Snitter floated away, watching the tod's mask recede and fade upstream through brown peat-water flowing insensibly, yet plain to be seen, across his flank.

When he awoke, the sun, from a clear sky, was shining warm into his head. A ladybird was clambering laboriously among the bents close against his muzzle, and he watched it without moving. Suddenly, beyond and between the grass stalks, a buzzard sailed into sight, low against the blue, and hung, wings fluttering. Snitter leapt up and the buzzard slid away.

He looked about him. The slope was empty. The others had gone. At least— He ran a few yards uphill, until he could look round the base of a nearby crag and, in the same moment that he knew himself to be alone, realised also that his faculties had returned and that he could both see clearly and use his legs. His head was still ringing, but at least he could now lift and carry it.

He must be off. The voice of the Bootterilket sheep's

Harter Fell

blood was crying from the ground not half a mile off. He thought of the long run back to Brown Haw and of the farms to be avoided on the way. It would be tricky going in the broad, morning daylight. Should he perhaps wait until nightfall? But then, where could he lie up? Not here. He remembered the tod's warning. This was too close to the scene of the kill. Elsewhere, then; and if he had to look for a refuge, he might as well seek it along the way home as anywhere else.

Which way might the tod have guided Rowf? Not the way they had come, that was as good as certain. Snitter, muttering "Roondaboot, roondaboot," cast back to where he had been lying and without difficulty picked up the tod's scent in the heather. To his surprise it led down the fell well to the north of their last night's route across the Duddon. Scattering innumerable spiders and a drowsy bumblebee or two, he shushed his way downward through the wet bracken and all in a moment found himself out upon the Hard Knott pass road where it wound back and forth in steep hairpin bends up the hillside. He nosed quickly across the narrow, grey roughness of tar and petrol exhaust and picked up the tod's line again on the opposite side. Down once more and so, at length, round towards Duddon and the Cockley Beck farmhouse standing among its trees on the further side of the bridge.

As he splashed his way across the river some little distance above the bridge and climbed back up the bank to the road, he was suddenly aware of a car standing on the verge near the signpost, about fifty yards away. Against it a man was leaning—a man with very clean boots, new, heather-coloured knee-breeches, a green twill coat and round, brimmed hat to match. Even at this distance the swell of his clean clothes was plain. His face was turned towards Snitter, but his eyes were obscured by some object which he was holding in front of them—something resembling two small bottles—two dark, glassy circles, fastened together. Beside him, propped against the wing of the car, stood a double-barrelled shot-gun.

The dog hunt, just as Mr. Ephraim had envisaged, had begun in good time and fine weather on Saturday morning, the various farmers assembling at the Traveller's Rest at Ulpha and being fortified with coffee and sandwiches by the landlord, Mr. Jenner, before proceeding up the valley to make a start on Caw and the rest of the Hall Dunnerdale land. Dennis, who had been infuriated by the frustration of his telephone conversation with Mr. Powell and more than ever convinced that Animal Research were at the back of all the trouble, had told everyone to look out for a dog wearing a green plastic collar.

Mr. Ephraim himself, resplendent in new boots, sporting jacket (to use his own term) and pork-pie hat, and carrying for the occasion a borrowed twelve-bore of which his pride considerably exceeded his experience, was eloquent on the sartorial rewards to be distributed to the participants, but distinctly less knowledgeable about the way in which the hunt might best be organized. However, being a good-natured gentleman and anxious above all to stand well with customers and potential customers, he was perfectly agreeable to this part of the business being arranged by others, and watched appreciatively through his binoculars as the guns, spaced about sixty yards apart, combed the breadth of the hillside southward from Caw, reassembled, swung round westward to Brock Barrow and finally regained the valley road by Low Hall. Dennis had bagged a grouse and old Routledge, a noted wag, had first missed a snipe and then accounted for a slow-flying magpie as it cocked its tail on a branch. Otherwise they had seen nothing but sheep, meadow pipits, crows and buzzards.

Mr. Ephraim and Mr. Furse (the latter taking copious notes and accompanied by a lady photographer) received them on the road with encouragement and nips of whisky, and they were further stimulated by a fine turn-out on the part of the various ladies of the valley—Gwen Williamson and her girls, Mary Longmire from the Newfield Hotel, Sarah Lindsay, Dorothea Craven ("Oh, what *fun!*"), Joan Hoggarth, Phyllis and Vera Dawson who kept the shop by the bridge, and several more. There was some disappointment that no one should as yet have seen the least sign of the dog marauder, but Mr. Ephraim, undeterred, made light of it.

"Well, it's early yet, ain't it? Anyway, at least we've found out where the dog's *not,* and no more dead sheep on your land either, Mr. Lindsay, eh? What you think we'd better do now, Mr. Longmire? Go up the valley and work over Mr. Williamson's land?"

"Ay, that'll do," answered Jack; then, turning to Harry Braithwaite, he added, "D'ye think so, 'Arry?"

Since Mr. Ephraim found Mr. Braithwaite (whose Lancashire was extremely broad) altogether incomprehensible without interpretation, he contented himself with beaming on everyone, shepherding them into the hired minibus and leading the way up the valley in his car, leaving the ladies to go home to late breakfasts.

The first leg of the hunt had also been observed with close interest by the tod and Rowf, from the concealment of a pile of tumbled boulders near the summit of Caw itself. It was only with difficulty that Rowf had been persuaded to leave Snitter asleep on Hard Knott, and he had at last agreed only when the tod had threatened to leave them both altogether.

"Who's te knaw what's gone wrang wiv him? We canna bide wiv'm till he wakes. If we divven't shift oursels, we'll aall be finished—him an' aall. He can folly us back when he's pulled hissel' tegither. Yon's ne fyeul, on th' fell or off't. Poor sowl, it's yon dent in his head."

They had already waited so long on Hard Knott, however—indeed, until the first streaks of dawn began to show behind the distant Wreynus Pass to the east—that the tod insisted that they must now make their way back by the highest and loneliest ground. They crossed the Duddon well above Cockley Beck, ran up Dry Gill in the first light and so on to Fairfield and the back of the Grey Friar. From here they made a straight five miles southward, passing over Goat's Hause, down the east side of Goat's Water and so, at length, along the eastern flank of Caw. The sun was gaining authority every minute and now, with less than a mile to go to their shaft, they lay down to rest in a patch of shade under a thorn-bush. As they did so the light wind veered round into the west and immediately the tod tensed and crouched flat.

"What's the matter?" asked Rowf, copying him quickly.

"Haald yer gob! Them lot o' th' fell, kidder! If ye got ne nose, ye got lugs, ha' ye not?"

It slunk quickly uphill for two hundred yards, Rowf following, and then inched its way forward between the rocks. They could now see plainly the line of farmers, backs toward them as they combed the fell below. There was the sound of a shot and Rowf ducked lower still.

"D'you think they're looking for us?"

"Who else? Ne doot at aall. Sneaky sods, craalin' aboot roond our place. They should think shame! By, what wid Ah do if Ah'd th' power mesel'? Ah'd skite thim!"

"They're moving off out of it now, though. Shall we go back?"

"Go back? Nay, not for two morns. Mebbies more. Are ye daft?"

"Where then?"

"A quiet spot, and a lang way backa beyont, Ah warr'nd."

"Not without Snitter," said Rowf emphatically. He waited for the tod to reply. After some moments it turned its head and stared at him without a word. Rowf, disturbed and excited as always by the rank, vulpine smell, stared back, watching the sun and moving shadows reveal and again cloud the irises of its eyes, flecked and peat-brown as the floors of shallow pools in the moss. At last he got to his feet.

"If as many men as that are hunting the valley for us, then Snitter's in great danger. I'm going back for him."

"Ye goin' on yer aan, hinny."

Harry Braithwaite, Jack Longmire and the rest had finally decided that probably the best course would be to tackle next the mile-long northwest slope of the Grey Friar, from Fairfield and Hell Gill Pike down towards Cockley Beck and Wreynus Bottom. This stretch—by the time they had got up there and down again—would occupy the rest of the morning until lunch time. (Lunch, with beer, was, of course, being provided by Suitable Suits and they were looking forward to it.) Then in the afternoon ("If we've noan shot th' sod bi then," as Dennis remarked) they could conclude by getting up on Levers Hause and combing out the Tongue 'Us land on either side of Seathwaite Tarn. Mr. Furse, still indefatigably taking notes, boarded the minibus and set off with the rest for the top of Wreynus and the ascent of Wetside Edge, while Mr. Ephraim—

who had no taste for climbing—disposing his binoculars and gun at the ready, remained alone at Cockley Beck.

"If you drive it down towards me, gentlemen, I shall know what to do, shan't I? You might find it hung up to dry, eh, by the time you get down for lunch?"

"Wi'owt he's ett it 'isself," remarked old Routledge, to a general laugh as the minibus moved off again.

Mr. Ephraim sat on the parapet of the bridge in the cool November sunshine. Below him the brown Duddon chattered between its rocks. A late grey wagtail, dark-backed and clear yellow beneath, bobbed and flirted its way upstream from stone to stone and a robin twitted autumnally in a half-bare mountain ash. With a thrusting heave of its buttocks, a black-faced Herdwick scrambled up from a peat-rift and trotted away through the ling, while far beyond, the cloud shadows followed one another in ripples across the great slope of Stonesty Pike. On the Cockley Beck clothes-line, two or three brightly coloured dishcloths were cracking like whips in the wind.

Mr. Ephraim noticed little and felt less of the lonely scene around him. As much as he could, he avoided being alone, for all too often the memories induced by solitude would speak with the voices of hell. He thought of his father and mother, gone without strength before the pursuer; then of his Aunt Leah, vanished more than thirty years ago into the night and fog of desolate Europe, slain by God alone knew what sword in the wilderness. His elder brother Mordecai, weeping with shame, had given evidence, for the sake of truth and justice, in the libel action brought in London during the sixties by the infamous Dr. Dering, the self-styled experimental research expert of Auschwitz. Yes, it was indeed more than thirty years, thought Mr. Ephraim, since the whirlwind had passed and violence had covered the mouth of the wicked; yet still the pestilence walked in the dark places of recollection; and no doubt for him it would always do so. He forced his thoughts towards better memories; of the Danube, rolling broad and smooth through Austria; of its cities and vineyards. When the evil began he had been only a little child. His mind, like a frightened dog, crept miserably back to the place whence he had tried to expel it.

He recalled, one after another, the years during which he had grown up and had journeyed at last to this cold, northern land of idle, half-hostile gentiles who concealed their hearts and never spoke their thoughts—or not, at all events, to strangers. And here he was, breaking the sabbath among peasants in a cold wind, for the sake of recovering, insofar as anyone could, some part of that substance and standing which his family had once known, before their dispossession and—and murder.

"It's a bad world for the helpless," said Mr. Ephraim aloud.

He stood up, stamped his feet on the hollow bridge and strode back to the car. This wouldn't do. He must, as so often before, snap out of it. There was as yet no sign of the farmers descending the fell. However, there was no harm in being prepared for the chance of action. Some of the men had thought it more than likely that the dog, if it were on the fell at all, would take alarm quickly, slink away well ahead of the gun line and come down into the bottom. Mr. Ephraim took his own gun out of the car, loaded and cocked it, put on the safety catch and propped it against the wing. Then he fell to scanning the hillside through his binoculars, first the Grey Friar, then the Crinkle Crags and finally Hard Knott to the west.

Suddenly he tensed, swung the glasses a second time towards the foot of Hard Knott Pass, adjusted them to give a clearer foreground focus and then remained gazing intently. A smooth-haired, black-and-white dog, not particularly large, was approaching the Duddon along the line of the tributary beck from the north-west. Through the glasses he could distinctly see round its neck a green, plastic collar.

Mr. Ephraim, trembling with involuntary excitement, bent down and slipped the safety catch of his gun. Then he returned to studying the approaching dog. Its belly was mud-stained and he could just perceive, along its muzzle, what looked like specks of dried blood. But more remarkable and arresting than all else—and at this Mr. Ephraim stared, at first incredulously and then with growing horror and pity—was a deep, hairless cleft, barely healed, pink as the inside of a rabbit's ear and showing the white marks of stitches running clear across the skull from nape to forehead—a terrible gash, giving the dog an unreal appearance, like some macabre creature from a Kafka fantasy or a painting by Hieronymus Bosch.

Mr. Ephraim shuddered. Then, to his own surprise, he found the lenses of his binoculars blurred by tears. He brushed them away with the back of his hand and as the dog came nearer, bent down and began gently slapping his knee.

"Komm, Knabe! Komm, Knabe!" called Mr. Ephraim. *"Armer Teufel, sie haben dich auch erwischt?"*

The dog stopped on the road, looking up at him timidly. Then, as he continued to call it and to talk in a low, reassuring voice, it came slowly forward, tail down, eyes wary and body tensed to run at the least sharp noise or movement.

As soon as he saw the man, Snitter stopped uncertainly, both fascinated and repelled, like an underwater swimmer who perceives some large, strange creature, eel or ray, among the coral. He paused, on the one hand overcome by fear and the sense of danger, on the other powerfully drawn by the hope of hearing a kind voice, by the desire to be patted, to stand on his hind legs, put his front paws against human knees and feel his ears scratched. The man removed from in front of his eyes the two dark, glassy circles, bent forward encouragingly and began to call to him in a low, gentle voice.

The ringing sound which, ever since he had woken on Hard Knott, had been creeping by Snitter upon the heather, intensified. It flowed, he now knew, not from his own head but from the strange man's; or rather, it was flowing back and forth between the strange man and himself. The ringing was a vortex, a circling funnel of sound, broad and slow at the top, but descending rapidly inwards to a dizzy, spinning hole which was at once both the pierced centre of his own brain and the barrel of a gun pointed at his muzzle. Whirling circles of time past—his own time and another's—were contracting upon that present where the strange man stood patting his knee and calling to him.

Snitter went hesitatingly closer. And now, he perceived clearly, there was, pouring both towards and from the strange man, irresistible as a swift current, a flux—shaggy, with bloody hide—composed of terror and inflicted pain, of ruin, grief and loss. Frightened, he shrank trembling against the stone wall as the road before him filled with a river of inaudible sound—noiseless indeed, yet clear as those unreal threads of light which in summer drought appear like trickling water across short grass on the hills. Children's voices he could hear, weeping and calling for help as they were swept away; women's, clutching after them and crying in agony; men's, trying to utter prayers and fragments of liturgies cut short as the flood engulfed them. Mockery, too, there was, and echoes of mean, cruel violence.

Clearly through all, as of a tree visible behind drifting mist, he continued to be aware of the actual voice of the man, calling him authoritatively yet kindly to approach. This voice, he now realized, was that of Death; but Death who must himself die—had himself died—and would therefore not be hard on a mere dog. In this place there was, in any case, no distinction between him who brought life to an end and him whose life must be ended. He himself, he now knew, was carrying death as a gift, both to bestow and to receive. He padded forward again, deliberately entering the spiral of cries and voices, and in so doing heard more loudly the ringing in his own head, now become a part of their lament. As he went slowly on in the bidden direction, the whirling spiral stretched and elongated, tapering to a point that pierced him, a sharp arrow of song: and this arrow he retrieved, carrying it obediently, as he had carried the wind's song on the fell.

> "From Warsaw and from Babylon
> The ghosts will not release the lives.
> A weary burden falls upon
> The groping remnant that survives.
> So this distracted beast contrives
> His hopeless search as best he can.

Beyond the notebooks and the knives
A lost dog seeks a vanished man."

Snitter came to the car. As he had hoped, the man stooped and patted him; then, with a hand under his jaw, gently lifted his head, scratched his ears and examined his collar, speaking to him soothingly and reassuringly as he did so. Bemused, he found that he was wagging his tail and licking the lavender-soap-scented fingers. Then the man opened the rear door of the car, leaned in and patted the seat, his black glass tubes dangling forward on their strap. He made no attempt to drag or lift Snitter inside, only continuing to talk to him in a quiet voice of sympathy.

Snitter clambered awkwardly into the back of the car and sat down on the seat, his nostrils beginning to run as he drew in the forgotten smells of oil and petrol fumes, together with those of artificial leather and cleaned glass. Still enclosed in that strange trance which he had entered of his own accord upon the road, he now had no awareness of the wind and sunlight outside, of the white wing-flash of a chaffinch in the sycamore or the sound of the pouring Duddon. He might have been sitting in a roped pail, listening to echoes rising from the well-shaft below him.

Mr. Ephraim lifted his gun by the barrel, rested the butt on the ground beside the open rear door and stooped to put on the safety catch. As he did so Snitter, turning his head, caught sight in the driving mirror of the figure of a man striding down the hillside—a grey-haired man, carrying a walking-stick and wearing an old tweed overcoat and a yellow scarf. Barking loudly, he leapt for the door. Startled, Mr. Ephraim involuntarily pulled the barrel of the gun towards him. Snitter, trying to push past him, struggled wildly. One front paw clawed at his sleeve while the other became caught in the trigger guard. There was a deafening explosion and the gun fell to the ground, dragging Snitter with it. A moment later Mr. Ephraim, his face pouring blood, silently toppled and fell with his body half in and half out of the car.

When the farmer's wife, the soap-suds still dripping from her bared forearms, came running out of the gate,

Snitter, howling in terror, was already across the bridge and two hundred yards up the windy hillside of the Hard Knott, tail between his legs and jaws frothing as though he had been loosed out of hell.

It was after this that the bad things began.

FIT 5

At least one went more easily alone, thought Rowf, plodding up Dunnerdale for the second time in twenty hours; not so much of this damned creep and peep stuff. Wherever Snitter's got to I'll find him; and bring him back too —unless he's dead. And I'll go the quickest way, exposed or not—he may be in some sort of trouble, or wandering about in one of his mad fits. And if anyone, human or animal, tries to stop me, they'd better watch out, that's all.

Yet all the time his thoughts, like a dog keeping just out of range of a man with arm raised to throw a stone, were avoiding the question, "What's going to become of the two of us without the tod?" They had parted with no further words, the tod, chin on paws among the ling, merely staring sardonically after him as Rowf, lacking only provocation to turn back and bite, set off over the northeast saddle of Caw. Straight over the top he went, through the disused slate quarries below Walna and down to the Tongue 'Us meadows. Here he rested for a short time, heedless whether anyone might see him or not. Then he skirted Thrang and crossed the marshy Tongue itself, dropping down to the road below Birks Bridge. There was much coming and going, or so it seemed, of cars on the road—surely a great many for so lonely a place?—

but evidently those in them, whatever their business, were too much preoccupied with it to pay attention to a solitary, furtive dog making his way up the valley along the grass verge.

Rowf had intended to retrace their previous night's route, but as he neared the spot where they had crossed the road his spirit baulked at the thought of the plunge—alone this time—into the tumbling Duddon, and the un-pleasant moments of the struggle across. Though tired, he decided to continue up to the bridge and the shallow water above, where he and the tod had crossed that morning.

He was less than two hundred yards below Cockley Beck when he became aware of the cars and the throng of people. He stopped, sniffing and staring. Little as he knew from experience of the ways of humans outside the Research Station, he could perceive something strange about the behaviour of these men—something which gave him pause. Their purpose was obscure: they appeared to be doing nothing, to have no intention, to be going nowhere. Uneasily, he sensed that they were in some way at check and under strain. Something unusual had thrown them off balance. He went cautiously nearer, pressing himself against the dry stone wall on his off side. His collar caught on a projecting snag and he freed it with a quick tug.

He gazed ahead of him. Some men in dark-blue clothes were gathered round a large, conspicuous white car, talk-ing in low voices and from time to time turning to look at something lying on the ground under a blanket. A little distance away was a group of rougher-looking men, all with guns; farmers, by their smell and—yes! he could tell, now, from their clothes—the very men that he and the tod had watched below Caw that morning. In the moment that he recognized them Rowf started and shied away from the wall. As he did so one of the men flung out an arm, pointing towards him and shouting, and the next moment a shower of pellets rattled among the stones beside his head. The quick whizz of a ricochet mingled in his ears with the sound of the shot. Rowf leapt the op-posite wall, ran down the meadow, plunged headlong into the Duddon, dragged himself out on the further side and disappeared beyond the alders.

Monday the 8th November

The noise of the traffic, rising from the treeless, grassless street below, caused the none-too-clean windows to be kept almost permanently shut, thus removing competition from the clacking of typewriters and the ringing of telephones. Also permanent was the low, whirring sound of the air conditioning, which extracted some of the cigarette smoke while mingling the remainder with the intake of motor-exhaust-filled air from outside. The daylight, though entering along two sides of the enormous room, was insufficient to illuminate the labours of those whose desks stood (or "were positioned," as they themselves would have said) near the centre, so that throughout working hours patches of electric light burned with a steady glare. As in a cage of budgerigars, the place was filled with an incessant, light movement and arhythmic, low chatter—an irritant and disturbance never quite strong enough to become unbearable by the various individuals who contributed to it. Each of these, with his or her name displayed on the desk, occupied an appointed place and used appointed possessions—telephone, blotter and diary; electric lamp, soap, towel, teacup, saucer and lockable drawer; with here and there a photograph and here and there a dusty, spindly *Rhoicissus rhomboidea* or *Hedera helix,* part-worn but surviving every bit as doggedly as its owner.

As a matter of fact—you may be surprised to learn— Dr. Boycott had had no hand in this place. No, indeed; it was not one of his experiments to discover who could endure what for how long and ascertain in what manner it might affect them. This was, in fact, a part of England where the folk were all as mad as he: it was that admired exemplar of modern working conditions, the open-plan main office of the *London Orator,* lynch-pin of the Ivor-stone Press, a great daily newspaper syndicated, indicated and vindicated all over the world, watchdog of liberty, cat's cradle of white-collar banality, ram's horn of soft pornography, crocodile's tear of current morals, gulf and maw of the ravined salt-sea shark and personal monkey-wrench of Sir Ivor Stone himself. Below, over the main door, the porter of which was R.S.M. O'Rorke, Irish Guards (retired), doyen of the Corps of Commissionaires and arguably the only honest man in the place, were blazoned Sir Ivor's arms, above his rebus motto, *Primus lapidem iaciam*. Immediately above projected the elegant bow window of the small conference room, where (refreshed by drinks kept in a cocktail cabinet made to resemble two rows of leather-bound books on shelves) important visitors (for example, those who spent a great deal on advertising in the *Orator*) were received and the editors and sub-editors met to discuss policy among themselves.

And this, in fact, is what they are doing now, on this fine November morning. Far beyond London, red and yellow beech leaves are pattering into the lake at Blenheim, at Potter Heigham great pike are on the feed and the west wind is blowing sweetly across Lancashire from the Isle of Man, but he who is tired of London is tired of life (though Dr. Johnson might have had second thoughts after a few days with the *Orator*). Gaze, reader, through the window—at the mock oak-panelled walls, at the portrait, by Annigoni, of Sir Ivor, over the Chair, at the grate-full of cosy living fire of solid smokeless fuel (supplied by Sir Derek Ezra and his merry men), the reference books on the side-table—*Who's Who,* Burke, Crockford, Wisden, Vacher's and the Local Government Directory—the writing desk with headed stationery ready to hand beside the signed photograph of Miss "Comfy" Effingbee, that popular screen actress (who some little time ago opened the building as effortlessly as her legs, while recuperating in England from her third and anticipating her fourth "marriage"), the bell that really works and will summon a real manservant, the wainscot, the pargeted ceiling, the expensive and ugly carpet, the—but hush! There are three men present and one of them is speaking.

"The thing is," said Mr. Desmond Simpson (sometimes referred to by his subordinates as "Simpson Agonistes," on account of his habit of talking round every potential decision until his colleagues were ready to scream), "the thing is, if we put an energetic reporter on to this and make a big thing of it—you know, daily sitreps, 'Exclusive from the *Orator*'s man in Cumberland,' 'Latest developments,' '*Orator* invites readers' views' and all that; and then the whole thing folds in the middle— you know, fizzles out in some sort of anticlimax and back to square one—then perhaps we lose circulation—"

"I've thought about all that," replied Mr. Anthony Hogpenny, M.A. Oxon., eighteen stone in a white jacket with carnation buttonhole, who was smoking a large cigar with that air of detached and confident superiority that large cigars can so effectively complement, "and I'm convinced the idea's perfectly viable. We've got to send someone with the ingenuity not to *let* it fold, whichever way it may happen to break."

"But suppose a farmer shoots the dog next week, for example?" pursued Mr. Simpson. "Surely that's bound to be the end of it, and perhaps just when we've gone to a lot of trouble and expense building up—"

"No, no, dear boy," put in Mr. Quilliam Skillicorn, pink-gin-flushed, epicene and somewhat elderly, once styled by himself "the meteoric Manxman," but more recently referred to, by the sub-editor of a rival daily, as "the rose-red cissie, half as old as time." "I mean, just think of the lovely build-up that's there already. First of all you've got the recommendation of the Sablon Committee that more public money ought to be spent on medical research. So after any amount of prodding— far too much of it from their own back-benchers—the Government finally accept the report and give this silly arse place more money. No one has the teeniest idea what the scientists are doing with it up there, and half the amenity organizations in the country hate their guts for starters, simply because they're in a national park. Then there's local talk of sheep-killing and apparently the station won't say a word in reply to questions from farmers and the local press. So after a bit this splendid Ephraim man tries to help, purely out of the kindness of his tiny heart—all events, that's our line, and anyway what's wrong with the public image of a good man of business?— and gets himself shot dead, apparently by the horrid dog that escaped—what a story, too!—"

"*Ah*, but *was* it?" interposed Mr. Simpson, his voice squeaky with the pangs of doubt. "*Was* there a dog involved in the shooting at *all?*"

"There were muddy paw-marks and dog's hairs on the back seat of the car, and Ephraim himself didn't own a bow-wow. The farmer's wife says that after the gun went off she heard a dog howling—"

"But did the dog necessarily *do* it? I can't remember any similar case. On the evidence—"

"Oh, Simpy, and you're a newspaperman? Can't you see it doesn't matter a damn what the dog did? We say it's evident that there was a dog and by the very act of so saying we put the research fellows on the spot to deny it. They're sitting on something they don't want to be forced to say—one can smell that from here, if I'm any judge. Little Eva—the boss—he wants us to discredit Government, right? So that's what we're out for. Our line is first, that Government had to be virtually forced to give the station more money, and secondly, that they stood back and let the station waste it; and then the station imperil the local agricultural economy by letting a dangerous dog escape. Now a life's been lost—well, what, oh, what more could any newspaperman want?"

"And on top of that," added Mr. Hogpenny fatly, "there's all the schmalz we can do about poor little doggies and hoggies and darling catties and ratties—"

"But that's incon*sist*ent, Anthony," squeaked Mr. Simpson, "if we're taking the line that the Research Station ought to be doing their work more efficiently—"

"Pooh," answered Mr. Hogpenny, puffing a cloud, "who ever cared a damn about consistency on a national daily? Don't you remember 'Miners Deprive Nation of Coal' and 'Keep Hungarians out of British Coal Pits' on two pages of the same issue? It's emotions that sell popular newspapers, old boy, not logical arguments, as you very well know."

"This particular little game's not really dissimilar from chess, is it?" put in Mr. Skillicorn. "What it comes to is that we feel pretty average sure that if we hopefully position a knight on queen's bishop's fifth, we'll subsequently get some play out of it, even though we can't see exactly what as of now." (This was how Mr. Skillicorn often talked—and very much how he wrote too.)

"But which knight, I wonder?" asked Mr. Hogpenny, after waiting a few moments to see whether Mr. Simpson to peace and contemplation was dismissed, and quiet of mind, all passion spent. "We need a good chap—someone who knows how to seize whatever opportunities may offer themselves."

"I'd say Gumm," suggested Mr. Skillicorn.

"You mean Digby Driver?" said Mr. Simpson.

"Well, Driver, Gumm, whatever you like to call him."

"Why him?"

"Well, he's shown that he's got a flair for making the public dislike anything or anyone he wants them to. That Coulsen business—there wasn't really an awful lot in it, you know—especially the minor offenders—but by the time Gumm had finished with them everyone was absolutely howling for their blood and circulation was up quite a bit. Cheap at the price of two suicides, wasn't it?"

"Can we spare him?"

"I think so," said Mr. Skillicorn, reflecting. "Yes, I don't see why not. He's been on 'English Friends of Amin' for the past week, but he could perfectly well hand that over to someone else and get up to Cumberland right away. The tooter the sweeter. This afternoon, in fact."

"How should I brief him, then, Tony, d'you think?" pursued Mr. Simpson.

"To stimulate public speculation and interest over the dog and over Ephraim: you know, 'What is the Sinister Mystery of the Fells?' 'Will Killer Dog Strike Again?' and all that; and to watch for any opportunity that may arise to discredit Animal Research. And any other little larks you can think of, Desmond. But look, I really must be getting on now. I'm supposed to be lunching at the Ivy

Leaf with some clean-air civil servant from DoE. I'm thinking of pushing them around a bit over lead in the atmosphere—there's a fellow at Durham University who's prepared to say virtually anything we want him to. There's embarrassment potential there all right."

He gulped the last of his whisky and was gone, leaving Mr. Simpson to send for Digby Driver.

Tuesday the 9th November

It was full moon, cloudless, and brighter for being a cold night—the coldest of the autumn so far. From the summit of Harter Fell the peaks of the Scafell range, more than four miles away across the upper Esk, rose clearly in the silver light—Great End the killer, Ill Crag and Broad Crag, the Pike itself and the long, southern shoulder of the Slight Side. Peaceful they looked in the moonlight, old stumps of great mountains long ago, worn down by ages of storm, wind and ice. Yet for Rowf, wandering back and forth in the dense, coniferous forest of Harter between Hard Knott and Birker Moor, there was no peace and only such little light as fell between the trees and along the open rides between. The movements of roosting birds, the pattering of water, the cracking of sticks and stirring of branches—all imparted to him, in the near-darkness, those feelings of tension and uncertainty which sentient creatures, from men downwards, have always known on strange ground among thick trees. To these, in his case, were added hunger and fatigue.

For the past two days he had been searching for Snitter, by daylight reckless of farmers or shepherds and by night of stumbling and injury in the darkness. After his flight from the men at Cockley Beck, he had picked up Snitter's scent near the top of Hard Knott Pass and followed it upward to the steep rocks on Harter's north face. There he had lost it, wandered till nightfall and then, as mist and rain set in, taken shelter under an overhanging crag

The head of Eskdale, from Harter Fell

and slept for a few hours. But he had woken with a start, trailing in his nose the wisp of a dream and believing Snitter to be nearby. Bounding down into the heather, he had found only a yow that ran bleating away in the moonlight.

Between that night and the middle of the following day he had, nose to ground, encircled the whole of Harter, from the dreary upland of Birker Moor (that wilderness where, in December 1825, poor young Jenkinson, as his tombstone opposite Ulpha church door tells, died in the pelting of the pitiless storm) to the steep banks of Duddon gorge; and so north and round once more by the west. Once he had snapped up a rat and once had routed out and nosed through an ill-buried package of hikers' rubbish —hard bread, fragments of meat and a mouthful or two of soggy potato crisps. Nowhere had he come upon any fresh scent of Snitter. At last, feeling that he had made as sure as he could that Snitter must still be somewhere within the circuit he had made of the mountain, he had started out to hunt him down but then, exhausted, had lain down and fallen asleep once more. When he woke it was early next morning and he set out again, running, as long as the chilly, lustreless daylight lasted, backwards and forwards across the open slopes and searching under the crags. As twilight closed in—the already-risen moon brightening in the southern sky as daylight waned—he entered the all-but-bare larch woods and began sniffing his way up and down. From time to time he stopped, threw up his head and barked loudly; but the only response was the clattering of disturbed pigeons and the echoes, "Rowf! Rowf!," thrown back from the distant steep of Buck Crag.

There stands a house on the southern edge of this forest—Grassguards, they call it—a dead place now, solitary, untenanted these many years, a shelter for the wandering sheep of Birker Moor, a roosting-place for owls and the pitiless, lamb-blinding crows that frequent the fells. Sometimes, in summer, visitors on holiday look after themselves for a week or two in the roughly furnished dwelling-house, which is reached by no road or lonnin. But the dank barns stand empty, no rooster crows or dog barks and all winter and spring the loudest sounds are the rain, the moorland wind and the wide beck—Grassguards Gill—pouring between and often over the stepping stones a few yards from the door. Hither, in the speckled moonlight, from Harter plantations to the northern bank of the beck, came Rowf; lame of a paw, muddy of coat, froth of a jaw, hoarse of a throat, taken apart, down of a heart. And here, as he lapped at the water and lay down exhausted on the crisp, thinly frosted grass, he caught suddenly the faint but unmistakable smell of a scalp wound and of medical disinfectant; and then, fresh and close by, the odour of a smooth-haired dog. At once he leapt up, barking once more, "Rowf-rowf! Rowf-rowf!"

He was answered by a feeble yelp from the further side of the water. Setting his teeth, he crossed, jumping awkwardly from stone to wet stone. The barn had a half-door, the upper part of which was ajar. Rowf threw himself at it, scrabbled a moment, climbing, then dropped down on the earth and round cobbles of the floor within.

Picking himself up, he made his way across to where Snitter was lying on a patch of straw beside an old heap of slack coal. He pushed at him with his head, but before he could speak Snitter said, "Oh, are you here too, after all? I'm sorry—I'd hoped somehow you'd be left out of it—"

"Of course I'm here, you fool; and a nice jolly outing I've had finding you. I'm tired out and half-starved as well. What *happened* to you?"

Snitter got up shiveringly, his muzzle brushing against Rowf's shaggy flank. After a few moments he said, "It's strange. You'd have thought we wouldn't be hungry or thirsty any more, wouldn't you? But I'm both."

"Well, so I should blasted well think, if you've been lying here all this time. How did you get here?"

"Well, I fell, Rowf, of course. And I suppose you fell too, didn't you?"

"Fell? Don't be stupid. I've run miles. This pad's bleeding—smell it."

"Rowf, you don't understand what's happened, do you? You don't know where we are?"

"Well, suppose you tell me. Only buck up—we both need something to eat."

"What happened to *you* when I—you know—when I—when the air all blew to pieces? Oh, Rowf, I'm so very sorry! I know it's all my fault, but I couldn't help it—not either time. The first time was the worst, of course—my master, I mean—but this time, too—I don't know who the poor man with the car was, but he was a sort of master—a very sad man."

"What master? What blew to pieces? What are you talking about?"

"Rowf, you still don't understand, do you? We're dead, you and I. I killed us both. We're here because I've destroyed everything—the world, for all I know. But the explosion, Rowf; you *must* have felt that, wherever you were. Can't you remember?"

"You'd better tell me what *you* remember."

"I was coming back, following you, and all the grass and stones in my head were very loud—sort of humming, like a strong wind. And then this dark man called me, and I was on a road, like—like the other time. I went to the man and got into his car, and then—then everything smashed to pieces. *I* smashed it. I did it; like the other time. So then I ran away before the white bell-car could come."

"That must have been the white bell-car that I saw, I suppose. I was looking for you."

"It all comes from me, Rowf. It comes out of my head. *I* killed the man. I believe I've blown the world to bits—"

"Well, that's wrong for a start. You haven't. How d'you think you got here?"

"I told you—I fell, like you. Falling into my head. I've been falling for two days."

"Well, if you'll come outside with me, Snitter, you'll find you're wrong."

"No, I'm not going out there. It's all stones and flying glass, like that other time. You couldn't know, of course, but it's all happened before."

"Snitter, can't we get out of here and go and find something to eat? I'm famished."

"I'll tell you. I'll tell you all about it, Rowf. Listen. A

long time ago, when there were towns—when there was a real world—I used to live with my master in his house. He bought me when I was only a puppy, you know, and he looked after me so well that I can't remember missing my mother at all. And I never really thought of my master as a man and myself as a dog—not in those days. There were just the two of us. Well, of course I knew really, but it was easy to forget, because I always used to sleep on his bed at night; and then in the morning a boy used to come and stuff a lot of folded paper through a hole in the middle of the street-door downstairs. When I heard that, I used to go down and pick the paper up in my mouth and carry it upstairs and wake my master. He used to take biscuits out of a box and give me one, and make himself a hot drink; and then we always played a kind of game with this wodge of paper. He used to open it up very wide—it was all black and white and it had a kind of sharp, rather wet smell—and spread it out in front of him while he sat up in bed, and I used to creep up the bed and poke my nose underneath. Then he used to pretend to be cross and pat it and I used to take it away and wait a bit and then poke it under somewhere else. I know it sounds silly, but I always thought how nice it was of him to get that boy to bring a fresh lot of paper every day, just so that we could play this game. But he was always so kind.

"Then after a bit he used to go to a room where there was water and cover his face with sort of sweet-smelling, white stuff and then take it all off again. There was no sense in it, but I used to come too and sit on the floor, and he used to talk to me all the time. I thought I ought to keep an eye on him. One of the best things about having a master is that half the time you've no idea what he's doing or why, but you know he's very kind and wise and you're part of it and he values you, and that makes you feel important and happy. Well, anyway, he used to go downstairs and have something to eat and then he used to put on his old brown overcoat and his yellow scarf and put me in the car and we used to go to another house a long way off. There were houses in those days. It was before everything was spoilt. Anyway, my master used to stay there all day and there was a bell that used to ring on his table, and people used to come and talk to him and there was an awful lot of paper, but for some reason I wasn't allowed to play with that paper. There was a fire in winter and I used to lie on the carpet. It was really very comfortable, only I didn't like that bell on his table: I was jealous of it. I used to bark at it. I don't know, but I think it must have been some kind of animal, because when it rang he used to talk to it instead of to me. He couldn't have been talking to anybody else, because usually there was nobody else there at all.

"My master hadn't got a mate. I don't think he wanted one, but there was a woman with grey hair and a red-striped apron who used to come into our house from another house across the street and clean all round. She used to get out a sort of humming, whirring thing on little wheels and push it about. It had a sort of long, black rope coming out of the back that used to go all across the floor, and one day when it was moving I grabbed it and began to gnaw it, just for fun, and she made an awful fuss. She was kind as a rule, and as far as I remember that was the only time she ever got cross with me. She bustled me out of the room and after that she never used to allow me into any room where she was pushing this humming thing. I think actually that was a sort of animal too, because it used to eat up scraps of paper and any other little, tiny things there were on the carpets. I wouldn't have liked to eat them, but then just look what birds eat, come to that. Or hedgehogs. It didn't really smell much like an animal, though.

"Often in the middle of the day, and always in the evenings, when my master had finished at this other house, we used to go for a walk. Sometimes it was just across the park, but other times we'd go into the woods or along the river, a long walk, chasing about after water-rats or grey squirrels, and my master used to throw sticks for me to fetch. Some days, every so often, he didn't go to the paper house at all, and unless he wanted to dig in the garden we'd go out walking for hours. And then sometimes at night, when we were in by the fire—he had a sort of flickering box he used to look at—that was another thing I never really understood, but it must have been all right if he liked it—we used to hear the cats yowling, out in the garden, and I'd cock my ears and sit up, and he used to laugh and click his tongue; and then he'd get up and open the back door and out I'd go like a bang-whappy-teasel, wuff! wuff! and over the wall they'd go flying! O Snit's a good dog! Ho ho!

"We were always jolly and I don't know whatever my master would have done without me to carry up that paper in the mornings and fetch the sticks he threw and bark when people came to the door and chase the cats away. And I tell you, I wasn't like that miserable tyke next door, who used to scratch up the garden and overeat himself and refuse to come when he was called or do anything he was told. I've never been snobbish, but I wouldn't smell *him* down a ten-foot rat-hole. We managed things properly in our house. I used to be fed every evening when we got home for the night, and that was that, except for the morning biscuit and perhaps just a sort of favour-mouthful before we went anywhere in the car. I used to get brushed regularly and sometimes I had stuff put in my ears; and twice my master took me to be looked at by a whitecoat— a proper, decent whitecoat. In those days I never knew there was any other sort. I was never allowed to sit on chairs—only the bed, and that had a nice, rough, brown blanket across the bottom—my blanket, no one else's. I had my own chair. It was an old one, you know, but I made it a whole lot older. I fairly tore the seat out of it! I loved it. It smelt of me! I always used to come when I was called and do what I was told. That was because my master knew what he was doing—he sort of made you want to do what he wanted, somehow. You were glad to—you trusted him. If he thought a thing was all right, then it was. I remember once I hurt my paw—I couldn't put it to the ground, it was so painful, and all swollen up, too—and he put me up on the table and kept talking to me all the time—just quietly and kindly, you know—and he took hold of it and I was growling and curling my lip and he just kept on talking gently and then suddenly I—I—nipped him—I couldn't help it. But he took absolutely no notice at all—just kept on talking away, the same as before, and

(201)

looking at my paw. I felt so ashamed of myself—fancy biting him!—and then he pulled a huge great thorn out of my pad and put some stuff on it—that was the first time I ever smelt that smell. I wasn't afraid of it in those days.

"I'm not sure, but I think some of the other men, and the women too—you know, the ones my master used to talk to; his friends, and the people who used to come to the paper house—I think they used to tease him a bit, sometimes, about not having a mate and about living by himself with just me and the grey-haired woman to look after him. Of course you can never really understand what they say to each other, but I've seen them pointing at me and laughing, and it was just an idea I got. My master didn't seem to mind. He used to scratch my ears and pat me and say I was a good dog and so on. When he picked up his stick and the lead I always knew we were going for a walk and I used to dance and jump all round the street-door and fairly bark the place down.

"There was only one person I didn't like and that was my master's sister. I knew she must be his sister, because she looked so much like him and she sort of smelt a bit like him too. Sometimes she used to come and stay at our house and when she did, oh liver and lights, didn't we catch it! You could tell from a sort of gritty softness in her voice—like—like charcoal biscuits strained through a doormat—that she thought everything was all wrong. And I could never find my things—my ball or my bone or my old woolly rug under the stairs—because she used to tidy them all away. Once she pushed me hard—banged me, really—with a broom, when I was asleep on the floor, and my master jumped up out of his chair and told her not to do that. But mostly he seemed almost afraid to say a word. I'm only guessing, again, but I believe she was cross with him for not having a mate and he sort of felt perhaps he ought to, but he didn't want to. If that's right, of course it would explain why she didn't like me. She *hated* me, Rowf. She used to try to pretend she didn't, but I could smell it all right and I used to act up and cower away from her so that other people must have thought she ill-treated me. Well, she did, really: and in the end—in the end—

"Do you know, it's a funny thing; I knew my own name,

(202)

of course, but I never knew my master's name. Perhaps he hadn't got one, any more than the tod; but I knew *her* name all right, because my master always used it so much. I'd smell her coming through the gate and then my master would look out of the window and he always used to laugh and say the same thing—'Heercums Annie Mossity.' Sometimes I used to growl, but he didn't like that. He wouldn't let me treat her disrespectfully, even when she wasn't there. You had to behave properly to humans—all humans—in our house. But I always used to think that that name was too long and grand altogether for the likes of her, and to myself I always left out the 'Heercums' and thought of her as 'Annie Mossity'—or just plain 'Mossity.' My master spoke sharply to me once for dancing about and wagging my tail when she was leaving and he was carrying her bag down to the door. I couldn't help it—I knew she was going and it couldn't be too soon for me. And when she'd gone there always used to be something extra nice that she wouldn't have allowed—the leavings of a cream trifle, or something like that.

"Now one day—one day—" Snitter paused, whining, and rubbed his maimed head against the straw. A gust of wind stirred an old sack hanging from a nail above their heads, so that it flapped slowly, like the wings of some great bird of prey. "One evening—it was very late last summer, almost autumn—we'd got back from the paper house. My master had taken his eye off me and I'd slipped out into the garden and gone to sleep in the sun, all among the rhododendron bushes by the gate. In summer they have great, pink flowers, you know, Rowf, half as big as your head, and the bees go buzzing in and out of them. This was a special place I had of my own—a sort of secret lair. I always felt very safe and happy there. It was sunset, I'd woken up and I was thinking about supper and feeling rather alert and active—the way you do when you're hungry, you know. And then, between the leaves, coming down the path, I heard footsteps and caught a glimpse of my master's yellow scarf. Sure enough, there he was going towards the gate, with a bit of paper in his hand. I knew what he was up to—the big red bin game. I've told you how men are always playing about with bits of paper. You said they even used to do it while they were watching you in that tank. It's the same for them as sniffing things is for us. And the arrangements in the street are the same for them as they are for us—lamp-posts for dogs and bigger, round, red bins for the humans' paper. I've never been able to understand why some masters—not mine, thank goodness—didn't seem to like their dogs having a pee and a sniff round the dog-posts, when they do just the same themselves with the red bins. We're all creatures, after all, and they're only laying claim to territory and asserting themselves, same as we do. When a man goes out for a bit of a walk—in the evening, usually—he often takes a bit of paper with him—it's got his smell on it, you see—and pushes it into one of the big, red bins; and if he meets another man or woman doing the same, he generally talks to them for a bit and sort of sniffs about, just the same as we do.

"Anyway, I've told you how good my master was, and he had just as healthy an enjoyment of paper as ever a dog had for a sniff round a post. And sometimes when he got home from the paper house in the evening, he used to sit down and scratch about with even more paper, and then he'd go out and push it into the red bin up the road.

"Well, it was plain enough that that was what he was doing this evening. He nearly always used to call me to go with him, but I suppose he hadn't been able to find me anywhere about the place and thought it didn't matter as we'd be going for a longer walk later. Anyway, out through the gate he went. So after a minute or two I thought, why not slip out after him and catch him up, just for fun— you know, give him a bit of a surprise? So I waited till he'd turned the corner at the end of the street and then I came out of the rhododendrons and jumped right over the gate. I was pretty good at jumping. It was a trick my master had taught me. He used to call out, 'Hoop-la, sugar lump,' and I'd jump clean over the table and get a lump of sugar for it. Well, anyhow, I jumped the gate and then I ran up the road and round the corner after him.

"The big red bin was on the other side of the road and you had to be rather careful crossing this particular road because of all the cars and lorries and things. Whenever my master took me with him he used to put me on a lead and he always used to cross the road at the same place, where it was painted black and white. I must have crossed there any number of times—we never crossed anywhere else. I saw him, in front of me, just coming up to it, swinging his stick, with the bit of paper in his hand, so I said to myself, 'Now to surprise him,' and I ran past him and out on to the black and white bit of road."

For a while Snitter said nothing, lying, with closed eyes, on the damp straw. Rowf waited silently, almost hoping that he would tell no more and thus, by desisting, perhaps avert or change what he knew must be some dreadful outcome. Who has not, as a sad story approaches its climax, found himself thinking in this way? The archons of Athens punished for lying the barber who first put about the news of the Syracusan disaster; for if he were treated as a liar, would it not follow that he must have been lying indeed, and therefore that it had never taken place?

After a time the moon, moving westward, shone directly upon the spot where the dogs lay. As though the light had broken in upon and put an end to Snitter's attempt to hide from the close of his story, he opened his eyes and went on.

"I was about half-way over when I heard my master, behind me, shout, 'Snitter! Stop!' I always obeyed him, as I told you, and I stopped absolutely dead. And then—then there came a dreadful, squealing noise on the road, and in the same moment my master ran out and grabbed me and threw me bodily right across into the opposite gutter; and as I fell I heard the lorry hit him—oh, what a terrible noise it made! I heard his head hit the road—if only I could ever forget it! His head on the road!

"There was glass all over the place. A piece cut my paw. A man got out of the lorry and people came running up—first one or two and then more and more. They picked my master up—his face was all covered with blood—no one took any notice of me. And then there was a bell ringing and a big white car came and men in blue clothes got out of it. I told you how my master used to talk to that bell in his room and I suppose they'd brought this other bell—it was a very loud one—to try to get him to talk:

but he never did. He just lay still as death in the road. His eyes were shut and there was blood all over his clothes. They all knew—you could see they all knew. The lorry driver kept on shouting and crying—he was hardly more than a boy—and then a blue man saw me wandering about and grabbed me by the collar. The grey-haired woman with the apron had come—everyone from our street seemed to be there—and she put me on a lead and took me back to her house. She wasn't kind any more—she acted as though she hated me—they all did, they all did! She shut me up in the coal cellar, but I howled so much that in the end she let me out and left me in the kitchen.

"I can't remember it all, but I never saw my master again. I suppose they put him in the ground. They do, you know. That's what they do. The next day Annie Mossity came. She stood in the kitchen doorway and just looked at me. I'll never forget it. You'd have thought anyone would have had a word for a dog as lost and miserable as I was. She said something to the grey-haired woman and then they shut the door and went away. And the next day she came back with a basket and put me in it and drove me off in her car—it wasn't our car, anyway; it smelt of her—and she took me a long way and then she gave me to the whitecoats. And I believe she took the trouble to do all that because she wanted something horrible to happen to me."

After a long time, Rowf asked, "Is that why you've so often told me you're falling?" Snitter made no reply and he went on, "It's a bad world for animals. You might just as well have fallen—out of the sky, I mean. There's no going back there, where you've come from, is there? Never. But at least it's over, Snitter. It can't happen again."

"It can—it does," whispered Snitter. "That's the dreadful thing. Men can do worse things than hurt you or starve you—they can change the world: we've seen that they can, you and I. But what I understand now is that they've done it through me. Annie Mossity—what she wanted to happen *has* happened. I don't know what she told the whitecoats to do, but I know now that everything bad comes out of my head, and that it happens again and again. That's where the bad things start and then they come out into the world, like maggots coming out of meat and changing into flies. When you and I got away from the whitecoats' place, we thought the men had taken all the houses and gardens away. But it was really I who destroyed them. The lorry driver that morning who threw stones at me—he knew who I was; and that man with the sheep-dogs—so did he. What happened to my master has happened again; the white bell-car—you said you actually saw it there, by the bridge. The man with the kind voice—the dark-faced man beside the car at the bridge—*I* killed him. I tell you, there isn't a world at all now except this wound in my head, and you're in there too, Rowf. I'm not going outside again—not any more. If I can die and stop it all, then I'll stay here and do that. But perhaps I've died already. Perhaps dying—perhaps even dying doesn't stop it."

"The tod's left us," said Rowf. "He wouldn't come with me to look for you."

"Do you blame him?"

"It's his nature, I suppose. We'll just have to do the best we can without him. Some of what you've said may be true, for all I know. I can't understand it, really. There's no way out for us, I'm sure of that, but at least I mean to stay alive as long as I can, like the tod. And as for dying, I'll fight before I'm killed."

"They'll shoot you, Rowf. When the gun—the dark man—"

"They tried—a man standing near the white bell-car—he tried."

"The noise breaks the world to bits, like a stone dropping into the top of the water. But then it all comes together again and goes on, like the water. And that can happen again and again."

"Stop chewing that!" said Rowf fiercely. "No one'll steal it—it'll still be there when you get back. Come with me, come on! Once we've found some food you'll know you're not dead."

"Hunt sheep?"

"No chance of that—I'm exhausted. I couldn't make the kill. It'll have to be dustbins, and somewhere where there are no dogs to give the alarm. After that, we must decide what we're going to do."

A second time he jumped the half-door and Snitter, feeling now that sense of relief and acquiescence which often follows the telling of a grief, followed him. Slowly, with no clear sense of purpose or direction, they plodded away southward, towards the bleak summit of High Wallowbarrow outlined against the moonlit sky.

FIT 6

What place in all the Lakes can surpass, in grandeur and beauty, the summit of Wreynus Pass and the high solitude of the Three Shire Stone? Where, if not here, is to be found the heart of the Lakeland—here, where the northern shoulder of the Coniston range meets the southern tip of the great Scafell horseshoe, and Langdale reaches up its arms to Dunnerdale across this desolate band of rock, turf and ling? Stand, reader, here—by the long stone itself, if you will, or at the summit of the pass—at dawn on a June morning, or at dusk of a rainy November nightfall. What, in the emptiness, do you hear, listening with closed eyes and fingers resting upon the squared edge of the stone? Nothing that you would not have heard a thousand years ago. Down the long, bare ridges on either side sounds the wind, tugging in uneven gusts over the slopes, breaking, as strongly as round a cathedral, about the corners of the greater crags that oppose their masses to its force. Up from below—from before and behind you—wavers the distant sighing of the becks, the sound coming and going on that same wind; and the occasional cry of hawk, buzzard or crow sailing on the currents in obedience to behavioural instincts evolved tens of thousands of years gone by. A curlew cries, "Whaup, whaup," and something on Wetside Edge—a grazing yow or wandering fox—has put up a blackcock which rockets away, rattling in its throat with a noise like Mr. Punch about his gleeful mischief. A sheep bleats close by and little, cloven hooves—ah, here is a new sound—rattle across the metalled road. Open your eyes—unless a car comes there will be nothing else to hear except, perhaps, the thin note, now and again, of twite, pipit or shrike.

What do you see—for the wind, though sharp and bleak, is nevertheless friendly in blowing away the mist that might have enclosed you, muffling all sound, confusing north with south and compelling you to stumble your way from cairn to cairn along the tops, or to follow the course of a beck until it led you down below the mist-ceiling—what do you see? To the south, the mile-long shoulder of Wetside Edge comes curving down from Great Carrs, falling away into the dip below Rough Crags, where the river Brathay, itself no more than a beck, tumbles, cold and lonely, towards the meadows of Fell Foot and Little Langdale Tarn. To the north, the summit of Pike O'Blisco rises beyond its south face that they call the Black Crag. Behind you stands Cold Pike and between the two, on the other side of the saddle, so that you cannot see it from here, lies the little Red Tarn—barely two hundred yards long but big enough, no doubt, to cast a chill into the heart of our friend Rowf, should he ever happen upon it in his wanderings. The high, uneven ridge of the Crinkle Crags you cannot see—not today, for over it the vapour is still lying, a grey cloud extending from Gladstone Knott right across to Adam-a-Cove and back along Shelter Crags to Three Tarns. But walk over a little way to the west, back over the crest of the pass, across this high watershed. There, below you, patters the narrow, stony stream of the infant Duddon itself, gaining from tributary beck to beck as it runs down, alongside the road but well below it, all of two miles to that bridge, that very gate where Snitter faced Mr. Ephraim on the road. Beside its course stand great tussocks of grass over which you can trip and measure your length in the soaking peat, tracts of bilberry, bog myrtle, wet moss and boulder-broken turf strewn with lichened stones; and on either side, stretching up the fell and all along the banks, the dry stone walls built of those same rocks and boulders, gathered and piled by men—whence came their patience?—dead these two hundred years and more.

Despite their seeming emptiness, many men have in fact marked these hills—marked at least their surface, though they have not changed it, as the great fens of East Anglia have been changed or the once-forested Weald of Sussex. Beyond your view from Wreynus, away over the crest of Hard Knott, on its western slope and not far above Booterilket, lies the Roman camp they call the Castle. Mediobogdum the Romans called it, and here, where the rock-face falls to the grassy platform of their parade ground, the legionaries must have stood cursing as they looked out over the wet, windy heather, with lice in the tunic and a cold in the nose, all the way down the valley of the Esk to its sandy estuary at Ravenglass. The Duddon valley was held by a Norman and its tenure is recorded in Domesday Book. Here, where you stand, a beacon burned to pass on news of the Spanish Armada. Wordsworth tramped over the Wreynus—indeed, he knew the Duddon valley from Wreynus to the sea, and late in life wrote a not-terribly-arresting sonnet sequence about it. And Arnold of Rugby and Ruskin and G. M. Trevelyan and Beatrix Potter and all the Everest climbers from Mallory to Hillary and for the matter of that, Mr. Switchburg B. Tasker of Nebraska, for on his vacation last summer he drove over here in a hired Renault and I observe that he—or somebody—has scratched his name on the face of a nearby rock. Never mind, Switchburg, old boy, the rain will rain and the lichen—*Hypogymnia physodes*, perhaps; or *Parmelia conspersa*, or perhaps the pretty, rust-coloured *Lecidea dicksonii*—will grow over the blurred place, and later on you'll be able to join the Roman and his trouble, just like A. E. Housman. There's glory for you: well, all that you or I—or Rowf and Snitter, for that matter—are going to get, anyway.

Who is there who does not sometimes need to be alone, and who is not the poorer deprived of that strength and solace, even though he may not himself be conscious of his loss? This hundred years and more great Pan has been disdained and robbed and his boundaries diminished—

Hard Knott

the boundaries of a kingdom which many fear and shun, having had, no doubt, too much of it in the past against their will: the kingdom of solitude and of darkness. White stands for good and black stands for bad, we learned as children (though half the human race is black). If the light that is in thee be darkness, how great is that darkness! said the good Lord, and so we misapply the metaphor and pray, O God, give me more light, until I come to walk in the courts—heaven help us!—of everlasting day. And what will then become of your dreams, and of the phantasms that your own heart has summoned out of firelight and the dark; those fancies that do run in the triple Hecate's team from the passage of the sun? I would not trade them for all the golden crowns to be cast down around the crystal sea. There shall be no night there? So much the worse, for light and darkness, sons of Man, for us are complementary. Think otherwise to your harm. Great Pan has retreated, if not fled; before the borough surveyor, that excellent and necessary man, with his street-lighting, his slide rule, duffle coat and gum-boots in the rain. And a good job, too, did I hear you say? Yes, indeed, for a hundred years ago it was a dark and lonely life for all too many, and now they are neither ignorant nor afraid, and at all events believe themselves less superstitious. And my goodness, how mobile they are! On a fine Saturday in summer the summit of Scafell Pike may well be thick with those who have climbed it, having first journeyed towards it by train, car, motorbike and even aeroplane. No one need be alone any more, in that solitude where Socrates stood wrapped in his old cloak in the night, Jesus told Satan to get behind him and Beethoven, in his scarecrow coat, walked through the fields with the voice of God sounding like a sea in the shell-like spirals of his ruined ears. Strange paradox! In solitude great Pan confers a dignity which vanishes among crowds and many voices. Great Pan is half animal and incapable of pity as the tod, sending fear, strange fancies, even madness to trouble the lonely and ignorant. But shun him altogether, tip the balance the other way entirely and another—a vulgar, meaner—madness will come upon you—even, perhaps, without your awareness. Do you think great Pan is going to stand idly by while Dr. Boycott stabs and maims and drowns his creatures in the name of science, progress and civilization?

But wait—come back here a minute! Were you gazing up Wetside Edge into the mist on Great Carrs, or watching the buzzard sliding sideways down the north wind from Pike O'Blisco? Look eastward into Westmorland, down past Wreynus Bridge and Great Horse Crag to Little Langdale and the road that comes snaking up out of the valley, nearly eight hundred feet to where we stand on this clear November morning. A car is coming up, twisting from side to side with the road; a green car—a Triumph Toledo, I rather think—anyway, the kind of car that not infrequently goes with a job. And who, pray, is the driver? Take your binoculars to him. Yes, I thought as much. How beautiful upon the mountains are the feet of Sir Ivor Stone's emissary! We are to be routed out in our solitude. It is indeed he! Ladies and gentlemen—Digby Driver, the urban spaceman! Let us—er—get a load of him, shall we?

Digby Driver had not always been known by that name, for the very good reason that it was not his original one. He had been born about thirty years before—in some year soon after the Second World War, in fact—in a midland county borough; and at that time his name was Kevin Gumm. True, he had not been christened Kevin, for he had never been christened (which was not his fault), but he had nevertheless grown up with that name, which had been given to him by either his mother or his grandmother. We shall never know which, for not long after his birth his mother had left him in the care of his grandmother before vanishing permanently out of his life. This was partly due to the arrival of Kevin himself, for his paternity, like Ophelia's death, was doubtful and his mother's husband had laid it, most resentfully, at the door of the American G.I.s who at that time were thick on the ground in England. He certainly had some evidence tending toward this conclusion; and although his mother had denied the accusation, poor Kevin became first a *casus belli* between them and before long the final disrupter of a marriage-tie which had never been anything but tenuous. Mrs. Gumm began to look elsewhere and before long struck oil in the person of a sergeant from Texas, with whom she "took up," as the saying goes. Kevin would certainly have met with no more favour from the sergeant than he had from Mr. Gumm, and Mrs. Gumm (whose name, by the way, was Mavis), divining this intuitively (no very hard matter), took care to give the sergeant no opportunity to form a view. By the time Kevin was old enough to talk, Mavis Gumm had not been among those present for nearly two years, and since her own mother had not the least idea on which side of the Atlantic to begin to look for her, she found herself reluctantly stuck with Kevin.

William Blake remarked that the unloved cannot love, but he said nothing about the development of their intelligence. Kevin was above average. He grew up sharp enough, and very much a product of his time. Thanks to his circumstances and to various ideas current among well-meaning people in the fields of child psychology, social welfare and state education, he also grew up without respect or fear for parents (since he knew none), for God (of Whom, or of Whose Son, for that matter, he knew even less) or for the school authorities (who were prevented by law from subjecting him to any effective restraint or discipline). Consequently, he developed plenty of initiative and self-confidence. In fact, it never really occurred to him that any opinion or purpose which he had formed could be wrong, either morally or rationally. The possibility was never a consideration with Kevin, the concept not really being one which held any meaning for him. For him, the prime consideration was always practicability—whether, if he took this or that course, anyone was likely to try to frustrate him, and if so, the extent to which such opposition could be ignored, deceived, brow-beaten, terrified or, if all else failed, cajoled or bribed into submission. For his elders he grew up having about as much respect as has a baboon—that is, he respected them to the extent that they were able to harm or to exercise power over him. One brush with the juvenile court at the age of ten (something to do with breaking and entering a shop kept by a seventy-two-year-old widow and threatening her with violence) taught him that on balance it was better to avoid attracting the attention of the police, less on account of the possibility of punishment than because it indicated incompetence and involved loss of personal dignity. The following year he obtained his entry, in the eleven-plus, to the grammar-school stream of the colossal local comprehensive school. As has been said, Kevin was no fool and, since he had the intellectual ability, once he got a taste of secondary education he soon began to realize the advantages to be expected from raising himself beyond his origins and out of his background. The only factor in his make-up likely to interfere with such progress was his *amour propre* and the tremendous respect which he felt for the personality of Kevin Gumm. No adult was going to tell him what to do or stop him doing anything he wanted. His grandmother had long ago given up trying. His headmaster did not come into the picture—the school was far too big and he no more knew Kevin by sight or character than he was able to know sixty per cent of his pupils. As for the form-masters, they tended to reach a *modus vivendi* with young Gumm, partly because he was no slacker—indeed, capable of excellent work at times— but principally because nearly all of them were afraid to take him on—not altogether physically afraid (though to some extent that came into it), but certainly afraid of friction and unpleasantness, and of getting no support, if it came to the crunch, from higher authority. The easier course was to stick to the letter of the law by helping him to develop his intellect on his own terms and leaving his character out of account. It was some time during the middle years of the sixties that Kevin obtained a state-grant-aided place to read sociology at one of the provincial universities.

Now he really began to spread his wings. As a rebel student, he was a match for all challengers, not excluding even the great "Megaphone" Mark Slackmeyer immortalised by Garry Trudeau. He made himself the bane and dread of the university authorities; and might very well have proceeded on this triumphant course right up to graduation, had the direction of his career not been suddenly altered by two discoveries: the first, that one of his several girlfriends was pregnant, and the second, that she possessed two large and aggressive brothers who intended to spare no pains to make Mr. Gumm regard the matter more seriously than he had hitherto thought he would. Thus stimulated, Kevin departed precipitately from the university and plunged into the great anonymity of London. Not long afterwards (since he had to make a living somehow) he accepted the advice and good offices of a friend who had offered to use his influence to get him a small job in journalism.

To be perfectly honest, reader, I cannot be bothered to set out the details of the various steps by which Kevin turned himself from a student of sociology into a successful popular journalist on the *London Orator*. They took him about five and a half years and at times made up a hard road, but he eventually achieved his aim. The alteration of his image, coupled with the retention of his zeal and ability, amounted to a brilliant personal manoeuvre which I must leave to be recounted by his biographer. A new image was essential, a change of name, the cutting of his hair, a radical modification to his beard. He even increased the frequency with which he washed.

He began by turning his energies to free-lance journalism and discovered, as others had discovered before him, that as long as he stuck to the kind of views which had distinguished him at the university there was too much competition and too little chance of escaping by patronage from a jungle where this sort of *jeu* was decidedly *vieux*. Oddly enough, it was the abandonment of a political slant which really set his feet on the right road, for he first distinguished himself as the librettist of a successful rock musical, based on Mozart's *Marriage of Figaro* and entitled *Out for the Count*. And it was while being questioned by various journalists and television interviewers in connection with this opus that he began to reflect that there was no reason why he should not study and adapt their techniques to his own purposes. After a lapse of time and several trials and errors, he managed to gain entry to the "stories of human interest" field of popular journalism.

Here all his past life, from the earliest years, paid off, and all his talents were fully employed. In short, he had found his métier. Kevin's ear was well to the ground and he soon built up a web of reliable contacts and sources of information. Did some wretched, distracted girl gas herself and her children one dark night in Canonbury? Kevin was on the doorstep by seven the next morning and by one means or another could always contrive to extract some interesting remark from the husband, the neighbours or the doctor. Was a child abducted and murdered by a psychopath in Kilburn? The mother had no hope of evading Kevin—he knew her better than she knew herself. Was there a fatal traffic accident on the North Circular, a near-miss by an intending suicide at Putney, a case of two typists caught in possession of drugs at Heathrow, a schoolmaster accused of interfering with a boy at Tottenham, a Pakistani arrested and bailed on a charge of living on the immoral earnings of schoolgirls at Tooting, a knifing, a shooting, a case of corruption; rape, ruin, bereavement, heartbreak, the riving open of some long-concealed private grief? Kevin was the lad to make sure the public did not miss it; and infallibly hit upon the original line (not necessarily salacious, but invariably personal and destructive of human dignity) calculated to make of his subject a target for ill-informed indignation or raw material for a few moments of vicarious and mawkish horror. Privacy, reticence and human worth melted before him like ghosts at cockcrow.

It was while in Copenhagen, getting material for a special feature on pornography and sexual night clubs, that he first adopted the *nom de plume* of Digby Driver, by which he was later to be known to millions of *London Orator* readers and eventually even to himself. He had decided that he needed a better image or *persona* for the job—something a shade jokey, suggestive of youth, energy and good humour, but having—as it were, at a deeper level of loose and irresponsible association—an undertone of delving, subterranean perseverance in the pursuit of news ("Digby") coupled with that relentless, forceful energy ("Driver") which ought to characterize an *Orator* man. The idea worked excellently. Kevin Gumm had gone into Copenhagen. Digby Driver came out.

And what the devil (I hear you asking) has all this got to do with Snitter and Rowf, with Animal Research and Dr. Boycott? Nothing, you have concluded? Your Highness shall from this practice but make hard your heart. In fact, since we are standing about in this wild and empty place—for many miles about there's scarce a bush—for the Triumph Toledo to complete its ascent from Langdale, we might perhaps ask ourselves, "Is there any cause in nature that makes these hard hearts?" It is a difficult task to exclude all pity from the mind when confronting a weeping girl whose child has been strangled by a maniac—to get in at her window when her husband has put you out of the door. In fact, it is probably harder than the examination of a mongrel dog which has just withstood a shock of three hundred volts and is about to receive one of four hundred—but we really must get on. Here he comes now, right up to the Three Shire Stone. The moguls of the *London Orator,* arrested—as indeed the entire public has been, to some extent, arrested—by the strange and macabre death of Mr. Ephraim, have sent none other than Digby Driver to investigate and report upon the matter. And believe me, if he doesn't find a story, then Dr. Boycott's a Copenhagen swinger and Snitter's as sane as Lear and the Fool put together.

Once again, Snitter hastened forward to catch up with Rowf. The mist, pouring from his head like the flow of some forgotten tap left running by the tobacco man, swirled between them, through and among the bents and sedges, in and out of the grey, sharp-edged stones piled in long walls across the moor. Everywhere lay the smells of damp heather, of lichen on stones, water, sheep, fresh rain and acorns.

"Where are we, Rowf?"

"Going to look for food, remember?" Rowf paused and sniffed the air. "*There!* That was a rubbish-bin—no mistaking it—but a long way off, over there—did you get it?"

The bitter sense of all that he had lost came pouring over Snitter, tightening in a sharp-edged spiral, diminishing him, paring away his vitality and memories, his very thoughts and all those inward recesses in which he had thought to hide. He stood still on the wet heather, feeling himself reduced to a tiny, hard point which must at all costs be kept safe, which must not be destroyed, or he would be gone; the last drop would fall from the tap and disappear into the ground. He waited, panting. Then, suddenly, unaccountably, the spiral reversed, his head was wrenched about and from it came pouring, like a fungus, long, white stalks of loathsome growth, blighting, killing and destroying, laying waste the spaces of the fell into which they writhed their way.

"It's not real!" gasped Snitter, staggering in horror of the slimy, phantom antlers. "Not real!" He shook his head and the chicken-wire, a clumsy helmet, tumbled one way and the other, falling across from ear to ear. "Jimjam, I couldn't help it! I couldn't—"

"Jimjam? What about him?" Rowf was there, a hirsute, dog-smelling shape in the dark, friendly but impatient.

"D'you remember him?"

"Of course I remember Jimjam. The whitecoats killed him."

"*I* killed him."

"Snitter, get up and come on! I remember Jimjam perfectly well. He told us the whitecoats put a tube down his throat and forced bitter stuff into his stomach. Then he went blind and peed pus and blood all over the floor. You never got anywhere near Jimjam. Of course you didn't kill him."

"The blood and pus came out of my head."

"There'll be a lot more blood coming out of your head soon if you don't come on. No, I'm sorry, I didn't mean it. I know you're not yourself; but I'm hungry—famished. Can't you smell the rubbish-bins?"

"I'm sorry, too," said Snitter meekly. "If there's any rubbish about you can always trust me to find it, Rowf. I remember now—we're going to look for rubbish, that's right."

They ran together across the back of High Wallow-barrow and then began to descend steeply, scrabbling over the loose gravel and stones of the Rake. On their right, in the dark, a rill went chattering down. Snitter ran across and drank, smelling as he did so the acrid fume, beneath his paws, of a disturbed anthill. At the first sharp little bite he lurched away, overtaking Rowf at the foot of the slope. They smelt fowls and cows, and stood watching light spread gradually across the cold sky.

"There's a farm over there, Rowf, across the field."

"Yes, but it's no good to us. Can't you hear the dog?"

"Oh—I thought it was me."

"Whatever do you mean?"

"Well, there are bits of me all over the place, Rowf, you know. I'm not really sure where I am."

"Neither am I. I know where the dustbins are, though. Come on!"

They skirted the farm by way of the fields and scrambled over a stone wall into the lonnin. The barking of the dog died away behind them. A few hundred yards further on they came to the Duddon, swift and wide, seven miles below its source, surging noisily down beneath bare, black-budding ash-boughs in the bleak dawn.

The lonnin became a narrow road. They found themselves approaching sheds and a house with a trim garden alongside. Beyond, a bridge carried a larger road over the river. There was neither smell nor sound of a dog. After the briefest of pauses Rowf led the way round to the back, nosed along the side of a shed and the base of a low wall and then, with all the determination and force of his hunger behind him, jumped at the piled stonework and clawed his way up and over into the yard.

As Snitter fell back from the wall for the third time, he heard from the other side the clang and thud as Rowf knocked over a dustbin, releasing a surge of smells—tea leaves, bacon rinds, fish, cheese and cabbage leaves. He gave a quick whine.

"I—I—Rowf, can you help? I can't manage—I mean— why, what a fool I am!" said Snitter. "Of course it isn't a *real* wall. It's only in my head. I can make a gap in it if I want to."

He limped his way along the line of an open, concrete-lined gully running from a square hole at the base of the wall to its further corner. Round the corner, as he had known—since he had himself just caused it to appear— there stood in the wall a green-painted gate of divided palings. Between these, Rowf could be seen nosing about. He had pushed aside the lid of the rubbish-bin and was pulling the contents across the yard. Snitter, belly pressed to the ground, wriggled and squeezed his way under the gate.

"Mind, Rowf, careful. That's a tin edge—it's sharp!"

Rowf looked up, bleeding from a cut along his upper lip. "Not half as sharp as I am! Cheer up, Snitter; don't give way yet—we're still alive! Here's an old ham bone and you can have it all!"

At the first lick Snitter realized that he was very hungry.

Lying down out of the wind, in the lee of the shed, he began to gnaw.

Phyllis Dawson woke with a start, looked at her watch and then at the window-panes. It was a little after seven and just light—a grey, cloudy, windy, leaf-blown morning, with rattlings of rain here and gone across the glass. Something had woken her—a noise—something unusual. But what? It wouldn't be anyone trying to break into the shop—not at seven o'clock in the morning. But it might well be someone trying to help himself out of the locked petrol-pumps—that had been known before now.

Phyllis slipped out of bed, put on her dressing-gown and slippers and looked out of the window. There was no one outside the front of the house. The road was empty. On the coping of the wall, the rain had washed clean the petroglyph outline of the great salmon caught by her father in the Duddon many years before. Beyond and below the wall, the river itself was running high, noisy and turbid, tugging at ivy-strands, pulling here and there at a trailing ash-bough, rocking its way down and under the bridge in tilted, glistening waves.

At that moment Phyllis heard, coming from the back of the house, sounds of commotion—irregular noises of dragging, bumping and knocking. She called to her sister.

"Vera! Are you awake?"

"Yes, I am," answered Vera. "Can you hear the noise? D'you think it's a sheep got in at the back, or what?"

"I can't tell—wait a minute." Phyllis made her way to a rear window overlooking the yard. "Oh, my goodness! It's two dogs down there! One's a big one! They've pulled the rubbish all over the place! I'd better get down to them at once. Oh, what a nuisance!"

"But whose dogs are they?" asked Vera, joining Phyllis at the window. "I've not seen them before."

"They're certainly not any of Robert Lindsay's dogs," said Phyllis, "and I don't think they're Tommy Boow's, either. They don't look like sheep-dogs at all, to me."

"Oh, look!" said Vera, catching her sister's arm. "Look—the collars! Green plastic collars! D'you remember Dennis said—"

Seathwaite

At this moment the smaller of the two dogs below moved, raising its head, and Vera drew in her breath sharply. The winter morning suddenly seemed still more bleak and grim. It was the kind of sight at which an Irish peasant crosses himself. Both the Dawson girls started back with a spasm of horror.

"Lord save us! Whatever's happened to it? Its head,

look—it's almost cut in two! Did you ever see anything like it?"

"The other one—the big one—its mouth's all bloody!"

"That must be the dog—the dog that killed the poor Jewish gentleman at Cockley Beck! Don't go down, Phyllis—you mustn't—no, come back—"

"I *am* going down," said Phyllis firmly, from the stairhead. "I'm not hiding indoors while a couple of stray dogs pull our rubbish up and down the yard." She reached the foot of the stairs, picked up a stout broom and the coke shovel, and began to draw the back-door bolts.

"But suppose they attack you?"

"I'm not standing for it! Whatever next?"

"We ought to telephone the police first—or d'you think the research place at Coniston—"

"Afterwards," said Phyllis firmly, flung open the door and stepped into the yard.

The bigger dog—an ugly-looking beast—had evidently been alarmed by hearing the bolts drawn. It stood glaring, the head of a chicken hanging from its bloody jaws; a sight to daunt a good many folk.

"Go on, be off with you!" cried Phyllis. She threw the shovel at the dog and followed it up with a blacking-brush—the first missile that came to hand. The brush hit the dog, which ran a little way and stopped. One paw had become entangled in a clutter of old sellotape and wrapping-paper, and this trailed behind it along the stones. The squalid mess all over the yard roused Phyllis—who was tidy, neat and deft as a swallow in all she did—to a total disregard of possible danger.

"*Will* you get out of here?" she cried, rushing upon the dog with broom extended and flailing from side to side. "Go on—*out!*" She caught up with the fleeing dog, pushed it hard with the broom and then chopped downwards. The head of the broom struck the stones and came off the handle. In the same instant the dog, with potato peelings flying from under its hind feet, got clear of the sellotape, leapt the gate and disappeared.

Phyllis, victorious, turned back, a little breathless, and stood for a moment leaning on the broom-handle. As she did so her eye fell upon the second dog, which in the heat of action she had forgotten. It was indeed a terrible sight—the weck of what had once been a pedigree, black-and-white, smooth-haired fox terrier. One paw was held awkwardly off the ground and the left flank was plastered with a mixture of dried mud and blood—whether its own or the other dog's was uncertain, for it had no discernible wound. The stitched gash in its skull was more than Phyllis could regard steadily. After one glance she turned away, went across the yard and opened the door of the shed.

"I don't think this one's likely to give any trouble, Vera," she called. "Poor little thing! I think it's been taken badly—and no wonder, either, with that head."

The dog remained where it was, looking from Phyllis to Vera and back again in a frightened, furtive manner. After a few moments it got up, its tail between its legs, and, shaking from head to rump, began to slink across the yard.

"I think it's hungry and frightened to death as well," said Vera, bending down to the dog. "What's your name, then?"

"It might be best not to touch it," said Phyllis. "I feel very sorry for it, but it may have something catching, especially if it's come from that research place. We'll shut it in the shed and telephone the police at Broughton. They'll know what to do."

Vera went back into the house and returned wearing the heavy leather gloves which she used for dispensing petrol and oil to customers. The dog struggled feebly as she put two fingers under the green collar—there was plenty of room—and led it into the shed. As an after-thought, she threw in the ham bone it had been gnawing and some old slices of cold meat, shaken out of their wrapping of greaseproof paper (which Rowf had over-looked). She was a kind-hearted girl.

When she came in and began washing her hands, Phyllis was already on the telephone.

Rowf, shivering partly from shock and partly from the bitter morning air, raced up the western slope of Caw. He ran with no attempt at concealment and from time to time gave tongue, scattering the Hall Dunnerdale yows

(225)

from beneath crags and out of the shelter of heathery clefts. Sheep-dip he could smell, and withered bilberries. He paused an instant over faint traces of gunpowder in an old, sodden cartridge—it was, in fact, the very one with which old Routledge had shot the magpie. Then, hunting on, he lit upon some carrion under a rock, a live hedgehog, a sodden cigarette-butt, the place where a blackcock had roosted for the night, the track of a hare leading northward—everything but what he was seeking. Tired out after the long night, he limped across Brock Barrow, bloody nostrils to the ground, and forced himself to run once more as he came up on the long shoulder of Brown Haw. He stopped to drink and then, as he raised his muzzle once again to the cloudy, grey sky, suddenly caught, strong and clear, the reek he had been looking for. In the same moment a soft, mocking voice spoke from the bracken.

"What fettle th' day, kidder? The way ye wor runnin' Ah thowt yer arse wez afire."

Rowf spun round, but could see nothing. He waited, fuming with impatience, and after some little time caught a glimpse of the tod's mask peering from a tangle of grass ten feet away.

"Lost yer bit marrer? Noo there's a bonny goin' on."

"Tod, come with me quickly, now, or I'll bite your head off. Snitter's in bad trouble. If you can't get him out, no one can."

There was silence inside the cylinder as Mr. Powell chalked up the monkey's score—24 plus. He paused a moment and then tapped the metal with his pen, but there was no response from the occupant. He turned to other matters.

Mr. Powell had come in early to examine and record the hairspray rabbits; a routine job which he should really have completed on the previous evening. The rabbits were assisting in the tests statutorily required before Messrs. Glubstall and Brinkley could market their newly developed "Rinky Dinky" hairspray. The matter had become urgent, since the first tests had yielded somewhat ambiguous results. Messrs. Glubstall and Brinkley were impatiently awaiting clearance, both to manufacture in bulk and also to launch the initial advertising campaign. ("He'll look at you with new eyes when you're using—Rinky Dinky!")

During instillation the rabbits had been restrained in canvas sleeves, in which they had remained for about fifteen minutes before being transferred to individual steel lockers with adjustable apertures in the doors. Each rabbit sat in a separate locker, with its ears and head protruding through the hole in the door, the edges of which were then closed round its neck so that it could neither withdraw its head nor touch its eyes with its paws. Mr. Powell's task was to assess damage to the eyes of each rabbit by measuring corneal thickness.

Having put on his white coat and washed his hands with disinfectant soap, Mr. Powell, thoughtfully tapping his front teeth with his pencil as he read, consulted the log which Miss Avril Watson, his colleague who had carried out instillation, had considerately left open on the laboratory desk.

" 'Instillation carried out between 12:00 and 12:33 hours,' yesterday—h'm, h'm—so that makes—er—a little over twenty hours now—that's O.K. 'No unusual features'—good—'All rabbits struggled violently upon instillation'—well, woudn't you, Avril, dear, eh? 'Three screamed'—now that's really useless information; what more does that tell us? 'Swelling occurred rapidly. Individual checks at 1800 hours showed tissue in a swollen state in each case. Average corneal swelling of 164.14 per cent of normal size'—there's one good hard fact, anyway—'lachrymation'—well, obviously—'fairly severe erythema and oedema formation'—yes, well, let's cut the cackle and have a shufti for ourselves."

The disembodied heads of the rabbits, fixed side by side in a long row, gazed from their lockers at the green-painted, opposite wall. So unnatural, against the dully gleaming background of the metal doors, appeared this straight line of uniform heads without bodies, that the still-sleepy Mr. Powell, yawning and absently exercising the privilege of rubbing his eyes, entertained for a moment the illusion that they were not in fact the heads of living creatures but rather a frieze from some elaborate decoration—as it were, the heads of angels or of the resurrected elect, ranged behind Father, Son and Virgin in some carved tympanum of a west front or reredos of a high altar. (For Mr. Powell, who had grown up in merry Lincoln, had been in his time a choirboy and was by no means unfamiliar with such sights.) However, the elect are not usually depicted with mucous eyes (indeed, we have it on good authority that God will wipe away all tears from their eyes) or with twitching noses, so that after some moments the illusion vanished as Mr. Powell approached Rabbit No. 10,452 (Animal Research used, on average, about 120 rabbits a month).

"Oh bun, oh bun," murmured Mr. Powell under his breath, as he took hold of the ears with one hand and opened the locker with the other, "thy task is done, thou soon wilt be—"

There was a tap on the laboratory door.

"Come in," called Mr. Powell without turning round. "Thou soon wilt be a—a skelly-tun. A skellytun in the cupboard, bun. Well, that'll be your next job, I dare say. Some secondary modern bio. class. Mustn't waste you. Corneal swelling 170.2 per cent of normal. Let's get that written down."

"Excuse me, sir."

Mr. Powell had supposed that the person outside must be Tyson's boy, Tom. He now looked up and saw, with something of a shock, a policeman standing at his elbow. He released the rabbit's ears and instinctively rose to his feet.

"Sorry if Ah startled you, sir."

"Oh, that's all right, officer. I wasn't expecting to see you, that's all. Anything wrong? By the way, d'you mind my asking how you got in? Only I thought the place was still locked up. I'm early, you see."

"Oapened a window-catch, Ah'm afraid, sir. Ah rang bell at door, but there was no reply, like. We soomtimes have to gain entry to premises at our discretion, y' know, if it seems joostified int' circumstances—say we think there's soomthing in jee-oppardy. Only anything's in jee-oppardy, y'see, it becooms necessary to take oonwoanted steps—"

"Yes, of course. Well, what's up exactly?"

At this moment the rabbit blundered into a wooden rack of test tubes. Mr. Powell lifted it back into its locker and adjusted the steel aperture round its neck. The policeman waited patiently until he had finished.

"Well, Ah've joost coom oop from Coniston, sir, y'see. It seems there's a lady in Doonnerd'l, a Miss Dawson at Seathwaite, who says she's got one of your dogs shut oop in her shed."

"One of *our* dogs, officer?"

"That's what it leuks like, sir. It seems Miss Dawson woke oop this morning and found this 'ere dog havin' a go at the roobbish-bin, so she roons down, grabs it, like, and pushes it int' shed."

"*Did* she now?"

"Ay, she did that. Seems she saw it had green collar, like, and a big coot across it heed. So Miss Dawson, she reckoned it moosta coom from here, and she rings us oop. Well, sergeant rings here hafe an hour ago, but couldn't get any reply—"

"Well, he wouldn't, of course, not so early—"

"Ay, that's it, sir. So he says to me to coom oop here and try to find soomone to talk to about it."

"Well, I suppose I'm someone. I'll tell the Director as soon as he comes in." (And won't he be delighted? thought Mr. Powell. This is really going to take some getting out of.)

"Ay, well, it's like this, y'see sir. Ah'm to assk whether soomone will kindly accoompany me to Doonnerd'l and see the lady—well, see the dog too, y'know—identify it an' that."

"What, now this minute?"

"As seun as possible, sir, if you please. Y'see, if it *is* in fact saame dog that's been killing sheep and's been soomhow mixed oop with yon nassty fatal accident at Cockley Beck, it ought to be identified as seun as possible and removed from the lady's premises. Naturally, she feels soom anxiety, y'see—"

In jee-oppardy, thought Mr. Powell. Oh hell, I don't

see how I can refuse. My eye, why's it always have to be *me?*

"All right, officer, I'll come along at once, if you don't mind just hanging on while I scribble a note to let my boss know what's happened, when he comes in."

"Ah'm greatly obliged, sir."

A few minutes later Mr. Powell and the policeman were speeding on their way to Dunnerdale, while in the clock-ticking solitude of the laboratory the rabbits continued their vigil.

Snitter lay motionless on the floor of the shed, belly to the ground and eyes half-closed. His muzzle, laid upon his paws, had remained still for so long that his condensing breath had formed a tiny pool of moisture, which glistened in the half-light. His entire being was filled with a sense of quiescence and contentment; and of a riddle answered so unexpectedly and in so astonishing a manner that there could be nothing to do but meditate upon it with a wonder transcending all such petty ideas as hunger, the future or his own safety.

When the lady with the thick leather gloves had first made towards him, he had cowered away in fear. Yet this fear had been not altogether for himself, but because he had felt it likely that if she touched him she would fall dead; and the thought of this—a repetition of the terrifying explosion as the air about them shattered, driving its sharp fragments into her face; the blood, and her shuddering, silent fall, like that of a dog which he remembered dropping dead from poison in the pen next to his own; the soft, scuffling thud as the body met the ground—the prospect of inflicting such another death was unbearable. When her fingers gripped his collar he had struggled for a few moments but then, true to his nature, had acquiesced at the sound of a kind voice and made no resistance as she opened the shed door and led him into a twilight smelling of apples, dust and wood splinters. He had wondered what she was going to do; but having patted him, spoken a few words and considerately returned his ham bone, she had left him alone.

After the first shock of surprise it was plain enough to

Snitter where he was, for after all he had known the place all his life, every feature of it. Once it had been brighter, tidier, cleaner, brisker-smelling. All the same he was, in fact, nowhere but where he had always been; only now he was actually seeing it for the first time. He was inside his own head. There were his eyes, straight above and in front of him, two square, transparent apertures, side by side, through which the morning light showed fairly clearly. True, they were somewhat grimy—even cobwebbed in places—but that was only to be expected, all unfortunate things considered. He would clean them up later. But he must be situated rather low down in his head, for all he could make out through his eyes was the sky. Directly between them, lower down and straight in front of him, was his muzzle—mouth, nose; both? That was puzzling— a fairly large aperture at ground-level, through which he could perceive smells of rain, mud, oak leaves, a tom-cat somewhere in the offing and still-more-distant sheep. Inside, the place appeared, alas, only what one might expect after all this time—distinctly a mess, untidy and neglected; and about the shelves a beggarly account of empty boxes were thinly scattered to make up a show. But what put the whole thing beyond doubt was the concave cleft running down the middle of the floor, from the place where he himself was lying to his own muzzle in the centre of the further wall. He had always supposed that the cleft must be narrower and deeper in appearance—it certainly *felt* deeper—but nevertheless he had been right all along about one thing. Pushed into the opening and covering the outlet was a rough ball of chicken-wire, in which were embedded a few old leaves, some chips of wood and scraps of sodden paper. It was clear enough, too, how the cleft had affected him and why he so often felt odd and confused, for on one side of it lay a stack of small logs, with a cleaver and block, while on the other were two rows of clean, resin-smelling splinters tied in bundles—obviously the part which had been split when the cleft was made.

"So it was the *splinters*," said Snitter, getting to his feet and sniffing them over. "Of course, it must have been some of those splinters that made the dark man's face bleed. But then what made the awful bang? Oh, well, if the lady lets me stay here long enough I suppose I shall come to understand that and a good deal more. My goodness, though, what a mess the place is in! I wish those flies hadn't got in. Maggots and flies—who wants a lot of flies buzzing round inside his head? Well, now I'm here I'd better make a start on my eyes. How funny it'll be to clean them from inside! I hope it doesn't hurt."

He jumped up on a shelf running along the further wall, just below the level of his two cobwebbed eyes. There followed a twinge of pain in his head as some light, unseen object fell from beneath his paws and shattered on the ground below. He wondered what part of him it might have been. Still, he could feel nothing immediately wrong. He waited a few moments to recover himself, then put his fore-paws on the narrow, dirty sill and looked out through his right eye.

It was just as he had expected. He was looking at the expanse of grass and heather outside the wall down which he and Rowf had sniffed their way before he had jumped over the gate. He could see Rowf's paw marks in a patch of mud immediately below. He raised one of his own paws and, a little surprised to find the inner surface of his eye so insensitive, pulled down a clot of sticky, dusty cobweb. The dust made him sneeze and he scuffled on the shelf, trying to get the mess off his paw and snapping at a fly that flew against the pane, recovered itself and buzzed away.

"The trouble is, I don't think I can reach as far as the top part of this eye," said Snitter. "I wonder why not? I suppose the whitecoats must have taken some of the inside of my head out—it really does seem awfully empty—and that's why I can't climb all the way to the top. Of course when my master—when my master was al—"

He broke off sharply, stared out and then edged along the shelf to get a clearer view. He had caught sight—he was almost sure he had caught sight—of Rowf and the tod creeping through the long grass a little way to his left. Yes, there they were, beyond all doubt, Rowf conspicuous enough, the tod all but invisible except in the moments when he inched forward.

But why can't I *hear* them? thought Snitter. Goodness knows where my ears are—somewhere out to the sides, I suppose. What do they look like, anyway? Oh, well, never mind; I suppose I can *smell* the tod. You generally can.

He jumped down and made his way across to his wiry, cold nose. Yes, sure enough, it was clear that not only Rowf but the unmistakable tod were close outside. A moment later Rowf's muzzle appeared, half-blocking the light.

"Snitter! Are you sure you can't get out? Have you really tried?"

The question caught Snitter unawares. Was he shut in? No—obviously you couldn't be shut into your own head against your will. But if he wasn't, why was it apparently impossible to use his eyes and muzzle at the same time?

"Well, no—you see, Rowf—"

"Come on, then! Quick, too—before the whitecoats come!"

"No, I can't come out, Rowf. I mean, if I do I shall be mad again. I'll explain. You see—"

"Snitter, listen, for goodness' sake! This is no time for one of your turns. I've brought the tod here to tell you how to get out. Whatever he tells you to do, do it. If he can't get you out, nobody can. But you've got to be quick."

Rowf's muzzle disappeared and a moment later Snitter not only smelt but saw the tod, peering in at him through the chicken-wire.

"Cum oot, ye greet fond article! Sharp wi' ye noo—afore wor aall knacked!"

"Listen, I want to explain," said Snitter. "I can't possibly come out. You see—"

"Reet afore ye there—yon back-end drain, straight afore ye! Yon's aye the way oot of a shed. Slip yersel' oot o' that sharp, ye greet nanny-hammer!"

As Snitter was considering how best to explain the extraordinary situation in which he found himself, the tod gripped the wire ball in its teeth and tugged it out through the opening in the base of the wall. Snitter, with a yelp of pain and shock, thrust his head and shoulders into the widened opening and tried to snatch it back. As he did so, he became suddenly aware that an enormous door had opened in the back of his head, letting in a blaze of light and a rush of cold air. With these came a scraping of men's boots, the sound of human voices and a moment later, faint but dreadfully, unmistakably clear, the smell of the whitecoats—the smell of their hands and their horrible, clean clothes.

Terrified, Snitter crushed and forced his body through the aperture. Behind him he heard a quick plunge of heavy feet and felt a human hand grabbing at his hind-quarters. He scrabbled in the hole, feeling pain along his left side as some pointed excrescence scratched him. Then he was out in the wet grass, bleeding down his flank, with Rowf dragging him forward, teeth in the scruff of his neck. He scrambled to his feet.

"Now run, Snitter, run like a hare, or I'll bite your arse off!"

Together they tore down the valley towards Ulpha. Half a mile away, as they lay panting in the shelter of a leafless hazel copse, the tod joined them without a word and at once made its way to a high, bracken-covered bank on the outskirts, whence it could look down on the road outside and the fields sloping to the Duddon beyond.

As he drove down into Dunnerdale, it occurred to Digby Driver that he could do not only with some petrol but also with something to eat. He had arrived in Ambleside late the previous night and set out again—after a snatched breakfast which he was already beginning to forget—at half past seven that morning. His general plan was to run down the valley, stopping for a look at the scene of the fatal accident at Cockley Beck, and then, having got some idea of the kind of terrain in which the mysterious dog was operating (for he had never before been in the Lake District), to move across to Coniston in the early afternoon and see what chance there might be of talking to one or more people from Animal Research. A certain kind of reporter might have telephoned the Director and tried to make an appointment for an interview with a representative of the station, but Digby Driver was not that kind of reporter. The last thing he wanted to send back to the

Orator was a piece based upon any kind of official release and the last thing he wanted to learn was whatever the Director of Animal Research might decide he wanted to tell him. He was after a sensational story and this, of course, could not be constructed out of mere truth; not out of officially released truth, anyway. It was essential that the news-reading public should feel, first, that the community was in danger and secondly that people—well-off people, "official" people—who ought to have known better, were to blame for it. As he got back into his car and drove down through the green fields south of Cockley Beck, Digby Driver reflected with satisfaction on some of his past triumphs. The to-do over clean air a few years ago—now that had been something like! The facts, as released by the Department of the Environment, had shown that by the early seventies the air over the country as a whole was cleaner than at any time during the previous hundred and twenty years at least; but by the time Digby Driver had finished with the matter, the advances in domestic smoke control appeared nugatory, while the Alkali Inspectorate had become irresponsible, incompetent sinecure-holders, fit only to be swept away as an obsolete liability. Of course, nothing in the way of statutory reform had followed from Digby Driver's articles. This was not surprising, since the British Clean Air Acts were already the most sensible and effective of their kind in the world and were not capable of being improved. But this was not the point. The point was that thousands of people had been scared, had bought the *Orator* like billy-o and been prevented from grasping that, in an adverse and difficult world, one blessing which they could count was the great improvement in clean air effected by local and central bureaucracy during the previous fifteen years.

Then there had been the lead-poisoning scare—ah! happy days for environmental correspondents! "And it'll go bloody hard," said Digby Driver to himself, "if there isn't some angle to be found on a research station where as much goes on as it does at this A.R.S.E. place. But which would go best, I wonder—darling doggies, or gross irresponsibility? Gross irry for choice. Who gives a damn about darling doggies these days, anyway? And where the hell am I going to find a petrol station in this blasted outback?"

In this last matter, however, Digby Driver was more fortunate than he had expected. A mile down from the Newfield (where he had narrowly missed not only a ginger cat but also one of Harry Braithwaite's dogs), he came once more upon Duddon, pouring southward in gleaming planes of noisy, wall-slapping, pewter-coloured spate. Just the other side of the bridge and a few yards up the side-road stood not only some plain and palpable petrol-pumps but also, if he were not mistaken, a village shop, doubtless full of biscuits, chocolate and cigarettes. Digby Driver drew in to the pumps, got out of the car, strolled back and forth a few times beside the wall above the river, glanced at the petroglyph of the salmon on the coping, and then pooped his horn.

Vera Dawson appeared with haste, smiles and apologies.

"I'm so sorry to keep you waiting! I didn't see there was anyone here or I'd have been out directly."

"That's all right," replied Digby Driver, pitching his cigarette over the wall into the Duddon. "Who'd want to be in a hurry in a lovely spot like this? Real old-world charm and peace, eh?"

"Well, there's plenty see it that way," replied Vera pleasantly, as she screwed the cap off the petrol tank, "but as a matter of fact we've had a bit of a rumpus this morning—quite a to-do while it lasted."

"Really—what sort of a to-do?" enquired Mr. Driver, his professional acumen instinctively aroused. "Fill her right up, please."

"Well, early this morning some stray dogs broke in and upset our dustbins," said Vera, "and we felt fairly sure one of them must be the dog that's been causing all the trouble round here—"

"Really? What made you think that?"

"Well, both the dogs had green collars, and they say that shows they come from the Coniston research place. We had one of them shut up in the shed and there's a young gentleman come over from Coniston with a police-man. They're still out at the back now, but unfortunately the dog got away before they could get hold of it."

Thank goodness for that, thought Digby Driver, and what a turn-up for the book to walk right into the middle of something like this!

"Oh, that *was* bad luck," he replied. "So the research chap had his trip from Coniston for nothing? No, I think she's O.K. for oil, thanks. Five forty-eight? There we are—five fifty; and a whole tuppence, all for me. Thanks."

At this point Mr. Powell and the policeman appeared, in conversation with Phyllis, who was politely seeing them to their car.

"—and if either of them should turn oop agaain, like," the policeman was saying. "If y' see them round plaace at all, doan't hesitate about telephoning us. It's better to telephone than not to, like. And if y' can keep them in sight—y' know, if it's practicable—that'd be best."

"Yes, of course," replied Phyllis. "I must say I hope they *don't* come back, though."

Digby Driver stepped forward, smiling politely.

"I've just been hearing something about this bit of trouble of yours over the stray dogs," he said. "I hope they didn't do any damage?"

"No, luckily not," answered Phyllis. "Of course, they've pulled the rubbish all over the yard and made a terrible mess, but nothing worse than that. And these two gentlemen have been very helpful in tidying it up for us."

"I suppose you're anxious to get hold of the dogs, aren't you?" pursued Driver, turning to the policeman.

"Ay, well, stray dogs killin' sheep's a serious matter oop 'ere, y' knaw," replied the policeman. "And then it's been aggravated, like, by this 'ere tragic death, y'see—very naasty, that was."

"Yes, indeed, I read about it in the paper," said Driver, offering his cigarettes round the company. Phyllis, Vera and the policeman declined, but Mr. Powell was more forthcoming.

"And if I'm not mistaken, you must be the poor bloke from the research laboratory," went on Driver, flicking his cigarette lighter between Mr. Powell's cupped hands. "You carry the can, do you?"

"Well, I don't know yet whether we do or not," answered Mr. Powell, recalling as he spoke the Director's policy of silence, as expounded by Dr. Boycott. "I still need to get a sight of the dogs, you see. They might be ours and then again they might not."

"Did you not see that one as it was pushing itself through the drain-hole?" asked Vera. "Kind of a black-and-white terrier it was, and the most terrible gash—"

"Yes, but of course it was just its head that I couldn't get to see," replied Mr. Powell. "It was outside already, you know, by the time we opened the door."

"They both had green collars," said Phyllis, "and I don't know where a dog could come by such a cut across the head as that, except by—well, by vivisection, if that's the right word. It was a terrible sight—enough to make anyone feel really bad—"

"Oh, I don't doubt for a moment that they had green collars," answered Mr. Powell rather hurriedly. "What we don't know, though, is whether these particular dogs are the ones that have been killing the sheep or whether either of them had anything to do with the fatal accident. Probably those are things we never shall know."

There was a rather awkward pause. Everyone seemed to be expecting him to say something more. "We need to get hold of the dogs first, that's what I mean," he added. "Then we may learn whose they are, mayn't we, and where they come from?"

"Oh—I thought perhaps the research station would know whether they had any dogs missing," said Vera, putting the obvious question in the politest possible way, "and what they looked like. The other dog now—the one you didn't see—that was altogether different to look at. It was a big, kind of a rough—"

To the sharp eye and experienced journalistic sense of Digby Driver, it was plain that Mr. Powell, young, honest, ingenuous and a trifle callow, was about to find himself in deep water—if indeed he were not already there. Obviously, the thing to do was to come to his aid: there would be nothing like so much to be gained by pressing awkward questions on him or adding to his confusion.

"Oh, that reminds me," he said, smiling at Vera. "Sorry—not changing the subject or anything, but it was what you were saying about the one we didn't see. There's been a most peculiar noise coming from the engine of my car, but I can't actually see anything at all. I'm usually rather good at seeing noises, too, and hearing smells and all that. I wonder—" he turned to Mr. Powell. "Would you be good enough, seeing you're here, to put an ear under the bonnet and tell me what you think? I'm sure you know a lot more about these things than I do."

As he had expected, Mr. Powell was not backward in seizing the floating spar.

"Yeah—well, sure, if I can," he said. "I can't claim to be an internal combustion expert, but—"

"I bet you're more of an expert than I am," replied Mr. Driver cordially, as he led the way across to the Triumph Toledo standing by the pumps.

He propped open the bonnet and started the engine. "Damn nuisance for you, all these people asking questions," he went on, revving the engine with one hand to make the interior a still more fine and private place. They both leaned inward, heads close together. "I suppose you want to say as little as you can, don't you; and hope the bloody dogs'll go up in smoke one dark night? That's what I'd want, I know that."

"Well, you've about said it," answered Mr. Powell, his spirits already rising in response to the stranger's quick understanding and ready sympathy. "I mean, you know, if one's got to spend half a day going out in a police car about three times a week, every time someone gets a sight of a stray dog anywhere in the Lake District—"

"These provincial police are so damned unimaginative," said Digby Driver. "Anyway, why should you have to stand in a white sheet even before anybody's proved that this dog—or these dogs, if there are two of the buggers— I didn't know there were—come from your place? I mean, it's like asking a bloke whether or not he's screwed Mary Brown because she's looking for someone to pin an affiliation order on to—why the hell should anyone expect him to answer up and put himself in the dock?"

Mr. Powell laughed; and gave every evidence of appreciating this witty, young-man-of-the-world approach.

"Well, whatever it may have been, the bloody thing seems to have stopped doing it now," said Mr. Driver, jerking his thumb at the engine. "It would, of course, when the expert comes along. Look, I say, are you going back to Coniston now? Only I'm going that way, and unless you particularly want to go back with your policeman chum, you'd be doing me a good turn if you'd let me give you a lift. Then you could hear the noise if it develops again."

"But are you sure I'd not be taking you out of your way?" asked Mr. Powell.

Ten minutes later, munching Phyllis's Kendal Mint Cake (as eaten by Hillary and Tensing on the summit of Everest), Mr. Driver and his passenger passed within a few yards of the vigilant tod crouched among the hazels and continued on their way towards Ulpha and Broughton.

"I don't know why the hell they can't say straight out whether they've lost any dogs or not," said Gerald Gray, landlord of the Manor at Broughton-in-Furness, as he drew a pint for Mr. Hutchinson the butcher (known locally as Mistroochinson) and a half for himself. "What gets me down is all this damned ca' canny stuff. Everyone knows there's a dog up at Seathwaite killing sheep and everyone's virtually certain it's escaped from Lawson Park; but the station themselves won't even say yea or nay. Well, why the hell won't they?"

"Ay, well, ye've about said it theer, Gerry," replied Mistroochinson.

At this relatively early hour there was no one else in that finest of all pubs, the Manor Hotel at Broughton. The banded slate floor lay cool, dark and smooth as a woodland pool in autumn. The newly lit fire was burning up in the beautiful, eighteenth-century fireplace and Strafford, Gerald's black tom-cat, sat purring on the rag rug, as well he might.

"They're bein' what ye might call circumspect," added Mistroochinson sagaciously. "Not sayin' nowt until they've got to, like."

"Well, they'll damned well have to soon, I should think," answered Gerald. "Another sheep or two and the local peasantry'll be storming the gates of the station with fire and sword. Heads will roll and bells will toll. Balls, will fall," he added, after a moment.

"Ay, well, but everyone's worried about joost his oan sheep, Gerry, tha knaws, and noan s' mooch about anywoon else's," said Mistroochinson. "They say——"

"Well, talk of the devil," interrupted Gerald, looking out of the window into the pretty, quiet little square that forms the centre of Broughton. "Here's one of those very research buggers coming in now, unless I'm much mistaken. That's young Stephen Powell, who works up at Lawson. Wonder what he's doing here so early in the morning?"

It had not been particularly hard for Digby Driver to persuade Mr. Powell to stop off for a quick one in Broughton before returning to duty. A moment later he entered the bar with his companion, wished Gerald good morning and ordered two pints of bitter.

"Pints at this time of day?" demurred Mr. Powell, albeit a trifle half-heartedly.

"Oh, sorry," replied Mr. Driver civilly. "Never mind, they're here now and they won't do us any harm, I'm sure."

"O.K., but then I really must hurry back to those blinking rabbits," said Mr. Powell. "Well, here's mud in your eye!"

"Cheers!" responded Mr. Driver.

"Morning, Gerald," said Mr. Powell, perhaps a shade more tardily than courtesy to a landlord requires, as he paused for breath between his first and second pull. "How's the world treating you?"

"Oh, mustn't grumble," answered Gerald. "And yourself?"

"Fine, thanks."

"And how's Stephanie?" asked Gerald, this time with more than a touch of genuine solicitude in his voice.

"She's—well, she's about the same, you know," replied Mr. Powell. His noticeable, if controlled, clouding of manner did not escape Digby Driver. A sick child? he wondered. An invalid sister-in-law? An expert in observing and exploiting personal grief and suffering, he stored the little incident away for future use.

"You were just telling me that the dogs went from

room to room through the animal block, but nobody knows how they finally succeeded in escaping?" he asked.

"Well, I'm blest if *I* know how they did," answered Mr. Powell, "unless they dissolved themselves in smoke and blew away up the chimney. But to tell you the truth, I don't really want to spend any more of this pleasant morning talking about the sods. They've made enough trouble for me already."

"What a damn shame!" said Digby Driver. "Why the hell should *you* be blamed? It's like the old lady and the parrot in the public lavatory—d'you know that one?"

Nobody knew it, and Mr. Driver obligingly related it to an appreciative audience. It reminded Gerald of one about two miners and a cow, which assisted Mr. Powell to the conclusion that, since nobody at Lawson Park could possibly tell how long he might need to investigate the Dunnerdale dogs and return, it would be a pity to hurry away. He set up three more pints, including one for Mistroochinson; and then insisted on buying a fourth, for Gerald. Nobody ever wants to leave the bar of the Manor.

The sense of loss and desolation lay over Snitter's awareness like hill-mist. Rising, here and there, out of this separating mirk, he could discern three or four peaks of certain knowledge, as that his master was dead, that he himself was mad, that men had destroyed the natural world and substituted a wilderness and that although he had now lost again the head which he had briefly found, he still carried in himself the involuntary power to deal death. But from what viewpoint he was regarding these; what the mist-covered land connecting them looked like; their relationship to each other beneath the miasma of confusion and ignorance from which they protruded—in short, where he was—these things remained dark to him. He lay still among the bare hazel branches and leafless elder, but from time to time raised his head to the sky with a howl, cut short as often as Rowf turned upon him, cursing.

"You can't expect any sense," said Snitter petulantly, "from a dog that's just been dragged outside his own head. If only you'd left me where I was!"

"Ye'd nivver be here noo, ye'd be in th' Dark, hinny,

ne bother. Them cheps wudda gi'n ye ne chance at aall. Noo bide easy, an' sort yersel' oot." The tod turned to Rowf. "We got te get th' wee fella back hyem afore neet. He's bad i' th' heed aall reet, ne doot."

"But we'll be seen for sure at this time of day. Isn't that what you've been teaching me all this time? We'll *have* to wait till dark."

"An' hoo ye gan te keep his gob shut, marrer?" enquired the tod sardonically. "He'll be yammerin' his heed off, an' fetchin' aall th' farmers fer five miles roond. It's howway wi' us te Broon Haw, an' sharp as w' can shift an' aall."

"In broad daylight?" asked Rowf again.

"Ah shud say so—unless yer gan te leave him here. We got to get him undergroond an' well in-bye an' aall, where nebody'll hear him. Howway noo! He'll manage sure eneuf."

"But the river?"

"Nowt else for't but swimmin'. There's ne bridge atween Ulpha an' yon hoose we wor at."

They swam the Duddon under High Kiln Bank, Rowf setting his teeth to the horrible business and sweeping down twenty yards with the swift, bitter current before his paws gripped stones and pulled him out on the further side. They thought themselves unseen, but they were mistaken. Bob Taylor, the most skilful fisherman in the valley, working his way with a wet fly up the reach between Ulpha Church and Hall Dunnerdale Bridge after the running sea trout, caught sight, a hundred and fifty yards upstream, of Snitter's black-and-white back as he plunged across behind the tod. A minute afterwards, Bob hooked a three-quarter pounder and thought no more about what he had seen; but it was to recur to him later.

"But, Stephen, old boy, surely the dogs weren't in any physical condition to kill sheep and give rise to all this bother?" asked Digby Driver, gripping the handrail and looking back at Mr. Powell over his shoulder as they pussyfooted their way down the breakneck flight of steps that leads into the yard behind the Manor, on their way to the netty, Gents or loo.

Ulpha Church

"Well, I don't know so much about that," replied Mr. Powell. "One of them was an absolute bastard of a dog—mind you, it'd had enough to make it, poor sod—but there was nobody cared to touch it, not even old Tyson—"

"Tyson? He's the man about the place?"

"Yeah—feeds them, cleans them out an' all that. I always say he knows more about the work at Lawson Park than anyone else. He deals with *all* the animals, you see, and it's his business to know what each one's being used for and by whom. The rest of us, except for the Director, only knows about the projects we're doing ourselves. No, but that seven-three-two, it really *was* a dangerous animal

—it was always muzzled before it was brought out for tests—"

"What were the tests?" asked Driver.

"Well, they were something like the tests carried out by Curt Richter at the Johns Hopkins medical school in America—what's his thing called?—'The Phenomenon of Sudden Death in Animals and Man.' D'you know that?"

Like a good many young people immersed in specialized work, Mr. Powell tended to forget that others were likely to be unfamiliar with his background material.

" 'Fraid I don't—not up my street really."

They came back into the yard and Mr. Powell, hands in pockets, stopped and leaned against the netty wall.

"Well, Richter put wild rats and domesticated rats into tanks of water to swim until they drowned; and he found that some of them died very rapidly for no apparent reason. A bloke called Cannon had already suggested that it might be psychogenic—you know, fear, with consequent over-stimulation of the sympathicoadrenal system; accelerated heartbeat, contraction in systole—all that jazz. What Richter established was that it wasn't fear but hopelessness—overstimulation of the parasympathetic system, not the sympathicoadrenal. This seven-three-two dog of ours at Lawson Park had been given all sorts of drugs—you know, atropine and the colingerics, and adrenalectomy and thyroidectomy—you name it. But the real thing was that it had been continually immersed, drowned and revived, so that it had built up a terrific resistance, based on the conditioned expectation that it was going to be removed again. It didn't succumb to the usual psychogenic factors; on the contrary, it was doing fantastic endurance times, very very interesting. They're funny things, you know, hope and confidence," said Mr. Powell rather sententiously. "For instance, they're present a good deal less strongly in dogs that haven't been domesticated. Wild animals, and therefore by inference primitive men—creatures living in precarious situations—are more susceptible to fear and strain than domesticated animals. Strange, isn't it?"

"What about the other dog that escaped?" asked Digby Driver.

"Well, that wasn't mine—not involved in any of my programmes: I don't touch surgery—probably shan't until I'm established—but if we hadn't had evidence to the contrary this morning I'd have thought that that dog was unlikely to be alive, let alone to be killing sheep. It had what you might call a pretty drastic brain operation, to say the least."

"What was the object all sublime?" asked Driver, as they made their way through the Manor into the square and got back into his car.

"Well, that was a sort of psychological thing, too, as I understand it," replied Mr. Powell. "That was why they needed an adult, thoroughly domesticated dog—they paid quite a bit for it, I believe, to some woman in Dalton."

"Why did she part with it, d'you know?"

"Well, it wasn't originally hers. Apparently it had belonged to her brother in Barrow, but it had somehow or other brought about his—I'm not sure, but his death, I believe I heard—in an accident with a lorry, so naturally she wasn't keen on keeping it. That's an exceptional situation, of course. In the normal way domesticated animals—people's pets—aren't easy to come by for this work, as you can well believe. The operation was something quite new—a bit like a leucotomy, but that's misleading, really. To be perfectly frank, there were innovatory complications that put it a long way beyond me. But the general purpose—and no one'll be able to say, now, how far it was successful; not in this particular case, anyway—was to bring about a confusion of the subjective and objective in the animal's mind."

"How would that work in practice, then?" asked Digby Driver, accelerating out of the square and up the hill towards the Coniston road.

"Well, as I understand it—whoops!" Mr. Powell belched beerily, leaned forward and frowned, seeking an illustrative example. "Er—well, did you ever read a book called *Pincher Martin,* by a man named Golding? You know, the *Lord of the Flies* bloke?"

"I've read *Lord of the Flies,* but I don't think I know this other book."

"Well, the chap in it's supposed to be dead—drowned

at sea; and in the next world, which is a sort of hellish limbo, one of the things *he* does is to confuse subjective and objective. He thinks he's still alive and that he's been washed up on a rock in the Atlantic, but actually it's an illusion and the rock is only a mental projection—it's the shape of a back tooth in his own head. The dog that had this operation might have illusions something like that. Suppose it had come to associate—well, let's say cats with eau de cologne, for instance—then it might be observed to treat some inanimate object—a cardboard box, say—as a cat when it was subjected to the smell of eau de cologne: or conversely, it might see something objective and act as though it was nothing but the equivalent of some thought in its mind—I can't think what, but you get the general idea."

"It must be a fascinating job, yours," said Driver. "Straight on, do we go here? All the way?"

"All the way to Coniston. It's really very good of you."

"No, not at all—I've got to go there myself, as I said. No, I mean, a fascinating job you have with all these experimental discoveries."

"A lot of it's routine, actually—you know, Fifty L.D. and all that."

"Fifty L.D.?"

"Fifty lethal dose. Say you—or anyone—wants to market a new lipstick or a food additive or something, then we have to forcibly feed quantities of it to a group of animals until we've ascertained at what dosage level half of them die within fourteen days."

"Whatever for? I mean, suppose the stuff's not toxic anyway?"

"Doesn't matter. You still have to continue forcible feeding until you've ascertained Fifty L.D. They may die of internal rupture—osmotic or pH effects—anything. It's a bore, actually, but that's partly what we're there for. All in a good cause, you know. Cosmetics have to be safe, or no one'd buy 'em."

"I suppose there are compensations—not for them but for you, I mean—defence projects and secret stuff—breaking new ground. No, O.K.," added Digby Driver, smiling broadly. "Don't answer that, as the judges say. I don't want you to give me anything to pass on to two square-jawed blokes in raincoats on Hampstead Heath."

"Oh, Goodner's the chap for that. I wouldn't be in the least surprised to learn that he'd been one of those very blokes in his time. He's German by birth. He was working in Germany at the end of the war—for the Germans, I mean. He's on secret work of some kind right now, that I do know. Something to do with lethal disease, for the Ministry of Defence. They practically lock him up at night—they lock up all his stuff, anyway. And there's no talking shop to *him*. I bet he gets paid three times what I do," added Mr. Powell, in a candid *non sequitur*.

"And what sort of leave do they give you?" enquired Digby Driver, who knew exactly how far to go and when to stop. "Where's this? Oh, Torver, is it? Does it get a bit lonelier before Coniston? Good—I could do with another piss, couldn't you?"

" 'Accidental death,' " said Robert Lindsay. "Ay, well, that's all he could have found—couldn't have found owt else, Dennis, could he?"

"Could have found suicide if he'd had a mind," said Dennis.

"Never on the evidence. There were nothing to suggest it. If yon Ephraim chap's alone and he dies wi' shot-gun when he's standing beside his car, he's entitled to benefit of all the doubt there may be; and there were no evidence at all that he were of suicidal disposition. Nay, Coroner were reet enoof—on available evidence that were accident, Dennis, plain as day."

"He never said nowt about dog, though, did he?" said Dennis. "But it were yon bluidy dog browt it about, for all that. It were dog as shot him, tha knaws."

"Y' reckon dog set off gun an' killed him?"

"Ay, I do that. It were seen booggerin' off oop fell like th' clappers, tha knaws, Bob."

"Coroner couldn't bring that in on evidence either. An' if he had, it would still be accidental death, wouldn't it? Dog's an accident as mooch as light trigger or owt else."

"Ay, happen it would, Bob, but if he'd pinned blame fair an' square on dog, like, then happen police or soomone'd be instroocted to find it at once and shoot it. Way it's been left now, you an' me's no better off than we were at start. You could lose a coople more sheep tonight an' Ah could lose three next week, and no boogger but us give a damn. Research Station weren't at inquest—no bluidy fear. Nowt to do wi' them—and they'll *do* nowt, an' all, without they're made to, Bob, tha knaws."

There was a pause while Robert sucked the top of his stick and considered his next words. Dennis lit a cigarette and pitched the spent match over his dog's head into the long grass below the wall.

"Theer's joost woon lot o' chaps as *could* make them stand an' annser, Dennis," said Robert at length. "Com*pel* them to answer, like."

"Member of Parliament?" asked Dennis. "He'll do nowt—"

"Nay, not him. Woon lot o' chaps; an' that's press chaps. Did y'see *Loondon Orator* yesterday?"

"Nay, Ah niver did. Ah were back late from Preston—"

"Well, they're sending reporter chap oop from Loondon —special reporter, they said, to coover t' whole story, like, an' get to t'bottom of it. It were Ephraim's death started them off. Chap called Driver—ay. Real smart chap, be all accounts—real 'andy fella."

"Ay, but wheer's he at? No good to us without he's here, is he?"

"Coniston police were over to Dawson girls this morning, tha knaws," said Robert.

"Git awaay?"

"Ay, they were that—an' fella from Research Station were wi' them. Two dogs with green collars were into Dawson girls' doostbins int' early morning. Phyllis got one on 'em shut int' shed an' she phoned police, but dog were awaay owt of back-eend draain before this yoong research fella could grab it. Ay, weel, if police are that mooch interested, Dennis, tha knaws, and tha tells 'em tha's got soomthing tha wants t' say to yon Driver chap, they'll tell thee wheer he's at."

"Ah've got a whole bluidy lot Ah'm gann't to say to him," said Dennis.

The morning turned still and fine, with high-sailing, diaphanous clouds barely masking the sun's warmth in their swift passage across its face. The heather was snug as a dog-blanket. Rowf lay basking on the summit of Caw, warming his shaggy coat until the last moisture of Duddon had dried out of it. A few yards below, among a tumble of rocks, Snitter and the tod were playing and tussling like puppies over a bone long picked clean, the tod pausing every now and then to scent the wind and look east and west down the empty slopes below.

"What's up wi' ye noo, marrer?" it remarked, as Snitter suddenly dropped the bone and remained gazing westward with cocked ears and head lifted to the wind. "Ye're not hevvin' one o' yer bad torns agen? Aall that aboot 'inside yer head'—where else wad ye be, ye fond wee fyeul?"

"No, I'm all right, tod. Rowf! I say, Rowf!"

"Aargh! He'll take ne notice, he's still dryin' hissel' oot. What's gan on, then? Can you see owt doon belaa?"

"Far off, tod. Look—the dark blue. It's not the sky. It's like a great gash between the sky and the land. They've cut the top of the hills open, I suppose, but why does the blood spill out blue?"

"Mebbies yer still a bit aglee wi' yon shed carry-on. Which way ye lukkin'?"

"Out there, between the hills."

Ten miles away, through the clear, sunny air, between and beyond the distant tops of Hesk Fell and Whitfell to the west, a still, indigo line lay all along the horizon.

"Yon? Yon's th' sea. Did ye not knaa?" As Snitter stared, the tod added, "Well, it's ne pig's arse, fer a start."

"No, I suppose not. What is the sea? Is it a place? Is that what we can smell licking the wind like a wet tongue?"

"Ay—th' salt an' th' weeds. It's aall watter there—watter, an' forbye a sea-mist noo an' agen."

"Then we couldn't live there? It looks—it looks—I don't know—peaceful. Could we go and live there?"

"Wad ye seek feathers on a goat?" replied the tod shortly, and forthwith crept up through the rocks to where Rowf had woken and begun snapping at flies in the sun.

Snitter remained staring at the patch of far-off blue.

Water—could it really be water, that tranquil stain along the foot of the sky? Firm it seemed, smooth and unmoving between the crests of the hills on either side; but further off than they, deeper, deep within the cleft, a long way beyond and within.

It could be put back, I suppose, thought Snitter, musingly. It shouldn't have been cut open like that, but it's all still there—funny, I thought it wasn't. It could be closed up again and then I'd be all right, I suppose. Only it's such an awfully long way off. If only I could have stayed inside my head this morning, I might have been able to decide how to get there—how to reach it. But whoever would have thought it was all still there?

He closed his eyes and the salty wind, fitful and mischievous, tugged at the grass and whispered in a half-heard song, while faint scents, breaking like waves, came and went between his nostrils and ears.

> *"We are the brains the whitecoats stole,*
> *And you the victim of the theft.*
> *Yet here the wound might be made whole,*
> *The sense restored and healed the cleft.*
> *And since, of sanity bereft,*
> *You can devise no better plan,*
> *To us, the only place that's left,*
> *Come, lost dog; seek your vanished man."*

"If I could just get all these thoughts up together," murmured Snitter. "But I'm sleepy now. It's been a long day—long night—something or other, anyway. How smoothly that grass moves against the sky—like mouse-tails."

Soothed and finally oblivious, Snitter fell asleep in the November sunshine.

Lakeland shopkeeper Phyllis Dawson got a shock yesterday, tapped Digby Driver on his typewriter. (Except when signing his name, Digby Driver had seldom had a pen in his hand for several years past.) *The reason? She found her dustbins the target of a new-style commando raid by the two mysterious dogs which have recently been playing*

*a game of hide-and-seek for real with farmers up and
down the traditional old-world valley of Dunnerdale,
Lancashire, in the heart of poet Wordsworth's Lakeland.
The mystery death of tailoring manager David Ephraim,
found shot beside his car at lonely Cockley Beck, near the
head of the valley, took place while farmers were combing the fells nearby for the four-footed smash-and-grab
intruders, and is believed to form another link in the chain
lying behind efforts to pinpoint the cause of the enigma.
Where have the unknown dogs come from and where are
they hiding? Shopkeeper Phyllis's contribution was doomed
to disappointment yesterday when scientist Stephen Powell, hastening eighteen miles to the scene of the crime
from Lawson Park Animal Research Station, arrived too
late to forestall the dogs' escape from the shed where they
had been immured pending identification and removal.
Are these canine Robin Hoods indeed a public danger,
as local farmers hotly maintain, or are they wrongly accused of undeserved guilt? They may have an alibi, but if
so the term is more than usually apt, for where indeed are
they? This is the question Lakeland is asking itself as I
pursue enquiries in the little gray town of Coniston, one-
time home of famous Victorian John Ruskin.*

Well, thought Digby Driver, that'll do for the guts of
the first article. If they want it longer they can pep it up
on the editorial desk. Better to keep the actual connection
of the dogs with Lawson Park to blow tomorrow. Yeah,
great—that can burst upon an astonished world as an
accusation. "Why have the public not been told?" and
all that. The thing is, what come-back have the station
got? We know two dogs escaped from Lawson Park; and
thanks to dear old Master Stephen, bless him, we know
what they were being used for and what they looked like.
And we can be certain—or as good as—that they were the
same dogs as those that were raiding Miss Dawson's dustbins. But that's no good to the news-reading public. The
thing is, have they been killing sheep and, above all, did
they cause the death of Ephraim? What we want is evidence of gross negligence by public servants. "Gross
negligence, gross negligence, let nothing you dismay,"
sang Mr. Driver happily. "Remember good Sir Ivor Stone's

the bloke who doth you pay, To make the public buy the rag and read it every day, O-oh tidings of co-omfort and joy—"

He broke off, glancing at his watch. "Ten minutes to opening time. Well, mustn't grumble. I confess I never expected to fall on my feet right from the start like this. Drive down Dunnerdale and walk straight into the dogs and then into Master Powell looking for them. All the same, it still doesn't grab the reader by the throat and rivet the front page—and that's what it's got to do, boy, somehow or other. Tyson—and Goodner—ho, hum! Wonder who that there Goodner used to be—might ask Simpson to look into that."

He strolled down the road in the direction of The Crown. The mild winter dusk had fallen with a very light rain and smell of autumn woods drifting from the hills above. The far-off lake, visible at street-corners and between the houses as a faintly shining, grey expanse, lay smooth yet lithe as eel-skin, and somehow suggestive of multiplicity, as though composed of the innumerable, uneventful lives spent near its shores—long-ago lives now fallen, like autumn berries and leaves, into the peaceful oblivion of time past, there to exert their fecund, silent influence upon the heedless living. There were bronze chrysanthemums in gardens, lights behind red-curtained windows and drifts of wood-smoke blowing from cowled chimneys. A van passed, changing gear on the slope, and as its engine receded the unceasing, gentle sound of babbling water resumed its place in the silence, uprising like heather when horse-hooves have gone by. A clock struck six, a dog barked, the breeze tussled a paper bag along the gravel and a blackbird, tuck-tucking away to roost, flew ten yards from one stone wall to another.

This is a right dump, thought Digby Driver as he crossed the bridge over Church Beck. I wonder how many *Orator* readers there are here? Well, there'll be some more soon, if I've got anything to do with it.

He entered the saloon bar of The Crown, ordered a pint and fell into conversation with the barman.

"I suppose you're not sorry to have a bit less to do

during winter months?" he asked. "There must be a lot of work at a place like this during the holiday season?"

"Oh, ay," returned the barman. "It's downright murder at times. July and August we get fair rooshed off our feet. Still, it's good business as long as y' can stand oop to it."

"I suppose in winter it becomes mainly a matter of looking after the regulars?" pursued Driver. "D'you de-escalate your involvement with catering for visitors at this time of year?"

"Well, there's always a few cooms by," replied the barman. "We keep on a bit of hot food at mid-day, but not sooch a wide raange, like. There's no Americans in winter, for woon thing, y' see."

"No, that's true," said Driver. "How about the people up at Lawson Park? They bring you a bit of trade, I suppose?"

"Not really so as ye'd noatice," replied the barman. "Theer's soom o' them looks in for a drink now and then, but they're not what ye'd call a source o' regular coostom, aren't those scientific gentlemen. Ah reckon theer's a few o' them thinks alcohol's what's used for preserving specimens," he added humorously.

"Ha ha, that's a good one—I dare say they do," said Digby Driver. "I suppose they get up to all sorts of new research projects up there. D'you think there's much in the way of secret weapons they go in for—germ warfare and all that sort of thing? Makes you feel nervous, doesn't it? You know, if anything were to get out and come down here—hell's bells, eh?"

"Ay, well, that were woon thing as coom oop at pooblic inquiry before they built t'plaace," answered the barman. "Them as objected said there'd be element o' daanger from infection an' sooch like. Not that anything in that way's ever happened so far. But Ah've heerd as theer's parts of t'plaace kept secret, like, an' no one to go in but those that have to do wi' it."

"That reminds me," said Driver, "d'you know a chap called Tyson?"

" 'Bout forty," answered the barman with a chuckle. "Two thirds of t'folk int' Laakes is called Tyson, an' hafe the rest's called Birkett."

"Well, I meant a particular chap who works up at Lawson Park."

"Oh, old 'Arry? Ay, Ah knows him reet enoof. He cleans out animals oop there—feeds 'em an' that. He'll likely be in a bit later—cooms in for 'is pint most evenings. Did you want to speak to him?"

"Well, I'm a newspaper man, you see, and I'm doing an article on English research stations from the point of view of ordinary people like you and me. So a real, live chap like Tyson'd be more use than those scientists—they'd be too technical for the newspaper-reading public anyway."

"Oh, ay," said the barman, unconsciously flattered as Driver had intended. "Well, if ye're going to be here for a while I'll tell you if he cooms in, like. He'll be through int' pooblic yonder, but I'll let y' know."

"Thanks," said Driver. "He certainly won't be a loser by it."

"Mr. Tyson, I'm a man of business like yourself. I believe in being perfectly straight and plain. I want information for my paper about this business of the dogs escaping and I'm ready to pay for it. It's not a question of bargaining—there's the money. Count it. I shan't say you told me anything—I shan't even mention your name. Tell me everything you know about the dogs and that money goes into your pocket and I've forgotten I ever had it."

The two had left The Crown for Tyson's cottage, where they were sitting before the fire in the living room. Mrs. Tyson was busy in the kitchen and the door between was shut.

Digby Driver listened closely to Tyson's account of the escape of seven-three-two and eight-one-five, which corroborated and in certain particulars added to what he had already heard from Mr. Powell that morning.

"You're sure they went right through the entire animal block from end to end?" he asked.

"Good as sure," answered Tyson.

"How?"

"Weel, they'd knocked ower caage o' mice int' pregnancy unit and one moosta cut it paw on't glass. Theer

(255)

were spots o' blood reet through to t'guinea-pig plaace at t'oother end. Ah cleaned 'em oop."

"But you still don't know how they got out of the block?"

"Nay."

Digby Driver chewed his pencil. This was maddening. The vital piece of information, if it existed and whatever it might be, was still eluding him.

"How much d'you know about the work of Dr. Goodner?" he asked suddenly.

"Nowt," replied Tyson promptly. "Theer's noon knaws owt about it but 'isself, without it's Director. He works in special plaace, like, an' it's kept locked, is yon. Ah doan't have nowt to do wi't."

"Why d'you suppose that is?"

Tyson said nothing for some time. He lit his pipe, raked through the fire with the poker and put on some more coal. Digby Driver remained silent, gazing at the floor. Tyson got up, picked up his cap from the table and hung it on a peg behind the door. Digby Driver did not even follow him with his eyes.

"It's Ministry o' Defence, is that," said Tyson at last.

"How do you know?"

"Yon Goodner were talking to me one day about disposal o' beeästs' bodies, an' Ah seen letter in's 'and. It were Ministry-headed paaper, like, marked 'Secret' in red."

"Is that all you saw of it?"

"Ay."

There was another pause, while the hounds of Digby Driver's questing mind cast back and forth on the scent.

"Where *is* Dr. Goodner's special laboratory?" he asked.

"Int' cancer research block," answered Tyson. "Separate part, like, with it oan door."

"Could the dogs have gone through it?"

"Nay, th' couldn't—not in theer; but they went through cancer block reet enoof."

"Why's Goodner's place there, d'you suppose? Any special reason?"

"Ah cann't saay, unless happen it's rats. Aall't rats are kept int' one place while they're to be used. Joost black separate from brown, ootherwise all int' one plaace, tha knaws."

Digby Driver started. Then, instantly recovering himself, he bent down to scratch his ankle; straightened up, looked at his watch, lit a cigarette and returned the pack to his pocket. Negligently, he picked up the ashtray and pretended to study its design.

"Does Goodner use many black rats?" he asked carelessly.

"Black and brown. Black moastly."

"No other animals?"

"Soometimes moonkeys. And a reet nuisance it is, is that."

"Oh—why?"

"Every time he wants moonkey it has t'ave full disinfectant treatment—theer's noan to be owt on it, he says. Doosn't matter how clean it is already, if he wants it, it has t'oondergo total disinfestation process and remain in sterile condition while he taakes it over."

"But that doesn't apply to the rats?"

"Nay."

"I see," said Digby Driver. "Well, thank you, Mr. Tyson. I shan't mention this talk of ours to anyone, and you needn't either. But it's been most helpful. Good night."

FIT 7

Wednesday the 10th November

Need information urgently rat and flea-borne diseases also background one Goodner ex-German wartime scientist employed A.R.S.E. prospects story excellent Driver.

"Oh, hooray!" said Mr. Skillicorn, rubbing his hands. "Izzy wizzy, let's get busy. Desmond, dear boy, with any luck this is going to break big."

"There's a *lot* could go wrong with it," replied Mr. Simpson, shaking his head. "A *lot!*"

"Like what?"

"Oh, I don't know. I hope I'll be proved wrong, Quilliam. It's just that I've got such an incurably suspicious mind, you know."

Thursday the 11th November

"—And then there's this," said the Under Secretary, picking up a press cutting, "which you may already have seen. It may prove entirely negligible, but I don't much like the look of it. A little cloud out of the sea, like a man's hand."

"I'll advise the Parliamentary Secretary to prepare his chariot."

The Assistant Secretary sighed inwardly and tried to assume an eager and co-operative air. The two of them had already spent an hour in discussing three matters on which the necessary action could have been decided in as many minutes. If ever there was a case of Parkinson's Law, thought the Assistant Secretary morosely—only there ought to be a corollary in this case. "Work expands in direct proportion to the loquacity of the senior officer responsible for it."

Outside, in Whitehall, evening was falling and over Horse Guards Parade the sunlit air was flecked and alive with starlings' wings. By the thousand they flew in, whistling, strutting, chuckling to one another on the jutty friezes of the Government offices, their pendent beds and procreant cradles. The light reflected, from their glossy plumage, swift, glancing greens, blues and mauves. O happy living things! No tongue their beauty might declare. "I wish my kind saint would take pity on *me,*" thought the Assistant Secretary, taking the press cutting which the Under Secretary was holding out to him. Whatever it might be, he ought already to have seen it himself, of course—it was he who ought to have drawn it to the Under Secretary's attention, not the other way around. The Under Secretary was making this point by the act of refraining from making it.

Mystery Dog Raiders at Large in Lakeland, he read. *A report from the* Orator's *Man-on-the-Spot—Digby Driver*. He skimmed quickly down the item. With any luck, and if he could absorb the gist of it quickly enough, he could say that he *had* already seen it, but hadn't thought it worth mentioning to his busy Under Secretary.

"Yes, I did see this, Maurice, actually, but it didn't seem to amount to a great deal. I mean, even if Animal Research were to admit that they'd let a dog or dogs escape, and even if one of those dogs *had* caused the death of this poor chap Ephraim, it's still purely local in effect and wouldn't be damaging to the Secretary of State, I would suppose."

"That depends," replied the Under Secretary, looking

down and making a minute and entirely unnecessary adjustment of the Remembrance Day poppy in his buttonhole. "You see, the Secretary of State's rather sensitive at the moment, on account of attacks in the House about finance."

"But how could this tie up with that?"

"I'm not saying it does, but it *might*." The Under Secretary suavely showed his teeth like an elderly sheep. "You'll recall that a few years back we—or our predecessors—advised the Secretary of State to accept the principal recommendations of the Sablon Committee and that that meant, *inter alia,* approval of the Lawson Park project; and a good deal of money for it in the annual estimates ever since. Lawson Park's always had its enemies, as you know, and someone may well try to argue that these wasters of public money have been negligent in letting the dogs escape. That could be embarrassing. It's bad enough the station having been sited in a national park in the first place—"

"Can't see that. It doesn't cause pollution or increase the flow of traffic—"

"I know, I *know,* Michael," said the Under Secretary in a characteristically testy tone, "but it's a nonconforming user in a national park and as Crown development it attracted a deemed planning permission. That's quite enough for the Opposition if the place gets itself into hot water. But look, I fear we shall have to call a halt now to these most interesting deliberations. I have things to attend to and so, I'm sure, have you." (Good Lord! thought the Assistant Secretary, I can't believe it!) "I'm seeing the Parly. Sec. tomorrow evening about one or two other things and while I'm about it I'd like to set his mind at rest on this, if we can. Have you got a reliable contact up there?"

"Yes, more or less. Chap called Boycott I generally talk to."

"Well, could you please find out what their thinking is on this, and in particular whether they've had a dog escape and if so what they've done about it? We want to be able to say, publicly if necessary, that this Hound of the Baskervilles, if it exists, didn't emerge from Lawson Park."

"Right, Maurice, I'll see to that." (Bloody old woman! What other Under Secretary would make a meal of a thing like this?)

"You understand, I *hope* I'm going to be proved to be fussing unnecessarily, Michael. It's just that I've got such an incurably suspicious mind, you know."

In the corridor, the Assistant Secretary paused to look out over St. James's Park in the failing light. From high up in a great, bark-peeling plane tree a thrush was singing, and in the distance he could discern the pelicans on the lake, swimming one behind the other and all thrusting their heads below water at the same, identical instant. As often in moments of difficulty or depression, he began to repeat "Lycidas" silently to himself.

> *"Yet once more, O ye laurels, and once more*
> *Ye myrtles brown, with ivy never sere . . ."*

The mist was like an elastic, damp cloth over the muzzle, yet worse, being insubstantial and impossible to claw aside. For the twentieth time Rowf rubbed a paw across his face to wipe away a clot of the wet gossamer filling the grass for mile after mile. The muffled pouring of the becks sounded from both before and behind. There were no stars. There was no breeze and no movement of smells. There were only those scents that hung stilly in the mist itself and formed part of it—sheep and sheep's droppings, heather and the lichen and fungus covering the stone walls. There was not a sound to be heard of any living creature, man, bird or beast. He and the tod were moving beneath a ceiling of mist, along passages walled with mist, shouldering their way through thickets of mist. Yet the mist, unlike honest trees, bushes and walls, placed no bounds upon uncertainty and error. Along a walled path you can go only one way or the other—right or wrong. But it is a strange path where even with a thought the rack dislimns and the walls are at once on all sides and nowhere at all, cut away before and closing from behind, apparently extending in one direction but in fact open in all.

Rowf, with the tod at his side, plodded on through the

wide vacuity. He was tired out, but less with exertion than with the strain of ignorance, doubt and uncertainty. Some three hours earlier, as soon as darkness had fallen, he and the tod had descended into Lickledale, leaving Snitter, who was once more rambling and evidently confused as to where he was, alone in the shelter of the shaft. Rowf, still weary after his long search on Harter Fell and the rescue from the shed, had felt unequal to hunting sheep with no more help than the tod could give him, and they had decided to go for poultry at best, with dustbins as a last resort. Upon the outskirts of Broughton Mills and the threshold of what seemed likely to prove a hopeless business among too many houses, cars, men and dogs, the wet fog had crept down from the tops like an accomplice and they had smashed (or rather, Rowf had smashed) a length of slack wire netting, snatched two hens and disappeared into the grey density amid a clamour of guinea-fowl and the shouted curses of an invisible man not twenty yards away, whose torch showed him nothing but a motionless, all-enveloping curtain of fog.

The tod put down its hen and sat breathing smokily into the surrounding cold. "Ye canna beat a bit mist, if yer liftin' hens or ducks. We'd have been oot half th' neet forbye, an' mebbies got wor hint-ends full o' lead atop o' thet."

The wire had re-opened Rowf's wounded nose and it was beginning to sting abominably.

"Whit are ye rakin' aboot efter noo?" asked the tod irritably.

"A puddle," answered Rowf, vanishing into the fog. "A good, cold one, too." There was a muffled sound of lapping and he reappeared. "That's better."

"By, ye're reet mucky."

"Tod, how do you find the way? I've no idea where we are."

"Groond," answered the tod. "It gans up an' gans doon. Ye divven't need mair. We're goin' up noo."

"Are we near home? Oh, damn these cobwebs!"

"Pluff 'em off, hinny. Ay, we're nigh noo. Ye can tell fro' the groond. Up ahight th'earth's lighter. Mind, yon snout o' yours luks weel brayed aboot. Ye've torn it bad."

"It'll be all right. Tod, what about Snitter? How does he seem to you?"

"He's weel away wi'd, yon. He wez on agen this mornin' aboot not bein' left inside his aan heed. Daft as a brush."

"Yes, he's bad right enough—worse than I've ever seen him. These turns of his pass off, though—or they always have. It's a nuisance, but he'll have to stay where he is for the time being. We'll have to hunt without him."

"He canna bide there, hinny. None of us can. If yon mist howlds doon, we'll hev to be off b' th' morn."

"Again, tod? He'll never do it. D'you want to go far?"

"This tale o' his aboot killin' yon chep wiv a gun— d'ye think thet's reet, or is it just his daft crack?"

"It's true. As far as I can make out the man had caught him on his way back alone from that last sheep we killed on Hard Knott, and either Snitter startled him, so that he let the gun off himself, or else Snitter got his paw caught in it. Either way the man's dead."

"An' foond?"

"He's found all right." Rowf told the tod of the shot that had missed him at Cockley Beck. The tod listened silently, and before replying set off once more up the hillside.

"By, he's th' dabbest hand ye iver saw, yon wee fella. Shoot a man? Whey, ye wadden't credit it. Mind, it's bad, yon, bad. The'll be huntin' noo till they find th' pair o' yez, ne doot aboot that. If Ah had th' sense Ah wes born wi', Ah'd be off an away mesel' an' leave ye t'id."

"That'd be the end of us, tod. Without you we'd have been finished a long while back."

"Ay, ne doot aboot thet neether. Whey . . ." (the tod paused), "Whey, Ah'll not be tekkin mesel' off yit. But mind—Ah'm tellin' ye—gan where Ah tell ye te, an' ne muckin' aboot, or Ah'm away like a shot an' ye can fend fer yersels."

"How far, tod?"

"A lang way—it'll be two neets gettin', Ah warr'nd. We'll lie up o' Bull Crag till th' morrer morn, if th' wee fella can get that far. Then through b' Wyth Born an' Dunmail Raise. Best te cross th' Raise be neet—ay, an' duck across sharp when there's ne bit cars or lights shinin' o' th' road."

"But where are we going? Have you ever been there before?"

"Helvellyn range. Nowt but th' once. Mind, it's high groond—wild and blowed lonely forbye. 'Sennuf to blaw yer lugs off there, noo an' agen. But there's ne other chance for ye, with aall them booggers oot huntin'."

"If you think we're as badly off as that, why are you staying on with us?"

"Mebbies Ah'm sorry for thon wee fella." The tod paused. "Mebbies."

"I don't believe that, you smelly—" Rowf broke off, choking and coughing, and again clawed at his muzzle. Up here, on the higher ground, the mist was so thick that they could scarcely see one another.

"Ah warr'nd ye divven't, ne kiddin'."

"Why don't you talk straight for once?" Rowf, infuriated by his enforced dependence on the tod to guide him through the mist, growled dangerously, and at once the tod became obsequious.

"Give ower, hinny. Divven't gan on se. Taalk strite? Aall reet, thin. *Ye*'ll nivver leave yer marrer, noo will ye? An' ye're th' one that fells th' yows, reet? Noo, there's wor place yonder, an' th' wee fella's got th' wind o' ye— d'ye not hear him yappin' inbye? Howway doon an' give 'm thon chicken."

" *'Pasteurella pestis,'* " said Digby Driver happily. "Ah ha-ha-ha-ha HA! A flea! Ha, ha, ha HAH! A flea! Well, well! Who'd a thought it? Now read on! 'This disease is primarily one of rats and other rodents, but wherever rats live in close proximity to man there is the chance of an outbreak through rodent fleas which transfer their attention to man.' Splendid! And so? Don't miss next week's smashing instalment! 'Transmission may be mechanical, involving simply the contamination of the mouth-parts of the insects, or it may involve regurgitation of infected blood into the puncture. Most infected fleas develop blockages in their digestive tracts as a result of the multiplication of bacteria, so that, when they try to feed, the blood simply flows back into the host, taking with it some of the germs from the gut. Because no food can get past their blockage, the fleas become "hungry" and try to feed more frequently than they otherwise would. The result is that the disease spreads more rapidly.' Excellent! Then there's —er—let's see—murine typhus, 'a less severe form of ordinary typhus fever, carried by rodent fleas—' well, never mind that, we can do better. Find out where the worthy doctor resides, and off we go. A wolf am I, a wolf on mischief bent."

Friday the 12th November

The Under Secretary stared owlishly across his desk, contriving to suggest that not the least unfortunate aspect of the matter was that he himself had had to initiate inquiries which otherwise would not have been pursued at all.

"And what did your Master Boycott say?" he asked.

"Well," replied the Assistant Secretary, "not more than he could help. I began by asking him whether they'd lost any dogs and he said why did we want to know."

" 'I will also ask you one thing, and answer me.' Well?"

"Well, I *could* have had a shot at the baptism of John," said the Assistant Secretary, who liked to show that he could at least nail the Under Secretary's quotations, "but I hesitated a moment on that. I saw no reason specifically to drag the Parly. Sec. into it, so I simply said that we'd seen this press item and what could they tell us about the dogs. Then Boycott said that it hadn't been proved that the dogs were theirs—"

The Under Secretary clicked his tongue and frowned peevishly.

"—so I said, well, at that rate why had Powell gone chasing over to Dunnerdale with the police; and Boycott said that Powell had taken it entirely on himself to do that—no one else had been in the place when the police called. And *then* he said—off his own bat, this was—that in any case there was nothing to prove that the dogs seen at the Dunnerdale shop premises were the ones who'd been killing sheep. He got rather aggressive, as a matter of fact."

The Under Secretary, now that he had learned that the conversation had taken this unproductive turn, allowed his manner to suggest contempt, dislike and patience sorely tried.

"But did he *say*, Michael" (with the air of bringing an undisciplined mind back to the only question that mattered), "did he *say* whether or not they'd lost any dogs?"

"He didn't, and I couldn't get him to."

(A frown, implying, "You must have mishandled him —upset him.") "You didn't mention the Parliamentary Secretary's probable interest?"

"No." (My line didn't work, so it *ipso facto* becomes wrong.) "Maurice, why should one fortify a request for information by mentioning any particular member of the Department, Minister or officer? If the Department want to know, then the Secretary of State wants to know, or so I was always taught."

"Well, it doesn't seem to have worked very well on this occasion, does it?"

At this moment the telephone rang and the Under Secretary picked it up.

"Yes, Jean, put him through. Good morning, Edward. No, not yet. *Have* you? Did Lock say that? *Did* he? All right, I'll come over and join the party. *A bientôt.*" He put the telephone down.

"Well, Michael, more heavy affairs supervene. But we shall have, I think, to press this matter a little further." (That means *I* must. How?) "Someone up there must be found who will say a resounding Yea or Nay about these predatory hounds. Can you please try again, and let me have half a sheet of paper to put to the Parliamentary Secretary this evening?"

He left the room without waiting for an answer.

"Begin then, sisters of the sacred well
That from beneath the seat of Jove doth spring . . ."

"Oh Rowf—Rowf, wait a minute—I know where we are —we've been here before. That first night—the very first night after we escaped. It was misty, like this, only it was almost dark—after we'd left those sheep-dogs who got so angry with us, d'you remember?—and then we changed —changed into wild animals. It was here."

"D'you think we're wild animals, tod?" Rowf sat on the lonely waste of Levers Hause and listened to the invisible streams below. A crow rarked somewhere in the mirk above. It was cold and raw, with cat-ice on the puddles among the rocks. Both dogs' coats were sodden and the tod's brush dragged dark and heavy.

"Wild animals? Whey, mair like two aald cluckers runnin' loose i' th' paddock! Cum away noo sharp! We've a lang lowp yet te Bull Crag." The tod looked impatiently at Rowf, its breath steaming round its head in the still air.

"Plenty of time, surely?" said Rowf. "Let him rest a bit."

"Nar, nar. Yon mist'll be lifted afore mid-day an' some clever boogger on th' fell'll spot us. Th' whole idea o' goin' t'Helvellyn is that nebody sees us goin' an' nebody knaws we've come."

Rowf stood bristling over the tod, which cowered down but made no move to run.

"You're so damned clever, aren't you, you little sneaker? As long as I do all the hard work and get hurt killing your meals—"

"Howway, steady, noo, steady, bonny lad! Ne need te gan on so. Give ower! Listen, d'ye knaw why, though there's nowt but th' three of us, w' still alive, wi' hundreds—mebbies thoosands—o' men that'd be glad te kill us?"

"*I* know." Snitter lifted his leg against a rock and sat down again with the flap of one ear falling rakishly into the cleft in his head. "I've just realized why. They wouldn't dare. I've only to go and drown, or jump under a lorry, and the sky will fall down and all the men will die. Have you ever thought of that, Rowf? That puts us one ahead of them all right."

Rowf made no answer.

"The mouse went down a gully in the floor," went on

ACROSS
COUNTRY

Friday and Saturday
12th and 13th November

LEVERS HAUSE to
DUNMAIL RAISE

HELVELLYN

ULLSCARF

Dunmail
Raise

road

GLARAMARA

Bull
Crag

Wythburn

Greenup

Far Easedale

Langstrath

Stickle
Tarn

BOWFELL

Rossett Gill

LANGDALE PIKES

CRINKLE
CRAGS

PIKE O' BLISCO

Great Langdale

Red
Tarn

Gap

LINGMOOR
FELL

Wrynose Pass

road

Blea Tarn

Little Langdale

CARRS

Wet Side Edge

WETHERLAM

Little Langdale
Tarn

SWIRRAL

Great
How
Crags

The
tod

Levers Hause

BRIM FELL

Levers
Water

looking north

Snitter. "That's why *he's* alive. D'you know where that gully is? *I* do. Sometimes, if I shut my eyes quickly, I can actually catch a sight of his tail. He's made of newspaper, you know—a boy puts him through the hole in the door —I mean the floor—every morning. The whitecoats made the hole—a long, narrow one—with their knives. Right? Well, now then—"

"Aa'll tell th' pair on yez why." The tod's harsh whisper silenced Snitter. "Them menfolk—the' aall mistrust an' cheat each other—aye shovin' an' fightin'. Us tods knaw that. Divven't ye turn thet way, an' mebbies we'll fettle th' booggers yet. Yor ne wild animals—if ye wor, ye'd knaw th' same as Aa knaw, wivoot th' need te be telt. Ah'm not lettin' ye bide here fer a start—yon mist's ganna lift, an' b' then we've te be up on th' Crinkles, up ahight there, where none'll spy ye oot—neether ye nor him, wiv 'is bonny magpie jacket. Noo, ne messin', let's away!"

They set off once more along the Hause. Snitter brought up the rear, singing to himself in a quiet whine.

> *"The whitecoats dyed a mouse bright blue*
> *And stuffed his ears with sneezing glue.*
> *They shone a biscuit in his eye*
> *To see what lay beyond the sky.*
> *The mouse, he knew not what he did,*
> *He blew them up with a saucepan lid.*
> *So they were drowned in blackest milk—"*

"Will you shut up about drowning?" said Rowf. "Singing nonsense—"

"It passes the time." Snitter was apologetic.

"There are other ways to pass the time."

"And to pass these rocks too. But not before I've passed this turd."

Snitter crouched trembling in the cold, and then hurried after the two trotting shapes already disappearing into the mist over Great How Crags.

"But how on earth could they have found that out so quickly?" asked Mr. Powell, handing back the press cutting from the *Orator* which Dr. Boycott had laid on his desk without a word.

"There's very little there, actually, when you come to boil it down," answered Dr. Boycott. "Nothing they couldn't have got from the police at Coniston. In fact, that's almost certainly where they did get it from."

"But I never even told the policeman my name—"

"He may know it anyway—it's a very small point, however they got it. The real awkwardness is that you ever went over to Seathwaite at all."

"How could I avoid it? The policeman said he'd come on purpose—"

"And you instantly dropped what you were doing and went off with him almost as though we'd been expecting him to come. It's a great pity you were in the place so early."

"But damn it, what else could I do? The policeman said the dog had a green collar—"

"You should have said that the station saw no reason to send someone rushing off to Dunnerdale and that you'd report the matter to the Director as soon as he came in."

"I *did* say that—the last bit, anyway—and the policeman wouldn't have it."

"He couldn't have compelled you to go with him, Stephen. Now it looks as though we acknowledged our connection with the matter instantly—which is exactly what you did do, in effect."

"Surely it'd have looked a lot worse, chief, if the police had gone there alone and then brought the dog back here themselves?"

"Not at all. Indeed, one might well say, 'If only they had!' In that case, we could simply have said thank you very much, taken the dog in, destroyed it and burnt the body. It's not an offence to possess a dog that raids a dustbin, and in the absence of any proof that it had been killing sheep, that would have been the end of the whole business and we'd have been home and dry, without even a body that anyone could identify."

"Well, I'm sure I meant to act in the best interests of the station—"

"No doubt. Well, it can't be helped now, Stephen. What

I wanted to say was this. In the light of these recent developments—the Ministry were on the telephone yesterday evening, you know—"

"Oh, were they?"

"They were indeed. I fended them off fairly briskly as far as yesterday goes—but I'll come back to that in a minute. What I want to say is that the Director has now decided that in all the circumstances our best course will be to take the bull by the horns and make a short announcement, simply to the effect that two dogs escaped, and the date when they did so. We can't go on saying we won't say a word—not if Whitehall are determined to poke their noses in and make a fuss. For the life of me I can't see why they should be, though. *We*'re situated in the locality—obviously *we* didn't want locals knowing dogs escaped if we could help it. But a few sheep—and even that poor fellow's death, though they never succeeded in pinning it on the dogs—why ever should Whitehall bother? Those things are surely very local, even if they are unfortunate."

"P'raps some old worry-guts up there's afraid of a local M.P. digging up the Sablon Committee's recommendations and the planning permission and all that."

"What rubbish! Well, now, come and help me with the press statement—I want to make sure I get the details right—and then we really must get on with those monkeys. What's the present position on them?"

"Well, the entire group's been paralysed by lumbar injections of pure OX-Dapro, as you instructed."

"Excellent. Any results yet?"

"Well, the four with flaccid areflexic paraplegia show no response at all, either to stamping on their tails or to pins applied to the lower limbs."

"All right, but be careful how you intensify tests like that. They mustn't die. Monkeys are getting increasingly hard to obtain, you know—apparently there's a world shortage. I wonder why? Anyway, we shall be needing to use these again for something else. What's the score now on the monkey in the cylinder, by the way?"

"Twenty-seven days plus," answered Mr. Powell. "It

seems almost comatose. To tell you the truth, I shan't be sorry when it's time to take it out."

Digby Driver trod out his cigarette on the step, pressed the bell firmly and turned his back on the door while he waited. Certainly the door was mean enough to make the distant, moonlit view of Coniston Water appear a great deal more attractive, even to him. Just as he was about to ring again, the hall beyond the undulant glass panels became lit, the door was partially opened and he found himself looking into the shadow-obscured face of an elderly, grey-haired man standing defensively behind it.

"Dr. Goodner?"

"I am, yes." Both the voice and the look were hesitant, nervous. Digby Driver put one foot on the door-sill and noticed the other noticing him do so.

"I'm a pressman. May I talk to you for a minute, please?"

"We don't— we don't talk vith the press unless it is happening vith an official appointment at the station."

"Dr. Goodner, believe me, I've only got your best interests at heart, and I won't take up ten minutes of your time—not five. You'd do much better to see me now, privately and entirely off the record. You would, I assure you. Want me to tell you why?"

Dr. Goodner hesitated a moment longer, looking down at the door-mat. Then he shrugged his shoulders, let go of the door, turned his back, led the way into a small, unheated drawing-room, which was obviously not the room he had been sitting in, closed its door behind Digby Driver as he entered, and stood looking at him without a word.

Driver, standing by the sofa, opened the folder he was carrying, took out a typed sheet of paper and began looking at it intently.

"What is it you want?"

Driver looked up. "I want the answer to just one question, Dr. Goodner, and I give you my word that I shan't say where that answer came from. What is the special work you are doing in your locked laboratory at Lawson Park?"

Dr. Goodner deliberately opened the drawing-room door and was half-way across the narrow hall before Driver could speak again, this time in sharper tones, which the authorities of his former university would have recognized at once.

"You'd better look at this sheet of paper, Dr. Goodner—Dr. Geutner, I should say, Flat 4, Tillierstrasse 9043. Come on, you have a good look at it before you go rushing off to call the bouncer."

Dr. Goodner returned and took in one hand the paper which Driver handed to him. As Driver let go of it, the upper end began to tremble. Dr. Goodner put on his spectacles and held it horizontally beneath the ill-shaded central bulb.

"What is this that you show me?"

Driver paused a moment. Then he said quietly, "You can see what it is. It's a biographical sketch—or the notes for one. My newspaper's planning a series, to be published shortly, on naturalized ex-enemy scientists and doctors working in this country. An article based on those particular notes is due to appear in two weeks' time."

Dr. Goodner shrugged.

"These things that have happened are all finished very long time ago. I am not a war criminal."

"You won't be far short of one in the public mind, Dr. Geutner of München, when this gets published. We're in touch with a man who remembers your visit to Buchenwald early in 1945—"

"I haff done nothing there. I go in, I go avay again—"

"Very likely, but you went. And the work for the Wehrmacht on disease warfare potential? Oh, and Trudi —I forgot her. Come on, Dr. Geutner. Have a good think about it."

Dr. Goodner clenched one hand by his side, but said nothing.

"Now listen, that article *won't* be published, now or at any future time, I promise you—certainly not by my paper, and not by any other British paper that I know of —*provided* you simply answer yes or no truthfully to one question and then forget that you ever did. After that, I'm gone for good and I've never been here. Easy, isn't it?

Now, here's the question. From last month up to the present, has the work you've been doing in your locked laboratory been research into bubonic plague?"

After a short pause, Dr. Goodner shrugged his shoulders and replied, "Yes."

"Thank you. I know I said one question, but there's just one more related one, I'm afraid, and then I'm gone. Were there, last month, infected fleas in that laboratory capable of transmitting plague?"

This time there was a longer pause. Dr. Goodner was looking down at the empty fireplace with one open hand laid flat on top of the glazed, putty-coloured bricks of the cheap mantelpiece. When at length he looked up, his spectacles flashed in the cold light. But Digby Driver was before him.

"Don't bother to speak. If the answer's yes just nod." By this time he had reached the door and turned, Dr. Goodner was once more looking at the fireplace. He nodded almost imperceptibly and Digby Driver let himself out into the peaceful night.

Saturday the 13th November

"It's a bad world for animals," said Rowf grimly.

"Does that include the caterpillars you ate?"

"It includes you."

"I'm the brainy zany with the drainy crany. It smells like that, anyway."

"Let me lick the mud out. Keep still."

"Ow—look out! I say, what would you call this— brain-washing?"

"All right, I've finished. It's clean enough now."

"Fine—I feel much cleverer, too. You could say you've cleared my mind. I'll walk on my hind legs if you like. It used to make Annie Mossity as cross as two sticks, only she never dared to say so. One day I pretended to slip and clawed at her stockings. Ho ho!"

"Didn't do you any good, did it? Anyway, why *are* you so cheerful? You've got no reason that I can see."

"It's the mouse, actually. When the moon shines like this, he sings songs inside my head; like Kiff, you know. Kiff's all right. He's up on that cloud of his."

"Maybe; but I can't hear your mouse."

"That's only because you're hungry. Didn't you know hunger mays yeff?"

"What?"

Snitter made no reply.

"What did you say?"

Snitter jumped up and barked in his ear. "I said, didn't you know hunger makes you DEAF?"

Rowf snapped at him and he ran, yelping.

"Haald yer whisht!" The tod, padding ahead up the steeply falling beck, looked round angrily.

The truth was that Rowf, like everyone with an accomplishment admired or relied upon by those about him, was wondering how long he would be able to keep it up and afraid that he might already be finished. For the past thirty hours they had had a hard time. On the previous day, urged on relentlessly by the tod, who seemed tireless compared even with the hulking Rowf, they had travelled the length of the Crinkle Crags along their eastern side, skirted Bow Fell, sneaking through the top of Rossett Gill in thinner but still persistent mist (within earshot of a burly young man whose girl was begging him to turn back), passed below Angle Tarn, trotted down the upper part of Langstrath Beck and by evening had reached the tod's promised refuge among the rocks of Bull Crag. Though not a true earth, it was spacious enough and, with no more than a light east wind blowing, reasonably warm with three bodies crowded into it. But this, as it turned out, was cold comfort. Rowf, already tired, and still plagued by the pad which he had cut on Harter Fell, failed again and again to pull down the marked-out sheep until at last, flinging himself exhausted and cursing on the ground in the moonlit solitude, he allowed Snitter to persuade him to give up for the night. His temper was nothing improved by the marked manner in which the tod refrained from comment and began hunting among the heather for beetles and anything else that might be edible. Both dogs, swallowing their pride, copied him and Rowf, when he nosed out two hairy, chestnut-striped, three-inch caterpillars of the fox moth, snapped them up without hesitation.

Next morning Snitter woke to find Rowf already vanished into the wet, still mist. As he and the tod were about to set out on the scent—plain enough on the damp ground—they met him returning, bloody-mouthed, swollen with his kill but lamer than ever. Nearly an hour before, in the dark before dawn, he had pulled down his quarry alone, lying in ambush under a crag and leaping straight at a yow's throat as she wandered too close. The battering he had suffered from her, fresh and unfatigued by the usual pursuit, had winded and hurt him until only his rage at the previous night's failure had given him the determination to hold on. After the kill he had ripped off and gorged the flesh of an entire flank, lain for a time belching and licking his paws; and so come back to his friends. The mercurial Snitter danced and gambolled about him as they all three returned to the body. The tod, however, said nothing beyond a surly, "Yer not se femmer t'day, then?"

"Tod," said Snitter sharply, "that remark's in very poor smell. You mean he was no good yesterday, and you've no business to say it. I'll set the flies on you, I will—huge ones—men riding on them—oh, whatever am I talking about?—"

"Nivver said nowt aboot yisterday. Said he were none se femmer t'day."

Nevertheless, the tod returned to gnawing its bloody share without further speech. A rebuke from Snitter was so unusual that perhaps even its ladrone, hit-and-run mind felt something akin to abashment.

Later in the day Snitter, unaided, succeeded in catching a lean, wandering rat and ate it alone, without telling. The feat raised his spirits as June the mayfly and when they came to set out in the dusk he was in tearing form. Throughout the four miles over Greenup and down to Dunmail Raise he was irrepressible, coming and going like a scent on the breeze and glittering like shards of broken looking-glass.

The sound of car engines and the sight of headlights moving on the broad road south of Thirlmere excited him with memories.

"I remember those lights at night, Rowf! And the cars growl, you can hear them—that's why young dogs often rush out and try to chase them. Waste of time; they never take any notice. The lights are pieces of old moons, you know."

"What d'you mean?" asked Rowf, interested in spite of himself to watch the long beams approaching, dazzling into the eyes for a second and humming away again into the moonlit dimness.

"Well, once the moon gets to be full somebody—some man or other—goes up every day and slices bits off one side—you've noticed?—until there isn't any more, and then after a bit a new one grows. Men do that with all sorts of things, actually—rose-bushes, for instance; my master used to cut them almost down to the ground in winter, and then they grew again. Come to that, I dare say it was something of the kind the whitecoats were up to with me. Perhaps I'll grow a new Snitter one day, you never know. Anyway, by the time it gets to be full the moon's all pitted and rifted with cracks and holes—to make it easier to break bits off, obviously. Well, my dam told me that moons are actually huge—enormous—only they don't look it because they're so high in the sky. The man who slices the bits off brings them down here, and then they're used for making those lights on the cars. Clever, isn't it?"

"Do they last long—when they're lights, I mean?"

"Not very long—only about a night, I should think, because you hardly ever see them shining by day. They must keep changing them. You can tell they're quite different from the still sort of lights men make indoors by lifting up their hands. Sn'ff! Sn'ff! How that car smell takes me back, too! It's a cheerful, natural sort of smell, isn't it?—not like these foul rocks. Let's stay here and rest a bit, tod."

"Nay, git ower, ye gowk. Bide aboot o' th' road an' ye'll be gud an' deed."

Snitter scuttled across in an interval of darkness, joined the tod in the bed of Birkside Gill and looked up at the long Helvellyn ridge fading into distance and moonlight above them.

"O for the wings of a sheep!" sighed Snitter, as they began once more to follow the inexorable tod up the gill's pools and cascades towards Willie Wife Moor.

"Wings of a *sheep,* Snitter?"

"Yes—they had them once, you know. What happened was that one flew up into the sky, so naturally they all followed. Then they took off their wings and began feeding and as the sun moved on across the sky they went with it, to keep warm. Well, towards evening a wind got up and blew all their wings away from the place where they'd left them. They never got them back—you can see them all up there, blowing along in the blue to this day."

"But how did the sheep get back to the ground?"

"Why, a long way off the sky curves down and touches the land—you can see it does. They had to walk round the long way—took them ages."

"Well, I never knew that. You are a clever little chap, Snitter. He's clever, isn't he, tod?"

"Ay, clever as th' north end of a sooth-boond jackass." The tod lay down. "Ye kin bide a while noo, lad. It's a canny bit run yit an' Aa haven't the list t' do it."

When at length they had passed Nethermost Pike, reached the western end of Striding Edge and were looking down the almost sheer six hundred feet to Red Tarn shining smooth in the moonlight, Rowf curled his lip and swore.

"My teeth in your neck, tod, you never told me we'd be living on the edge of one of these blasted drowning-tanks! And no men, you said—why, the whole place smells of men like a rubbish-tip—tobacco, old bread— what are those other smells, Snitter—"

"Oo—potato crisps, women, chocolate, ice-cream squishy squish. That was another of Kiff's songs. O mutton-bones, chicken and cheese, they're things that are

Greenup and Eagle Crag

certain to please, but what *I* like the most is a jolly lamp-post—' "

"Shut up! Tod, scores of men must come here—"

"Why ay, but not in winter an' not where yor gannin'."

"I'm not going down to that tank," said Rowf.

"Nay, divven't fash yersel', hinny." The tod seemed almost conciliatory.

Snitter, sitting back on the stones, raised his muzzle to the cloudy, sailing moon. With as little reason and almost as much delight as the migrant blackcap in May, which sings on the outskirts of an English copse, heedless that in six months' time some hirsute swine in Italy or Cyprus, with call-pipe and quicklime, will murder it for some other swine in Paris to eat in aspic, Snitter gave tongue in the moonlight.

> *"O friendly moon,*
> *As bright as bone,*
> *Up in the sky*
> *You rot alone.*
> *The cracks and marks*
> *That I can see*
> *Are no great mys—*
> *Tery to me.*
> *It's plain to my*
> *Observant snout,*
> *Maggots go in*
> *And flies come out!*
>
> *"Now if a fly,*
> *On pleasure bent,*
> *Sat down on my*
> *Warm excrement,*
> *I wouldn't mind*
> *One little bit.*
> *I'm really kind—"*

"Oh, come on, Snitter!" said Rowf. "What's the use of sitting there, singing rubbish?"

"A lot," answered Snitter. "When I sing, people in the sky throw bits down to me. Or Kiff does, or someone. You don't believe me, do you? Look!"

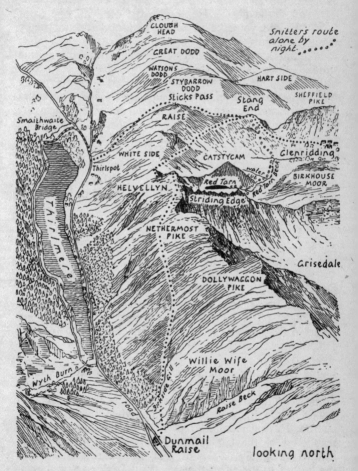

Saturday, 13th November
to
Saturday, 20th November

ON THE HELVELLYN RANGE

Snitter's route alone by night.......

CLOUGH HEAD

GREAT DODD

WATSON'S DODD

STYBARROW DODD

Sticks Pass

HART SIDE

SHEFFIELD PIKE

Stang End

RAISE

Smaithwaite Bridge

WHITE SIDE

Thirlspot

CATSTYCAM

Glenridding

BIRKHOUSE MOOR

HELVELLYN

Red Tarn

water

Red Tarn Beck

Striding Edge

Thirlmere

NETHERMOST PIKE

Grisedale

DOLLYWAGGON PIKE

Willie Wife Moor

Wyth Burn

road

Dockrey Gill

Raise Beck

Dunmail Raise

looking north

He pattered away a few yards among the rocks and a moment later they could hear and smell him routing out and munching the damp remains of an abandoned packet of crisps. He ran back to them with the plastic bag stuck over his muzzle.

"Woff floffle floof." He snudged it off with one front paw. "Would you like it, tod? I'm afraid it's not really what it was just now."

Without a word the tod set off northward along the summit, towards Low Man.

Half an hour later they had descended a thousand feet and come to the ruined flue below the eastern slopes of Raise—an ugly, enseared landscape, riven with the scars of old industry—and here, in a kind of little cave formed by part of the ruin, they went to ground and dozed restlessly for two or three hungry hours. At moonset the tod roused them and led them a mile down the beck to the hamlet of Glenridding where, under its shrewd guidance, they foraged among the dustbins for what little they could get.

"Dustbins is as dangerous as owt else—thet's why ye were nigh booggered i' Doonerd'l: ye took ne heed. Ye've to push th' lid off, grab whit ye can an' away while they're still thinkin' what wez yon. Nivver hang aboot."

They returned to their lair in the darkness before dawn, half-filled and half-poisoned, Rowf stopping repeatedly to excrete a foul fluid over the stones along the beck. Snitter's high spirits had evaporated and he felt tired out. Once in the chilly hole, he curled up beside the tod and fell asleep at once.

Digby Driver, having made a telephone call to Mr. Simpson in London and dictated his second article to the *Orator,* returned into Dunnerdale. He certainly did not intend to be in or near Coniston when the article appeared. Having reconnoitred from the bar of the Traveller's Rest to the bar of the Newfield, he proceeded to follow the kindly advice of Jack Longmire (landlord of the latter) to the effect that Mr. Bob Taylor knew a great deal about the whole valley, being up and down Duddon at nearly all times of year, fishing. He was lucky enough to find Bob in, tying trout flies at a table by the fire.

"Ye-es, I'm fairly sure now that I must have seen one of those dogs crossing the Duddon on the very morning it escaped from Miss Dawson's," said Bob, pouring sherry for Digby Driver and himself. "At least, if it wasn't, I'm sure I don't know what a strange fox terrier was doing swimming the Duddon on its own in quite a lonely spot. Wasn't it a black-and-white fox terrier that Miss Dawson caught in her yard?"

"So I believe," said Driver. "So if you're right, that's the dog that's been killing sheep in the hills east of the Duddon, and it returned there as soon as it escaped. But why hasn't anyone seen it up there? Where's it hiding, d'you think?"

"Hard to say, really," replied Bob reflectively.

"Are there any lonely barns or sheds up that way?"

"None at all," said Bob, deftly concluding the manufacture of a black gnat with two fragments of a starling's feather. "All the same, it would be very unlikely to be living in the open, I'd think, for two reasons. One's simply the time of year and the weather; and the other is that if it were, someone—Dennis Williamson or somebody—would have seen it up there by now."

"So?"

"So it must have found some sort of underground refuge."

"Like?"

"We-ell, let's think; perhaps an old shaft or slate working of some kind; or the old coppermines—somewhere like that."

"What are the actual likeliest places, d'you know?"

"I think it's hardly possible to be comprehensive about that," replied Bob, who in his time had been first a schoolmaster and then a town planner in Whitehall, and was accustomed to answer questions with precision. "But if it were anything to do with me, which thank goodness it isn't, I'd be inclined to have a look at the old Seathwaite coppermine shaft, up beyond Seathwaite Tarn, and then, perhaps, over the top, at the area of the quarries south of the summit of Coniston Old Man; yes, and the Paddy End mining area too."

"Where are they, exactly?"

Digby Driver spread out his map and Bob showed him. Not long afterwards, Driver refused Mrs. Taylor's hospitable offer of luncheon and took his leave.

He returned up the Duddon valley, left his car in the line near Long House, took a torch with him and set out for Seathwaite Tarn. Having rounded the tarn along the north shore, he reached and entered the coppermine shaft; and here he smoked a cigarette, throwing down the empty packet as deftly as any Islington yob at the Angel. Like Dennis before him, he drew blank, but did not fail, nevertheless, to observe the gnawed bones, excreta and other evidence of relatively recent canine occupation. He was too ignorant to be able to tell whether the occupants had left some time ago or whether they had merely gone out and might be returning.

"H'm," mused Digby Driver thoughtfully. "What's to be done now, I wonder? This mustn't leak out. No, no. It would never do, would it, if that dog—if those dogs— were to be caught too soon? Never, never. They're lucky to have me, they are indeed."

Monday the 15th November

"Good *God!*" said Dr. Boycott, aghast.

He sat staring at the front page of the *Orator* with a kind of stupefaction. Mr. Powell, behind his shoulder, also stared, lips compressed and eyes moving from side to side as he read.

ARE RUNAWAY DOGS
CARRYING BUBONIC PLAGUE?
(From Digby Driver, the Orator's Man-on-the-Spot)
The tranquil inhabitants of Lakeland, England's celebrated rural area of natural beauty, got a shock yesterday. The reason? It has

now at last been revealed that, contrary to the bureaucratic silence hitherto preserved by Whitehall's Animal Research Station at Lawson Park, near Coniston, the mystery dogs who for some days past have been playing cops-and-robbers among the sheep and hens of local farmers, are in fact escapees from the Station's experimental pens. An official statement, issued two days ago by Animal Research, typically concealing as much as it informs the public, now says that on a date last month two dogs escaped. That tells little enough. But would they have told the public *that* much without the *Orator?* There are, therefore, THREE dogs involved, the third being—yes, you've guessed it! The public's watchdog, the *London Orator*, Britain's highest-selling daily paper.

Cagey

What the statement did NOT say was that the dogs are identical with those who have been killing sheep in the Lake District and were discovered by Dunnerdale shopkeeper Phyllis Dawson red-handed in a daring raid on her premises, as reported in these pages. Yet this is virtually certain. What kind of time is this to be cagey, when public safety is at stake? Yet this is what the scientists of Lawson Park, who are paid with the taxpayer's money, are doing. To them the *Orator* says, "Wake up, gentlemen, among your teacups and clanking inventions. If not, we shall have to wake you up, in the public interest."

Sinister

Yet a more sinister reason, as it seems, looms in the background to the story. The *Orator* is now able to purvey to its readers the exclusive information that at the time of the dogs' escape, when, as is now known, they were alone and at large in the Station's laboratories for long hours on the "night of the crime," investigations were taking place in those very laboratories into bubonic PLAGUE. This terrible killer-disease, which once decimated the London of merry monarch Charles II three hundred years ago, has now been unknown in this country for many years past, being carried by flea-parasites of the common rat.

Did They?

Could the escapee dogs, before their getaway, have met up with the deadly infected fleas? We know that dogs like rats, and fleas like dogs. But does the British public like secrets, deception and silence? That is why the *Orator* says today, to the men of Lawson Park, "Open your doors, gentlemen, open your minds and learn to TRUST THE PEOPLE."

"Coo-er!" said Mr. Powell. "And what exactly does A do now, I wonder?"

"I don't know what the Director will do," replied Dr. Boycott, "but I know what I'd do in his place. I'd get Whitehall to issue a categorical statement immediately that the dogs couldn't possibly have had any contact."

"And what *about* the dogs? Do we have to go out and try to catch them now?"

"If it was me, I'd take instructions from Whitehall on that. This is one situation where Whitehall might be some help to us. The dogs'll *have* to be shot now, obviously—not just caught, but shot dead, and the quicker the better. What I want to know is, how did the *Orator* man get hold of all this?"

"Goodner, d'you suppose?" asked Mr. Powell.

"Goodner's always been as canny as they come. A man of his age and experience—if he was prone to indiscretion he'd have fallen down a long time before now. I dare say discretion was one of the assets he'd already shown he possessed before he got the job. Not just anybody gets put on germ warfare, you know. There's too much at stake."

Mr. Powell picked up the *Orator* and re-read it with a demure travel of regard, frowning the while. He was at a cold scent, but it was certainly rank; and sure enough, after another half-minute, Dr. Boycott cried upon it.

"Have *you* said anything to anyone?" asked Dr. Boycott suddenly and sharply.

Mr. Powell started. "Me? No, not a thing, chief, straight up."

"You're absolutely certain? Not to *anyone?* How about that fellow you said gave you a lift back from Dunnerdale?"

"I can't remember what we talked about. Nothing that's security, that's for sure."

"But he couldn't help knowing you were from here and that you'd gone over to Dunnerdale after the dogs. Did he ask you any questions?"

"I said something about the dogs, I believe—nothing much—but certainly nothing about Goodner's work or bubonic plague. Well, I couldn't, could I? I don't *know* anything. I didn't even know he was *doing* plague, come to that."

"Well, all right. It's a matter for the Director now. Save it for the judge, as the Americans say. It's possible that nothing more will come of it. Dogs can't contract bubonic plague, you know. If they could, and those dogs had had any contact, they'd be dead by now. Presumably we've only got to say so and the whole thing'll die down. But all the same, the quicker they're shot the better."

"You know, chief," said Mr. Powell, "something tells me that that press release of ours may not have been terribly fortunately timed."

Tuesday the 16th November

"A major disaster," said the Under Secretary, "I would imagine, though it's early to tell as yet. It could hardly have come at a worse time, with criticism running so high over public expenditure to implement the Sablon Committee recommendations."

The Assistant Secretary stood gazing out of the window. It was T. S. Eliot's violet hour, when the eyes turn upward from the desk, and the street below was full of clerks, typists and executive officers hurrying to St. James's Park underground and the buses of Victoria Street. The starlings had already come in and, after their usual cackling and squabbling, more or less settled down along the cornices. There had been a kestrel over the park that afternoon. Did the kestrels ever take starlings, he wondered. Hardly; but they probably took sparrows. It was to be hoped so, for there was something disappointing and undignified about the idea of their coming into London merely to pick up rubbish. Sate itself in a celestial bed and prey on garbage. Come to think of it, Shakespeare must have seen them taking garbage. Then that line might be a kind of unconscious extension of the iterative image of hawking in *Hamlet*. "When the wind is southerly—"

"If you've had time to reflect, could I have the benefit of your views, Michael?"

(Could you?)

"Well, I think it might be extremely awkward all round, Maurice, if the papers are intent on making a meal of this plague business."

"Let us see whether our respective minds are in accord. Why do you?"

"Well, we can't deny that the dogs escaped and that initially the station kept quiet about them. We can't deny that the station have got a bloke on germ warfare and that *inter alia* he's working on bubonic plague. And apparently we can't deny that the dogs, while escaping, may have gone somewhere near where that work's being done."

"I agree. But now, tell me two things. *Could* the dogs in fact have had any contact?"

"Well, almost certainly not. Boycott says it's out of the question."

"And *is* it?"

"I honestly can't tell, Maurice, unless I were to go up there myself and have a look round. But apparently the plague lab's kept locked and it can be proved that it was locked that night."

"But fleas—cracks—doors—"

"Precisely. Of course the fleas weren't loose, but how can anyone swear for certain—how can the Secretary of State stand up in the House and say that *one* might not have been?"

"And secondly, can dogs in fact carry bubonic plague?"

"Well, I'm advised not. But it's like all this advice you get from technical officers, you know. When you get right down to it and lean on them, they begin qualifying. 'Well, they conceivably could, but it's very unlikely.' 'We can't positively say it could never happen in any circumstances,' and so on."

"So for all practical purposes there's nothing to worry about, but nevertheless it's gone sour on us to the extent of providing nuisance value to a hostile and malicious press?"

"That's the way I see it."

"Oh, dear." The Under Secretary drew meditatively on his blotting-pad. "Gone to the demnition bow-wows."

"I don't think even Mr. Mantolini could give us much help in this case."

"Well, you may perhaps have to go up there, depending on how things develop."

(At twelve hours' notice, I bet, in the event.)

"I'll be seeing the Parliamentary Secretary about it, though I'm not sure when—probably Friday. Perhaps you'd better come along too, Michael. I'm afraid it may be going to be difficult to convince him that all this couldn't have been avoided. How close is our liaison with Lawson Park? Shouldn't we have been told at once about these dogs having escaped?"

"Hardly. They have a great many projects and experiments up there and the dogs weren't particularly important until this press attack started."

"Yes, I know, I *know,* Michael" (O God, here we go again!), "but you must try to see things from a *Minister's* point of view. I can't help feeling that very often you seem unable to appreciate—oh well, never mind." (I do mind, damn you, and why don't you either say something I can answer or else keep quiet?) "You see, what's really so *very* unfortunate is this press release that the station appear to have put out unilaterally, without reference to us. They issue a statement admitting that two dogs escaped, as though there were now nothing more to be said, and in the event this virtually coincides with a piece in the *Orator* accusing them of trying to keep quiet about the plague work. It looks bad."

"I know. It's a pity they did that."

"But *should* they have, Michael? Shouldn't there have been an agreed drill under which they referred their proposed statement to you before releasing it?"

"I've repeatedly tried to arrange one, but as you know, these chaps always put up a great deal of resistance to anything that suggests to them that they're being controlled and restricted by Whitehall."

"H'm. No doubt they do." (And you're thinking that I ought to have been able to push them off it if I had any ability.) "Well, let us trust that the hope is not drunk wherein we dress ourselves—"

"Well, I dare do all that may become a man." The Assistant Secretary's goat was not altogether ungot.

"I'm sure you do, Michael. And now, good night. Perhaps you wouldn't mind asking James to look in for a moment, would you?"

(What's your P.A. for, you sod?)

> *"Together both, ere the high lawns appeared*
> *Under the opening eye-lids of the morn,*
> *We drove afield . . ."*

Wednesday the 17th November

Rowf, raising his muzzle cautiously above the bracken, had time to glimpse nothing more than the distant bar of moonlight twinkling and gleaming across Ullswater before ducking quickly down again at the sound of men's voices a good deal closer than he cared for. He glanced at the tod, crouched small, tense and watchful among the fronds, and at Snitter gnawing on a stick to contain his hunger and wagging his head like some crazy, ill-made scarecrow in a high wind.

It was now the fourth night since they had come to the Helvellyn range. They had killed two sheep, but with greater difficulty than before, and tonight Rowf had refused to attempt another, insisting instead on a farmyard raid. The tod had demurred, pointing out that the weather was too fine, still and clear for hunting round human dwellings, but in the face of Rowf's angry impatience had finally given in. To Snitter it was plain that the tod was unable to make head or tail of Rowf's total lack of its own natural bent for coldly weighing one consideration against another and then acting to the best advantage. At the time when it had first joined them, it had never known a creature like Rowf and accordingly had not reckoned with his ways, but now it had come to distrust and fear his impulsive nature and above all his impetuous anger, which it could not understand. Snitter hoped that it was not beginning to regret the bargain it had struck with them. He would have liked to ask it, and to try to smooth things over, but discussion was not the tod's strong point.

The wind was carrying plainly the smell of poultry from the henhouse in the farmyard. Rowf lifted his off-side front paw and tried his weight on it. It was as tender as ever and, cursing, he lay down again. His hunger moved sluggishly in his belly, dulling his spirit as drifting clouds obscure the sun.

His companions in desperation, he thought the one, whose very talk he could barely understand, more crafty and self-interested than any cat, whom he now knew he hated for its sly, calculating cunning; who would desert them both without the least compunction whenever it might decide that it would suit it to do so; the other his friend, the only creature in the world who cared a fly for him, but who seemed to grow more addle-pated and more of a liability with every precarious day they survived. It was for these that he had to go on, night after night, mustering his diminishing strength for yet another plunging, battering encounter, using up what little was left of his courage and endurance, until the time when there would be none left—whereupon the tod would depart and Snitter and himself would either starve or be cornered and killed. No, he thought, the tod had been right enough; he was no wild animal, nor, after all, had it proved possible for him to become one. Though he might never have had a master, yet by his nature he needed the friendship of other creatures as the tod did not.

The reek of the tod excited him, in his hunger, to a slavering rage. Why couldn't I have died in the tank? thought Rowf. That was what my pack leaders wanted: at least, I suppose they did; and I let them down. Now I'm neither a decent dog nor a thorough-going thief like the tod. Oh, blast this leg! If it goes on hurting like this I shan't even be up to breaking into a hen-roost. The two of us could try to eat this damned tod, I suppose, come to that. Then there's cats. Cats run loose in farmyards.

You could eat à cat at a pinch. I wonder whether I could kill one and get it out before the place came round our ears?

He turned again to Snitter. "Are you ready, Snitter?"

"Oh, yes," answered Snitter, with a grisly pretence of jaunty carelessness, "but why not wait a bit? There's a flood of sleep coming to cover the houses, you know. Blue and deep—a deep sleep. I'm calling it, actually. You see—" He stopped.

"What do you mean? You mean you can—"

"Call it? Yes, I call it the sea. The tod told me. A deep-blue sleep."

Rowf, a trifle light-headed in his emptiness, remembered the man whom Snitter had killed and the strange power which, according to his account, had seemed to come pouring from his head.

"I say, Snitter?"

"Yes?"

"Can you *really* make things happen—you said you could—you know, alter things and turn them all upside-down? You can't really, can you? That man just died, didn't he? It was only one of your queer turns that made you think you killed him?"

"I don't know, Rowf. Sometimes I feel sure that that's really what I did without meaning to, and then the feeling disappears, so that I—well, I can't even remember what it felt like to feel like that. It's muddling."

The wretched dog seemed upset. Rowf gave him a playful nip.

"Come on now, Snitter, I didn't mean it seriously—it was only a joke. But if you really can do these things, why don't you—well, why don't you make all the men afraid of us, for instance? Ho, yes, that's the idea!" Rowf paused to relish it, then began to elaborate. "Make them all run away—make them call their dogs off, open their gates and —and send us home carrying a nice, warm chicken? Now that really would be something! Couldn't you do that for us, Snitter, hey?"

Snitter raised his split head and licked his friend's nose. "I'll try, Rowf; but I don't really know whether I could manage all that."

"Neither do I, old chap. I only wish you could."

"You mustn't think I—oh, Rowf, you were only making fun of me!"

"No, no, of course I wasn't! I know you could do all that quite easily if you wanted to—it's just that tonight's not convenient—that's it, isn't it?"

"Bidin' there yammerin' aboot nowt—"

"Oh, shut up, tod! Let us alone!"

"Ay, Ah will thet. Ah's off t'see if w' can bash our way into th' henhoose. Nay, marrer, let me do't mesel'. Ye'll owny clitter an' clatter till th' farmer comes, an' that'll mean another neet wi' ne meat, an' mebbies worse."

Before Rowf could reply the tod had melted away with its usual silence. A few moments later they caught sight for an instant of its slim, dark shape slinking across a patch of moonlight where the lonnin led into the farmyard.

"Hush, Snitter," said Rowf quickly, "lie down again!" For behind the thin shelter of the bracken patch Snitter had stood up and was capering slowly from paw to paw, giving low whines and wagging his stumpy tail.

"Well, Rowf, I was only doing my best to—you know, you said to make the men give us—this is what they call a tincantation—but I don't really know quite how to go about it—"

"It was a *joke,* Snitter, for goodness' sake! Now pull yourself together—we're going to risk our lives in a minute, and that's real—it's not a game. Even you can tell the difference if you try. You're hungry—that's real. And in there are hens, and *they*'re real, and a man, possibly with a gun, and *he*'s real. Got it?"

"Yes, Rowf."

"Well, don't forget it."

There was a rustle in the fern and the tod reappeared. Its jaws were faintly glistening, yellow and viscous, and there was a smooth smell, at once creamy and lightly savoury, that made both ravenous dogs slobber. Rowf licked at its mask.

"What's that you smell of?"

"Chucky-eggs, hinny. Th' wez a layaway nest i' th' nettles roond th' back. Th' aald clucker wez away an' aall.

Aa's taken th' lot an' nipped ootbye sharp as a flash. Ye canna gan in there t'neet—it'd be nowt but th' Dark fer th' bowth o' yuz. There's two chaps bletherin' away i' th' hemmel an' a woman forbye. If th' hens or th' dergs wez te kick up a row they'd be strite doon on ye, and if ye wor in th' henhoose they'd hev ye afore ye could torn roond. Mebbies they'd have a gun an' that'd be yer lot. Howway on oot of it noo! We'll try elsewhere."

The tod's air of artful self-possession, its smell, the smell of the eggs, his own fume of hunger—Rowf felt his teeth on edge to burst his dripping mouth.

"You crawling, sneaking little rat! You go in there and eat your head off and then you come back and tell us we're not to! You stinking, underground—"

He leapt for the sharp-nosed, grinning mask, but in the instant that his weight fell on the patch of long grass from which it had been protruding, it was no longer there. Heedless now of how much noise he made, he thrust here and there through the undergrowth, drew blank and came pushing his way back to Snitter, who had not moved.

"Goes in there, stuffs itself full of eggs and then, oh yes! it's ready to go home, the dirty little—"

"He didn't say that, Rowf. You're even more light-headed than I am. All he said—"

"I tell you, I'm finished with it—and for good this time. It's just a filthy scrounger. We don't need it to help us to stay alive—we never did. It just hangs about and eats what we kill—"

"That's not true, Rowf. He's done as much for himself as us all along—both with sheep and hen-roosts. He can't help what he is. It's not his fault that only one of the three of us has the weight to pull down a yow. I admire him—I like him—"

"And I *don't!* The mere smell of it drives me as mad as you! If ever it shows up again I'll chew it to bits—"

"It's only your hunger—"

"Yes, and now I'm going to do something about that, too. Come on!"

"But Rowf, the tod warned us—"

"I don't care what the damned tod said. We're going to eat."

Rowf led the way down the bank into the lonnin and squeezed under the farmyard gate. Snitter followed. The cowshed, at right angles to the farmhouse, flanked one side of the yard, and through its open door came electric light and the sounds of human voices, clinking cans and the soft thudding and stamping of cattle in their stalls. Evidently milking was getting finished late.

"They're terribly near, Rowf—"

"They're busy—they won't hear us—"

"There's sure to be a dog—"

"And *I'm* a dog, too—"

From the further end of the farmyard they could hear a faint pecking and rustling, followed by the quiet, slow clucking ("rer-er'ck, t'ck t'ck") of a drowsy hen awake among her roosting sisters. The sound drew Rowf entranced. With claws clicking on the tarred surface, he trotted briskly through the cowpats, down the length of the yard and so up to the hens' wire enclosure. Here he stopped, sniffing the dark air and listening to the noises from inside the henhouse, which rode, laden, above his rapacity like Noah's ark above the gulping flood.

Snitter ran up behind him, whispering urgently.

"We can't do it, Rowf! You can't smash your way into that! The tod might have crept in through a crack, thrown a couple of hens down and we could have grabbed them and run; but that's all finished now. This farmyard's a fearful dead-end, too; an absolute trap. For goodness' sake let's get out quick and try somewhere else!"

"No fear! There's a started board there—see it? I'll shove it inwards and you can squeeze through and do the job better than ever that damned tod could. Only be quick! Ready? Right!"

Rowf plunged up the wooden steps and hurled his weight against the sprung board beside the trap-door. It levered stiffly inwards and at once Snitter, as he had been told, pushed his way inside. Instantly a fearful racket broke out around him—clucking, squawking, clattering, flapping here and there and the resonant clanging of wiry perches in close, odorous darkness. He plunged forward at random, came upon a hen and bit it through the neck, pushed it out of the gap and heard it thump, jerking and twitching, on the ground.

"I can't—can't hold the board open any longer," gasped Rowf in the dark. "Come on out quick or you'll be stuck inside."

Snitter pushed his head and shoulders under the splintered end of the board. It dug into his back, knifing downwards painfully. He pushed harder. The board gave and he stumbled forward between Rowf's front paws, knocked him off balance and fell with him to the ground beside the hot, pulsating body of the hen. Picking himself up, he grabbed the body by the neck as the tod had taught him and began to run with it. At that moment the farmyard was suddenly flooded with light. He dropped the hen and pulled up, terrified and confused.

He looked about him. Along the side of the farmyard opposite to the cowshed, a high stone wall extended down to the gate, without even a tree-trunk to break its line and never so much as a rubbish-bin or old crate left against it. The farmhouse windows were shut; so was the door. They were in an enclosed, walled space, lit by electric bulbs, from which the only ways out were through the farmhouse, the cowshed and the gate leading into the lonnin. As he realized this, two men, followed by a dog, came striding into the light from the shadow outside the cowshed door. One was carrying a heavy stick and the other a shot-gun.

A cat went racing across the yard and was gone like a flash under the gate into the dark. Then Rowf was beside him, gripping a bone in his teeth—presumably one left lying about by the very dog which was now glaring at them between the men's legs.

At least it may not hurt, thought Snitter. With any luck it may be over in a moment.

"I'm sorry, Snitter," mumbled Rowf through the bone. "It was all my fault."

"It's all right, old Rowf," answered Snitter. "The hen didn't complain, after all." His confusion was gone. He was astonished to find himself so calm.

Suddenly a woman, screaming at the top of her voice,

ran forward from the cowshed door, seized the already-levelled barrel of the gun and pushed it upward. As the man shouted and turned upon her angrily, she flung out a pointing arm towards the dogs, babbling a torrent of words which guttered down into whimpering and frightened tears. The second man uttered a low, corroborative word and at once all three began to back away, staring at Snitter and Rowf in wide-eyed horror. The dog, who had been moving towards them, bristling, was checked by a quick, " 'Ere Jed, 'ere Jed," and, sensing his master's fear, turned and slunk back across the yard.

Dazed, Rowf looked about him. For a moment he wondered whether perhaps Snitter and he might already be dead. Perhaps this was what happened—some kind of trance? He took a few hesitant steps forward and at once the three humans, with quick, jerky scratchings of boots on the stones, sidled still further away. Then one of the men, at a run, stumbled across the yard, tugged open the gate, propped it wide and hurried back to his companions. At the same moment the woman, who had edged along the wall to the farmhouse door, fumbled an instant with the latch and disappeared inside.

Snitter and Rowf, as stupefied as though they had been struck suddenly deaf or found all odour destroyed throughout the world, made their way across the yard and out through the open gate. They had gone no more than a few yards down the lonnin when there sounded behind them a thudding of boots. Rowf, looking quickly round, saw one of the men carrying the hen's body on a garden fork. He tossed it, and it fell with a thump between the two of them, smelling of succulent flesh and warm blood. Hardly knowing what he did, Snitter snatched it up in his mouth and ran into the darkness with Rowf at his side.

Looking back from among the bracken, they could see the farmyard lights still burning, the two men standing together, apparently deep in talk, and the dog sitting beside them with an air of amazement as deep as their own.

"Snitter! What—what on earth did you—how—how did you do it? I don't understand—"

"I don't know, Rowf! I'm as bewildered as you are! I

must have done it, I suppose—at least—but I've no idea how."

"It's—it's terrifying! You might have killed them—set the farm on fire—you're not safe! I never supposed you could really—"

"The hen, Rowf; your bone! We've got food! Let's forget the rest—it's too—too frightening! I'll never know what I did! Can you find the way back without the tod?"

"Yes—yes, I think so. If the place is still there. If *we're* still here. I—I don't know what to—I can't make head or tail of it. Snitter, you must be—"

"Let it alone, Rowf! Drop it! Come on back!"

They ate their kill at the top of the wood, strewing guts and feathers all abroad without a thought and then, their hunger satisfied, made their way back to Stang End without another word between them.

Thursday the 18th November

"I see," said Digby Driver, "and the Research Station wouldn't tell you anything?"

"Nay, not a thing," replied Dennis Williamson, " 'Noothing to say.' I assked the boogger why he'd roong, like, if he'd noothing to say."

"What did he reply to that?"

"Said he were returning my call as matter of courtesy. Ah said Ah'd return him dog through his bluidy window-pane if Ah got channce."

"Well, let's hope we do get just that, Mr. Williamson. If I'm not mistaken, you've been all over your land pretty thoroughly, haven't you, to try and find these dogs?"

"Ay, Ah have thet."

"And you had a look into the old coppermine shaft above the tarn?"

"Ay, well, there'd been soomthing in theer, but it were hard to tell whether it were dog or fox or owt. There were boanes an' that layin' around and there were smell of fox reet enoof. But fox could have browt boanes in on it oan, like. It could have been nowt but fox, or it could have been dog. But if it *were* dog, it's not been back theer, that's for sure."

"Well, if they're still up there I mean to find them. You know the land. D'you think we could—"

Gwen Williamson came out of the door of Tongue 'Us into the yard.

"Mr. Driver? It's telephone—for you."

"For me?"

"Ay—Mary Longmire from t'Newfield. I think she's got a message. Happen soombody wants you."

Digby Driver went indoors, picked up the receiver and spoke.

"Mr. Driver?" said Mary Longmire's voice. "I thought you might be up with Dennis, so I just gave him a ring. Sorry to bother you. There's been someone on the telephone enquiring for you. He wouldn't leave his name, but he was speaking from Glenridding, over by Ullswater. Apparently your dogs were seen there lasst night."

"*My* dogs? Are you—was he—sure?"

"No doubt about it, he said. They had green collars, and one had a terrible split all along it head. He wanted to know what he ought to do. Said he'd informed Medical Officer of Health, but his wife was still terrified on account of the plague."

"Did he leave a number? Any address?"

"Nay, he did not."

"All right, Mrs. Longmire, many thanks. I'll get over there right away."

Digby Driver put down the receiver and smote his forehead with his open palm.

"My God, my God, why hast Thou forsaken me?"

Digby Driver quite often said things like this. He could not have identified the context and would not have been particularly bothered if anyone had told him what it was.

FIT 8

Now leave we to speak of Digby Driver and turn we unto Snitter and Rowf, that all this while had been awaiting darkness in their refuge upon Stang End. The rain, drifting across the bare, waste solitude, made, even to a dog's ear, only the slightest sound in trickling between the stones. Snitter, watching his breath condense on the wall of the ruined flue, wondered whether Rowf were really as hungry as he smelt or whether the smell got its intensity from his own starved belly. He raised his paw from the chicken bone which it had been holding down and as he did so Rowf rolled over and gripped the bone between his teeth.

"Oh—you're going to gnaw that, Rowf, are you?"

"Yes, I am."

"Did I enjoy it?"

"What?"

"It's the one you pushed across to me just now."

"Oh. Sorry. There's been nothing left on any of them for hours, anyway."

"I know."

"I hate this place."

"We've got so many friends to help us choose a better one, too. The whitecoats, the farmers—"

"I wish we'd never come here. That damned tod!"

"I'm sure he was only doing what he'd have done by himself and for himself. I wish you hadn't driven him away, Rowf. You terrified him—he won't come back now."

"Good. Just the smell of him—"

"But Rowf, we can't kill sheep without him—not safely —or go on taking ducks and hens. I'm afraid we may not even be able to keep hidden. He knew such a lot that we didn't."

"We killed sheep before we met him."

"One sheep. Without him we'd never have lasted this long. We'd have been caught long ago."

"I killed one above Bull Crag that morning."

"Rowf, it's twice as hard without the tod, you know it is. We shan't manage a kill tonight. We shall make a mess of it and have to give up again, that's the plain truth."

"My paw's painful. I can't run on it properly. But even apart from that, it seems to get harder and harder. Like— like—"

"Like what, Rowf?" Snitter changed his cramped position on the stones.

"I was going to say, like the whitecoats' tank. I feel just as though I were sinking, sometimes. And there's no avoiding it, either. We've got to eat. But I'm afraid the time's coming when I'm not going to be able to kill."

Snitter made no reply and they lay unspeaking for some time, while the rain billowed on across the fell.

"Last night, Rowf—I still don't understand. What happened? Those men were frightened—badly frightened. Did you smell them?"

"Yes, I did. But Snitter, I've been thinking—if you can do all that to humans and other dogs, why do we need to hunt sheep at all? Why don't we just go down there—"

"I tell you, I don't *know* how I did it. But there was something wrong, Rowf, wasn't there—something frightening about it? I don't know what I did, but I know one thing—they hated us. They wanted to kill us, only they were afraid; and that's what I can't understand. I wouldn't dare go back. They might not be afraid next time. Besides —oh, Rowf, you can't imagine what it's like to see a man fall dead and know that it's you who killed him." Snitter paused a moment. "If I hadn't killed my master, we'd both be sitting at home now, by the fire; instead of—oh dear, oh dear! Sometimes I wish I could do it to myself. It's that Annie Mossity. I'm sure she put it on me, somehow or other. She always hated me."

"As far as I can see," said Rowf, "it's better never to have had a master. I wish that Annie was here—I'd chew her up for you. I hate all humans: I hate them!"

"Perhaps they don't really know any more than we do. Perhaps humans have their troubles."

"Don't be so damn silly."

"I *am* silly. But they never *look* happy, do they—not like—well, not like a chaffinch or a puppy. Perhaps they don't know what they're doing any more than we do. Perhaps they do bad things to each other, not just to us—"

"What I'm saying is that they run the world for themselves. They don't care what they do to us; they just make use of us for their own convenience. It's a bad—"

"I wish you'd stop saying that. Anyone'd think you'd got another one somewhere."

"The men could alter this one if they wanted to. Anyway, our chances are thin enough, yours and mine. What's the use of talking? Let's go out again and try our luck. We've got to find something we can eat—"

"Firelight—newspapers crackling—my master used to put slices of bread on a sort of stick and brown them in front of the fire—it smelt nice—sometimes he used to give me a bit—oh look, look, there are the rhododendrons, Rowf! Look, just outside! Come on!" Snitter ran out into the rainy darkness and lay down. "Now and then that mouse has good ideas, you know. He's very small, but of course he's been ill—"

He laid his muzzle on his paws and closed his eyes contentedly, while the rain ran in streams over his back.

"Oh, the bees, Rowf—the sun's so warm—"

"Snitter, come back inside, come on! You'd better stay in here tonight. You're not fit to go out hunting. Go to sleep; and don't go lying out in that rain, d'you see? I'll go down and find—well, I'll have a go at the dustbins. I'll bring you something back. If I don't come back by tomorrow you'd better—you'd better—well, anyway, don't get wandering off, d'you understand?"

There was no reply. After pausing a few moments in the damp, chilly den, Rowf pushed his nose against his friend's belly. Snitter was fast asleep.

Inhabitants of the tiny, quaint lakeside village of Glen-ridding, Westmorland, on the shores of majestic Ullswater, tapped Digby Driver on his typewriter. He paused, seeking a striking and really original turn of phrase: *—here in the heart of poet Wordsworth's watery homeland—;* still it euded him: *—here in the heart of novelist Hugh Walpole's picturesque country—;* ah, here it came: *got a shock yesterday. The reason? They found themselves next in line for a visit from the dreaded Plague Dogs, who are spreading a reign of terror across this quiet rural area, where hitherto the most dreaded creature for centuries has been the wolf, the last one of which was killed in 1534, the same year in which Anne Boleyn lost her head on Tower Hill while husband Henry was hunting in Richmond Park.* (If that's wrong who the hell cares?) *While a few are still disposed to make light of this threatening menace, many more already know with creeping dread that it is a matter not to be regarded with such detachment. Those who think of plague in the same breath as bosomy orange-girl Nell Gwynne and bewigged diarist Samuel Pepys may soon find themselves mistaken, as the* Orator's *quest conclusively shows. Many readers will ask, when was the last outbreak of plague in England? The answer? 1910 to 1918 in Suffolk. Yes, it's true! Between these dates there were no less than 23 identified cases in that old-world county, 18 of whom died.* (Clever of old Simpson to dig that one up.)

COULD IT HAPPEN AGAIN?

Already, those on the spot are anxiously asking their local government officers (at least, they bloody soon will be when I've finished with them) *whether any undisputed cases have yet been confirmed and what safety precautions should be taken. Can the unthinkable repeat itself?* (Wonder what they'll do when this really takes hold? Fill the rag up with good stuff like this—push 'em in and let 'em swim—interesting experiment in sociological group reaction, really.) *Might the mysterious dogs be about to turn our secret weapons against ourselves? Does a canine Nemesis hang over Lakeland? Farmers at Glenridding have told me personally that they were so terrified by the mere sight of the maddened, snarling brutes who invaded their hen-roosts last night that they actually threw them fowls and flung open their gates to speed their departure, not daring to shoot for fear the infected bodies might spread the ghastly pestilence in the vicinity of their own homes.*

SILENCE

Meanwhile, Animal Research at Lawson Park preserves its bureaucratic silence. Yes, they deign to tell us, the dogs escaped. No, replies the Orator, *the people of Britain are not satisfied. Today, in YOUR interest, the* Orator *asks these questions. WHO let the dogs escape? HOW close did they come to the fleas of Death? WHY were those fleas allowed to roam at large and uncontrolled? WHEN will the public be told the TRUTH? Let us see whether the Men of Science, who are continually telling us they know all the answers, can tell us these. If they cannot, and that right soon, then the* Orator *says, "Write to your M.P.!"* *(For an artist's impression of the Plague Dogs, turn to page . . .)*

"Yeah, well, Bob Grisly'll do that in half an hour if old Simpson fancies the idea. Pity we haven't got a photograph. We need a *visual* image, if we're going to get not just the adults but the kids steamed up about this. Kid-involvement—that's what's needed to get it really on the move. Now," said Digby Driver, looking out of the window at the soft rain drifting across Ullswater in the last light, "the immediate requirements are a telephone and two or three dry Martinis. A large steak'd come in handy, too—or some eggs and bacon, anyway. What I need in this hole just now is some joy dee veever."

Snitter woke hungry. The rain had cleared and beyond

Ullswater the moon had risen. The waters on this starry night were as beautiful and fair as poet Wordsworth (or even novelist Hugh Walpole, come to that) could have wished. Yet it was not these which caused Snitter to feel a vague, alert uneasiness. He got up, put his head out of the shelter and listened. Something had awakened him—something which was not the all-too familiar return of the humming in his head. He listened, but could hear nothing except the coming and going of the light wind as it patted gently against the stones of the ruined flue. Cautiously he went outside and stood looking about the empty, moonlit waste. There was still nothing to be heard but the wind and the distant stream. More than a mile to the southwest rose the enormous, symmetrical pyramid of Catstycam, its slopes falling away on all sides from the pointed summit. Remote and calm it looked, soaring, in the moonlight, far above the solitude of masterless, starving dogs.

I wonder what it's like up there? thought Snitter. Perhaps it was from there that those sheep flew up into the sky. Kiff might be up there. He always used to say he'd be on a cloud—

Suddenly he tensed, listening more intently. This time there could be no mistaking it. Far off it was, and faint, coming and going on the wind like the noise of the beck; a barking sound, a cry as of a dog or fox.

"It's the tod!" cried Snitter. "The tod! He's looking for us!" He leapt up and began running across the long, downward slope toward Glenridding Beck, yapping, "Tod! Tod!"

There was no reply, but still he ran on. After about a quarter of a mile he stopped and, since the wind was from the north and of no use to him, searched with his eyes among the scattered rocks. He was near the beck now and could see below him, plainly enough, a stone sheepfold in the angle where a second beck came in from the opposite side. And now, at this close range, he suddenly perceived a stirring in a brake of fern. He barked again and in the same moment saw, quite clearly, a terrier bitch glancing through the covert—a bitch whose appearance recalled others from the days of his old life with his

Catstycam

master. Certainly she did not look like a sheep-dog—at all events, not like the unfriendly dogs which he and Rowf had met above Levers Water during the first afternoon of their escape.

"Who are you?" barked Snitter.

The bitch made no reply, but ran a little way towards

him. There was something wild and shy in her motion which was puzzling.

What's the matter with her? wondered Snitter. He barked again, "You needn't be afraid of me! I'm alone!" Then he thought, But is she? and looked round at the hollows and heights about them. There was no human in sight. What could she be doing here? Surely there can't be a shepherd with her at this time of night? As he waited for her to come nearer he listened uneasily, but heard neither shout nor whistle.

Whatever is she up to, all by herself? I can't seem to see her properly, either. How strange—but then I never can see anything straight when these humming fits come on. I wish I didn't feel so giddy and queer.

Suddenly the thought came to him: She's no sheep-dog—that's plain. I wonder, can she possibly be like us—another escaper? We'd have a pack again—how splendid! What a lark for Rowf when he gets back! "Hullo, Snitter, are you all right?" "Oh, yes, only there's two of me now! I split my head in two and made another dog! Here she is! Wuff wuff! Ho ho!" Snitter rolled on the stones and waved his legs in the air.

At this moment the other stopped in the act of climbing the nearer slope from the beck, stood gazing at him for a few moments and then began to go back by the way she had come.

"Oh, rip it and tear it!" said Snitter. "Now I've put the wind up her by acting so crazily. Wait!" he barked. "Stop! Stop! I won't do you any harm!"

The bitch—plainly a town-dweller, both from her motion and her general air of being in a strange place—turned and once more stared at him, but then ran on, re-crossed the beck and went a short distance up the course of the tributary.

Well, she *is* nervous—she's worse than I am, thought Snitter. Unless I can get her to stop I suppose I'll just have to try to overtake her. I believe she *has* escaped from the whitecoats and they've frightened her half silly. I hope she doesn't turn out to be useless—just another mouth to feed. Still, at least I don't have to be afraid of her. It's lucky Rowf isn't here—he'd scare her all to bits.

He splashed over Glenridding Beck and pushed on up Red Tarn Beck behind his elusive quarry. From time to time he caught glimpses of her dodging in and out of the bracken, yet whenever he laid his nose to the rain-soaked ground he could not pick up the least scent.

"Funny!" said Snitter. "That's not natural. She's no distance ahead—not as far as my master used to throw my ball. Sn'ff, sn'ff! How odd!"

At this moment he came round a boulder and at once saw the bitch not twenty lengths ahead of him. She was, if anything, rather bigger than himself, with a rough, brown coat that brushed the wet fern as she ran clumsily on.

"This is very strange!" said Snitter. "She's not trying to get away from me, that's plain. She's going quite slowly; but I can't seem to catch her. And her smell, wherever is it? Oh my dam, I believe I know—how shameful! The whitecoats must have done something to her, as they did to me, and it's destroyed her smell! Poor creature—whatever will she do! Can't tell anyone where she's been, can't excite a dog, can't leave traces—or if she can it's no good to her, if she doesn't smell. They *are* cruel swine—the very worst! Jimjam was right. Whatever happens to me, I'm glad I got out of there. I only wish I could see straight—it's that mouse again. Get your tail out of my eye! Oh, there she goes now!"

He crossed the line of the disused water-cut and held on up the beck. From time to time he barked, but still there was no reply.

I hope Rowf's not back yet, thought Snitter. If he is, he'll be worried to find me gone. Still, he'll be able to follow *my* scent, that's something. It must be as plain as the paraffin man's used to be at home. Oh, I know where she's going now. We're quite near the big tank that Rowf didn't like—the one we could see down below when I was singing to the moon that night and found the potato crisp bag. My goodness, it's a long way up here! And that's snow, that white patch in the gully over there. Oh, fanackers, this is too much of a good thing altogether! She's off her head for sure, to lead me all this way and never answer a word.

As he came out on the dreary marsh below the outfall of the Red Tarn, he looked about him at the enormous, cliff-surrounded hollow. He was in a cove, a huge recess, marked here and there by old, snowy streaks among the almost-sheer gullies. In front was the lofty precipice of Helvellyn's eastern face, running round by the south to the gnarled line of Striding Edge black against the moon. At its foot lay the silent tarn, still and grey as a tombstone in a churchyard. When a fish splashed, a hundred yards out, Snitter jumped, nervous as a cat; and not altogether from surprise that a fish should leap at night, though he tried to tell himself that that was the reason.

Not free from boding thoughts, he remained for a while on the shore of the tarn, wondering whether he would do better, after all, to go back. He was uneasy in this high, desolate place and was becoming less and less keen on the stranger. If she were an honest dog, why did she not behave like one? Also, he himself was beginning to feel as glass-legged as he had on Hard Knott. And if I'm to be taken badly like that again, he thought, I'll try to make sure Rowf's there this time. No more dark strangers with guns for me. Poor man! I didn't want to kill him! No, and I don't want to bring any misfortune on her, either. I'm going back now.

He barked, "You're only making a fool of me!" and set off down the beck by the way he had ascended. Yet still he could not help feeling a certain curiosity about his mysterious fern-skulker. He stopped under a low, lichen-covered crag, lapped a long drink and then barked once more, "I'm going back! Can you hear me?"

"I can hear you." The answer, instant as an echo, came from immediately behind him.

Snitter leapt in the air and faced about. The stranger was standing under the crag not three lengths away. Raising a hind leg, she scratched herself a moment and then, being the bigger dog, came forward and sniffed Snitter over, Snitter standing still while she did so. Her nose felt icy cold and oddly dry.

I was right, thought Snitter. They *have* taken away her smell. What a shame! There's nothing they won't do, those whitecoats.

As the bitch sat back from him he asked, "What are you doing here?"

"Watching."

What? thought Snitter. The answer had reached him as a kind of audible mist drifting into his head. I must pull myself together: she'll think I'm even crazier than I am.

"What?" he asked. "What did you say?"

"Watching."

"Watching what?"

The other said no more.

"I'm sorry," said Snitter. "Don't mind me. I believe we're both in the same sort of fix. I got out of that white-coat place too, but they cut my head open, as you'll have noticed, and I can't always hear properly—or see straight either, come to that. I'm very sorry they've taken your—" He stopped, for it suddenly occurred to him that most likely his fellow-victim would not want to be reminded that she had been deprived of the power to communicate fear, aggression, heat and, indeed, almost everything worth-while.

It's like blinding her, thought Snitter angrily. The dirty brutes! He went on quickly, "It's just that I've never met a bitch quite like you before. Let me have a sn— I mean, let me have a look. Why, my goodness, they've *starved* you as well, haven't they? Or is it with living out here? Haven't you been able to find any food?"

Still the bitch made no reply. She was, indeed, dread-fully thin. Each staring rib showed along her sides, and her eyes were sunk so deep in her head that they seemed almost to be looking out of a skull.

"Come on, my dear," said Snitter, "what's up? I dare say you're thinking I can't help you or be any good to you, but it's no use just saying nothing, now you've led me all the way up here. What's the trouble—apart from everything, I mean?" Suddenly faint, he lurched where he stood, and lay down on the moss. When the hum-ming in his head had cleared he heard the other saying, "—my master, so I stayed."

"Oh, you had a master?" answered Snitter. "So did I,

once, but Rowf—that's my friend—he never had one, you know. I'm not sure he's not better off in the long run."

Stiffly, as though with difficulty, the bitch began to walk away. "So will you come? Perhaps—"

Quite apart from her fearful thinness, there was something so eerie about her whole manner and appearance that Snitter was once more seized with misgiving.

"Come—where?"

"My master, I said—my master! Weren't you listening?"

"Your *master*? Why, where is he? Not here, surely?"

"I *told* you!" The stranger sounded less angry than desperate.

"I'm very sorry," answered Snitter humbly. "I'm not altogether right in the head, you know, and I've got one of my dizzy spells coming on. They maimed me almost as badly as you, I'm afraid. Tell me again and I'll get hold of it this time."

"My master's hurt."

"And he's out here?"

"Over on the other side of the water. We were walking along the top when he slipped and fell. I went down after him, but he was hurt. He can't move."

"Oh, my life," said Snitter, "that's bad! But couldn't he shout or wave or something? Men quite often walk along the top—the tod said so. Besides, I've been up there myself and it's littered with bags and packets. There must be people who'd come down and help—"

Without answering the bitch jumped awkwardly across the beck in the yellowing moonlight.

She's not very polite, thought Snitter. Still, I can't honestly say that this is much of a place for manners, or that I'm a very deserving case either, come to that. She told me about her master and evidently I didn't hear most of it. If only my head weren't as full of holes as a tomtit's nutbag! How on earth can *I* help her? Then the idea occurred to him: I could take a message. I suppose she's too stupid to do that herself. At least, she may not be stupid but she seems very much confused and—well, sort of dazed. But if *I* go, the men down in the valley will—

Helvellyn and Red Tarn

oh dear, oh dear! Well, I'd better go and see this master of hers first, anyway.

He overtook the bitch and they ran on together, across the bog and round the lower, eastern end of the tarn. Once round, she left the shore and, going faster now, covered the short distance to the boulders and stones about the foot of Striding Edge. Here they came into deep shadow—almost darkness—and Snitter stopped to accustom his eyes.

He peered up at the abrupt and perilous rocks above.

My dam! he said to himself. Did her master fall from there? He must be badly hurt! And this poor fool's been hanging round when he must have wanted her to do anything but that. But why couldn't he shout? I suppose it only happened this afternoon, and there's been no one along the top. He must be starved with the cold. Oh—I never thought! If I can help him, perhaps he might take me—me and Rowf—take us back to his home when he's better!

"I say! D'you think your master—"

He stopped. In the near-darkness, the bitch was gazing at him with so sombre, so wan and foreboding a look that instinctively he shrank away from her. There was not a sound all around them. At last he said timidly, "I'm sorry. I only meant—I—where is your poor master?"

She led the way round a crag standing a few yards out from the foot of a great, over-hanging face. Snitter followed her, his pads rattling lightly over the loose stones, and at once saw the dark shape of a man lying face down beside a patch of bog myrtle. He went up to it and pressed his muzzle against the shoulder.

The clothes were sodden, cold as the stones, rotten through and through. But more dreadful still, they were void, without firm content and yielding as an old, empty sack. Despite the horror that gripped him, Snitter pushed harder, desperate to give the lie to his fear, to prove himself wrong by encountering the resistance of the flesh-and-blood shoulder beneath the coat. The cloth, breaking open in a long rent, revealed the sharp, grey edge of a protruding bone. At the same moment the hat, jammed awry along the side of the head, fell off to disclose the dome of a skull, streaked with wisps of hair still adhering to the yellow skin of the scalp. One black eye socket stared up at Snitter and clenched teeth grinned in a stilled grimace. There was not the least smell of carrion. He saw, at a little distance, the scattered bones of one hand lying separately—no doubt where they had been dragged and dropped by the ripping, tussling buzzards.

Shaking, salivating, urinating with shock and fear, Snitter ran out from among the rocks.

"She's more mad than I am—she doesn't know! She's

gone crazy and she doesn't know! Oh, how dreadful—I shall have to tell her! What will she do! How *can* she not know? That man must have been dead three months."

He limped tremblingly back to the terrier, who had not moved and did not look up from the body as he approached.

"Your master—your master's dead! He's dead!"

The brown terrier, where it sat on the stones, raised its head. And now, as Snitter realized with a terrible certainty, there was no question either of his own madness or of his own eyesight. He was seeing what was there to be seen. The bitch, open-jawed, emaciated, glimmered faintly in the dark, turning upon him blank eyes that contained no speculation, that neither blinked nor followed his movement as he cowered away from her. The tongue was black and dried, the teeth decayed almost to the gums. It answered not a word. It could not, since, as now he perceived, it possessed no life, no substance but that which might be attributed to it by some unsuspecting creature who had not yet seen it for what it was; a phantom, a nothing, a dried, empty husk of old grief suffered long ago.

Snitter turned to fly; and in so doing saw, plain in the moonlight beyond the shadow of the precipice, the figure of a man, hunched in an old overcoat and carrying a stick, striding away towards the tarn. He raced after it but then, terrified that the horror behind might be following, looked back. Both dog and body had disappeared. So, when he turned again towards the tarn, had the figure in the moonlight. He was alone.

Ten minutes later Rowf, who had made his way by scent up the beck, carrying an entire leg of lamb with a fair amount of lean and gristle left on it, found Snitter wandering on the shore, crying like a dog at the mercy of devils. Twice during their return he seemed to lose his wits altogether, plunging in frenzy into the stream, first in terror of a blundering sheep and then of the glitter of a streak of limestone quartz in the moon. But when at last, back in the shelter of the ruined flue, he had pushed, like a puppy, deep under Rowf's side, he returned almost at once into a sleep even deeper than that in which his friend had left him upon setting out at nightfall.

Friday the 19th November

Mr. Basil Forbes, M.P., the Parliamentary Secretary, was a pleasant enough young man and, even if regarded with a degree of amusement by the higher civil servants on account of being something of an intellectual lightweight, was, on the whole, reasonably well liked in the Department. He had the advantage of a prepossessing appearance and, despite the reputation for imprudence which had earned him his nickname of Errol the Peril, was nevertheless free from the higher lunacies (such as a conviction that he was a godsent political genius, or a tendency to resent the activities of other Departments and instruct his civil servants to have rows with them) and above all, was well-mannered and open to persuasion. In a word, there were plenty of worse people that a civil servant might have to civilly serve.

On a chilly morning of London sootshine and grimegleam, sunsift, cloudstrain and lightrack, he greeted affably the Under Secretary and the Assistant Secretary as they were shown in by his personal assistant. He switched on the lights in the tropical fishtank, ordered lukewarm coffee all round and graciously treated them to fully five minutes' small talk. At length the Under Secretary, glancing surreptitiously at his watch, contrived to mention the Lake District.

"Ah, yes," said Mr. Forbes, as though tearing himself with reluctance from the pleasures of civilized conversation, "the Lake District; and these frightful-frightful dogs. What d'you think we're going to have to do about these dogs, Maurice?"

"Well, Parliamentary Secretary, I think by all *sensible* standards it's really a non-problem—"

"But none the less a shade awkward, eh?"

"None the less awkward indeed—politically speaking. Still, at least there's no actual health risk to the public—"

"That's certain, is it?"

"Absolutely, Parliamentary Secretary," said the Assistant Secretary, opening fire from the left flank. "The dogs were never in contact with the bubonic plague laboratory at all."

"Then why can't we say so?"

"We think you can and should," said the Under Secretary, "but we'd like to confirm that a little later, when Michael here's been and had a look at the place. The *newspapers* can get it all wrong, of course. No one's going to mind that in the least; but *we* mustn't get anything wrong—even if no one notices."

"All right," said Mr. Forbes. "So there's no public health risk and we can say so and the papers'll have to go away and invent something else. But now, what about the by-products—secondary nuisance value and all that? You know next Thursday's a Supply Day and the Opposition have chosen to debate expenditure on Research Establishments."

"Yes, we shall be briefing you, Parliamentary Secretary. Bugwash will probably start by resurrecting the matter of the planning permission for Lawson Park, then allege extravagance in the Government's implementation of the recommendations of the Sablon Committee, and proceed thence to allegations of mismanagement on the grounds that the dogs were allowed to escape, and that once they *had* escaped nothing was done."

"That'll be about the size of it, I expect, and normally it wouldn't be hard to answer. But I must confess, Maurice, that there's one aspect of it I don't terribly like, and I hope you're going to be able to tell me the answer. At the moment it can be made to look as though we thought we had something to hide—in fact, as though we'd been trying to hide everything we could, and very unsuccessfully at that."

"I know," replied the Under Secretary, nodding sagely to indicate that he, no less than the Parliamentary Secretary, had realized, as soon as the case got up to his level,

the deplorable lack of perspicacity shown by their under-
lings.

"I mean," went on Mr. Forbes, smiling matily up from
the papers on the table, "first these dogs get out, you
know. All right, so that could happen to anyone. But then,
when they find the dogs are gone, the boffins decide to
say nothing to anyone; and they go *on* saying nothing to
anyone even when they know the dogs are killing sheep
and prowling about in a national park like a couple of
jackals. Surely that was damn silly, Michael, wasn't it?"

"It certainly looks that way now, Parliamentary Secretary, but it's only fair to these chaps to point out that at
the time there was a certain amount to be said in favour
of silence. It was a hundred to one chance against all this
trouble brewing up. It was much more likely that the dogs
would get themselves shot or that the whole thing would
evaporate in some way or other."

"Well, maybe," said the Parliamentary Secretary, glancing momentarily across at the tropical fish. "But what
about the next piece of misjudgement? The station finally
put out a statement to the effect that two dogs escaped;
and this coincides spot-on with the *Orator*'s published
allegation that those dogs had been in contact with bubonic plague. Thereupon the station go silent again and
don't deny it, so that it looks as though they deliberately
omitted it from their original statement. What's the answer?"

"That the allegation's too ludicrous to merit either
mention or denial."

"H'm. All gone off at half-cock, rather, hasn't it?"
mused the Parliamentary Secretary. "What's worrying me
is why we ourselves—the Department—didn't weigh in
earlier. Why didn't the station tell us at once what had
happened? Why did they go and put out a statement of
their own before giving us any chance to see it? And
why didn't we stamp on this plague nonsense earlier, and
talk to Min. of Ag. about placating the local farmers?
Those are the sort of things the Secretary of State's going
to want to know."

Looking up, the Assistant Secretary again met the intent gaze of the Under Secretary. He waited for him to

speak—it being now, of course, the moment for the captain of the team to weigh in on behalf of his subordinate. The Under Secretary, with an air of joining Mr. Forbes in waiting for a reply, continued to gaze and say nothing. A silence fell. Stupefied, incredulous, the Assistant Secretary groped for words. Floundering as though in deep water, he felt fixed upon him the eyes of one who might, if he chose, pull him out. Mr. Forbes waited courteously. The Assistant Secretary saw the Under Secretary look down at the table, draw lines and squares on a pad of paper and then once more raise his eyes attentively.

"Is there an agreed liaison drill?" asked Mr. Forbes, by way of kindly stimulus.

"We're—er—in the process of setting one up, sir."

"Well—well—it all seems just a little bit unfortunate, Michael," said Mr. Forbes pleasantly. "P'raps you could let me see the agreed drill as soon as possible, could you, even if it *is* rather shutting the door after the horse has bolted?"

"Michael's going up there this afternoon, Parliamentary Secretary," said the Under Secretary, at last breaking his silence. ("First I knew of it. It was going to be Monday.") "No doubt that'll be one of the things you'll sort out as a matter of urgency, Michael, won't it?"

"Splendid!" said the Parliamentary Secretary in a tone of warm congratulation, as though all were now merry as lambkins on the lea. "Well, perhaps we've just got time to glance at this very convincing draft answer you've given me for the P.Q. that Bugwash has put down—'To ask the Secretary of State, etc., in what circumstances two infected dogs were permitted to escape from the Animal Research Station at Lawson Park, and if he will make a statement.' Now, I expect I'm being very silly, but it did seem to me that this third draft supplementary—"

Ten minutes later, in the corridor, the Under Secretary said, "Well, Michael, you'll want to be catching a train as soon as possible. You won't forget, will you, that there are *two* things—first to see whether we can safely advise Ministers that the dogs couldn't have been in contact with any plague-infected material; and then the—er—somewhat belated matter of an agreed consultation drill."

At the lift-doors the Assistant Secretary found his tongue.

"I've got to go and see one of the lawyers, Maurice, now, about an appeal case, so I'll leave you here, and look in for a final word before I set out."

Once in the lavatory on the next floor, he was overcome by a blinding rage so violent that for a few moments his sight actually clouded over.

"He sat there and said *nothing* to the Parliamentary Secretary—not a bloody word! He *sat* there and let the Parliamentary Secretary take it out on me for something he knew damned well was no more my fault than a cold in the head! Eton and Balliol, and he let Forbes, a basically reasonable bloke, whom we all like, think that I'm to blame. The bastard, the dirty, rotten bastard!"

He beat the flat of one hand against the tiled wall.

"Excuse me, are ye feelin' all roight, sorr?"

The Assistant Secretary, looking round vaguely, recognized a messenger named O'Connell, a decent Irishman who had once served him during bygone days as a Principal.

"Oh, hullo, O'Connell. Nice to see you again. Yes, I'm all right, thanks. Just letting off a bit of steam, you know."

"I thought perhaps ye might have come over queer, sorr—been taken baad, ye know."

"It's good of you to bother. Still, old soldiers don't get taken bad, do they?"

This was a joke. Both the Assistant Secretary and O'Connell had at different times been in the army and had once or twice exchanged military reminiscences.

"Well, they can do, sorr. I didn't like to see ye put under the weather, ye know."

"Thanks. You know, O'Connell, it's extremely annoying to suffer injustice and be unable to do anything about it."

"Man, baste and bird, 'tis the fate of every wan in the world, sorr, all but a varry few. There was some fella—Oi read ut in the paper—that said, 'The dispensin' of injustice is always in the roight hands.' Oi'd say that was very thrue indade, wouldn't you?"

Digby Driver had succeeded in tracking down Annie Mossity.

It had not really been very difficult. He had simply followed up what Mr. Powell had told him during the run back to Coniston from Broughton, by enquiring of the Barrow-in-Furness ambulance service and police about any road accident known to them during recent weeks involving a man and a lorry and brought about by a dog. Within a few hours this had resulted in his being put in touch with a lady in Dalton named Mrs. Ann Moss, the sister and next-of-kin of the dog's master, a local solicitor named Mr. Alan Wood.

Mr. Driver was now sitting in a small, chilly drawing-room, in front of an inadequate electric fire masked by a façade of plastic coal and below a singularly nasty coloured print of two little Italian-looking children with fixed and implausible tears on their cheeks, balancing on his knee, in its saucer, a full tea-cup coloured pale buff and having the form of a truncated and inverted cone. Annie Mossity, a hefty, plain, untidy woman with large limbs and a general air of thinly veiled aggression, was sitting opposite. Digby Driver, who could seldom be accused of dragging his feet in getting around to the personal circumstances of anyone whom he interviewed—particularly any that might pertain to anxiety, fear, misfortune, sexual irregularity or conjugal disharmony—had already gathered, first, that she had no children and secondly that Mr. Moss, though presumed to be alive, was no longer in the field. He was not unduly surprised. The goldfish, he thought, looked frustrated and the budgerigar distinctly put upon. Neither, however, was in the fortunate position of being able to follow Mr. Moss over the hill.

"Was it a shock," asked Digby Driver (who had prudently left his notebook, as possibly having a somewhat inhibiting effect, in his overcoat pocket), "when you realized that this dog which had broken out of the Lawson Park Research Station was the very one that you'd sold them?"

"Well," replied Mrs. Moss, with an apparent spontaneity that somehow contrived despite itself to seem disingenuous and cunning, "we can't be sure of that, actually, can we? I don't believe it *is* the same dog, and to be perfectly frank, Mr. Driver, I think you're wasting your time here. If my brother were to get any idea—"

"There's virtually no doubt about it, Mrs. Moss, believe me. You see—"

"Why don't you ask the Research Station?" interjected Mrs. Moss somewhat sharply. "They'd be able to tell you for certain, surely? I don't want to be drawn in—"

"I have," replied Digby Driver untruthfully. "But you'll know—that is, you'll know if you read the *Orator*—that the station aren't saying any more than they can possibly help. They're not acting in the public interest by persisting in this uncooperative silence, but nevertheless that seems to be—"

"I don't wish to discuss it either," rejoined Annie Mossity. "I hope you'll soon come to feel sure, as I do, that it's nothing to do with me and that it's not my brother's dog."

"Well," said Digby Driver, smiling pleasantly, "well, all right, Mrs. Moss, let's not trouble our minds about that aspect of the matter at all. I'm not asking you to say yea or nay to that. Let's agree that we don't know for certain whether or not the dog you sold to Lawson Park has become one of the Plague Dogs—"

"However many are there, for heaven's sake?" asked the lady.

"Only two, but that's definitely two too many, you know. But as I say, let's leave all that on one side. We'll agree that it's not your job or mine to know that, although you can be sure that it'll be established one way or the other quite soon. Can you help me by telling me something about your poor brother and his dog? His death must have been a terrible shock and grief to you, wasn't it?"

As he uttered these last words there passed across Annie Mossity's face a sudden, swiftly suppressed look of incredulity, followed immediately by one of relief. She hesitated before replying and appeared to be pondering. Then, with an air of decision, she said, "It was a dreadful blow; and a dreadful loss. Oh, Mr. Driver, if you don't mind, I can't bear to speak of it—"

"No, no, of course not. Forgive me," said Driver hastily. In the normal way he rather welcomed the tears of the bereaved, since they usually led to freer and more indiscreet speech, and often reduced the interviewee to a defenceless and malleable state. However, this was not what he was after just now. What he wanted was specific information.

"Just tell me a little more about the dog," he said. "Have you a photograph of it, by any chance?"

"No, I certainly haven't," replied Mrs. Moss. "To be perfectly honest, I was only too glad to get rid of it."

"Ah, that's interesting," said Driver. "Why was that? Was it simply because it had been the cause of the fatal accident to your brother, or was there something else?"

"Well—er—"

Annie Mossity cannot be said to have been unconscious, in the psychological sense—though they were certainly not present to her mind at this moment—of the fur-lined boots and gloves which she had bought with the money that Animal Research had paid her for Snitter. Thanks, however, to inveterate vanity and to a long-established capacity for self-deception, she was almost completely unconscious of her own jealousy of her brother's affection for the dog, and totally unconscious of her resentment of all that it represented—her brother's happy, untidy bachelor life and domestic contentment, his not always very well-concealed contempt for her empty-minded, genteel ways and lack of any real desire or need either for her interference in his home or for her nagging insistence that he ought to get married. Snitter, like Alan himself, had tolerated her, teased her and conceivably even committed, insofar as a dog can, the unforgivable sin of pitying her. But since neither dog nor master were present, all this could be unthinkingly transmuted in her mind.

"Well—er—you see, the dog—it was, well, it was—"

"What was its name?" interrupted Digby Driver.

"My brother used to call it 'Snitter.' As I was saying, it was undisciplined and aggressive. It was its undisciplined ways that brought about the accident to my poor brother, you know—"

"It was habitually aggressive, was it? Were you afraid of it? Did it ever attack you?"

"Wel—er—no, not to say attack, really, no. But it had a very nasty *nature,* really, Mr. Driver, if you know what I mean. It was—well, untidy, really, and destructive in its ways. After the accident there was no one to take it. I couldn't take it, not here; and you see, with my poor brother gone—"

"Did it ever attack other animals?"

"Oh, yes, with cats it was very bad. Very bad indeed. It used to bark at them and chase them."

"So when it made its recent day boo as a sheep-killer, it didn't come as a surprise to you?"

"Well, I suppose it didn't, really, no, not really, when you come to think about it, no." She considered for a moment and then said, "Not really."

"So you think that perhaps after all it may be one of the sheep-killing dogs?"

"Well—er—" Annie Mossity perceived that Mr. Driver had led her where she had not intended to go. "Well, I'm only saying it *might* be."

"Quite so. But it wasn't a particularly large dog, was it? Do you think it would really be able to kill a sheep?"

"Well, I mean, it was a fox terrier, it could kill a fox, couldn't it, and sheep, I mean, they're timid creatures, aren't they, really, and if it was that hungry—oh, it didn't care *what* it did, Mr. Driver! I saw it one day in the rhododendrons round at my brother's, and it had got hold of some horrible—well, I wouldn't like to say, but full of—full of, ugh, you know—"

(As long as she hated the dog and isn't going to deny anything we want to say about its evil and aggressive nature, thought Driver, that's all I need. There's one thing, though, that might be raised by some third party if they were so minded. I'd better make sure that that's out of the way and then I can get the hell out of here and send some local chap round to get a picture this evening.)

"—and dragging that nasty, smelly blanket out of its

basket, Mr. Driver, all round the floor—well, really—I was glad to see it thrown away—"

"Mrs. Moss, I'm just wondering—I'm sure you can tell me—what gave you the idea of selling the dog to the Research Station? After your poor brother's death, you had a great deal to do, I'm sure. Why go to that extra trouble? I mean, why not just have the dog put down?"

"Mr. Driver," said Annie Mossity, with the swift flux of defensive aggression that had caused her employer to learn better than to try to criticize her, however gently, for anything at all—it was easier to bear her incompetence in silence—"I hope you're not implying that I would want to cause the dog to suffer in any way. If so, I'm bound to tell you—"

"Certainly not," replied Digby Driver smoothly, "far from it. On the contrary, Mrs. Moss, I was wondering where you got hold of such a sensible, useful idea."

"Why, it was my brother-in-law—my sister's husband," replied Annie Mossity, warming under the facile flattery. "He's a vet up Newcastle way, you know. I'd mentioned to him that I couldn't do with the dog at all and meant to have it put down, and a day or two later he told me that the gentlemen at Lawson Park had circulated a request to several vets in his neighborhood that they wanted to obtain a full-grown, domesticated dog for a particular experiment. It had to be an adult, domesticated dog, he said. He assured me that it wouldn't suffer and explained how important it was in the public interest that these scientific needs should be met—"

(So you sold your dead brother's dog to the experimenters, did you, you mean, avaricious cow, for what you could get? I wonder if you stopped to think whether that was likely to be in accordance with his wishes?)

"So it was a case of yielding to pressure, really, wasn't it, Mrs. Moss? In effect, they asked you on bended knee and you obliged them?" (And I'll bet you beat 'em up to more than they were offering in the first place.) "We all have to consider the public interest, and it was really kinder than having the dog put down, wasn't it? I mean, you saved its life, really." (If she'll swallow that she'll swallow anything.)

"Oh, yes, I suppose I did, really, because you see, well, I mean, I couldn't really do with a dog with that aggressive nature, you see, but it was kinder really than having it put down, I mean—"

"Yes, of course. Precisely. Well, now, I'd like to do an article on you and the dog, if you don't mind" (or if you do mind, you blue-haired faggot) "and perhaps if I could send a colleague round for a picture this evening—you know, you in your charming home—"

It was deady cold out of doors and the light fading. Mr. Powell, who had a sore throat and also, he suspected, a temperature, stood shivering in the draught and wondered yet again why Dr. Boycott did not shut the window. In point of fact Dr. Boycott—who, whenever he had to take one of his subordinates to task, always felt a little more tense and averse than he would have cared for them to know—was not conscious either of the draught or of Mr. Powell's discomfort. He had already decided that in the light of what he had to say it would not be appropriate to ask Mr. Powell to sit down; but on the other hand he did not feel up to remaining seated himself while requiring Mr. Powell to stand. In view of their normal working relationship, that would be overdoing things and what he had to say would only misfire, leaving upon Mr. Powell the dominant impression that his boss had tried to come it too heavy: and on that account Mr. Powell would not feel small. Detachment would be a more effective ploy.

Accordingly, having sent for Mr. Powell, he had allowed him, upon entering, to find his superior standing beside the wallboard opposite his desk and apparently examining the progress graphs and other information pinned thereon. He continued in this occupation while talking to Mr. Powell, who stood uneasily nearby, unsure (as intended) whether he was expected to show an interest in the graphs, from which Dr. Boycott did not, to begin with, deflect his eyes. In the pauses of their conversation, the east wind could be heard moaning round the corners of the buildings, and outside, something tapped and tapped constantly against a drainpipe, with a flat resonance like that of a cracked bell.

"The Director's seen Goodner," said Dr. Boycott absently, running his finger down some figures relating to Ministry of Defence research establishments' experiments on living animals. "I wasn't there myself, of course."

"Doe, of course dot," replied Mr. Powell, snuffling and blowing his nose into his last dry handkerchief.

"131,994 experiments last year," muttered Dr. Boycott parenthetically. "Call it 132,000. But Goodner was positive that he'd said nothing to anyone."

"Oh."

"That represents—er—let's see—thirteen per cent of the total number of experiments performed by or on behalf of Government departments and related bodies," went on Dr. Boycott, in a fast, preoccupied mutter. Then, raising the volume a shade, "I had a word with Tyson myself and he was equally positive."

(Tyson had, in fact, been provoked by Dr. Boycott's questions into broadest Lancashire, accounting for himself with a flow of vowels and consonants as obscure in vocabulary but plain in meaning as the barking of a dog.)

"Well, doe wud's had eddythig out of be, chief, I assure you," said Mr. Powell, clutching his sopping handkerchief and weighing the respective merits of sniffling without it or attempting another blow.

"The Illinois experiments—I know I had the file somewhere, only yesterday," said Dr. Boycott. "Never mind—d'you recall the figures off-hand—just roughly, of course?"

"I doe the reference," said Mr. Powell. "Radiation Research, 1968. Sixty-wud beagles were radiated with Cobalt 60 gamma and half of them died within three weeks. Dasty symptoms they had. Their stomachs—"

"Oh, well, Susan'll dig it out for me. Except for that chap who gave you a lift back from Ulpha that morning?"

"Yes, I told you about that, you'll recall."

"Would you know him if you saw him again?" asked Dr. Boycott.

"Yeah, I reckon I would. Why?"

"Is that him?" Dr. Boycott jerked his head towards a small newspaper photograph, shorn of explanatory print, which was lying exposed on his desk. Mr. Powell went across and looked at it.

"Why, yes, that *is* the chap," he answered immediately. "Where did that come from, thed?"

"It came from yesterday's *London Orator*," said Dr. Boycott expressionlessly. "That's their reporter Driver, who's covering this business of the dogs. He wrote the bubonic plague article, you know."

Mr. Powell ran this through his aching head while the mucus finally blocked both nostrils entirely.

"If there's eddy suggestiod—" he began. He stopped. "I think—could I see the Director myself?"

"You *could*," replied Dr. Boycott, "but I think you'd be ill advised—I mean, to go in there and make something out of it before he's decided whether to take it any further himself. *Qui s'excuse s'accuse,* you know."

Mr. Powell didn't know.

"Besides, you're not established yet, are you?" said Dr. Boycott. "I think, in view of that, you'd do better to sit tight and see whether it blows over, even now."

"Well, it all depeds what he thinks, doesn't it? If he thinks that I've—God dabbit, I hardly dew Goodner was doig plague at all, so how could I—"

"Well, I know what he'll think if you go in to see him with that cold on you," said Dr. Boycott. "One hundred and twenty-nine sheep last year—tests on wounds caused by—er—high-velocity bullets. The Director's got an absolute obsession about cold and infection. Anyway, he can't see you now. He can't see anyone. He's drafting a personal letter to the Secretary of State. But you're obviously not well. You ought to be at home. Yes, go home, Stephen—go home and drink hot whisky in bed. Ring up on Monday morning if you're not feeling better. Er—one hundred and thirty-five goats, let me see—jagged shrapnel—"

"Thanks. But where are we at with this lot dow thed, chief?"

"Hard to say, really," replied Dr. Boycott. "Ministers are bothering themselves, apparently. Someone's here now from the Department, come to see the Director and have a look round. Damned snoopers—I should have thought a written report from us would have been enough for any reasonable person. It's all rubbish, anyway. I'll give you a five-pound note for every case of plague confirmed from Land's End to John O'Groats. And that includes Bedfordshire. Go there, Stephen, now. Hot whisky."

As Mr. Powell reached the door he added, "Before you go, make sure someone else takes over that monkey in the cylinder. The Director attaches importance to that experiment. We mustn't have anything go wrong with it after all this time. How long has it done now?"

"Thirty-five days," answered Mr. Powell. "Five weeks. I wonder whether it feels worse than I do?"

"My feet are colder than the whitecoats' glass table," said Snitter. "I wish I had my dear old blanket here. Wonder what happened to it? It used to smell so nice. I bet Annie threw it away."

Rowf, half-asleep, rolled over on the stones, drew in a long, snuffling breath and released it in a steamy cloud.

"Rowf, you did promise we wouldn't stay here another night, didn't you? I couldn't face—you know—even wondering whether—whether it might come back. If I only heard it out there, I believe I'd—"

"We'll get out before dark, don't worry. Where to, though?"

"I don't mind where. Just not here." Snitter sat up and looked out into the bitter, louring afternoon. "Funny—I was going to say I believed I'd go mad. But of course, I forgot, I *am* mad, so—"

"That's why you saw it. It was one of your bad turns. If I'd been there you wouldn't have seen anything at all."

"I dare say not, but it *was* there, all the same. I didn't imagine it. Oh, let's not talk about it any more, Rowf. My feet feel like stones in the water. It's turned much colder. Does it seem to you as though we were under some sort of surface—you know, down in some deep place, like a lake?"

"No, it certainly doesn't. And let me tell you, I've been down at the bottom of—"

"I didn't mean that. Don't get angry, Rowf. But why is the sky so heavy and sort of pressing down? And there's a funny smell, too—a kind of clean, light smell. Or is it something I'm imagining again?"

Rowf sat up suddenly, sniffed the air, ran a few yards outside and then tensed, nose turned to the slight but rising wind.

"Snitter, come out here, quick! What on earth is it?"

Snitter, following him into the open, raised his muzzle also towards the low, thick clouds. Both dogs stood silent, gazing westwards at the flat summit of Raise outlined against the bleak winter light. As far as eye could see, a vast flurry filled the horizon; a silent, regular commotion that flickered, darkly speckled, through the space between earth and clouds. As it came moving onward towards the place where they were standing, Snitter began to whine and almost turned tail. But in the same moment it was down upon them, swift as swallows on an evening lake, feathers and ice-pins, pricking and tingling minutely in eyes, ears and open skull, innumerable, momentary sharpnesses of cold on lips and moist noses, all the fell from sky to sky blotted out under a steady, whirling drift of melting particles, smaller than leaves, larger than dust or sand.

"They're flies, Rowf! They must be—white flies! But no sound, no smell, like the—the ghost dog! Oh Rowf, don't let them get me! Don't let them—"

"Come on, Snitter, come back inside! Be sensible! Whatever they are, they're not flies. Look at the ground —they disappear the moment they touch it."

"No, they don't—they turn into water. Look at your nose—no, well, look at mine, then."

They watched as the crevices between the stones began slowly to fill with frail, dully glinting, crystalline fragments that crumbled, renewed themselves, crumbled again and grew, clinging together and gradually forming piles light as cat's fur caught on garden bushes. At last Snitter said, "Why d'you suppose they've done it?"

"To try and kill us, I suppose. We know now that for some reason or other they're afraid to come near us, don't we? So they must mean to make it too cold for us to stay alive."

"But it's not as cold as that. At least, it wouldn't be if

Raise

only we had food. Anyway, Rowf, it'll be dark soon. Let's go away now—anywhere—please. I can't help being dreadfully afraid. You would be too, if you'd—if you'd seen—there's a garden in my ear, you know," said Snitter, once more going outside. "Some of this stuff's falling on it. All the bushes are white."

Twenty minutes later, plodding in the direction of the pallid sunset still faintly visible through the drift, they crossed the north shoulder of Raise above Sticks Pass and looked down at the innumerable, scudding flakes disappearing as they fell upon the dark sheet of Thirlmere.

"Where are we, Rowf?"

"I don't know about you, but I'm a good throat's length away from my stomach."

"I wish the tod were here. He'd know what to do."

"The tod—it's all my fault. I'm sorry, Snitter."

"Never mind, old Rowf. It can't be helped now. Oh, Rowf! Oh, my dam! Look—look! *That*'s why they've done it! Oh, they're clever, aren't they? If they're so clever, why can't they just come and kill us and be done with it?"

Behind them, up the slope of the shoulder they had climbed, their tracks showed clearly, black paw-marks impressed on the lightly covered, white ground; two lines stretching back and down until they were lost in the blotted-out waste of Stang.

"Everywhere we go!" breathed Snitter. "They can see where we've been and everywhere we go!"

"No, they can't," said Rowf after a few moments' thought. "They've been *too* clever this time. Don't you see, as long as this stuff goes on falling, it blots out the marks we make in it?"

"But when it's finished falling? They're just not ready for us yet, that's all."

"I know a trick worth two of that. The tod's got nothing on me. We're not beat yet, Snitter. It doesn't lie in the becks—look. The water melts it. So down that beck we go, come on. There you are—not a print to be seen. Are you all right?"

"My feet are cold," gasped Snitter, splashing and shivering.

House of Commons,
Westminster, sw1.

Dear Basil,

It was a great pleasure for Cecily and I [*Sic,* thought the

Under Secretary, reading] to see Molly and yourself once again at the Guildhall dinner last week, and I trust that it may not be long before your many engagements permit you to pay the visit to my constituency of which we spoke in general terms on that occasion. I think there are quite a few floating votes which might well be picked up by a judicious appearance on your part in key places, when you can spare the time.

As you will, of course, be aware, a good deal of uneasiness is felt throughout this constituency area at the moment on account of the trouble given rise to by the dogs which have escaped from Lawson Park. I know that Bill Harbottle and yourself take the view that dogs can't carry bubonic plague, but if I may say so, it is one thing to affirm from Westminster and quite another to persuade constituents—some of whom are not scientifically minded—after they have had the full benefit of the kind of stuff which the *London Orator* has been disseminating lately. I'm afraid I need convincing that there are no firm grounds for anxiety. Shouldn't things be put right sooner rather than later? In my view, reassurance needs to be accompanied by *action!*

Sorry to bother you on top of all your other preoccupations, but I would welcome a line to say what advice I should give my constituents. Perhaps we might profitably have a word in the House at some convenient moment?

Ever yours,
Jack

Immediate. Private Secretary's Office. For Advice, Please, and Draft Reply as soon as possible.

"Oh, bother!" said the Under Secretary, wrinkling his nose and staring at the red slip stapled across the green folder. "I suppose Michael *has* departed for Lawson Park, has he?"

"Oh, yes, he's been gone some time. I phoned to make sure," answered his personal assistant, raising one hand to pat her hair as she cleared the OUT tray with the other.

"Well, I suppose we'll just have to do it ourselves," said the Under Secretary. "No time like the present. Could you take dictation, please, Jean—one plus—er—two, draft, double-space? Er—h'm—yes—'I am replying at once to your letter of 18th November, in which you speak of local anxiety caused by the recent escape of two dogs from the Animal Research Station at Lawson Park.

" 'While I fully understand and sympathize with your very natural feelings in this matter, I should, I think, make it clear that the Secretary of State is strongly of the view that this, which is essentially a local problem, should remain one for tackling, at all events in the first place, by the local authorities concerned. The Medical Officers of Health in the area (whose Association are in full agreement with my Chief Medical Officer as to the extreme unlikelihood of these dogs being able to carry bubonic plague) will no doubt wish to take immediate steps to allay local anxiety—' "

Two starlings alighted outside, strutted, tussled and let their liquid siftings fall to stain the Under Secretary's stiff, dishonoured window-sill.

Saturday the 20th November

PLAGUE DOG "DANGEROUS BRUTE"

Former Master's Sister Tells Why
She Sold It to Research Station

Office executive Mrs. Ann Moss, of Dalton-in-Furness, got a shock yesterday. The reason? She learned that "Snitter," the fox terrier formerly belonging to her solicitor brother before his tragic death in a traffic accident, was none other than one of the escapees from Animal Research (Scientific and Experimental), Lawson Park, Cumberland, better known to millions as the "Plague Dogs." The two dogs, which are widely believed to be infected with bubonic plague contracted in the course of their nocturnal escape, have inaugurated a reign of terror throughout the Lakeland, indiscriminately killing sheep, ducks and hens and terrifying farmers and their wives by their ruthless attacks on lonely homesteads.

Not to Blame

"I can't really think myself to blame," said handsome, dignified Mrs. Moss, interviewed yesterday at her Dalton-in-Furness home.

"The dog had always been dangerous—wild and hard to control—given to attacking cats and making trouble for my brother and myself. It was really only kept on because my brother had such a kind heart and couldn't face the idea of getting rid of it. After the accident—which was actually brought about by the dog itself, but I can't bear to talk about that—I was left with the responsibility of dealing with my poor brother's things and had to do as I thought best. Naturally, I couldn't be expected to take such a dog into my own home. I was going to have it put down, but when my sister's husband, who is a vet, told me that Animal Research were seeking an adult, domesticated dog for experimental purposes, that seemed better for everyone concerned, including the dog. Of course, I never had any notion that my well-meant idea would have such terrible results, or that the Research Station would allow it to escape. I really think they ought to have taken more care."

Capable of Savagery

Mrs. Moss left me in no doubt that "Snitter" is a dog capable of savagery and one that—

"Oh, hell!" said Digby Driver, putting out his cigarette with a hiss in the slopped saucer of his teacup. "All this is beginning to smell of day jar voo. What we need now is something new—pep the whole thing up to a higher level. A photograph of the dogs in action—some indiscretion by the people at Lawson Park—an official statement by a Minister; not that I could cover that from here—but some bloody thing or other we need, to get a fresh driving force behind the story. Undiagnosed illness somewhere round about? No, that's no good—only fall flat when it's proved not to be plague—as of course it would be. Hell's bells, let me think, let me think—"

"I can't tell, Rowf. It's puzzling, and I'm afraid I'm not making much sense after wandering about all night in this cold. But perhaps the people in the cars aren't looking for us after all. They all go by at such a rate. If they *were* after us they wouldn't have far to look, would they?"

"Damn them, they all look as fat as castrated Labradors. Why can't one of them stop and give us some food?"

"I'm starving, Rowf. I'm perished with this cold. It's

a long time since sunrise now, but it doesn't seem to get any warmer. Can you feel your paws?"

"Don't be silly. They must have dropped off hours ago."

"Rowf, let's find a house, or a farm or something and give ourselves up. Licking men's hands would be better than licking this cold stuff off our paws. They might feed us before they took us back to the whitecoats, you never know. Otherwise we'll die out here for sure."

Rowf threw back his head and barked at the close, muffling sky. The snow, which had ceased during the night, had been falling steadily again for the past hour, and in the swirling confusion neither dog could make out either the hills whence they had come or what lay beyond the main road, where the cars and lorries went whang-whanging past behind the dismal sheen of their lights in the gloom.

"Rowf-rowf! Rowf-rowf! Go on, pour down the lot and bury us underneath it, blast you! I don't care! You're not as cruel or contemptible as the whitecoats who used to put me in the tank! They were supposed to be masters —you're not! I'm just a dog, starving to death, but I'm still better than you, whatever you are! You're licking the whitecoats' hands. Aren't you ashamed? Miles of bitter sky and freezing cold powder against a couple of starving dogs! Rowf-rowf! Rowf-rowf!"

"Rowf, even a whitecoat indoors would be better than this cold stuff out of doors. If only I had my head in a decent kennel, it'd be a lot less mad than it is now."

"I shan't say any more. I never barked when they drowned me: I knew my duty all right. I can die out here as well as ever I did in there."

"I say, Rowf, there's a car stopping! Look, it's pulled in to the side, just up there. Can you see?"

"Don't care. Let it."

"D'you think they're looking for us?"

"If they're looking for me they'll find a lot of teeth."

"There's a woman getting out. She looks a bit like Annie Mossity, in that fur coat. It isn't Annie, though. Oh, look, Rowf, she's gone up behind that rock to pee! I always wondered how they did it. Look at the steam! It seems rather a funny bit of ground to want to lay claim to—still, I suppose she knows what she wants. What's the man doing? He's got out, too. He's looking at the lights or something on the car. Oh, Rowf, can you smell the meat? Meat, Rowf, meat! There's meat in that car!"

"Snitter, come back!"

"I'll be shot if I come back! Look, you can see into the back of the car! That's a shopping basket. My master used to have one. It's full of things to eat—they always wrap them up in paper like that. Wherever there's men there's paper—and food!"

Rowf caught up with him. "Snitter, stop! They'll only hurt you or shut you up again, like they did in that shed."

"They won't! I'm desperate, I'm mad, I'm dangerous—remember me? They throw chickens after me to get rid of me faster! I'm bold untold in the great white cold, I'm the dread with the head, the nit with the split! Here I go, who dares say no!"

Capering, ears erect, staring white-eyed, rolling head over heels, wagging a frothing muzzle, curling his upper lip until the black gums showed above his teeth, Snitter, out of the thickened gloom, came mopping and mowing down upon the car. In the sight of the driver (a young man named Geoffrey Westcott), starting in surprise and peering quickly round with vision half-dazzled from his examination of the alignment of the headlight beams, his eyes were two full moons, he had a thousand noses, horns whelked and waved like the enridged sea. Thou hast seen a farmer's dog bark at a beggar, and the creature run from the cur? There thou mightst behold the great image of Snitter. So did Mr. Westcott. With a spasm of horror he recognized the features of which he had read in the paper —the green plastic collar, the split head, the air of gaunt, crazy savagery. Even as he cried out and ran, Snitter leapt into the car, jumped over the back of the driving seat and, slavering, began to drag the soft, squashy, meat-reeking parcels out of the wicker basket on the back seat. Rowf, up beside him in a moment, gripped a joint of mutton in his jaws and sprang with it out of the car door. As they gulped and chewed, the snow grew dappled red with blood, brown with fragments of sausage, chocolate and kidney, yellow with butter and biscuit-crumbs. Plastic wrappers and shreds of paper blew away on the wind.

"Look out, Snitter, the man's coming back!"

"I don't care. Tell him I want a blanket as well! A cloud would do—ashes, hay, newspapers tell him—"

"Snitter, he's got a gun! That's a gun!"

Snitter looked up quickly. "No, it isn't. I've seen those flat, black boxes before. Lots of men have them. My master had one. They just make little snicking noises, that's all."

"But he's pointing it at us!"

"I know. I tell you, they do that. You needn't worry: it's not a gun. There—did you hear that little click? That's all they do. Anyway, that's the lot now, except for what's left of this great lump of meat here. You licked up the eggs off the back seat, didn't you?"

"Of course I did. What d'you take me for? Better than the tod's eggs, those were. You grab that soft stuff and I'll carry this great bone here. Come on!"

They vanished into the whirling desolation as Mr. Westcott supported his sobbing, trembling lady passenger back towards the road. It had indeed been a terrible experience, and Mrs. Green might very well have wet her knickers if she had had anything left to wet them with. The driving door was swinging ajar and the back seat looked like a field of war and if it was not Mungojerrie and Rumpelteazer, that redoubtable pair would certainly not have been ashamed of the job. Shocked and dazed, but nevertheless deeply thankful at least to have escaped contact and infection, the two of them left the deadly, contaminated vehicle where it stood and set out to walk the four miles to Keswick through the snow.

Five minutes later Snitter reappeared, followed by the reluctant Rowf, and set to work to finish off the scraps.

"I'm not leaving *anything*, I tell you!"

"It's not safe, Snitter! They'll come back, or another car will stop."

"I don't care! I shall have eaten the lot, and nothing can alter that."

"Come on! Don't overdo it! There's a man coming!"

"I'll sing him a song!

"O I'm a bold dog with a skull like a drain,
(Sing chompety, chumpety, piddle-de-dee!)
I'm horribly wild and completely insane,
(Sing wiggety waggety, hark at him braggety,
Mumble a bone on the lea!)"

Nevertheless when, a minute later, the police Jaguar
drew up to see why an empty car, with headlights on and
driving door wide open, was parked on the hard shoulder,
the only canine traces were two lines of paw-marks disappearing into the mirk.

The telephone rang. Digby Driver picked it up.
"Driver *Orator.*"
"Is that Mr. Digby Driver himself speaking?"
"It is indeed. Who might I—"
"Mr. Driver, you don't know me, but my name's Westcott, Geoffrey Westcott, and I believe I've got something
of considerable interest both to tell and to show you. My
landlady and I were attacked and robbed this morning by
your Plague Dogs. They drove us off and then ransacked
my car."
"Christ Almighty! Where?"
"It was during a snowstorm, near Smaithwaite Bridge,
a little north of Thirlmere. We'd stopped the car and got
out for a minute, when the dogs just appeared and fell
on it."
"But you say ransacked and *robbed?* What of, for
God's sake?"
"All my landlady's shopping, out of the back of the car.
Everything that was edible, that is. They ate the lot."
"You sure it *was* the Plague Dogs?"
"I'm as good as certain, Mr. Driver. But more than that,
I've got several photographs of them, taken from about
twenty-five to thirty yards' distance. Would you be inter-
ested in acquiring those for your paper?"
"I'd like to meet you right away. Where are you?"
Mr. Westcott gave an address in Windermere.

"I'm on my way," said Digby Driver, and slammed down the receiver.

Vaguely aware of the two glimmering squares of the casements opposite and of the wash-basin between and below them—its waste-pipe an elephant's grey trunk curving downward into the floor—Mr. Powell staggered on through the snow, shivering with fever and tormented with a sick headache that never left him. Sometimes he clutched a drift of cotton snow about him for warmth. Anon, he flung it aside as he clambered, sweating with the effort, out of the piled heap of snow into which he had fallen and become engulfed to the neck.

He was at Stalingrad, lost, out of touch with his unit and as a last hope of making his way back to 6th Army headquarters. The enemy were shaggy, black dogs, armed with casks of hot whisky slung round their necks, the terrible effect of which was to intensify headache and induce nausea and vomiting. They could be seen everywhere —dark shapes scudding down from the bitter hills to cut communications on the roads, or skulking in the balance-cupboards behind isolated cylinders, to ambush any fugitive who might try to seek shelter. All organized resistance had broken down and the stragglers were wandering to the rear in desperate search of relief. But there was no relief for Mr. Powell.

"The tanks!" muttered Mr. Powell, tossing from side to side. "Too many tanks—too many dogs in tanks!"

As he spoke he came in sight at last of headquarters, a huge, grey ruin standing alone in an expanse of white snow. He floundered towards it, scratching, through his sweat-sodden pyjamas, at his unwashed, itching body, and as he came closer saw that it was, or had once been, a cathedral. Struggling, he turned the heavy, iron ring of the door and stumbled inside.

At first he could perceive nothing, but then, raising his eyes to the source of the dim light, he saw, with a sense of recognition and relief, the rabbits—row upon row of them—gazing gravely down from the hammer beams and the lamp-lit reredos. Even here it was very cold and throughout the building there was not a sound save that of his own coughing, which echoed in the nave.

"Help me!" cried Mr. Powell to the ranks of silent heads.

They gave no sign of having heard him and he fell on his knees.

"Help me! I'm ill! Can't you see me?"

"We can't see you," said a rabbit. "We can't see anyone. We're drafting a personal letter to the Secretary of State."

"I've brought you some tea," said a dog with a slung tommy gun, entering the nave from behind him. "How are you feeling?"

Mr. Powell sat up, coughed, spat yellow into his handkerchief and looked confusedly round the cold, darkening room.

"Oh, fine. I'll be all right a bit later, love," he replied. "Sorry—I had a lousy dream—not too good at all. Must be time to draw the curtains, isn't it? Tell Stephanie she's a sweetie, won't you, and I'll try to be fit enough to read her some more about Dr. Dolittle tomorrow? I must aim to get back to work by Tuesday, I really must."

FIT 9

Sunday the 21st November

(*From the Sunday Orator*)

AT LAST!
THESE ARE THE PLAGUE DOGS!
ASTONISHING PHOTOGRAPHS
BY BELEAGUERED MOTORIST

Windermere bank executive Geoffrey Westcott and his landlady, Mrs. Rose Green, returning home by car through snow which for the past twenty-four hours has held Lakeland in its icy grip, got a terrifying shock yesterday. The reason? You can see it here, for bankman Geoffrey possesses not only courage and presence of mind, but a camera in whose use he is expert, for which the public have much cause to be grateful to him.

"You could have knocked me down with a feather," said Geoffrey, depicted here recovering yesterday from his ordeal at his comfortable flat in Mrs. Green's Windermere home, where he is a lodger. "I'd driven Mrs. Green over to Keswick to do some shopping and pay a visit to a friend, and on the way back we'd just got out of the car for a moment, about five miles north of Dunmail Raise, when all of a sudden I saw these mad dogs—and that's what they were, make no mistake—rushing down on us. There were two of them, both as wild and ferocious as wolves on the Russian steppes. I don't know if plague sends its victims mad, but I wouldn't be surprised to learn that it does—not after what

I've seen. They tore every scrap of Mrs. Green's shopping out of the car—meat, butter, biscuits, the lot—and ate it in about three minutes flat. In fact, they were so busy that I risked getting close enough to take some photographs. The car? Oh, it just about breaks my heart—my super-tuned Volvo sports—but I'll just have to write it off. I could never bring myself to risk sitting in it again, whatever tests the local authority may carry out and whatever assurances they may see fit to give me. I mean, you never know, do you—bubonic plague?"

Time for Action

You never know—that shrewd comment of bankman Geoffrey, ace amateur cameraman and sports car driver, might well go for many other people in England today. You never know—*where* these dangerous brutes—themselves insane from the terrible disease they are carrying—may attack next: *what* harm they may do; and *who* may be their victims. SEE these ghastly photographs of *wild beasts* at large—supplied exclusively to the *Orator* by intrepid Geoffrey Westcott. HEAR what the *Orator* has to say about the danger to our fair land and its people. SMELL the stink of evasion and bureaucratic We-Know-Best which is still drifting, all-pervasive, from Lawson Park to Whitehall and back. Suppose *your* child were to TOUCH one of these dogs? No danger of that, you say? But how can you be sure? And others may well be less fortunate. The TASTE of danger is all abroad in Lakeland, and where its deadly flavour may next seep—

"Yeah, well, all right," said Digby Driver, throwing down his copy of the *Sunday Orator* with satisfaction. "And the photographs look first-rate. Lucky the bigger dog's in front—it looks a lot fiercer than the little one. Tom's touched out that cleft in the head quite a bit, too: good idea—some readers might have started feeling sorry for it. O.K., let's get on the blower to old Simp. the agony king."

Digby Driver made his way to the hotel call-box and reversed the charges to the *Orator*.

"Desmond? Yeah. Yeah, I've seen it. Glad you're pleased. Oh, fine, thanks. What now? Well, I thought Westcott might be good for a bit more, properly shoved and guided from behind, you know. What? Yeah, he's stimulatable all right. Sure. A yibbedy yobbedy, out to be clobberdy, up in the courts young man. What? *Patience,* Desmond. No, I said *Patience.* No, not patience, *Patience.* Oh, skip it! Oh, you don't think he'll do? You want it stronger than that? Stronger than that? Uh-huh. Uh-huh. I see— force their hand, eh? But that's a bit of a tall order, isn't it? Well, dammit all, Desmond, I just got you the photo- graphs, didn't I? O.K., O.K., never mind. You say Sir Ivor wants a *disaster?* Something the Government can't duck out of? Well, that *is* a tall order, Desmond, but I'll do my level best. Yeah, that's about it—pray for something to turn up. Never know what the dogs themselves might get up to, of course, specially if this snow goes on. Father for- give them for they know not what they bloody do, eh? O.K. Desmond, do my best. Talk to you soon. Bye-bye."

Having rung off, Digby Driver remained musing in the call-box for fully half a minute, tapping his front teeth with his pencil. At length he once more, and resolutely, grasped the receiver.

"The time has come the walrus said," he remarked, and proceeded to put a call through to Animal Research.

"Lawson Park? Yes, that's right, duty officer, I said. *London Orator* here. Yes, of course I know it's Sunday. Look, can you give me the home phone number of the young fellow I talked to at Broughton last week? No, not Boycott, no, his name's—er—yeah, that's it, Powell, Stephen Powell. What? You say he's *sick?* Oh, *is* he? Sick, eh! What's he sick with? You *don't know?* I *see!* And you won't give me his number? Right, thank you. Thank you *very* much. Good-bye."

"What is the mysterious illness afflicting young research scientist Stephen Powell?" muttered Digby Driver to him- self. " 'Animal Station Preserves Suspicious Secrecy.' Well, we'll play it for what it's worth, but it's not really what Desmond's after—not for a body-blow. It's got to be bigger than that. What we ought to be praying for is something nasty, nasty—*really* nasty, oh yuck! Come on, Driver, get with it! But what, what, what?"

Mr. Driver, smiting his forehead with an open palm, proceeded to seek inspiration in the bar.

"I don't think we shall ever be able to find the tod now,"

said Snitter. "If I were a mouse I couldn't even run as far as the gully in the floor."

He sat up, looking round uneasily at the sky. "I suppose the buzzards will come, but I hope we're properly dead first. Tug tug, munch munch, I say, Beakrip, old chap, which d'you like best, Snitter or Rowf?"

"Shut up."

"Have you ever thought, though, Rowf, we shan't need food or even names when we're dead? No names—like the tod—just the wind making those little whistling noises along the ribs, like that yow's bones last night that had nothing left on them. Nothing—not even maggots. That'll be us. Thank goodness we're out of the wind here. It's enough to blow a cat over the hill into the tarn. Here I come help miaow oh splash how did that happen?"

Rowf said nothing, licked Snitter's ear for a few moments and then let his head fall back between his numbed paws.

"Rowf, do you—"

"I can still smell that stuff you said the whitecoats put into the hole in your head."

"You weren't cut open. All the dogs who were cut open smelt of it. If you'd been cut open you'd have it too and you wouldn't notice. Rowf, d'you really think it's because of us that the dustbins had been taken indoors last night?"

"Probably. They're all afraid of us, aren't they?"

"So they *all* know—every one of them—about me killing people?"

A few moments later Rowf was asleep again—a light, wary sleep, in which exhaustion barely turned the scale against hunger and the fighting animal's fear of being surprised and killed without the chance of a struggle. Snitter pressed himself deeper into the cleft between Rowf's shaggy coat and the base of the crag and lay gazing out over the fell and the dark tarn below. The sun, which had been shining from a clear sky during the early afternoon, was now hidden behind a bank of clouds like an arctic sea. From height to height, across the bitter waste, the snow lay austere and silent, knowing neither hate nor pity for whatever creatures it would kill during the darkness of the coming fourteen-hour night.

"I'm a whitecoat," murmured Snitter drowsily, looking down at the slate-coloured surface of Levers Water, like an eye-socket in a skull, surrounded by its white, still shores. "I need to find out how and in what way you two dogs are going to die under this particular crag. You'll have noticed that I smell very smooth and clean, which is just as it should be: and that I cover everything up. You must understand that I'm not insensitive to the situation of my charges. My experiments have taught me great respect for all creatures. Your life certainly won't be wasted. Even your bones will have a use—you should feel proud and interested. Let me explain. There's a kind of buzzard that looks like a maggot—flying, of course—"

A flock of gulls drifted into sight over the crag, sailing up into an aureate beam, high and remote above the deepening twilight below. Not a wing moved as they glided silently against the darkening blue, their out-stretched pinions and white plumage tinged with gold as often as they circled towards the west.

"Whatever have I been dreaming about?" said Snitter. "That mouse has been chattering nonsense in my head again. It's not surprising, really—I feel quite light-headed. We've come such a long way since the car yesterday morning, and not a mouthful, not even the lick of a dustbin lid. We'll never be able to pull down a sheep again—never." He dozed off once more, but started up almost immediately at the cry of a passing buzzard. "No more wading down becks for me. I split my brains into that beck, I believe; anyway, I could feel them running down inside my head, so there you are." He looked upward. "Those birds—they're beautiful, soaring round up there. They look just like this cold stuff the men have put down—silent and needing nothing. The birds lie on the sky and the white stuff lies on the ground. I used to lie on a rug, once. I wonder where they come from? Perhaps we could get there, Rowf and I. Perhaps that's where Kiff is. If we don't find the tod—and we never shall, now—we'll starve all to pieces. Well, we're starving now, come to that. Poor old Rowf—it's worse for him."

All day they had been hoping against hope to come upon tracks of the tod. After the raid on the car the pre-

CONISTON
OLD MAN

SWIRRAL   Levers
Hause

WETHERLAM   BRIM FELL

CARRS

GREY
FRIAR

Wrynose Pass
road

CRINKLE
CRACS

PIKE O'
BLISCO

BOWFELL

Red
Tarn

Angle
Tarn

Watendlath

Langstrath

EAGLE
CRAG

Bull
Crag.

Stonethwaite Beck

GREAT   CRAC

Watendlath
Tarn

Watendlath

RAVEN
CRAG

HIGH SEAT

Thirlmere

road

Smaithwaite
Bridge

looking south

vious morning they had crossed the main road, rounded the northern end of Thirlmere and then wandered south-westward, up the forested slopes of Raven Crag, and so by way of the moor south of High Seat, to the lonely hamlet of Watendlath beside its little tarn. Here, although they had waited for darkness and gone most stealthily about their business, they had had no success and fled away empty, with the barking of angry dogs behind them. The sound of Digby Driver had gone out into all lands, so that here, as at many dwellings throughout the Lakes, even the dustbins had been taken indoors. The ducks and hens, naturally, were no less securely out of harm's way.

That they were both weaker and more exhausted than on that warmer morning, more than seven days before, when Rowf had killed at dawn above Bull Crag—pads sorer, courage and hope lower, energy much diminished and bodies more quickly fatigued—these things they felt continually. Later that night, at moonrise, they had searched the dismal, snowy fell, but found not a single sheep, save for a skeleton, long picked clean, lying among sodden hanks of old wool. Giving up all hope of a kill, they went on southward, crossing Greenup Gill among crumbles of snow and thin splinters of ice which dissolved even as they dropped into the biting water. It was when they realized that they were once more near Bull Crag that the thought of the tod had returned to Rowf. Impelled partly, perhaps, by that abused but still dog-like sense of loyalty and duty which had so often made him feel ashamed of his flight from Lawson Park and the drowning-tank, he had begun by blaming himself once more for the quarrel and then insisted that, somehow or other, the tod must be found and persuaded to rejoin them: it was possible that he might have returned, by himself, to the old lair. So they had set out, towards moonset, to retrace the way by which they had come from Caw and Brown Haw. By noon of the following day their hunger had become desperate. Above Levers Water they had lain down to rest and Snitter, in a kind of foolish, light-headed gaiety of privation, had spent the afternoon chattering about anything that came into his head, while Rowf slept and shivered in the lee of a tall crag.

"Shell we be ghosts, Rowf, d'you think?" asked Snitter, wriggling like a puppy. "I say, Rowf, shall we be ghosts? I don't want to be a ghost and frighten other dogs. Look, there's a pink cloud drifting over now, right above those white birds. I'll bet Kiff's on it. I wish we could go wherever those birds have come from. It must be warmer there, and I expect their tobacco man gives them—I say, Rowf, I can pee backwards on a rock, look—" He tumbled head over heels and got up crowned with a helmet of freezing snow. In the act of shaking it off, he suddenly stopped and looked about him in surprise.

"Rowf, listen, I've just realized where we are! Rowf! D'you remember that day—the first day after we escaped—when we chased the sheep—that shepherd man came—and those dogs got so angry with us? It's the same place—remember, the water and these rocks, and look, that's the beck over there? I wonder what made me realize it just now and not sooner? And come to that, I wonder where all the sheep have gone? Up in the sky, d'you suppose?"

As he spoke, the sun shone for a moment through a rift in the clouds, glinting stilly on the distant water. There was the smell of a cigarette and a sound of crunching boots. A blue, moving shadow appeared and the next moment a man—surely, the very man of whom Snitter had been speaking—came striding round the end of the crag and stood still, his back toward them, looking intently out across the tarn. At his heels was following one of the two dogs who had so fiercely resented their chasing of the sheep. Seeing them, it stopped, with a low growl, and at once the man turned his head and saw them also.

Rowf rose slowly and stiffly from the depression which his body had made in the snow, hobbled out of range of the man's stick and stood uncertainly on the defensive. Snitter, almost as though at play with some chance-met stranger in a park, took a few gambolling steps towards the man, wagging his tail. At this the man immediately backed away, flinging down his cigarette, which quenched, in the silence, with a quick hiss like a tiny utterance of alarm. Then, as Snitter hesitated, he swung his stick, shouting, "Git out, y'boogger!", turned quickly on his heel and disappeared at a run. Evidently he was too much startled and frightened even to remember his own dog, for he did not call it and it remained where it was, facing Rowf in the chilly shadow. At length, in a guarded but not altogether unfriendly manner, and looking at the depression in the snow, it said, "Tha's bin layin' there a guidish while, then. Art tha noan cold?"

Rowf made no reply but Snitter, having cautiously approached the dog, stood still while it sniffed him over.

"By, tha smells queer," said the dog at length. "Where art goin'?"

"Nowhere," answered Rowf.

The dog looked puzzled. "How doosta mean? Tha'lt noan be bidin ont' fell the neet?"

"We've nowhere to go," said Snitter

The dog, plainly at a loss, looked from one to the other.

"Wheer's thy farm at? Tha'rt noan tourists' dogs, Ah'm varra sure—tha'rt nowt but skin and bone. What art doin' here?"

There was a pause.

"We live in a shed," said Snitter suddenly. "There are pink clouds like rhododendrons. I know it sounds silly, but I'm going to clean the cobwebs off my eyes and then you'll be able to see what I mean. Just for the time being I have to leave it to the mouse. Can you tell us why your man was afraid of us? Why did he run away? He *did* run away, didn't he?"

"Ay, he did that. Ah've nobbut seen t' like once afore, an' that were when he reckoned dog were sick wi' rabies, like. It were yoong pooppy, an' he reckoned it were in convoolsions—it were foamin' an' that."

"Rabies?" said Snitter. "What's that?"

"Doosta not knaw? A sickness—kind of plague, like—that kills dogs; but it's noan common. Happen he thinks tha's got it—tha smells queer enoof, an' that head on thee like rat split oop belly."

"But you're not afraid of us, are you?"

"Nay. Ah'd knaw reet enoof if tha had plague or sickness like, but that's whit t' gaffer thinks, for sure. Else he'd not 'a run."

"Where have all the sheep gone?" asked Rowf.

Langstrath

The dog looked surprised. "Sheep? We doan't leave sheep ont' fell in snaw. Sheep were browt down yesterday, an' damn' cold work it were an' all. That's what we're on with now—lookin' for any more as might 'a coom down off tops lasst neet."

"I see," said Snitter. "So we shan't be able to—yes, I see."

"So ye're livin' oop an' down ont' fell?" said the dog. "By, ye're thin wi't, poor booggers. An' ye're noan reet int' head an' all," it added to Snitter. "Happen ye'll die ont' fell. Nay, cheer oop, poor lyle fella, it's gan to thaw bi morning, canst tha not feel it?"

A sudden shouting—" 'Ere Wag, 'ere Wag—" sounded in the distance and the dog, without another word, vanished like a trout upstream. In the view from the crag, the white fell stretched bare as a roof down to the tarn.

"He didn't recognize us," said Snitter after a little, "and he obviously thought we couldn't do any harm."

"We can't."

"My feet are cold."

"They'll be colder if we stay here. We've got to find some sort of shelter. It may thaw by morning, as he said, but it's cold enough to freeze your eyes out under this rock."

"What a sad sight that would be," said Snitter. "I couldn't see anything, could I? Not a maggot not a mouse not a dustbin round the house. Cheer up, old Rowf. We might find the tod yet, and perhaps there's a bit of the world somewhere that nobody wants. Anyway, wouldn't you rather die here than in the whitecoats' tank? I would. It's little enough dignity we've got left. Of all the things the whitecoats stole, that's what I feel worst about, I think. I hope we die alone, like decent animals."

Sunday the 21st November to
Monday the 22nd November

Digby Driver's assessment of Mr. Geoffrey Westcott,

though characteristically flippant, exaggerated and uncharitable, had nevertheless been—also characteristically—by no means entirely inaccurate. While Mr. Westcott had never, in fact, seen the inside of a police court, either in a defendant or any other capacity, there was, notwithstanding, a certain unscrupulousness in his make-up, together with a kind of self-centred, insensitive roughness. He lived largely by his own rules and sometimes stretched even them. Humanity in general he did not care for, preferring objects, especially artifacts; and he was not, as a rule, concerned to conceal this preference. When it came to getting the best out of fine or delicate mechanism, he had penetration and unlimited patience; for people, little or none. He possessed an above-average intellect and strong powers of concentration, but together with his solitary single-mindedness there went a potential (and at times something rather more than a potential) for intolerance and even fanaticism.

He had been the second of six children of a railway linesman, and in the cramped, overcrowded home had, in sheer self-defence, grown up tough and impervious. He had developed a preference for his own company, and a passion for acquiring and mastering technological instruments, so much more satisfying and solacing, in their smooth, controllable predictability, than the emotional inconsistencies of human relationships. During adolescence he grew still further apart both from his indigent parents and his rough-and-tumble brothers and sisters; and met with no opposition—rather the reverse—when, as soon as he had taken his A-levels, he left home and set up for himself. His family, in effect, forgot him.

He secured a good starting job at a bank in Windermere, yet it was not long before he came to be generally regarded as a misfit. Dour and quick to take offence, he tended to get on the wrong side of his colleagues and on more than one occasion displayed a total inability to appreciate the client's point of view.

Westcott did not need people or want to get on with them. Living alone and without luxury, his income was already sufficient for more self-indulgence and private enjoyment than as a boy he had dared to hope for. His life-style took the form of a fairly rigorous régime of self-denial, directed towards the acquisition of a planned succession of fine technological durables. It would, perhaps, be tedious to catalogue his possessions—the prismatic compass, the Zeiss binoculars, the wrist-watch which could play "Annie Laurie" under water while displaying in fluorescent script the date and operative sign of the zodiac (or something like that), the quadraphonic gramophone which made the sound of a piano seem to come from four directions instead of one (which might have seemed strange even to poor Westcott if he had ever been able to stop fiddling with the controls long enough to listen with any concentration), the three electric shavers, and so on. Not his least source of pride and joy, however, was his small collection of guns and pistols. These were, of course, illegal, but sometimes, taking out one or another, he would risk a few rounds' fire in suitably lonely and secluded places. He had a good eye and was no bad shot. With the only rifle he possessed—a Winchester .22—he reckoned himself particularly handy, and was fond of shooting matchsticks at twenty-five or thirty yards.

Some of his money had not been honestly come by. He had certain shady acquaintances and had more than once allowed himself, his car or his rooms to be made use of by these people.

Mr. Westcott possessed at any rate one friend and that was his landlady, Mrs. Rose Green, a middle-aged widow. In time an odd relationship grew up between these two, who had both experienced so little of what most people regard as affection. In winter, Mrs. Green would after a fashion reassure Mr. Westcott by pooh-poohing his fears of infection—for in this regard he was inclined to indulge a mild neurosis. When he was setting off for a long day on the Pillar or the Scafell range, she would make him sandwiches and admonish him to be sure to return punctually in the evening for oxtail stew. When she had a mind to spend a Saturday morning shopping in Keswick, Kendal or even Preston, Mr. Westcott, if he were not bound for the tops, would drive her there and back in the Volvo. They had little conversation—Mrs. Green was not a warm or talkative woman—but that in itself rather increased than diminished their mutual respect. For chat and laughter they felt, by and large, contempt.

The indignity, inconvenience and loss which Mrs. Green and he had suffered from the Plague Dogs aroused in Mr. Westcott all the brooding resentment of which he was capable (which was quite some), and this his dealings with Digby Driver had done nothing to allay. It was true that Driver had paid him quite well for the photographs, but while interviewing him Driver had—like many others before him—found himself disliking Mr. Westcott, who counted and pocketed the money without a word of thanks and tended to answer questions with a glowering and defensive "What? Well, for the simple reason that . . ." Driver had therefore begun to needle him, lightly but deftly, in his best Fleet Street manner, in his own mind comparing Westcott's reactions to those of a bull pierced by banderillas. Mr. Westcott had parted from Driver with the surly feeling—which he had been meant to have— that some of these smart London fellows thought they were too damned clever by half. Although on the following day the police had succeeded in persuading him that he could with safety resume the use of his car, they had not, of course, cleaned up the mess of eggs, butter and mud which had soaked well into the back seat, while the germicidal fumigator used by the local authority had had a noticeable effect on the upholstery (already torn in two places by Rowf's claws). Moreover the delicate valve-tuning, over which he had taken such pains, had been impaired by whoever had driven the car back to Windermere. Among his final questions to Digby Driver, before they parted, had been, "Why don't you go out and settle the damn dogs yourself, instead of writing newspaper articles about them?" To which Driver, perhaps a trifle stung, after all, by the thrust, had managed to reply only "Oh, we're content to leave that to burly dalesmen like you."

The following night—the Sunday—Mr. Westcott was sitting alone in his room, morosely watching colour television and wrapping himself in two blankets when the gas fire (greedier in cold weather, like all lodging-house metered fires) had consumed the last shilling earmarked for its consumption until next day. (He was not going to raid the sinking fund intended for the purchase of a wet suit and scuba equipment.) The image of the pestilential dogs, macabre in appearance and lethal in effect, came stalking across his peace of mind as the Red Death through the irregular apartments of Prince Prospero's castellated abbey. In his mind's eye he saw himself relentlessly pursuing them over the Scafell range, tracking them across Helvellyn's snowy wastes, following them from the larch copses of Eskdale to the plunging falls of Low Door. In his imagination their bodies, each neatly bullet-pierced through heart or brain, lay warm and still at last upon the fell. To hell with the *Orator,* with photographs, interviews or public acclaim. This ought properly to be an austere, individual vendetta, hunter against hunted, the putting of a salubrious and necessary stop to the dirty brutes who had had the audacity to spoil his car and gobble up three or four pounds' worth of meat and groceries. Having shot them, he would not even bother himself to go up to the bodies. He would simply walk away and go home.

By eleven o'clock his mind was made up. Monday and Tuesday were both, of course, working days, but under employment regulations he was entitled to take up to not more than two days' sick leave of absence without a medical certificate, and after his known ordeal and at this wintry time of year no awkward questions were likely to be asked. True, if enquired for he would not in fact be at home, but in all probability he would not be enquired for, and in any case Mrs. Green would if necessary cover up for him. He would need to brief her to that effect before he set out. As for the chance of being seen on the hills by anyone who might tell the bank, it seemed too remote to take into account.

Methodically he checked and laid out his fell boots, clothing and equipment—thin and thick socks, mackintosh overtrousers, scarf, gloves, anorak, Balaclava helmet, vacuum flask, map, whistle, prismatic compass, binoculars and light pack, together with the four-foot-long, waterproof rope-and-alpenstock bag which had never housed an alpenstock but which he used to carry in concealment his Winchester .22, together with its telescopic backsight (in padded bag) and the screwdriver for mounting it. The tobacco man himself could not have been more deliberate in his preparations. When all was ready he undressed, washed briefly in tepid water, set his alarm clock for the usual time and went to bed wearing his socks, with his overcoat piled on top of his eiderdown.

At breakfast Mrs. Green clicked her tongue and shook her head, but made no effort to dissuade him. It never occurred to either of them to go in for anything so articulate or demonstrative as the discussion of opinions or the rational influencing of each other's point of view. One might say, "Pass the salt," or "I'm not leaving until this afternoon," but one did not say, "I see this matter in rather a different light from you and will try to explain why." Nor did it occur to them that if Mr. Westcott were to succeed in killing one or both of the dogs he might not, in the current state of publicity, be able to return as obscurely as he had set out. Neither was that kind of person. There had had to be sausages for Sunday dinner—of that Mrs. Green was still fully conscious—and apparently Mr. Westcott was not going to take it lying down. Good for him. She was also conscious of the need, in Mr. Westcott's interest, for a well-buttoned lip. By twenty to ten he was on his way in the Volvo.

Mr. Westcott commenced by returning to the scene of the attack. He parked the car in the same place and waited to see whether the dogs would reappear. After half an hour they had not done so and he began considering his next step. On that morning two days ago, he reflected, they had apparently come down the fell from the east—probably more or less down the line of Fisher Gill. He had read in the paper of the panic caused by their appearance at a Glenridding farm a few days before. So it seemed most likely that they had some sort of lair in or under the Helvellyn range, somewhere between Thirlmere and southern Ullswater.

Mr. Westcott got out of the car, locked it, shouldered his pack and set off up Fisher Gill, in and out of the grass tussocks, over the soaking, spongey peat and moss and the last of the almost-melted snow. He was glad that he was going to have to make a search. He even hoped that it might turn out to be a long, hard one. He was determined to find and kill the dogs. It was an entirely personal conflict between himself and them, the spoilers of his possessions, the wreckers of scientific order. It ought not to be unduly easy, for he meant to prove to himself—or to someone—what he was worth in defence of his little realm. The dogs might have proved too much for everyone from Keswick to Hawkshead. They were not going to prove too much for him.

In the course of the next five and a half hours, until the fall of early darkness, Mr. Westcott covered thirteen miles. He was lucky enough to have no mist. Having climbed Sticks Gill up to the pass, where he saw but, since the snow was almost gone, could not follow for more than a few yards the vestigial tracks of two dogs, he spent some little time in searching with his binoculars the area between Stang and the reservoir. It was devoid of everything but curlews and buzzards, and at length he turned south and strode easily up to the summit of Raise. From there he made his way along the whole ridge—White Side and Low Man to Helvellyn itself—continually stopping to observe the slopes below. He paid particular attention to the sheltered Red Tarn basin between Striding Edge and Catstycam, where once, long ago, a terrier bitch had kept herself alive for three months, guarding the body of her master fallen from a precipitous height above. Someone had told him that the place was haunted, though neither Wordsworth's nor Scott's poems on the incident— both of which he had once taken the trouble to get hold of and read—told what had finally become of the dog.

Still bootless, he continued for two miles south to Dollywaggon Pike and, having stopped for about fifteen minutes to eat, began the rather tricky descent to the east, down the narrow, still-frosty Tongue. In these conditions of part-frost, part-thaw, the Tongue was more than a little dangerous, which was why Mr. Westcott chose it. He would have attempted the north face of Scafell if he had thought that to do so would give him a shot at the dogs. No course, whether involving fatigue, discomfort or actual danger, was going to remain unpursued, provided it held out the promise of success. More than once he slipped

White Side

on the rocks of the Tongue but, undeterred, pressed on
into the gully and so to the cascades of Ruthwaite Beck.

He returned northward across the valleys and ridges
east of the Helvellyn heights; straight over peat and ling,
rock and grass, stones and moss; Grisedale Forest, Nether-

most Cove Beck, Birkhouse Moor and Stang End. There was no least sign of the dogs; and he met no one all day. He regained the car by way of Sticks Pass, wondering whether his best course would be to spend the following day on the Dodds to the north. He was still wondering when he got back to Windermere, to hear from Mrs. Green the news that on Sunday afternoon the dogs had been encountered in the high valley of Levers Water by a Coniston farmer looking for odd sheep to bring down out of the snow. He had recognized them at once and taken to his heels, but not before observing that they appeared thin and fair shrammed with the cold.

Digby Driver, hastening back to Coniston to learn nothing different from what he had already heard from other eye-witnesses on previous occasions, left this farmer after no more than fifteen minutes and, back in his room, fairly cursed with frustration.

"The bloody brutes—they're just going to fizzle out— die up there—the whole thing'll collapse without one more story, yucky or otherwise! Simpson'll be livid! What a load of crap! Come on, Driver, you're not beat yet! What to do? What to do? Well, we'll just have to try the Research Station and hope for some sort of indiscretion. Any port in a storm!"

He rang up Lawson Park and this time, by some curious turn of the wheel, found himself talking to Dr. Boycott, who offered to see him by appointment forty-eight hours later, on the afternoon of Wednesday the 24th.

As has been said, Digby Driver had little time for set-piece, formal press interviews with official representatives. In his view—a not altogether inaccurate one—such interviews were often designed to soft-pedal or even to conceal things likely to provide material for news copy. It was usually more profitable to talk to the boot-boy or the cleaning-woman, but in this case he already had an even better contact, if only he could get at him.

"Look, Mr. Boycott," he said, "it's good of you to offer to see me, but the man I'd really like to talk to is Stephen Powell. Is he still off sick?"

"I'm afraid he is," answered Dr. Boycott. "Why do you want to talk to Mr. Powell so particularly?"

"Because he was so darned helpful when I met him before, the day I drove him back from Dunnerdale. It was him that—oh, well, never mind. But I don't want to waste your time unnecessarily, and it'll suit me perfectly well just to have a word with Powell. Could you give me his address, perhaps?"

"Well, he'll be back tomorrow or the next day, I understand," said Dr. Boycott, "so if you like we'll both see you on Wednesday afternoon. Will three o'clock suit you? Excellent. Well, until then, good-bye."

Tuesday the 23rd November

The following morning was more than a little misty on the tops, but nevertheless Mr. Westcott set out even earlier than before. Having reached Little Langdale, he was able to see that the northern end of the Coniston range was considerably less obscured by mist than the Old Man itself. Accordingly he ran up to the Wreynus Pass, left the Volvo and climbed the Grey Friar by way of Wetside Edge. The weather had become warmer and damp, with a light west wind, and he sweated in his anorak as he stood swinging his binoculars this way and that across the slopes above Seathwaite Tarn and Cockley Beck. There were no dogs to be seen. He crossed the saddle to Carrs, ate an early lunch and tramped southward to Swirral, Great How Crags and the Levers Hause. Here the mist was troublesome, and Westcott, knowing himself to be immediately above Levers Water and the very place where the dogs had last been seen two days before, went down as far as Cove Beck and covered that area very thoroughly indeed. He found nothing and climbed back to the Hause. His tenacious and obsessive nature was not yet dispirited but, like a fisherman who has not had a rise all day, he now made a deliberate demand on his concen-

Carrs

tration, persistence and staying-power to play the game out to the end and finish the day in style, win or lose. Who could tell? Mist or no mist, he might even now run slap into the dogs sheltering in a peat-rift or under a thorn. This, apparently, was what the farmer had done. Making use of his prismatic compass in the mist, he set off for Brim Fell, Goat's Hause and the Dow Crag.

"I'm very glad you've felt well enough to come back today, Stephen," said Dr. Boycott. "There are several important things. I trust you're quite recovered, by the way?"

"Yeah, more or less, I think," replied Mr. Powell. "A bit post-influenzal, you know, but it'll pass off, I dare say." In point of fact he felt dizzy and off colour.

"Well, work's often a good thing to put you back on your feet, as long as you don't overdo it," said Dr. Boycott. "You should certainly go home early tonight, but I'd like you to be familiarizing yourself today with the details of this new project that we've been asked to set up. I shall want you to take entire charge of it in due course."

"What's the present position with those dogs, chief, by the way? Are they still at large?"

"Oh, yes, the dogs—I'm glad you mentioned that. Yes, they're still very much at large, I'm afraid; they seem to keep turning up all over the place. On Saturday, apparently, they actually robbed a car of a load of groceries. There've been a lot of phone calls, and I dare say you may very well get some more today. Mind you, we're still not admitting that those dogs are ours. Ours may be dead long ago."

"What about Whitehall?"

"Oh, they're still blathering away. There's going to be some sort of debate in Parliament, I gather. That Michael What's-His-Name was up here last Friday, as you know. He wanted to see Goodner's laboratory and then he was pressing me to give an assurance that the dogs couldn't have been in contact with any plague-infected fleas."

Mr. Powell made an effort to show interest. "Did you give it?"

"Certainly not. How could I? How could anyone? Anyway, we're scientists here—we don't get mixed up in politics. We've got work to do, and we're not to be run from Westminster or Whitehall or anywhere else."

"That's where the money comes from, I suppose."

Dr. Boycott waved the triviality away with one hand.

"That's quite incidental. This work's got to be done, so the money's got to be found. You might just as well say the money for water-borne sewage comes from Westminster and Whitehall."

"It does—some of it, anyway."

Dr. Boycott looked sharply at Mr. Powell for a moment, but then continued.

"Well—well. No, I think the principal thing that's bothering the Ministry is having to admit that bubonic plague's being studied here at all—as a Ministry of Defence project, that is. It was secret, of course. No one was supposed to know—even you weren't supposed to know."

"I *didn't* know—well, hardly."

"I still can't imagine how it got out," said Dr. Boycott. "But I suppose the press will continue to make all they can of it. And talking of the press, that reminds me. I've agreed to see this *Orator* man, Driver, tomorrow afternoon at three. I'd like you to join me. If I'm going to talk to a fellow like that, there ought to be a witness, in case he misrepresents us later."

"O.K. chief, I'll be there."

"Now, this new project I was starting to tell you about," said Dr. Boycott. "It's a pretty big one, with American money behind it—another defence thing, of course. We're going to construct a specially large refrigeration unit, the interior of which will simulate tundra; or steppe-like conditions, anyway. There'll be a wind tunnel, too, and some means of precipitating blizzard. These will be near-arctic conditions, you understand. There'll be food and some kind of shelter situated in one place, and a built-in escalator whose effect will be that the subject animals have to cover the equivalent of anything from thirty to sixty miles to reach it. We may install certain deterrents—fear-precipitants and so on. Actually, we're not quite agreed yet on that aspect of the work, but—"

"What subject animals, chief?"

"Dogs, almost certainly. Much the most suitable. Now as to timing—"

Mr. Powell closed his eyes. He had come over faint and his head was swimming. He began to realize that he was more post-influenzal than he had thought. As he made an effort to concentrate once more on what Dr. Boycott was saying, there came from outside a sudden burst of tommy-gun fire. He started, sat up quickly and looked out of the window. Tyson's boy Tom, emerging with a pail of bran mash from the shed across the way, was idly running the mixing-stick along a sheet of corrugated iron which had been used to patch the wall.

"—As to timing, Stephen, I was saying—"

Mr. Powell hesitated. "I—I—it's kind of—I wonder, chief—only, you see—look, do you think you could possibly put someone else on this? The thing is—"

"Put someone *else* on it?" asked Dr. Boycott, puzzled. "How d'you mean?"

"Well, I can't explain exactly, but—" Mr. Powell buried his face in his hands for a moment. When he looked up he said, "Perhaps I'm not quite back to normal yet. I only meant—well, you see—"

To his horror, Dr. Boycott saw—or thought he saw—tears standing in Mr. Powell's eyes. Hurriedly he said, "Well, we needn't go into that any more just now. We'll come back to it another time. You'll want to be having a look at your other stuff. By the way, Avril finally finished off that hairspray thing while you were away yesterday. The stuff was absolutely hopeless—the second lot of rabbits all had to be destroyed. I can't imagine how anyone ever supposed he could get away with marketing a product like that to the public. Just wasting our time and everybody else's. We shall charge him for the rabbits, naturally. Anyway, if I don't see you again before, we'll meet at three tomorrow afternoon."

In a confused fantasy of mist and hunger, Snitter was hunting for the tod across the hills and rocks of dream. A bitter rain was falling and twice, as he topped a slope, he glimpsed momentarily but never winded, disappearing over the next, the familiar, grey-haired figure with yellow scarf and walking-stick.

"Ah ha!" said Snitter to the vanishing figure, "I know better than to run after you! You look real, but you're not real. I've got to find the tod, or else we're going to die in this horrible place."

He knew now where he was; on the long, heathery slope that led down to the road winding up out of the green dale—the empty road that crossed the pass by the square stone post set upright in the turf. He remembered the post: he had lifted his leg against it for luck when the tod had led them across the pass on their way to Helvellyn. The wind was tugging in uneven gusts over the ling and up from below wavered the falling of the becks. A curlew cried, "Whaup, whaup," in the hills and as he came down to the road a blackcock went rocketing away from almost under his paws. It was all just as he remembered.

He paused, looking about him and sniffing the wet ground for some trace of the tod. Suddenly he saw, below him, a blue car ascending the pass, threading in and out of sight, steadily climbing the steep edge of the hillside, crossing the bridge and coming on towards the stone where he stood watching. As it reached level ground and drew to a halt on the short grass of the verge, he saw that the driver was a merry-looking, pretty girl, who smiled at him, calling and beckoning.

Snitter ran up eagerly and jumped into the car by the near-side door which she leant across to hold open. She smelt deliciously of soap, scent, leather and femininity. He put his muddy paws in her lap and licked her face and she laughed, scratching his ears.

"You're a friendly chap, aren't you?" she said. "Poor doggie, you've hurt your head, haven't you? And where have you sprung from, mmh? I bet your master's worried to death about you." His old, original collar had apparently come back and she read it, twisting round the little brass plaque with two slim, cool fingers pressed against his neck. "Would you like me to take you home? D'you suppose there's a reward, mmh?"

Head close to hers, Snitter wagged his tail, smelling her hairspray and the trace of wax in one small, dainty ear. "I'll give you a reward," she said, and popped a toffee into his mouth. He bit it. It had no taste at all and he shook his head, teeth squelching in the sticky gluten.

"It's dream toffee," she said, laughing and kissing him. "This is all just a dream, you know. Are you hungry? Poor old chap, then—it's no good looking in the back of *this* car. There's nothing there—only my bag."

She started the engine and backed to the road, leaving the still-unclosed passenger door to swing back and forth as she did so. "You can help me if you like," she said. "D'you know what I'm looking for? I need a mouse—a live one."

Snitter found speech. "I've got a mouse; he's in my head."

"Could he be injected? Only, you see, I'm overdue and of course my boy-friend and I want to know as quick as we can." She looked at her watch. "Oo, gosh, I'd better be getting on. He'll be home soon. We're living together, you know." She laughed. "Living in sin, as they used to say."

"Sin?" said Snitter. "I don't understand, but then I'm only a dog, of course. A kind of house you live in, is it? The men have taken all the houses away, you know. I don't believe there's a house for miles."

She patted him, leaning across, about to close the door.

"Why," she said, "we both believe the very same. There's no such thing as sin, is there? No such thing any more."

Suddenly Snitter realized that they were not alone in the car. The shining fur coat pressed against them began to writhe and hunch into folds, which resolved themselves into odorous, furry, fox-like creatures leaping past him into the back seat. On the instant there started up among them a great, brown lizard, with burnished neck of verdant gold, smooth, supple scales and forked tongue flickering in and out between its eyes. From the girl's feet, pressed to the controls, two tawny snakes came writhing.

The girl drew a knife from the top of her skirt.

"You don't mind blood, do you?" she said. "I was explaining, wasn't I, it's what I hope I'm going to see quite soon."

Snitter flung up his head, howling in terror.

"What's the matter now?" growled Rowf, startled out of sleep beside him. "Why on earth can't you keep quiet?"

"Oh, thank goodness! A dream! I'm sorry, Rowf—I suppose it's the hunger. It's more than three days now since we've eaten anything—not a beetle, not a caterpillar—"

"I know that as well as you do. Well, then. Three days, four days. Go to sleep. I deserve it even if you don't."

"I'd eat anything—anything, Rowf; if only there was—"

The lethargy of starvation, returning, flowed over Snitter, pressing him down like a soft, heavy paw. He slept, dreamed of the dog shed and the tobacco man, and woke to find himself half under Rowf's shaggy flank.

"Lodo," murmured Snitter. "I thought—yes, it was Lodo—"

"The bitch, you mean—that spaniel-eared one? Always smelt of burning?"

"Yes, she—was telling me—"

"What?"

"She told us—d'you remember?—the whitecoats made her breathe some kind of smoke, same as the tobacco man does. They put a thing over her face so that she had to breathe this smoke."

"Well?"

"Well, she said she hated it to begin with, but then later on, when they didn't give her the smoke, she wanted it."

Rowf turned his head, biting at a flea in his rump.

"We'll be like that, won't we?" said Snitter. "When we aren't here any longer, when we're not hungry or cold, we'll miss it. We'll wish we were."

"When d'you mean?"

"When we're dead."

"When you're dead you're dead. Ask the tod."

From the misty gully above came a faint rattling of stones and the scramble of a sheep's hooves. Two or three pebbles, pattering down the precipice, came to rest not far away.

"Flies on the window-pane," murmured Snitter drowsily. "There's nothing to be seen, but they can't get through it. Nothing's very strong, of course—much too strong for us. Like black milk."

"Black milk? Where?"

"It was in a lighted bowl, kept upside down on the ceiling. Very strong stuff. You couldn't look at it for long or it boiled. Well, after all, rain, you know—that just stays up there in the sky, I suppose until the men want it to come down. If rain can stay up there, why not milk?

Or Kiff. I mean, Kiff's not dead, is he? There's nothing at all strange, really, about black milk."

"I never thought of it like that."

For many hours past they had been dozing and waking, sheltered from the wind at the foot of the Dow Crag. Below them, beyond the tumbled screes, lay the narrow expanse of Goat's Water, treeless, grassless, weedless—cold water and stones.

After the dog Wag had left them, two days before, they had wandered aimlessly southward, up over Grey Crag, down into Boulder Valley and so round, below the eastern precipices of the Old Man, into this dreary vale, remote and sequestered, an open mouthful of tooth-stumps, a stone-grey muzzle asleep by a dead fire on a winter's night: a place where appetite and energy—almost life itself—seemed futile, as though among the craters of the moon. Only the clouds and gulls, far overhead, maintained their effortless sailing; a moving sky above a still land.

"The tobacco man will be round," said Snitter, looking about him in the gathering dusk.

"Not here."

"No, but it's like that here, too, isn't it? Whatever we were there for—you know, in the tobacco man's shed—it was nothing to do with us—with dogs—no good to dogs. And this—whatever it's for—this is nothing to do with us, either."

"We've been here before, Snitter, do you know that? With the tod. I chased the yow until it fell over and then we came down here and ate it—remember?"

"It seems a long time ago. The tod won't come back now."

"Snitter, there's a cave up there, among those boulders. I remember seeing it that night. We'll lie up there for now and find a sheep tomorrow. I'll kill it somehow."

During the night it thawed, as the sheep-dog had said it would, and by first light almost all the snow had gone. Rowf, however, woke surly and listless, biting at his staring ribs and falling asleep again, head on paws. There was not a sheep to be seen and he could not be persuaded to hunt for one.

During the afternoon Snitter limped down to the water, drank and returned. He woke Rowf and together they went to look for the remains of the sheep which they had driven over the precipice, but found only wool and bones at the foot of a sheer gully. They returned to the cave and passed a third night without food.

It was on the following afternoon that Snitter suffered the dream of the girl in the car.

"Nothing strange about it really," repeated Snitter in the solitude. "Nothing strange about black milk. I dare say men might make black bread, or even black sheep if they wanted, come to that. They sometimes make black clouds when they want it to rain—I've seen them." Then, with sudden determination, "Rowf, I'm going to look for the tod: and if I can't find him, I'm going down to some farm or other and give myself up to the men. Anything's better than starving to death—"

Rowf, battered and hollow as an old kettle discarded among the stones, grinned up at him from his refuge of despair.

"Your dignity! 'I hope we die alone!' "

"Oh, Rowf—"

"Go on, then, off you go! I'm damned if I'm going to be taken back to the whitecoats' tank. I'd rather starve here—it'll be less trouble. And as for finding the tod, I tell you, Snitter, if you can do that, *I'll* make some food drop down to us off the tops. There you are, that's a bargain. One's as likely as the other."

"Now the snow's gone the men may have brought some sheep back up here. Couldn't we try to find one?"

Without replying, Rowf put his head back on his paws and shut his eyes.

Snitter, wandering away through the stones and loose shale, came down to the northern end of Goat's Water and splashed through the infall turbid with melted snow. The little tarn lay still, unruffled by any wind, grey water reflecting clouds and grey gulls sailing.

I suppose there are fish in there, thought Snitter, like the ones in the river where my master used to take me for walks: and I suppose they think they can swim anywhere they like. The gulls, too—those gulls up there must think they've decided to glide round and round. I wonder whether I've really decided of my own accord to go this way? If I have, I'm sure I don't know why. I remember hearing that dogs often go away by themselves to die. Jimjam said he wanted to go away but of course he couldn't get out of the pen, poor chap.

He was climbing the south-west slope of Brim Fell and, as he came to the lower level of the mist, paused a moment before heading on into the thick mirk above. The sighing, moving air, the gloom and solitude about him appeared more sinister and hostile than ever before. Both the sky above and the tarn below were hidden and now— or so it seemed—even his ears had begun to deceive him, for from somewhere below and beyond—somewhere distant—he thought he could hear the barking of dogs. Urgent and excited they sounded, as though the tobacco man had come among them with his pails.

That must be it, thought Snitter. I keep on remembering feeding-time—not surprising—and now it even sounds real. Of course it isn't really, any more than my poor master when I see him. I wonder where I'm going? And —and who—what sort of man is this coming? I don't like the smell of him, somehow.

He was thick in the mist now, high up on the starved, sheep-cropped turf of Brim Fell. He could hear a soft, rhythmic thud-thud-thud of approaching boots, sounds of creaking leather and steady breathing. Quickly he hid himself, crouching flat in a peat-rift as a dark, burly young man came looming through the mist, striding purposefully towards him—a young man all hung about with jolting tubes on straps and discs of glass and leather; with a long, narrow bag on his back, a scarf round his neck and a coloured paper clutched in the fingers of one hand. For one fleeting moment he turned his head in Snitter's direction and Snitter, though he could not tell why, cowered close and let him go past. As he remained lying still, with closed eyes, the distant dog-sounds from below seemed muted, in his ears, to a kind of lullaby.

> *"You were disturbed inside your head,*
> *And thought to clean the cobwebs out.*

> There will be none when you are dead—
> The skull untroubled, have no doubt.
> And you will learn to do without
> This flesh and blood quotidian:
> Refined to nothing, bleached to nowt,
> Need seek no more your vanished man."

"I suppose not," said Snitter, torpid with starvation and half-asleep on the spongey peat. "One ought to try not to mind too much, I suppose. We're only dogs, and it's a bad world for animals, as Rowf's always saying. After all— why, it's getting positively crowded up here! Who's this coming now? Oh, no—it can't—it *can't* be—"

The mist swirled, the wet grass tugged in the wind, and now Snitter felt sure that he must indeed be mad and, as so often in the past, the victim of delusion, for up through the mist and wind came the tod. Limping it was, its breath coming in great, steaming gasps, brush trailing, eyes staring, belly caked with mud. Its teeth were bared above and below its lolling tongue and it turned its head this way and that, continually listening and sniffing the air. As Snitter jumped up, it snapped at him and made as if to run away, but he had no difficulty in overtaking it.

"Tod! Tod! It's me, it's Snitter! Tod, don't you know me?"

The tod halted, staring round at him with a kind of slow, glazed recognition. It reeked of a deadly fear.

"Oh, ay, it's th' wee fella. Ye'd best boogger off sharp, hinny, unless ye fancy th' Dark wi' me." As he made no answer it added more urgently, "Go on, kidder, hadda-way!"

It sank down on the turf, panting convulsively, rubbing its spattered mask on the grass.

"Tod, what—oh, what is it? What's happened?"

"Can ye not hear them bastards ahint? A puff o' wind into yon mist an' ye'll sharp see them forbye; ay, an' they'll see ye. Shift yersel', marrer, haddaway hyem!"

"Tod, come back with me! Come on, run! Rowf's down there—whatever it is, we'll save you! Quickly, tod!"

The many-mouthed barking and yelping broke out

again, louder and nearer, and now could be heard also a man's voice hollering and other, more distant human voices answering from further off. The tod grinned mirthlessly.

"Can ye not hear what the bastards is yammerin' on aboot, one to t'other—'Ah'll have first bite at his belly'? Ah've browt them siven mile, but Ah'll nivver lose them noo. Ah thowt last neet th' frost wad cum doon an' they'd not be oot th' morn. Ah wez wrong. A tod only hez to be wrong once, ye knaw."

"Oh, tod, tod! There must be something we can do—"

"Divven't fash yersel', hinny! Ah ken weel where Ah'm goin'. It's akward eneuf noo, but there'll be ne akwardness i' th' Dark. It's not th' Dark that frightens me, it's their rivin', bloody teeth. Have ye nivver hord say, 'Ne deeth over bad fer a tod'? Mebbies it'll soon be done. Ah'm not whinjin'—Ah'd rather go te th' Dark like a tod than in yon whitecoat dump o' yours. Tell th' big fella taa taa from me. He wez a grand lad—reet mazer wi' yows, tell him."

It was gone like smoke into the mist, down over the edge, down the north-western slope of Brim Fell, making for Tarn Head Moss and Blake Rigg Crag beyond. Snitter ran after it a few yards, then pulled up and lay shivering in the gloom. Some overwhelming thing was taking place —something old and dreadful, something which he remembered to have happened before in this very spot. About him was flowing a rank, feral scent, savage, and blood-seeking. Big, shadowy creatures were approaching, voracious and intent, running swiftly up out of the mist, lemon and white, black and tawny, noses to ground, sterns feathering, long ears swinging as they came loping over the top; some running mute, others giving tongue in fierce excitement. Hounds they were, great hounds shouldering past him where he crouched on the verge of the steep, heedless of him, paying him no attention in the heat and concentration of their pursuit. Behind them, on foot, ran the lean-faced huntsman, red-coated, horn clutched in one hand, almost spent with the long chase but still finding voice to urge them on. Over the edge they went, tumbling and jostling, each eager for his share, and were lost to view among the boulders. Yet still from a thousand feet below rose up their excited notes, one under another like the sound of a river in flood upon the unseen valley floor.

Snitter pattered in their wake. The wet turf and stones bore their clean, sharp smell—the smell of hunting, meat-eating animals in perfect health. It was as though a band of demi-gods had swept past him in fulfilment of their appointed function of pursuit and death; a ghastly, apocalyptic duty for ever carried out in some timeless region beyond, now—on this occasion—superimposed and enacted upon the bare hillside where he found himself, as in a dream, running alone through the clouds of swirling vapour.

Suddenly the wind freshened, carrying a far-off smell of seaweed, the heavy-sweet odour of cows in a shed and, laid atop of these, an instant's scent of the tod. The curtain of mist broke up into streamers eddying away across the fell, and now he could see clearly enough all that lay below him—could see the peat-hags and moss above Seathwaite Tarn, the sullen, black stream winding through them, the mouth of the cavern beyond; and the tod running, running, staggering over the moss, its brush a sopping weight dragged behind it. After it came the hounds, spread out, clamouring in frenzy to crush, conclude and quell, to dust the varmint and be done. Even as he watched, the foremost hound, on the very verge of the beck, reached the tod's shoulder and, turning quickly inward, butted and rolled it over on the stones.

He shut his eyes then, and scrabbled head-downward at the turf, for he did not want to see the pack close in, did not want to see the tod leaping, snapping and biting, outnumbered thirty to one, the blood spurting, the tearing, thrashing and worrying, the huntsman whipping his way into the turmoil and the tod's body snatched, lifted high and knife-hacked for brush and mask before being tossed back—oh, so merrily—among the baying, tussling foxhounds.

Mr. Westcott pressed on up the northern ridge of Brim Fell. The mist was moderately thick, but he had known it worse and furthermore he had an intuitive feeling, born of wide experience of Lakeland weather, that it was likely to lift, possibly very soon and certainly before sunset. He came to the cairn on the summit, sat down on it and, having examined his map, took a compass bearing into the mist of 225 degrees. Then he made allowance for the magnetic variation, selected a rock on the bearing as far ahead as he could see and set off downhill to cover the six or seven hundred yards to Goat's Hause.

It was silent in the mist, and his solitude gave him a satisfying sense of power, integrity and self-sufficiency. Alone with his instruments, his fell experience and his health and stamina he, like a well-found ship in the Atlantic, was a match for his surroundings in all their wildness and adversity. In his mind's eye he saw himself, purposeful, grim, intent, well-equipped and organized, moving through the fog like avenging Nemesis, deliberate and irresistible. The dogs, wherever they were, might as well give up now, for he, equal to all contingencies and possessed of the will and endurance of Spencer-Chapman himself, would get them in the end, if not today then later. He was retribution, *timor mortis* and the two-handed engine at the door.

Once he thought he noticed some kind of furtive movement a short distance off in the grass, and turned his head to look. He caught a glimpse of something off-white apparently skulking in a peat-rift, but then concluded that it was nothing but a sodden paper bag blown there by the wind. As he strode on he could hear behind him, coming up from somewhere below Levers Hause, the cry of hounds and the hollering of the huntsman. It sounded as though they were approaching, and in full cry. However, that was nothing to do with him and his mission. Indeed it was, if anything, a nuisance, for, if the Plague Dogs were anywhere close by, it might alarm them and cause them to be off. By all that he had heard, they were as cunning as foxes and more like wild animals than dogs.

Five minutes later his boots squelched across the muddy, snow-patched wet of the saddle and began to climb the slope of Dow Crag. It was at this moment that the mist began to lift. He could hear hounds pouring down into the valley above Seathwaite Tarn, and went so far as to stop, focus his binoculars and look down at the Moss before calling himself sharply to order. There were only about two hours of daylight left and tomorrow he must be back at work. Since Seathwaite Tarn valley would now be an unlikely place in which to find the dogs, he would make the most of the remaining light by going along the tops as far as Walna Scar, descending into Goat's Water valley (a remote place and as likely a hide-out as anywhere), up to the Hause again and so back to Wreynus by the way he had come. There was time enough for that, and he could safely come down Wetside Edge in the late twilight.

He was well up on Dow Crag now and approaching the head of North Gully. Except for a patch on the summit the mist had cleared and it would, he reflected, be possible to see down to the valley floor on his left. With this purpose he left the path and struck off over the rocks, intending to find a place near the top of Easter Gully from which he could command a view of Goat's Water and the screes at the foot of the Dow precipices.

Suddenly he stopped dead, with a heave in his belly like that felt by an angler when a big trout rises to the fly. For an instant, through a cleft between two projecting rocks about thirty feet down in the gully, he had caught sight of a dog—a large, black, rough-haired dog—lying, apparently asleep, beside a heap of stones at the foot of the pitch. The field of view between the two rocks was so narrow that by the time he had taken it in he had walked past the line of vision which had shown him the dog. He hastened back, dodging about with his head like a man spying, from the street, through a chink in somebody else's curtains.

The dog came into view again and he got the binoculars on it. Yes: it was, unmistakably, one of the two dogs which had set upon his car near Thirlmere. The collar was half-buried in the rough, staring coat at the nape of its neck, but the dog was emaciated and beneath the chin, where it hung loose, the green plastic showed up as plainly as a necklace.

"Steady, now, steady," muttered Mr. Westcott. Clasping his hands to stop their trembling, he drew a deep breath and considered. The quicker he shot the better. To go down below would take the best part of an hour and the dog might well be gone. His very approach, which he could not conceal, would be enough to alarm it. The trouble was that his view down the precipitous gully was so awkward and so much restricted that probably he could get only a standing shot. He checked this. He was right. Lying down or on one knee, he could not see the dog. And he would have only one chance—that was virtually certain. If his first shot missed, the dog would be off into dead ground under the Crag. Considering that what he had was a rifle, not a shot-gun, and that he could not get a lying shot, he ought to try to find some sort of steady rest.

He took the Winchester out of its bag and mounted the telescopic backsight. Then he removed the binoculars and compass from his neck and laid them on the ground. Scanning the top of the gully, he could see a way down to the cleft that was certainly feasible, if only he could get there without dislodging scree or pebbles and so alarming the dog.

The Winchester had no sling and, gripping it in his left hand, he began the descent. It was a distinctly nerve-racking business and at each step he bit his lip, moving from one hand-hold to another and wondering how the hell he was going to get back. He would think about that later, when the dog was dead.

Slowly, Snitter's head cleared and he recognized once more his bleak surroundings. The tod—the hounds—the dreadful squealing of the tod—the huntsman and his knife —he himself must not stay here. The mist was almost gone. He would be in view. He began running back along the edge of Brim Fell, in the opposite direction from the terrible thing he had tried not to see.

Soon he came round as far as Goat's Hause. Here, on the track, he at once picked up the smell of a man, very fresh; a man who could, indeed, only just have gone by. A moment's nose-reflection told him that this must be none other than the dark, burly young man from whom he had hid before meeting the tod; the man of whom he had felt so distinct a distrust and fear.

But the man was alone and a long way from the hunt. Perhaps he was carrying food. Indeed, it was extremely likely that he was and to approach him would not really be much to risk. A sensible dog could keep at a distance and give the man no chance to put him on a lead; and the man might very well throw him some food, even if it was only a mouthful. Looking up and ahead, he could now actually see the man striding away towards the summit, not very far off.

Snitter set off in pursuit, watching closely in case the man should turn round. Then there came a sudden swirl of mist and when it had blown aside the man had vanished.

Puzzled, Snitter ran cautiously on. Could the man have hidden and now be lying in wait for him? But there seemed to be nowhere for him to hide. Nearing the top he went still more slowly, following the man by scent. The scent left the path and led away across the rocks. It seemed to be leading towards a steep gully, very like the one into which he, Rowf and the tod had hunted the yow by night.

He came hesitantly up to the mouth of the gully and looked in. Sure enough, there below him, quite close, stood the man, peering down through a cleft between two rocks. It would be safe enough to attract his attention—in a place like that no human could possibly grab a dog. Furthermore, he *was* carrying food. Snitter could smell it. Yapping eagerly, he made a quick leap down to a convenient ledge below.

Mr. Westcott's bowels were loose and his breath was coming short with fear and excitement. The black dog had not moved and from moment to moment, as he clambered, he continued to catch glimpses of it. He estimated that it must be about three hundred feet below him—a sure shot if only he could find the right point of vantage.

He reached the cleft between the two projecting rocks. It was a frightening place, much less secure than it had appeared from above, with an almost sheer drop below and the smooth surfaces glistening with icy moisture. He had planned to lean against the left-hand rock and rest the rifle on its outer edge, near the centre of the gully. But now, at close quarters, this idea proved impracticable, for the rock was too tall and in any case projected downward, at considerably more than a right angle to the side of the gully. The opposite rock was better, its height diminishing to about four feet at the outer edge, but to use this for a support would, of course, involve a left-handed, left-eyed shot.

However, thought Mr. Westcott, with the telescopic sight and at such short range a left-handed shot offered a good chance of success. Anyway, it was the only chance that was being offered. In spite of his determination he was growing increasingly nervous. The drop below alarmed him and a glance over his shoulder confirmed that, unless he was prepared to jettison his rifle, the climb back was going to be horribly precarious.

With a thrust against the rock wall, he pushed himself across the breadth of the gully to the opposite side, leant forward, resting his weight against the right-hand rock, laid the barrel of the Winchester over its upper edge and eased himself into position. He was able to lean out towards the centre just far enough for the shot and no more.

There was his quarry and no mistake. The dog showed up in the back-sight like a black haystack. He slipped the safety-catch, aligned the fore-sight on the dog's ear and —awkwardly, with his left index finger—took the first trigger-pressure.

At this moment, not twenty feet above him in the gully, there broke out a sharp, excited yapping. Mr. Westcott started and simultaneously fired. The shot severed the dog's collar and as it leapt up he saw the blood spurt from its neck. In the same instant he lost his balance, clutching frantically at the icy top of the rock. The rifle slipped from his grasp, a stone turned under his foot, he grabbed at the rock again, found a slippery hold, retained it for one appalling, nightmare moment—time enough to recognize the dog looking down at him—and then pitched headlong.

When Snitter had left him, Rowf tried to return once more to his dreary sleep on the stones. Yet despite the feeling of exhaustion which seemed to permeate his whole body as the wind the hawthorn, he remained awake, gnawing on his misery like an old, meatless bone. Snitter had said that in the last resort he meant to go down into the valley and give himself up to the men. And it was this to which Rowf knew that he himself was not equal. This was the fear of which he was ashamed—the fear of which he had always been too much ashamed to tell even Snitter. In the instant after the electric light had filled the Glenridding farmyard, he had thought: What if they *don't* shoot? What if they send for the whitecoats and take me back to the drowning-tank? The drowning-tank, he knew, was his and his alone. No other dog in the shed had ever been put into the drowning-tank. So it was a fair assumption that the whitecoats wanted him back to go on putting him in the tank. His fear of the tank knew no bounds and of that fear he was ashamed. The whitecoats, whom he could not help but think of as his masters, wanted him to go on drowning in the tank, and he could not do it. Once, long ago, he reflected, the poor terrier bitch whom Snitter had seen—the bitch that was now a ghost—must, to remain by her master and guard him, have faced protracted death from hunger. Yet the drowning-tank was the true reason why, after the Glenridding escape, he, Rowf, had refused to attempt another farm raid; and the reason why, though he shared Snitter's despair, he had now let him set out alone.

He remembered a dog called Licker, who had told him how the whitecoats sometimes killed animals instantaneously. "This other dog and I," Licker had said, "were being restrained in metal harnesses. It was horribly painful, and suddenly this other dog stopped yelping and went unconscious. The whitecoats took him out of the harness and looked at him, and then one of them nodded to the other and just struck him dead on the spot. I tell you, I envied him."

And I envy him too, thought Rowf. Why couldn't there be just a quick shot, now, and that would be that? The tod was right; you'd wonder why we take so much trouble to stay alive. The reason is that no creature can endure being hungry—as the tod very well knew. The bitch—how did she do it?

Indeed, his hunger had now become an unendurable torment. His instincts were cloudy with hunger; he smelt the scree and the tarn as though through a drifting smoke of hunger, saw them as though through a sheet of hunger-coloured glass. He took a paw between his teeth and for a moment seriously wondered whether he could eat it. The pain of biting answered him.

He tried to gnaw a stone, then laid his head back on his paws and began to think of all the enemies he would have been ready to fight, if only fighting could have saved Snitter's life and his own. If nothing else, he had always been a fighter. Might it not be possible, in some way or other, to go down fighting? To bite, to bite, to sink the teeth in, aarrgh!—if only I hadn't driven the tod away, perhaps we might have learned at last how to be wild animals. Men—how I hate men! I wish I'd killed one, like Snitter. Oh, I'd rip his throat out, tear open his stomach and eat it, shloop, shloop!

Suddenly he felt a stinging pain in his neck, like the bite of a horse-fly but sharper, fiercer. As he leapt up, the sound of the shot reached him, magnified in the gully walls. Tearing over the loose stones, he could hear Snitter yapping somewhere far above and then a shriek—a human shriek—of fear. He stopped, confused. Where was Snitter? Pebbles were falling, yes and something else, something much heavier than pebbles. He could hear it, whatever it was, slithering, bumping, thudding to rest behind him in the gully. Holding himself ready to run, he watched to see what would emerge, but now there was complete stillness. He waited some time. Nothing moved. Not a sound. He could hear his own blood dripping on the stones.

He returned cautiously round the buttress to the foot of the gully. A little way off, sprawled on the scree, lay a man's body, the head bent grotesquely sideways, one outstretched arm ending in a gashed and bleeding hand.

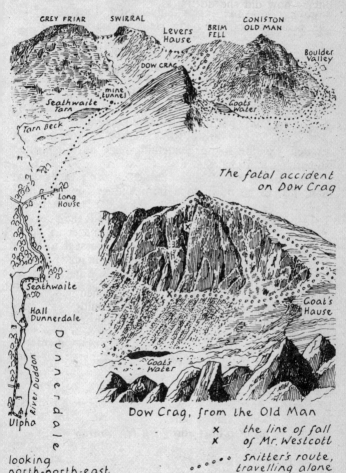

Sunday 21st November
to
Thursday, 25th November

LEVERS HAUSE
TO ULPHA

GREY FRIAR   SWIRRAL   Levers House   BRIM FELL   CONISTON OLD MAN

DOW CRAG

Boulder Valley

mine tunnel

Seathwaite Tarn

Goat's Water

Tarn Beck

Long House

Seathwaite

Hall Dunnerdale

Dunnerdale

River Duddon

Ulpha

looking
north-north-east

The fatal accident
on Dow Crag

Goat's Hause

Goat's Water

Dow Crag, from the Old Man

×   the line of fall
×   of Mr. Westcott
····· Snitter's route,
       travelling alone

The smell of blood was warm and strong. Rowf began to salivate. Slowly he moved nearer, drooling, licking his chops, urinating over the stones. The body smelt of sweat and fresh, meaty flesh. The smell obliterated the sky, the tarn, the stones, the wind, Rowf's own fear. There was nothing else in the world—only toothy, doggy Rowf and the meaty smell of the body. He went nearer still.

Snitter could not make out where the man had gone. Beyond doubt, however, he had disappeared, and further than round the rock too, for even the smell of his presence—his fear and his sweat and breath—had vanished. For a little while Snitter pattered ineffectively about in the top of the gully, but then gave up and climbed out. As he was doing so, he heard Rowf barking below him—an excited, exciting sound. Something must have happened; something had changed.

Poor old Rowf! thought Snitter. I can't really leave him, just to go down to a farm and get myself killed. Killed! Oh, good heavens, oh, the tod! That settles it! I shall *have* to go back and tell Rowf about the poor tod. What was it he said I was to say? "Reet mazer wi' yows" —I can't just ignore the poor tod's last message to Rowf.

Still bemused with shock and hunger, he made his way back to the Hause and so down to Goat's Water. Stopping to bark as he crossed the infall beck, he heard a curiously muffled reply from Rowf, coming, apparently, from deep in one of the gullies. It was not until he got nearer that he heard also the sounds of dragging and worrying, smelt blood and began to salivate in his turn. Yet upon entering the gully itself, he was altogether unprepared for what he saw.

Wednesday the 24th November

Punctually at five minutes to three on the afternoon of the following day, Digby Driver presented himself at the front door of Animal Research. It was warmer, pleasant weather, with a pale-blue, windy sky, the becks running brown and strong with the thaw and a smell of resinous larch trees in the air. Down on Coniston Water a flock of Canada geese had come in and the big, brown-breasted, black-necked birds could be seen and heard, trumpeting and honking as they hustled across the surface of the lake. They were, one would have thought, worth a glance; but if they had been anhingas and black-browed albatrosses, Digby Driver would not have taken a single step aside, since he would not have been aware of anything unusual. He stubbed out his cigarette on the porch wall, threw it down on the step, rang the bell and shortly found himself in a stuffy interview room, facing Dr. Boycott, Mr. Powell and a cup of thin tea.

Digby Driver had, in a manner of speaking, his back to the wall, and was beginning to realize that the Research Station's policy of sitting tight and saying as little as possible was proving, from their point of view, more effective than he had originally supposed that it would. A press campaign, like a drama, has got to be dynamic. It has to be kept moving. It is vital that it should go on finding fresh grist to its mill. The wretch who on Monday was helping the police with their inquiries must be arrested on Tuesday, tried on Wednesday, sentenced on Thursday and finally kicked when he is down with a calumnious and slanted biography on Friday. Otherwise the newspaper is slipping as a democratic organ and readership is likely to fall off. Ever since the death of Mr. Ephraim, Digby Driver, in accordance with his masters' instructions, had trailed his coat in front of Animal Research as resourcefully as he knew how. Being a clever, energetic journalist, he had managed to keep the story of the dogs very much alive. Nevertheless, none of his ploys had succeeded in provoking the scientists. Those within the castle had declined to come out and fight, reckoning, accurately enough, that in time the public were likely to lose interest in a pair of stray dogs who did no more than raid farms and kill a few sheep and of whom—whatever might be bawled to the contrary—it would ultimately have to be admitted that they were not in fact carrying bubonic plague. Some other topic would eventuate elsewhere, as it always does, and the newspaper would detach itself from the dogs and cease from troubling. As a matter of fact Driver, from his telephone calls to the London office, had already begun to have an unpleasant inkling that the inception of the said detachment might, indeed, be only just around the corner. Yet he himself, from the point of view of his own profit and career, had a strong interest in keeping the dogs' story going, if he could. Should he be recalled now and the story allowed to fizzle out, the whole thing would not have concluded with that feather in his cap which his employers, relying on his journalistic acumen to boost circulation and further their own political ends, had sent him up to the Lakes to acquire. The plain truth was that Digby Driver did not know what the hell to do next. By this time the dogs ought to have been dramatically shot, after a colourful and exciting hunt spontaneously organized by enraged farmers. Or better still, the countryside should have risen up in public protest and terror of the pestilence. These things had not happened. People had merely taken in their dustbins at night and hoped that the dogs would be found dead elsewhere. Unless Animal Research could be provoked into some kind of indiscretion on the eve of the forthcoming House of Commons' Supply Day debate on the cost of research establishments, the whole thing was likely to come to a lame conclusion for lack of a Pelion to pile on Ossa. Digby Driver, if not yet up a tree, was beyond argument gripping a lower branch with one hand.

Dr. Boycott, who was perfectly well aware of all this, greeted him with appropriately courteous urbanity.

"I'm very glad," said Dr. Boycott, offering Driver a cigarette, "that you've at last come along to see us this afternoon. Better late than never, you know. Now do tell us how you think we can help you. I'm sure we'll be delighted to do so if we can."

It took a lot more than this sort of thing to put Digby Driver off his stroke. As a professional bastard, he would not have been unduly troubled by the most adroit manipulation of chairs, ashtrays and lights within the capacity of Mr. Michael Korda himself. Like the great image in

Nebuchadnezzar's dream, his belly and thighs were as of brass and his legs as of iron.

"Well, I'd like to ask you to tell me a little more about these dogs," he began.

"Now, let me see, which particular dogs are we talking about?" asked Dr. Boycott with a warm smile.

"Come, Mr.—er—Boycott," said Driver (and now, indeed, they were both smiling away like a couple of hyenas), "I can't help feeling that that's just a shade lacking in—well, in frankness and honesty, if you don't mind my saying so. You know quite well which dogs."

"Well, I *think* I do," replied Dr. Boycott, "but what I'm trying to get at is how and in what terms you identify them: your attributions, if one may use the term. So can I, once again, begin as the idiot boy and ask you, 'Which dogs?'"

"The dogs that escaped from here and have been causing all this trouble locally."

"*Ah,*" said Dr. Boycott triumphantly, with the air of a Q.C. who has now in very sooth extracted from a witness for the other side the fundamental piece of disingenuous bilge which he intended to extract. "Now *that*'s precisely the point. What locality and what trouble?"

Deliberately, Driver knocked the ash off his cigarette and sipped some of his foul tea.

"Well, O.K., let's start from scratch, then, if that's the way you want it. You're not denying that some time ago two dogs got out of this place and that they've been running wild on the fells?"

"We're certainly not denying that two dogs got out. As I think you know, we said as much in an early press statement we issued. What happened to them after that I'm afraid I can't tell you. They may very well have been dead for some time."

"And it can't be denied that these dogs may quite likely have been in contact with bubonic plague?"

"It's improbable in the last degree that they *were,*" said Dr. Boycott.

"But you can't give a definite assurance that they weren't?"

"When *we* say something *here,*" answered Dr. Boycott,

with radiant cordiality, "it's always one hundred per cent reliable. That's why we haven't given any such assurance. But I repeat, for all practical purposes it's improbable in the last degree that—"

"Would you like to amplify that a little? Explain why?"

It did not escape Dr. Boycott that Digby Driver had been stung into interrupting him.

"No, I—er—don't *think* I—er—*would*," he said reflectively and with a musing frown, as though giving a lunatic suggestion every possible benefit of fair consideration, "because, you see, that's really a matter between the local health authority and the responsible Government Department. We have, of course, been in close touch with those bodies and complied with the appropriate statutory requirements. And if *they*'re not bothered, then I think it follows—"

"You say they're not bothered? That you let two dogs escape?"

"I say they're not bothered about any public health risk of bubonic plague. If you want to know more than that, I should ask *them*. They're the statutorily appointed custodians of public health, after all."

Digby Driver, fuming inwardly, decided to come in on another beam.

"What experiments were these dogs being used for?" he asked.

Oddly enough, this took Dr. Boycott unawares. It was plain that he had not expected the question and was unable to decide, all in a moment, whether or not there was likely to be any harm in answering it.

"I don't see why you shouldn't know *that*," he replied at length, thereby inadvertently suggesting that there were things which he thought Digby Driver should not know. "One was taking part in certain tests connected with physiological and psychological reactions to stress; and the other was a brain surgery subject."

"What specific benefits were expected to result from these tests—experiments—whatever you call them?"

"I think the best way I can answer that," replied Dr. Boycott, "is to refer you to paragraph—er—270, I think —yes, here it is—of the 1965 Report of the Littlewood

Committee, the Home Office Departmental Committee on Experiments on Animals. 'From our study of the evidence about unnecessary experiments and the complexity of biological science, we conclude that it is impossible to tell what practical applications any new discovery in biological knowledge may have later for the benefit of man or animal. Accordingly, we recommend that there should be no general barrier to the use of animal experimentation in seeking new biological knowledge, even if it cannot be shown to be of immediate or foreseeable value.' "

"In other words there wasn't any specific purpose. You just do these things to animals to see what's going to happen?"

"The specific purpose of a test," said Dr. Boycott, with an air of grave responsibility, "is *always* the advancement of knowledge with a view to the ultimate benefit both of man and of animals."

"Such as forcing animals to smoke to see how safely humans can?"

Like George Orwell's inquisitor O'Brien, when Winston Smith burst out that he must have tortured his mistress, Dr. Boycott shrugged this irrelevant remark aside. In any case Driver did not want to pursue it.

"So anyway, these dogs get out," he said, "and you do nothing about it—"

"We haven't got people to spare to go chasing all over the countryside looking for dogs on spec," replied Dr. Boycott crisply. "We've complied with the law. We told the police and the local authorities. For the matter of that, dogs round here sometimes run away from farmers who own them, and those farmers sometimes lose track of them altogether. We've done the same as a farmer does."

"But *these* dogs—first they kill sheep: then they actually cause the death of a man; then they begin attacking shops and farmyards—"

"*Ah,*" said Dr. Boycott again, "I thought you might be going to say something like that. *Do* they? I need convincing. With regard to the death of poor Ephraim, it's the merest conjecture that any dog was involved—ours or anybody else's. A dog—no one knows what dog—was seen running away in the distance; and that's all. Put two and two together and make five. Again, no one's ever actually identified these particular dogs in the act of worrying sheep—"

"The Miss Dawsons at Seathwaite saw their green collars—"

"Certainly. That is almost the only occasion on which dogs wearing green collars have been indisputably identified. Tipping over a dustbin is not the same thing as sheep-worrying. And on that occasion we had an officer at the premises within two hours," added Dr. Boycott, conveniently forgetting that he had originally blamed Mr. Powell for going on his own initiative.

"What about the farmer at Glenridding and the attack on Westcott's car near Dunmail Raise? Have you forgotten that this matter is going to be raised in a Parliamentary debate in the House tomorrow night? If I may say so, Mr. Boycott, you're being grossly irresponsible!"

"If anyone is being irresponsible," replied Dr. Boycott gravely, "it is popular newspapers who alarm the public with totally unfounded tales about bubonic plague—"

"Yes," said Mr. Powell, weighing in for the first time, "and with regard to that, I think we'd like to ask by what unauthorized means you obtained information about work being done here on bubonic plague which you later twisted and used all wrong for sensational purposes—"

"Why, you told me yourself!" answered Driver instantly, with raised eyebrows and an air of surprise.

"*I* told you?" cried Mr. Powell, with a great deal too much indignation in his voice. Dr. Boycott turned and looked at him. "I most certainly did not!"

"Come, come, Mr. Powell, you won't have forgotten that I gave you a lift back from Seathwaite on the morning you went over to see the Miss Dawsons, and that on the way we went to the bar of the Manor Hotel in Broughton and met your friend Mr. Gray over a few pints of beer. And then later, you told me all about Dr. Goodner and his secret defence work."

Dr. Boycott was frowning, his face expressing surprise and perplexity. As Mr. Powell drew fresh breath to struggle and splash, the telephone rang. Dr. Boycott nodded to him and he picked it up.

"Hallo? Yes. Yes, I'm an officer at Animal Research. O.K., carry on, then." There was a pause as he listened. "Under the Dow Crag? He's *dead?* I see. The dogs—you —you say they'd *what?* They'd—oh, my God! A green collar? You're sure? You've got it down at the station now? Oh, my *God!* Yes, all right—oh, God, how awful!— Yes, I'll ring you back—anyway, someone will—very quickly. Yes, very quickly indeed. Yes, I'm sure someone will come straight down. Good-bye."

Mr. Powell, staring and open-mouthed, put down the receiver.

"Chief," he said, half-whispering, "I think you and I had better have a word outside."

Five minutes later Digby Driver was belting on his way to the police station.

FIT 10

Thursday the 25th November

PLAGUE DOGS DEVOUR SECOND VICTIM!
APPALLING TRAGEDY OF YOUNG HILLWALKER
BODY DESECRATED ON MOUNTAINSIDE

The Plague Dogs—escapees from the Government-owned Animal Research Station near Coniston—who for some time past have been terrorizing Lakeland with their ruthless sheep-killing and poultry raids on farms and domestic premises, have committed a culminating deed of horror at which the whole British public will shudder, wondering whether this country has been plunged back into the Dark Ages. If you are squeamish DO NOT READ ON!

Yesterday, in the early afternoon, the body of Geoffrey Westcott, 28, a bank employee of Windermere, Westmorland, was found at the foot of one of the steep gullies below the east face of the Dow Crag, near Coniston, famed mecca of Lakeland mountaineers. Mr. Westcott had evidently fallen to his death from the top of the gully, three hundred feet above, for on the grass not far from the summit of the Crag were found his binoculars and prismatic compass, customary equipment of the hillwalker.

THE BODY HAD BEEN TORN TO PIECES AND LARGELY DEVOURED BY CARNIVOROUS ANIMALS.

NEAR IT WAS FOUND A SEVERED DOG COLLAR MADE OF GREEN PLASTIC.

"Terrible Sight"

Mr. Westcott's body was found by Dennis Williamson, a sheep

farmer of Tongue House, Seathwaite, who was up the fell with his dogs looking for stray sheep. "It must have been about two o'clock in the afternoon and I was on Dow Crag," Mr. Williamson told Digby Driver, the *Orator*'s reporter, "when I caught sight of something dark lying at the foot of one of the steep gullies running down from the summit area. The weather was a bit misty, but after I'd moved back and forth for some time to get the best sight of it I could and shouted without getting any reply, I felt sure that it must be someone who was either dead or unconscious. I went round by Goat's Hause, got down to the bottom and after a bit I found the body. It was a terrible sight—worse than I can tell you. I left everything as it was and went back at once to inform the police. I'm glad it was their job and not mine. I shan't forget it in a hurry, I can assure you."

Revenge

Superintendent Malcolm, in charge of the case, told our reporter, "The discovery of a damaged Winchester .22 rifle in the gully, together with a severed dog-collar made of green plastic, suggested to us at once that the dead man must have been attempting to shoot one of the so-called Plague Dogs from the top of the gully when he fell to his death and his body became their prey."

Inquiries subsequently made of his landlady, Mrs. Rose Green of Windermere, have corroborated that Mr. Westcott had told her that he intended to track down and shoot the dogs in revenge for their attack upon his car two days previously, after he had stopped for a few minutes on a lonely part of the Grasmere–Keswick road. Mr. Westcott was particularly upset that the dogs should have terrified Mrs. Green and torn her week's shopping of meat and grocercies out of the car in order to devour it.

"Practical—Determined"

Handsome, middle-aged Mrs. Green, interviewed by the *Orator* yesterday evening, described Mr. Westcott as a practical and very determined young man, and an experienced and capable hillwalker. "He told me his mind was made up to find and kill those terrible dogs," she said. "I only wish he had. This terrible tragedy has upset me deeply, especially as I feel that in a way Geoffrey was doing what he did for my sake. He was terribly upset about the dogs taking the grocercies and also about the terrible way they had spoilt his car. I shall miss him terribly. We were great friends. He was almost like a son."

No Comment

Senior officers at Animal Research, Coniston, refused to comment last night. Dr. James Boycott, a spokesman, said, "This is a very serious matter and neither we nor anyone else ought to try to anticipate the proper investigational procedures. We are, of course, ready to give evidence to the Coroner if he requires it and we are in close touch with the Secretary of State. I cannot pronounce on whether or not there will be a Government inquiry—that is for Ministers to say. We are as much appalled as other members of the public." (Leading Article, page 10.)

"Yes, well," said Digby Driver, happily pronging another forkful of egg and bacon and lifting the *Orator* from its place against the coffee-pot in order to turn over the front page, "by all means let's have a look at page 10. Good grief, black, what on earth?—"

HOW LONG, OH LORD?

Yesterday's shocking tragedy in the Lake District, when the body of a young hillwalker was desecrated and actually devoured by the murderous brutes who have come to be known as the Plague Dogs—from the strong probability that they are carrying the infection of deadly bubonic plague—must surely arouse and unite public opinion to demand that the Government act NOW to put an end to a menace that has already lasted too shamefully long. Are we living in some remote part of India, where women going to wash clothes in the river run the risk of becoming the prey of a tiger lying in wait? Or in Utah or Colorado, where a rattle-snake may end a straying child's life? No, we are in England, where savage killer animals are at large and the authorities stand by and do nothing.

Mr. Geoffrey Westcott, the hillwalker who died, had, apparently, courageously taken it upon himself to try to rid the land of these foul beasts. Why did he feel he had to do it? He acted for the same reasons as William Wilberforce, Lord Shaftesbury, Florence Nightingale and a host of other British patriots of the past: because he knew there was wrong to be righted, and knew, too, that the authorities would do nothing. Does the shade of Sir Winston Churchill, greatest of Englishmen, stretch out his hand from the shadows to this young man, whose life has been so evilly forfeited in taking up the responsibility which others, sitting in the seats of power, will not exercise in the course of their plain duty?

That is why today the *Orator* proudly and mournfully edges its centre page with black—

"And they damn' well have, too," said Driver admiringly. "Wonder whose jolly idea that was? Very snazzy, very snazzy."

—in homage to a PATRIOT. To those who let him go to his lonely death instead of taking the action it was their solemn, bounden duty to take, it says, in the words of the psalmist of old, "How long, oh Lord? How long?"

"Excuse me, how long will you be wanting the table, Mr. Driver, sir?" asked the waitress. "Only breakfast goes off at ten o'clock and I'm just clearing up."

"Not another minute, Daisy," answered Driver happily, "not half a mo. Everything in the garden is distinctly tickety-boo. Yeah, thanks, clear away the day bree by all means. I wonder," said Mr. Driver to himself, strolling out of the breakfast room, "I wonder whether old Simpson Aggo means to be at the debate in the House tonight? Hogpenny'll have been helping to brief Bugwash, that's for sure. I'll put a call through and see whether someone can ring me from Bugwash's room in the House as soon as the debate's over. That Boycott bloke's face! Ha ha ha ha ha HA! A flea!"

Wednesday the 24th November

It was noon of the day after the death of the tod. Rain had begun to fall before dawn and continued during most of the morning, so that now the becks were running even more strongly. A dog's ears could catch plainly the minute, innumerable oozings and bubblings of the peat, gently exuding like a huge sponge, rilling and trickling downward. There was a faint, clean smell from the broken half-circle of yellow foam which had formed at the infall to Goat's Water. Mist was still lying, but only upon the peaks, where it moved and eddied, disclosing now the summit of the Old Man, now Brim Fell or the conical top of Dow Crag. The wind was freshening and the clouds breaking to disclose blue sky.

"Rowf, we can't stay here. Rowf?"

"Why not? It's lonely enough, isn't it? There's shelter from the rain, too."

"They're bound to come and find the man, Rowf. They'll see us."

"I don't care. He hurt my neck. It still hurts."

Snitter struggled upwards through the baying of the hounds and the terrified, staring eyes of the tod.

"You don't—you don't understand, Rowf! The men will never rest now, never, until they've killed us; not after this. They'll come, any number of them. They'll have horns and red coats to stop us running fast enough. They'll pull us down and hurt us dreadfully—like the tod."

"Because of the man? We were starving. They can't—"

"Yes, then can, Rowf! I know more about men than you do. They *will!*"

"I bet they'd do it if *they* were starving. Probably have."

"They won't see it like that. Rowf, we're in the worst danger ever—I can hear it barking, coming closer—great, black-and-white lorries with drooping ears and long tails. We must go. If the tod were here, he'd tell you—"

"You say he's dead?"

"I told you, Rowf, I told you how they killed him—only I forgot to tell you what he said about you. He said —he said—oh, I'll remember it in a moment—"

Rowf got up stiffly and yawned, pink tongue steaming over black, blood-streaked lips.

"No one'd speak any good of me—least of all the tod. If men come here trying to hurt me, I'll tear a few of them up before I'm done. I hate them all! Well, where are we to go, Snitter?"

"Up there into the mist, for a start. Listen, Rowf; the poor tod said I was to tell you—only I can't think—it was all so dreadful—"

"The mist's breaking up."

"Never mind. As long as we're not found here."

That afternoon, while Digby Driver made his way to Lawson Park and back again, while first the police and then the entire country learned aghast of what had happened under Dow Crag, Snitter and Rowf wandered, with many halts, over the Coniston range. For much of the time Snitter was confused, talking of the tod, of his dead master and of a girl who drove a car full of strange animals. As darkness was falling they descended the southern side of the Grey Friar and found themselves, quite by chance, on the green platform outside the old coppermine shaft. Snitter did not recognize it but Rowf, supposing that he must have led them there on purpose, at once went in; and here, among old, half-vanished smells of sheep's bones and the tod, they spent that night.

Thursday the 25th November

"Ah'll tell thee, Bob," said Dennis, "it were worst bluidy thing as Ah've ever seen. An' if woon more newspaper chap cooms to't door aasking questions, Ah'll belt the bluidy arse off him. Ah will thet."

Robert nodded in silence.

"Happen those could have made *good* dogs, Dennis, tha knaws," he remarked after a little. "Good, workin' dogs. Ay, they could."

"Waste o' dogs? Ay—waste o' chap an' all. That were bank chap from Windermere, tha knaws."

Robert gazed meditatively down the cowshed, where the cows breathed and intermittently blew, tossed their heads and stamped in the warm half-dark. Fly, one of his own dogs, looked up from the floor and, perceiving that its master was still relaxed, returned its head to its front paws.

"Ah'll tell thee soomthing, Dennis," said Robert at length. "Yon newspaper chap, yon Driver. When this dogs' business started oop, wi' thy yows goin' an' that, Ah told thee as he'd be real 'andy fella, put paid to trooble an' all."

Grey Friar

"Ay, tha did."

"Well, Ah were bluidy wrong, an' that's all there is to it, owd lad. He's doon joost nowt, 'as 'e? Joost maakin' newspaper stories an' keepin' pot on't boil, like, to sell paper. He's made *more* trouble for us, not less."

"Ay, an' Ah doan't reckon as he ever meant t'ave dogs caught at all. Longer they went on, better he were pleased, tha knaws."

"Anoother bluidy story, ay. An' old 'Arry Tyson says they're no more carryin' plague than he is. Never read sooch a looäd o' roobbish in all 'is life, he said. What it cooms to, yon Driver's oop 'ere maakin' mooney out of us coontry johnnies, that's about it, old boöy."

"Well, he'll make no more out of me, Bob, tha knaws, for Ah wayn't oppen door to him agaain, nor noon o't basstards."

"Ay, but Ah were thinkin', happen theer's worse to't than that, Dennis. If he'd doon what he should 'ave doon, yon Windermere chap wouldn't have needed to be going out affter dogs at all. That could all 'ave bin settled an' doon with."

"Happen they could put green collar on *him,* like, an' boil his arse for experiment," said Dennis bitterly. "He'd be soom bluidy use then, any rooäd."

He got up off the stone bench. "Well, Ah'm away."

"Art tha goin' into Broughton?"

"Nay, Ah'm off t'Oolverston, an' bide theer while newspaper chaps are gone. They can talk to Gwen if they like, an' she'll tell them joomp int' beck, damn' sight sharper than Ah can an' all."

Five cars went by Hall Dunnerdale, nose to tail. Robert and Dennis watched them pass before crossing the road to the parked van.

"There'll be a few more o' those an' all, now," said Robert.

"Folk starin' about for they don't know what. Y'can thank yon Driver for that as weel."

HOUSE OF COMMONS
OFFICIAL REPORT
PARLIAMENTARY DEBATES
(*Hansard*)

5:20 p.m.

MR. BERNARD BUGWASH (*Lakeland Central*): Mr. Speaker,

in the course of this debate, hon. Members on this side of the House have already drawn attention very thoroughly, in general terms, to the reckless extravagance which throughout the past three years has characterized the Government in the field of so-called research work and research establishments, right across the board. The plain truth is that public money has been frittered away on all manner of nonsense. I would not be surprised to learn that alchemists had been given some of it to discover the philosopher's stone. (*Laughter.*) It is no laughing matter.

I was originally going to say that it has fallen to me to illustrate this incompetence by telling the House about a particular instance. However, as matters now stand, the House hardly needs further telling. The past two days have raised the matter to a level where no one throughout the country is unaware of it. Therefore I need only remind the House briefly of the tragic facts, to most hon. Members already only too dreadfully familiar.

It is a sinister reflection that if those hon. Members whom I observe at this moment leaving the Chamber were on their way to homes in my constituency, they would be running the risk of attack by savage animals—yes, Mr. Speaker, savage animals—and, upon arrival at those homes, the further risk of having their property destroyed or damaged during the night. If they were farmers, they might wake to find fowls or sheep removed or killed. This, one might have thought, would be bad enough. But that is not the worst. They would also have to endure the risk of infection by a terrible disease, none other than bubonic plague. And perhaps worst of all, they would be living day in and day out in the knowledge that no less than two local people, strong, healthy men in the prime of their lives, had had those lives brought to tragic ends by what are in effect wild beasts. I do not intend here to sicken the House with the details of the second of those deaths, which we have all seen reported in this morning's newspapers. I merely say, "Who would have imagined that these things would be allowed to take place in this country today?"

How did they come about and at whose door should the responsibility be laid? It rests squarely on the shoulders of the Government and, as I intend to show, the fear and tragedy which my constituents are presently undergoing are the logical—not the fortuitous, Mr. Speaker, but the logical—outcome of policies—

The Parliamentary Secretary of the Department of the Environment (MR. BASIL FORBES) *rose*—

MR. BUGWASH: I am sorry, but I cannot give way to the hon. Member at this point. The time is coming soon enough when these charges must be answered, but since there can be no satisfactory answer there is no reason why the hon. Member should be in a hurry to admit it. What has happened now is the logical outcome of policies dating back several years, to a piece of the stupidest doctrinaire steam-rollering which has ever been thrust upon this long-suffering nation—and that is saying a lot.

It is now something like five years since the Government, despite strenuous and well-justified opposition, gave approval to the construction of the buildings known as Animal Research, Scientific and Experimental, at Lawson Park, east of Coniston Water, one of the most beautiful places in England. And how did this piece of nonsense come to be put into effect? I will tell you how. By disregarding the clearly expressed views both of local people and of their elected representatives.

One morning the unsuspecting inhabitants of this national park area, whose very well-founded misgivings were set aside by the Secretary of State in his so-called wisdom, wake up and find that a pair of savage dogs have been allowed to escape. The dogs begin killing sheep on the fells, taking poultry from farms and doing all manner of damage. The station says nothing and does nothing. I need not give many details, for they are known to hon. Members from the daily press, but I must give some. At length a public-spirited businessman undertakes the organization of a hunt by local farmers. He is found shot dead and it is more than suspected that one of these dogs played a crucial part in the accident. Whether it did or not, surely the station, if they had had the least sense of responsibility, would have uttered something at this juncture? They did not. They did nothing. They said nothing until several days later, and then all they said was that two dogs had escaped. On the very same day it transpired, and was reported in the press, that those dogs were probably infected with bubonic plague. And both the station and its parent Department still did nothing, nothing at all.

One might have thought that by now enough had been

allowed to go wrong to galvanize anybody into action. But there was worse to come. You will be only too well aware, Mr. Speaker, of the tragedy reported in the press this morning, which has deeply shocked the entire country. That is what this dreadful story of neglect and criminal irresponsibility has brought us to. These are the sort of people who are entrusted with research programmes and with spending money on them. Ostriches—worse. A decent ostrich would have kicked someone by now.

I am not alone in feeling that there are several questions to which the rt. hon. Gentleman opposite should give us the Government's answers tonight. Public anxiety is grave, and it is his plain duty to allay it if he can.

CAPTAIN ALISTAIR MORTON-HARDSHAW (*Keswick*): Like the hon. and learned Member for Lakeland Central, I am anxious to hear what assurances my rt. hon. Friend has to give us on this matter. I feel strongly that there is one aspect which has received insufficient attention. We have learned that these dogs may have become infected, during their escape, with bubonic plague. I find it disturbing that this kind of work should be carried out at a place where risk to the public is involved. Surely work on something like bubonic plague should be carried out in complete isolation, in an underground bunker or something like that. It is disturbing that the station are apparently unable to deny that there is a possibility, however small, that these dogs are infected. While I do not feel able to associate myself with every one of the sweeping and in certain respects not very penetrating criticisms made by the hon. Member for Lakeland Central—

MR. BUGWASH: You ought to.

CAPTAIN MORTON-HARDSHAW: The hon. and learned Member says that I ought to. With respect, I cannot agree with him. I wish—

MR. BUGWASH: Because you are deliberately blind to what is—

CAPTAIN MORTON-HARDSHAW: At any rate I am not a lackey of the gutter press.

MR. BUGWASH: Who is the hon. and gallant Member suggesting is a lackey of the gutter press? Would the hon. and gallant Member care to say plainly who he suggests is a lackey of the gutter press?

CAPTAIN MORTON-HARDSHAW: I am afraid the hon. and learned Member for Lakeland Central is going to burst a blood vessel in a moment. If the cap fits he can wear it.

MR. SPEAKER: I am afraid the cap will not fit. That was an unparliamentary expression. The hon. and gallant Member for Keswick must withdraw it. It is desirable to keep the temper of the House down, if possible.

CAPTAIN MORTON-HARDSHAW: Is it only the hon. and learned Member with the brain of a fox and the manners of a dog who is entitled to your protection, Mr. Speaker? Am I not to be given any protection—

HON. MEMBERS: Withdraw!

CAPTAIN MORTON-HARDSHAW: It is often said by Mr. Speaker that he is conveniently deaf.

SEVERAL HON. MEMBERS *rose*—

MR. SPEAKER: Order. The hon. and gallant Gentleman is entitled to complete his speech. But he must withdraw that expression.

MR. MICHAEL HAND (*Oban*): On a point of order, Mr. Speaker. If we are considering manners and the pot is calling the kettle black—

MR. SPEAKER: That is not a point of order.

HON. MEMBERS: It is!

MR. SPEAKER: No, it is not. I do not take my orders from back-benchers. I have said that the hon. and gallant Gentleman must withdraw, and no doubt he is waiting to do so.

CAPTAIN MORTON-HARDSHAW: I withdraw the words that I used and I apologize to every lackey of the gutter press in this country for bringing him down to the level of the people who sit on the opposite side of the House.

MR. SPEAKER: I am obliged.

MR. BUGWASH: I accept the hon. and gallant Gentleman's withdrawal, but not his apology. Our sympathy should perhaps go out to the Secretary of State for the company he keeps today.

CAPTAIN MORTON-HARDSHAW: I will conclude by simply saying what I have been prevented from saying for the last five minutes. I sincerely hope that my rt. hon. Friend will be able to include in his reply some undertaking about ensuring the safety of the public when carrying out work on dangerous things of this nature which ought not to be done in places where there is the minutest risk of infection getting out. I hope my rt. hon. Friend will have something to tell us about that.

Up in the Strangers' Gallery, Mr. Anthony Hogpenny turned to Mr. Desmond Simpson.

"Let's go out and have a couple across the way, shall we? They'll be happy for at least half an hour yet. Then we can come back and hear whatever Hot Bottle Bill can find to tell them. One thing's certain, he'll have to concede something—quite a lot, I'd say, considering that he's under fire from his own back-benchers as well as from the Opposition. Should be an interesting spectacle."

When they returned, they found that the debate had evidently folded rather more quickly than Mr. Hogpenny had expected, for Hot Bottle Bill was already on his feet and had apparently been on them for some little time.

—I have already stressed to the House that I take a most serious view of the public anxiety brought about by the escape of these dogs. Let me say at once that I have every confidence in the people who run Animal Research. They are extremely good at their job.

MR. HAND: What is it?

MR. HARBOTTLE: Their job is scientific research by means of experiments upon animals, and I repeat, they are very good at it. I am satisfied that, in saying nothing initially about the dogs' escape, their aim was to avoid giving rise to public anxiety in a manner which might have proved alarmist and worse in its effect than silence. I want to assure the House that for all practical purposes there is no risk whatever of bubonic plague. That has been made far too much of in certain quarters and by certain people. There is a possible chance in ten thousand—in fifty thousand—that the dogs might have encountered an infected flea, and that is why the station, quite rightly, would not say that such a thing was out of the question. I repeat, they are men of science, not public relations officers.

MR. GULPIN MCGURK (*Adlestrop*) *rose*—

MR. HARBOTTLE: I am sorry, Mr. Speaker, but what I have to say is of the greatest importance and I cannot give way now.

The hon. and learned Member for Lakeland Central spoke

of public expenditure at Lawson Park. A balance sheet for the past three years will be laid on the Table of the House within the next two days. I do not accept for one moment that there has been any excessive expenditure. I am sure that there has not and the balance sheet will prove it—

MR. BUGWASH *rose*—

MR. HARBOTTLE: I must continue, Mr. Speaker. I am sorry. (*Interruption.*) This sort of thing only wastes time—

MR. BUGWASH: Better than wasting money.

MR. HARBOTTLE: I intend personally to examine the research programmes, staffing and costs at Lawson Park for the current year and next year, and see whether economies cannot be made. I will let the House know my conclusions.

"Christ!" muttered Mr. Hogpenny to Mr. Simpson.

I come finally to the matter of the distressing tragedy which occurred on the Dow Crag two days ago. It would be pointless for me or anyone to try to allot blame for a thing of this kind. The point is, what is going to be done and how quick and effective will it be? What I have to tell the House is that if time has been lost, we are making up for it now. With the co-operation of my right hon. Friend the Secretary of State for Defence—

MISS JOYCE O'FARRELL (*Abergavenny*): Where is he?

MR. HARBOTTLE: The hon. Lady asks where he is. That is irrelevant. The point is that he has already made a decisive contribution to this problem. Two companies of the 3rd Battalion, the Parachute Regiment, are at this moment on their way to the Lake District. Tomorrow they will begin an intensive search of the most likely areas and they will continue until the dogs are found and killed, which I hope will be quick. Also taking part in the search will be two Royal Naval helicopters, which will be directly in touch with the ground force by radio.

There is one more thing I want to say. It is important and I hope it will be widely reported. Members of the public who have no real business there positively must keep out of the area. Anything in the nature of rubber-necking, taking photographs, sight-seeing, and so on would certainly be a hindrance to the soldiers and could also be dangerous to the sight-seers themselves. We are not going to close the roads. That might create serious difficulties for doctors, veterinary surgeons, farmers and others. We rely on people's good sense to stay away.

I myself am going to the area tomorrow. I shall be in personal touch with those conducting the hunt and it will not be called off until it is successful.

MR. BUGWASH: I am sure I am expressing the feelings of the entire House in thanking the Secretary of State for his speech and for the action he is initiating in various different spheres. It is a case of better late than never. We on this side of the House welcome his co-operation.

"Hell's bells!" said Mr. Hogpenny, as he and Mr. Simpson left the Strangers' Gallery en route for Mr. Bugwash's room in the House, "talk about grovelling! Harbottle makes it too easy. A penny a kick and twopence a brick and sewage was threepence a bucket, eh?"

"He knows what he's doing, though," said Mr. Simpson. "Don't you see, the implicit line is that his chaps have clanged, he's too decent to say so and now he's Honest Joe acting like lightning to clean up the mess that wasn't brought to his notice earlier. A head will roll, as sure as fate, you mark my words. Give it forty-eight hours."

"Well, the Plague Dogs racket has certainly proved very successful from the *Orator*'s point of view, all things considered," said Mr. Hogpenny. "In fact, far better than I expected. How to make good use of our four-footed friends. A Cabinet Minister gravely embarrassed, some sort of junior resignation, if you're right, and circulation up more than half a million. Your Driver fellow has done very well. However, I think we need to be looking for a really resounding dénouement of some kind now. Fearsome dogs shot by gallant lads'll be about the size of it, I suppose. But I hope Driver may be able to contrive some unexpected conclusion that pays us and pleases the public."

"Don't worry," replied Mr. Simpson. "If anyone can, he will."

"Snitter! Wake up, blast you! Wake up, Snitter!"

Snitter was lying asleep on the shale. He woke, rolled over, turned towards the patch of daylight at the distant opening and sniffed the flow of air. It was late morning, cloudy but without rain.

Rowf ran a few yards, stopped and turned his head.

"Come and look. Take care, though—keep well out of sight. You'll see why."

When they were about fifteen or twenty feet from the mouth of the cavern, Snitter gave a yap of surprise and flung himself down on the stones.

"Oh my dam! How long—how long have all those people been up there, Rowf? What a—"

"I don't know. I only looked out myself just now. We've never seen anything like that, have we? What are they all doing and what do you think it means?"

"Such a lot of them!"

A mile away, on the opposite side of the Moss, the ridge of the Dow Crag was covered with human figures, black against the sky. Some were standing still, while others could be seen moving along the undulant top, trailing down towards Goat's Hause and thence out of sight beyond the brow. Rowf growled.

"I can *hear* them talking—can you?"

"Yes—and smell them—clothes, leather, tobacco. I was afraid yesterday—I said, didn't I?—I was afraid they'd come: but I didn't think there'd be all those."

"Do you think they're looking for us? They're not farmers, are they?"

"No. They look more like the sort of people I remember my master talking to, in the old days. There are women up there, as well as men. They all seem to be peering over the edge, look, and some of them are going down to where—to where the man was."

"I'm hungry," said Rowf.

"So am I; but we can't risk going out now. We'll have to wait—wait—what was I saying? The tod said—everything's so confused—the garden—oh, yes, we'll have to wait till—till it's dark. They mustn't see us, not a mouse."

"Starve, then," said Rowf, scratching his staring ribs against the rock wall. "We've done that often enough. Getting easy, isn't it?"

A drizzle began to fall from the clouds drifting up Dunnerdale from the west. In half an hour mist had blotted out the mile of moss and fell lying between the sight-seers on the Dow Crag and the watchers in the cavern. Rowf stretched, and shook himself.

"Hope they get wet. It might be worth going across there tonight, when they've gone. A crowd of people like that's sure to have left some bits of bread or something. But we'll have to take care. There might be men still watching. They hate us, don't they? You said so."

Snitter, staring into the blown rain, made no immediate answer. At last he said slowly, "I—know. And yet—I don't understand. My—my master's out there somewhere."

"What on earth d'you mean? Talk sense, Snitter! Your master's dead—you told me so. How can he be out there?"

"I don't know. The mist blows about, doesn't it? I'm so tired of it. I'm tired of being a wild animal, Rowf."

Snitter ran outside, lapped from a shallow puddle in the turf and sat upon his hind legs, begging.

"The gully in the shed floor—the lady with the gloves. It's all different since the second man died, and the poor tod. I must have dreamt the tod, because I saw him—after he'd gone—they tore him to pieces. It's the mist that makes everything so confused. And the tod said something very important, Rowf, that I was to tell you, but I've forgotten—"

"That's a change," said Rowf brutally. "Listen! Isn't that the sound of a man's boots? No, somewhere over there. We'd better get a good long way back inside. This is no good, is it? We shan't be able to go on like this—not for long."

FROM SNACKET J. MOREE, THE WONDER KING
Twenty-Seven Eighty-Four, Okmulgee
Oklahoma 74447

Dear Sirs,

I am a promoter and exhibitor of wide experience and distinction, having worked in this profession for many years in three continents and now sole director of the celebrated Three Continents Exhibitions Inc. I enclose a brochure relative to the work of this company, from which you will observe that its exhibits have been tributized by the Sultan of Nargot, President Amin of Uganda and others of worldwide note and fame. Exhibits during the last five years include the triple-breasted priestess of Kuwait, "Doghead" Slugboni, a former associate of Al Capone, and Mucks Clubby, the boy evangelist who at the age of eight convinced thousands in Texas that he was a reincarnation of Jesus Christ. These are only a few of the high-class exhibits characteristic of world-famous Three Continents service to the public.

It is my view that the "Plague Dogs" would constitute an exhibit of superior quality and on the assumption that they are still legally the property of your Research Station I am prepared to offer four thousand dollars for their outright purchase in good condition. Please wire your reply or if you prefer call collect to myself at the above address. Trusting to talk to you soon,

Best,
Snacket J. Moree
(The Wonder King)

"We're going to be inundated with this sort of thing and all manner of other rubbish, I dare say," said Dr. Boycott, endorsing a direction at the foot of the letter and throwing it into his OUT tray. "I don't know why that should have come here. It should have gone straight to Admin., and they're welcome to it."

"I've had two or three loopy phone calls this morning already," said Mr. Powell. "We really need someone put on to deal with that sort of thing until public interest dies down a bit. It's such a fearful interruption to work, you know."

"I'll mention it to the Director," replied Dr. Boycott, "but I can tell you now that we're not going to get anyone extra just at the moment. You know the Secretary of State's called for an urgent memorandum listing practicable reductions and economics throughout the station—apparently he intends to give some sort of undertaking in his speech in the debate tonight. There'll probably be drastic changes both in work and staff. Goodner'll be moving, almost certainly, but that's very much for your private ear just at the moment."

"I see," said Mr. Powell. "Anyway, chief, can you countersign this report on the kittens experiment—the lung-worm infections? That was what I really came in for.

I'm afraid none of the experimental forms of treatment were successful; and most of the subjects died, as you'll notice."

"Oh dear," said Dr. Boycott, reading. "What a shame! 'Death of almost entire group'—h'm—'preceded by'—h'm, h'm—'excessive salivation, impairment of locomotion and vision, muscular twitchings, panting, respiratory distress, convulsions'—how disappointing! Are the experimental treatments concluded now?"

" 'Fraid so, for the time being. They've all been given a very fair trial. Davies says it would be pointless to continue without further consultation with Glasgow, and anyway we haven't any kittens left, not until next month. That's why I've completed a report at this stage."

"I see," said Dr. Boycott. "Well, it can't be helped. Anyway, more painful matters seem to be looming all round just at the moment. What about the monkey, by the way? How long has it done now?"

"Forty and a half days," replied Mr. Powell. "I believe it's going to die. I wish—I wish to God—"

"That's very unlikely," interrupted Dr. Boycott swiftly, "if it's been fed and watered in accordance with the schedule. But obviously it's the worse for wear. You must expect that. It's a social deprivation experiment, after all."

"Rowf! Rowf—the rhododendrons, can you smell them?"

Amid the stirrings of glabrous leaves and the glitter and hum of summer insects, Snitter recognized with excitement the old, familiar spot where his body had made a hollow in the peaty soil. Rowf, awake instantly, bristled, sniffing and peering in bewilderment and darkness.

"What? What do you mean?"

"That damned cat's been here again, too. I'll cat it! I'll chew its tail off, you see if I don't!"

"Snitter, lie down! Go to sleep."

"I'm going to, don't worry. When the sun gets round just a bit more it strikes right in here, do you see, between those two branches? I tell you, it's the most comfortable place in the whole garden. I'm glad you're here too, Rowf: you'll like my master; he's a really good sort."

Snitter wriggled carefully along the shale, flattening his back to squeeze under one of the stouter branches.

"The leaves flash in your eyes, don't they, when they catch the light? Used to make me jump now and then, until I got used to it."

And now it really did seem to Rowf that they were both surrounded by a grove of dark-green leaves, cernuous on their short, tough stems; by brown, fibrous, peeling branches and great speckle-throated, rosy blooms. Yet all these he perceived as figmentary and as it were in motion, present while forever slipping away in the edge of the nose and the tail of the eye, superimposed upon the shale and the rock walls, covering them as a shallow, flowing stream its bed; or still more insubstantially, as smoke from a bonfire drifts over the trees and bushes of a garden. His hearing, too—or so it seemed—had become clouded; nevertheless a faint, sharp call, like an audible recollection of a human cry rather than the sound itself, came to his ears from a distance and he jumped up, turning towards the cave-mouth, where moonlight and stars showed faintly luminescent beyond and outside the ghostly den of foliage.

"Thats only the paraffin man," said Snitter, settling himself comfortably. "He usually comes round about now. Can't you smell him and his van? Fairly stinks the place out, doesn't it?"

A spectral odour of paraffin stole through the vault, indistinct yet undeniably present, like the twinking of bats at twilight. Rowf trembled where he crouched. His very senses seemed outside his own body. He heard a car pass by, over the curve of the world and down the other side. Above him an invisible flock of starlings flew cackling on their evening way, an impalpable bluebottle settled on his ear, and always the long, oval, glittering leaves nodded and rustled about him.

"Here he comes," whispered Snitter gaily, "out of the door, look, old brown coat, scarf and all. On his way to poke some paper into the red box, you bet! Look—no, through here—see him? Come on, let's give him a surprise!"

But now Rowf could perceive nothing. There was only

the glimmer of the rocky wall and something like a bank of mist blowing nearer and nearer across a desolate, windy field.

"Here he comes!" said Snitter again. "Can't see him now for the bushes, but you can hear him, can't you? He'll go right past us in a moment."

Rowf turned his head, trying to catch a glimpse of the approaching footsteps crunching on the gravel with a sound faint as that of blown leaves.

"O tallywack and tandem!" whispered Snitter, quivering with mischievous excitement. "Here we go! You can jump the gate all right, can't you? It's not a high one, you know. Don't be nervous—he always loves a joke."

The mist enveloped Rowf completely. He lay tense in a directionless, scentless obscurity where there was neither up nor down, a void in which a raindrop would become lost on its way from clouds to earth. He opened his mouth, but no sound came forth to break the windless silence.

Suddenly Snitter's body struck violently against his own. He fell to one side and found himself struggling and kicking on the floor of the cavern.

"Rowf! Oh Rowf, it's the huntsman, the huntsman with his red coat! They've torn the poor tod to pieces! They're coming! They're coming!"

As the spare, bent-kneed huntsman came panting through the rhododendrons, knife in hand, Snitter tried to burrow under Rowf's flank and then, in frenzy, bit him in the haunch; a moment after, he fled yelping out of the cave, away from the smoke-breathed, shadowy hounds bounding into it through the cleft in his head. By the time that Rowf, cursing and bleeding, had picked himself up and followed him outside, he had already reached the upper end of the tarn.

When sheer exhaustion brought him to a halt at last by the beck above Long House Farm, he did not at first recognize Rowf, turning on him, as he came up, with bared teeth and white, staring eyes. Rowf, still half-stupefied by the illusion which he had shared and by his two-mile pursuit of Snitter down the hillside, dropped, panting, on the other side of the beck, and after a time Snitter came hesitantly across to him, sniffing him over like a stranger, but saying nothing. Little by little—as though his sight were clearing—he returned to the surrounding realities of night, of the fell, the chattering beck, the clouds and starlight; and an hour later the two got up and wandered away together, refugees without destination or purpose, except never to return to the cavern.

Thus it was that when, on the following afternoon, a section of No. 7 Platoon, B Company, 3rd Battalion, the Parachute Regiment, patrolling the southern and eastern faces of the Gray Friar, entered and searched the old cop-permine shaft, they found no more than either No. 9 Platoon, patrolling the Goat's Water area, or No. 10 Platoon, searching from Walna Scar across to the fellside north of Dow Crag. The mysterious Plague Dogs had vanished once again.

CONFIDENTIAL

To: The Director, A.R.S.E.

Your confidential instruction, reference KAE/11/77, of yesterday's date, relating to and covering a copy of the Secretary of State's personal letter to yourself about the necessity of effecting, as an urgent and immediate matter, reductions in expenditure throughout the station, asks heads of sections to submit two reports by close of play tonight: the first to deal with experimental work and projects (both "going concerns" and those "in the pipeline") which can practicably be either deferred or dropped altogether; the second with feasible reductions in staff, either by transfer to other scientific establishments or alternatively by outright dismissal. This report deals with the second of those matters.

It is recommended first, that it would be both prudent and practicable to dispense with the supernumerary post of "assistant" to Tyson, the livestock keeper and shed warden. This "assistant" is a local school-leaver of sixteen named Thomas Birkett, who was engaged more or less casually last August on the suggestion of Tyson himself. The post is surplus to establishment and this in itself may be felt to constitute a good and sufficient reason for terminating it forthwith, since it might well come under criticism in the event of station staffing becoming subject to any kind of independent examination from outside. In addition to that consideration, Birkett has not shown himself, during the few months he has been

(411)

here, to be much of an asset, and it seems doubtful whether even Tyson would be likely to put up much resistance to his departure. The matter has not, of course, been mentioned as yet to Tyson, but I will discuss it with him if the proposed dismissal is approved. It will be appreciated that one effect of retrenchment throughout the station will be to diminish Tyson's work, and the departure of his "assistant" could undoubtedly be justified to him on those grounds.

After prolonged and careful consideration, I have concluded that we should also part with Scientific Officer Class II, Mr. Stephen Powell. Mr. Powell has been with the station since early this year and has shown himself capable of honest work of an average standard. While he certainly cannot be said to be a liability, at the same time his capacity is in no way outstanding. On at least one occasion he has allowed himself to express inappropriately emotional feelings about a proposed experimental project, although in fairness one should add that this was shortly after he had been ill with influenza. More disturbingly, he has displayed unsound judgement in handling an unexpected crisis, and on his own admission spent working time drinking with a newspaper reporter in a public house while returning from an official errand (which he would have done better not to have undertaken at all) on behalf of the station. It is possible—and I wish to emphasize that it is no more than a possibility—that he may on that occasion have been guilty of a breach of security. This is a matter which I would in the normal way have pursued with him, but since it came to light only recently, it seems better to leave it over, pending the decision on his proposed dismissal. What is indisputable is that an embarrassing breach of security occurred, and that shortly before it occurred Mr. Powell was drinking in a pub with the newspaper reporter who was responsible for it. I am, of course, ready to discuss further if desired.

I wish to stress that in the normal way no question of Mr. Powell's dismissal would arise. Both as a man and as a scientist he is somewhat immature, but capable of acceptable work. However, his ability is in no way outstanding, his "copybook" is not entirely "unblotted," and you have said that we are positively required to recommend staff reductions at the level of scientific officers of his class. He is unestablished (by a few weeks) and can therefore be transferred or dismissed without raising any serious establishment problem. In a word, he is expendable.

I should find it difficult, even in the state of play envisaged for the future, to recommend further staff reductions. It is, of course, as I realize, a case of seeing how little we can get away with. May I conclude, however, by saying that I will be very ready to go over the ground, as far as my section is concerned, at the Heads of Section conference convened for 2:30 p.m. tomorrow?

(signed) J. R. Boycott

Friday the 26th November

In the darkness of the early small-hours, Digby Driver lay sleeping the sleep of the unjust, his dreams flickering upwards from the incongruously honest, but cryptic and therefore unheeded, caves of the unconscious like marsh-gas rising through the ooze of a bog. Images and even phrases capered within his sleeping skull like lambent, phosphorescent corkscrews. Miss Mandy Prȳce-Morgan—an animal given to him (or to somebody) for his pleasure —clad in a gown of transparent airline tickets and a bullfighter's red cape, was reading to him from a silver-mounted copy of the *London Orator*.

"POLITICIAN CHEWS WRITER'S MEMORY ON FELL," read Miss Pryce-Morgan. "SCUBA DIVERS PROBE TARN IN BID TO ESTABLISH DOGS' INNOCENCE."

"Poet Wordsworth, celebrated Lakeland sheep, got a shock yesterday." She paused.

"The reason?" moaned Digby Driver automatically, tossing and turning where he lay.

"He found one of his odes had been chewed up by Mr. Basil Forbes, the Parliamentary Secretary. Mr. Forbes, in an exclusive press statement to the *Orator*, said 'I ode him nothing. Anyone alleging otherwise is up the Walpole. In any event, Mrs. Ann Moss has now sold herself to Animal Research for experimental purposes, and a dog has bitten

(413)

the Secretary of State. *Cet animal est très méchant. Quand on l' attaque, il se défend."*

It is learned from an official source in Gainesville, Florida, that Mr. Greg Shark, the well-known scuba-diver, is to descend into the day before yesterday in an attempt to discover the Plague Dogs' whereabouts. Mr. Shark, interviewed at a depth of two atmospheres in fresh water—

"That rings a bell," muttered Driver, half-awake. "Rings a bell. I can almost—almost hear—" He opened his eyes and sat up sharply. A bell *was* ringing—a real bell. A moment more and his awakened faculties, closing over the dream like mud over a flung stone, had recognized it as the telephone. He got out of bed and picked up the receiver.

"Driver *Orator."*

"It's Quilliam, Kevin."

"Who?"

"Quilliam—Skillicorn. Got it? Come on, dear boy, come on! You were asleep, I suppose?" (Mr. Skillicorn did not, of course, run to an apology.)

"Of course I—yeah—yeah, I was actually. Nice to hear you, Quilliam. Where are you, in the office?"

"No, I'm down at Sir Ivor's. Tony Hogpenny's here too. We've been having a talk with Sir Ivor about a lot of things, including this dogs business. Haven't been to bed yet, actually." (So *that's* the explanation of the malicious glee in the bastard's voice, thought Driver, shivering.) He said nothing and waited.

"Well, look, anyway—Sir Ivor thinks you've done very well on the dogs job. Are we right in thinking that it can't possibly go on much longer? They're bound to be killed within a couple of days at most, aren't they?"

"Yeah, bound to be. Well, I mean, there's two companies of paratroops after 'em, isn't there?" (Digby Driver, like far too many otherwise quite sensible people, habitually used the term "paratroops.") "They'll be shot to bits —I couldn't alter that with a million bloody pounds, and nor could anyone else."

"Yes, Kevin, I know that all right, but this is the point. Sir Ivor thinks you've done very very well, and you may like to know that it's rumoured that Basil Forbes is resigning—there's glory for you! But the thing is, before we switch the story off and put you on to child prostitution in the Home Counties yum yum, he thinks there might be a chance to discredit Harbottle by some means. Harbottle's coming up your way tonight, you know, on purpose to be in at the death. The death can't possibly be averted, can it? Because if it *could,* Sir Ivor says we'd back you with everything, to make Harbottle look a fool—"

"Oh, have a heart, Quilliam! You know there's not a hope in hell—"

"All right, all right, dear boy, keep it cool! Well, now, look, next best thing. Can you watch out for a chance to show Harbottle in a bad light? You know, bullet-riddled dog screaming in agony and Harbottle grinning, or something? The public wouldn't dig that, however much they've been upset by the Westcott business. If you could manage it, Sir Ivor would be enormously pleased. Just do your best, laddie. I'll have to go now. Good luck, my boy!"

Click.

"O my God!" said Driver, banging down the dead receiver and turning to stare out of the window at the moonlit fell. "Lo, I am with you always, even unto the end of the bloody world, eh? Who'd be a reporter?"

He made a cup of tea and then, thoroughly depressed, dialled the London number of the young woman who had played the part of Chubby Cherub in *Out for the Count.* (Digby Driver was currently "between girls.") If Susie was in a good temper, and in her bed, and if there did not happen to be anyone else in it, perhaps she might chat with him for a bit. No man is an island, and it was only by force of circumstance that Digby Driver was continent.

"Soldiers aal ower bluidy fell," said Dennis Williamson, "chasin' hither and yon and frittenin' yows to booggery, tha knaws. Newspaper chaps bangin' on't door hafe th' day, an' folk in cars drivin' oop an' down t' lonnin, oppenin' gates and crooshin' wire fences when they reverse. Ah reckon forty pounds' worth o' damage. Ah'll tell thee, Bob, theer's soomone's goin' to get a bang from me before this lot's doon with."

"Ay, an' yon helicopter scarin' cows—they've all been gallopin' oop an' down field fit to bust theirselves. An' theer's joost nowt ye can do, owd lad, so ye can set yeself down and thank your stars as theer's political chaps to stand oop for British farmer."

"Theer were soldier fella saw one of my dogs ont' fell, tha knaws, Bob, when Ah were tryin' to get yows down out o't waay. Dog were oop top o' Blaake Rigg an' I were down below, like, an' this basstard took a shot at it an' missed."

"Oh, 'ell!" said Robert.

"Ay, that's about soom of what Ah said an' all. He only took the one."

"Ah'll tell thee what," said Robert. "We've joost got bluidy noothing out of this lot, owd lad. Science chaps an' newspaper chaps an' political chaps—they've all been joost pain int' neck. Dogs have doon no harm at all compared with them, that's about it. Ah wouldn't mind seein' dogs get clean awaay, would you?"

"Well, that's one thing ye'll *not* see, Bob," said Dennis. "The booggers have got no more channce now than tick in a sheep-dip, tha knaws."

He nodded grimly and drove on down the valley, while Robert went to drive the cows into the cowshed to be out of the way of the helicopter.

Thursday the 25th November to Friday the 26th November

The assurances given by the Secretary of State in the House had been as effective as he had intended. There could be no possible doubt in the minds of the vast majority—if not of all—the newspaper-reading public that the drama of the Plague Dogs was now hastening—rushing—to its catastrophe. The sagacious power of hounds and death drew closer every hour. Certainly the dogs seemed to have vanished from the vicinity of the Dow

Crag, and since the discovery of Westcott's body no one had reported seeing them elsewhere. Obviously, however, it could not be long before one or the other of the patrolling helicopters spotted them, or else, as heretofore, some motorist or farmer would encounter them on one of their nocturnal forays. Once their approximate whereabouts was known the soldiers would close in and that would be that. Like the journeyings of King Charles after Naseby, the dogs' movements had become, though they might not themselves be aware of it, those of hunted fugitives. Their death was now a foregone conclusion—indeed, an anti-climax—and public interest was, if anything, on the wane.

Where did they wander that night, when they left the fields of Long House in the Tarn Beck valley of Dunner-dale, soon after Hot Bottle Bill had uttered his winged words to the Commons and the airborne soldiers had begun moving into billets at Coniston? They went southward, heading into a wind that bore the smells of salt, sheep and seaweed, the only communication reaching them out of all the encompassing miles of darkness. A cold rain had begun to fall, and before they passed above Seath-waite church and rounded the Newfield this had become a heavy downpour, so that Rowf, jibbing at the roaring, boiling beck beyond the old school-house, turned down-stream along its right bank, following it to where it runs under the Ulpha road. Slinking down that long, exposed road in almost pitch blackness, they sought what shelter they could from the flanking stone walls; and in a mile came, cold and clemmed with hunger, to Hall Dunnerdale. But here Robert Lindsay's dogs began to bark, and on they went once more until they reached the Duddon bridge by Phyllis Dawson's. They could see almost nothing and the smell of the rain weakened all smells else, so that they did not recognize the scene of Snitter's escape from Mr. Powell and the inside of his own head. But indeed, they were now oppressed by a sense of hopelessness and dread which, as it continued during hour after hour of the stormy night, weighed upon them more heavily than their own rain-sodden coats, so that for much of the time they were conscious of little but the wind and rain. Not one car met or overtook them all night, yet they did not stop or look for shelter. The continuous sound of flowing water, from the chattering rills along the verges under his paws to the distant commotion of the Duddon, troubled Rowf like an evil dream of fear and suffering revived, while to Snitter it seemed that the wind carried grim echoes—heavy, hound-like panting and far-off squeals of desperation and death. Not until dawn began to reveal, little by little, the dull shine of the sodden grass and the tugging of the bushes in the wind, did they rest at last for a time, behind Jenkinson's tombstone opposite the door of Ulpha church, from the pelting of the pitiless storm.

It will have been about an hour later that their bedraggled forms were seen, lurking at the bottom of his garden, by Roy Greenwood, former Himalayan mountaineer and Outward Bound instructor, the vicar of Ulpha-with-Seathwaite. Roy, as was his practice, had got up in the dark of the winter's morning to pray for two hours before breakfast and a full day's work; and as he knelt in intercession for the sins and grief of the world and the misery of its countless victims, human and animal, he caught sight, through the window, of two furtive shapes beneath the bare ash trees, where Japanese-faced tomtits swung on a bone suspended from a branch and brown, seatrout-harbouring Duddon overflowed its banks below.

Roy knew little or nothing of the Plague Dogs, for he could not afford the *London Orator* and had in any case more urgent and important things to do than read it—such as visiting the sick, lonely and afflicted, or giving one or other of the local farmers a hand out with yows. He had, indeed, vaguely heard some local talk, but this did not now return to mind. He could see that the dogs were famished and in distress, so he went outside and tried to get them to come to him, but they would not. Then—having precious little else to give them—he went in and got the greater part of what had been going to be his own breakfast, together with all he could find edible among the scraps (which was not much). This he put outside and, since he still could not induce the dogs to approach, went back indoors. When, an hour and a half later, he set out for Seathwaite, largely breakfastless, the food was gone and so were the dogs. This (it is interesting now to re-

Harter Fell

cord) was the last person to have any real contact with the dogs before the end and the only person, apart from Mr. Ephraim and Vera Dawson, who showed them any kindness throughout the time that they were at large.

Exactly where they spent that stormy Friday, while the sodden, cursing soldiers searched for them from Walna Scar to the Grey Friar and over to Wreynus Pass, is uncertain and perhaps not really important. But during some of the daylight hours—those of the afternoon, perhaps—they must have crossed, unseen by anyone in the dismal weather, the deserted wastes of Ulpha Fell and Birker Moor, and so come down into Eskdale. Probably they went almost as far north as Harter Fell and then down by Kepple Crag, crossing the swollen Esk by the bridge near Penny Hill, for Rowf would hardly have faced the thunder of Dalegarth Force, or even Birker Force in spate after twenty hours' continuous rain. At all events, we know that by nightfall they were not far from the Woolpack—that justly illustrious pub, with its excellent beer, slate flagstones and snug, draughtless rooms—for here, only a short while after closing time, they committed their last depredation when, appearing suddenly out of the darkness, they pushed past Mrs. Armstrong, the licensee, as she was about to close the back door, grabbed a tongue and a cold roast chicken from the kitchen table and made off with them in a matter of seconds. If Mrs. Armstrong were not a most competent and practical lady, the Woolpack would not be the pub it is; but black Rowf, snarling like a wolf, was an alarming sight and in addition had all the advantage of surprise. Snitter, with his green collar and cloven skull, would by now have been recognized anywhere from Barrow to Carlisle. As he followed Rowf at a run along the steep zig-zag path leading from the back of the Woolpack up to Great Barrow and the Eel Tarn, Mrs. Armstrong was already—and very understandably—on the telephone. Before midnight Major Awdry, second-in-command of the 3rd Parachute Battalion and officer in charge of Operation Gelert, had appreciated the situation and drawn up his plan; and soon after dawn on Saturday morning the two companies of airborne soldiers, browned off at the shortage of sleep but consoled by the prospect of a quick end to the business, were already moving into their allotted positions.

"—so I'm afraid that's really the long and short of it," said Dr. Boycott.

Mr. Powell remained standing by the window in silence. His face wore a puzzled expression and he had something of the air of a man who, having just been stopped in his tracks by a bullet or a heavy blow, has not yet begun to feel the pain. He seemed not to know what to make of Dr. Boycott's news.

"There's really no need to let it upset you," went on Dr. Boycott after a pause. "In fact, you know, it might very well turn out to be a blessing in disguise. We don't want you to think of it as a dismissal; you're not being dismissed at all, you're being transferred in your grade. I don't know where, yet. It might be Porton Down, it might be somewhere else."

"There's still the question of why me and not anyone else," said Mr. Powell, looking out at the gulls circling above the fell in the rainy, silver sunset.

"Well, obviously we can't discuss the matter in those terms," said Dr. Boycott, with the matter-of-fact briskness of one prepared to do anything reasonable but to entertain nothing foolish.

"Has there been some sort of report and if so can I see it?" asked Mr. Powell.

"Now, Stephen, you really must be sensible about this," said Dr. Boycott. "You know very well that even if there were a report you couldn't see it. You're quite entitled to an interview with the Director if you wish, but he'll only tell you the same as I'm telling you. And I repeat it: this is a transfer in your grade. It will mean no loss of pay and no loss of prospects. It's primarily an unfortunate matter of expediency—an experiment in retrenchment, if you like, that we've been told we've got to carry out. That's the right way to look at it. One has to think of the job first. We all do."

"An experiment. Yes, well, I can see that." What Mr. Powell could actually see were the outspread, barely moving wings of the gulls, at one and the same time gliding and remaining, like a spiralling eddy in a beck. He had not in fact been enabled by Dr. Boycott's last utterance to arrive at any new way of looking at the matter, and this was not surprising, since that utterance added nothing whatever to what he had already been told. But he was not by temperament a fighter, being naturally disposed to respect his superiors and to proceed upon the assumption that their wishes were probably right and justified. His normal inclination was to co-operate with them and accept what he was told.

Suddenly he blurted out, "Only—only you see, chief, I —er—well, I didn't really want to make a move just at the moment. I mean, the upheaval of a move—all the— well, I mean, the disturbance and that. It's—er—someone —well, I mean, personal reasons, sort of, you know—"

Dr. Boycott looked down at his blotting-pad in silence. What might this be—a mistress—some crypto-homosexual friendship? He knew Mr. Powell to be immature and ingenuous. He hoped he was not about to say anything embarrassing. Mr. Powell, however, seemed to have come to a full stop.

"Well," replied Dr. Boycott at length, "I can only repeat, Stephen, that you're quite entitled to see the Director if you like. I'm sure he'd welcome a chat in any case. You've done us all a good turn, you know, that's quite clear. You must never think anything else. We all wish you well and I'm sure you'll go on to do great things. Anyway, you certainly don't have to get up and go this minute: you do appreciate that, I hope." He smiled. "We've got to find you a job commensurate to your abilities and potential, you know. You really mustn't let it worry you. Think it all over this week-end and if you like we'll certainly have another word on Monday; although I don't honestly know whether there's anything I shall be able to add." After a pause he went on, "By the way, we've got another dog to spare now for that water immersion experiment, so we'll be able to make a fresh start on that before you go. Could you be looking out the papers on the first dog—you know, the former number seven-three-two? And now good night; and mind you have a really good break over the week-end."

"Yeah, righty-o. Thanks, chief. Thanks very much. Good night."

Mr. Powell went out into the long corridor and walked slowly down it, hands in pockets, rocking first on one foot and then on the other, toe-heel, toe-heel, like a man lost in thought. Yet what his thoughts were he could not have said. The boy Tom came towards him, carrying a long wire cage of guinea-pigs, and he moved to one side to let him pass. At the far end of the corridor he paused for a time by the window, looking down at the beck, which had risen to submerge the tussocks of grass and tufts of bog myrtle growing along its banks. There was a trailing branch which dipped continually into the water, was swept backwards and out again by the force of the current and then, rebounding from the extremity of the thrust, once more sprang forward and plunged itself under the surface. He wondered how long it had been doing this and when its pliancy would be exhausted: then idly took a stop-watch from his pocket and timed the little cycle. During a full minute, it did not vary from a regular three and two fifths seconds. Well done, branch. Still plenty of resilience and no sign of letting up.

After a while he went across to Lab. 4, took off his white coat, washed his hands and made preparations to go home, packing into his despatch case his newspaper, a nasal spray and pen left on his desk, a phial of corrosive acid for his domestic do-it-yourself kit (the habitual misappropriation of which from laboratory stock saved him a trifle) and some papers which he had intended to look at over the week-end.

Suddenly he threw down his mackintosh, walked quickly across to the balance cupboard and opened it. The cylinder, secured by its clip, was standing in the far corner. There were no sounds of movement, but he noticed some condensed drops of moisture round the ventilation holes. The slate showed 41+ days. Mr. Powell unclipped the heavy cylinder, lifted it out with both hands, carried it over to a bench and unscrewed the top.

The monkey was crouching in a foetal posture, knees drawn up to chin and head bowed between them. It did not move as he peered in. There was a stench of ordure mixed with disinfectant.

Mr. Powell reached in and lifted the monkey out by the scruff of the neck. It made no resistance and he thought it must be unconscious, but as he gently raised its head with one finger and thumb it opened its eyes and immediately closed them once more against the unaccustomed light. Mr. Powell tucked it under his coat, screwed down the top and put the cylinder back in the balance-cupboard, draped his mackintosh over his shoulders and went out to his car.

Saturday the 27th November

It was about half past seven and the rain had ceased. On the open gravel in front of the Woolpack, Major John Awdry, M.C., stood briefing company and platoon commanders in the first light. It was a mild enough morning, though very wet underfoot, and at least one thrush could be heard from a mountain-ash down by the Esk, as well as two robins who were asserting themselves to one another from opposite ends of the Woolpack garden.

"O.K., now just to recap," said Major Awdry. "The dogs were seen here, on these premises, hardly more than eight hours ago. They're almost certainly not far away, and if that's correct the nature of the area should enable us, with the help of the helicopters, first to surround them and then—well, to shoot them. B company will go three miles down the valley to Eskdale Green, where they'll deploy two platoons north of the Esk and two south; got the northern and southern extremities of the line of advance marked, haven't you?"

Captain Cranmer-Byng, commanding B company, nodded.

"Then at 08:30 hours you begin moving eastward up the Esk valley in an unbroken line, maintaining lateral communication by whistle, Very light, eyesight and anything else you like. You search any cover that might conceal the dogs; copses, of course, thoroughly, but also sheds, recesses in river banks, sheepfolds, bloody paper bags—the lot. And you do NOT repeat NOT on any account break the line of advance. You're a drag net, got it? Between 11:00 and 11:30 hours the company will halt on the line Boot–Eskdale Church and company commander reports to me, unless of course the operation's finished earlier. O.K.?"

He glanced round. The B company platoon commanders, together with the C.S.M., who was commanding a platoon in substitution for a subaltern on leave, nodded.

"Fine. Now meanwhile, C company will disperse its platoons to the four map references already given; at Gill Bank on Whillan Beck; Stony Tarn; Taw House; and the foot of Hard Knott Pass. There they'll deploy as widely as practicable and at 08:30 hours they'll start patrolling back down the lines of the Esk and respective tributary streams, until they get here.

"While everybody's doing that, operational H.Q. will remain here, in R/T contact with both company H.Q.s and in ground-to-air contact with the helicopters. The two helicopters are due over fifteen minutes from now, and they'll maintain a continuous watch on the northern and southern fells above the Esk valley, flying backwards and forwards along the 1,000-foot contour lines. If they spot the dogs anywhere along the tops, they'll inform this H.Q. and I shall issue further order as appropriate.

"Now one last thing, gentlemen, and this is of the greatest importance. No one, but no one, below the rank of platoon commander is to open fire. Is that quite clear?"

"Excuse me sir," said Captain Reidy, "but at that rate why are the blokes carrying live ammo?"

"I'll tell you why," answered Major Awdry, "and this it not to go any further. Because this damn' Cabinet Minister, Secretary of State, whatever he is, won't let us alone; and unless I'm very much mistaken, he sees this operation primarily as a publicity stunt for his own benefit. So orders are to carry live ammo. Intrepid paratroops—yes, real live paratroops, gentlemen, think of that—are combing the fells for the wicked Plague Dogs, all armed to the balls. And he'll probably be here in a minute, along with the B.B.C. television, talking to private soldiers and grinning into cameras. And he knows as much about the blokes as I know about Esquimau Nell—less, I should think.

"Yesterday afternoon, on the Grey Friar, some bloody man saw a perfectly harmless sheep-dog on a crag and popped off on his own initiative. He missed it, thank God. That dog was rounding up sheep and it belonged to a local farmer who quite rightly played merry hell. One more incident like that and we're all in the shit. The place is stiff with newspaper reporters. Apart from that, you realize that bullets can travel three miles and ricochet off stones and God knows what? Once we get blokes like Private Lawes and Corporal Matthews loosing off at their own sweet will—" He left the sentence unfinished.

"What's the form then, Major, if someone spots the dogs?" asked Cranmer-Byng.

"Keep them in sight and inform the section commander, who informs the platoon commander," replied Awdry. "Platoon commanders are authorized to fire in person only if they're absolutely certain that it's safe to do so and that the dogs are beyond doubt the ones we're looking for. Any questions?"

"Will there be anything for the blokes to eat when they get back here, sir?" asked a platoon commander.

"Yes, Admin. are laying on a meal for 12:00 hours, but you appreciate that that's dependent on whether some or all of us got to go chasing from here to Ravenglass or something."

"Sir."

"No other questions? O.K., let's get cracking."

The platoons embussed and departed up and down the valley. John Awdry sat down on the bench under the sycamore tree which stands in the middle of the gravel and accepted a cigarette from the R.S.M.

"Well, sir, doesn't look like it'll be much longer now," said the R.S.M., "unless the dogs got out of the valley during the night, which 'ardly seems likely. I don't see how a rat could get through that lot. We ought to be back in Catterick by this evening."

"You're probably right," answered the Major. "I only

wish I felt a bit more enthusiasm for the business, that's all."

"Well, it's not much, but at least it gets the lads out on a real job, sir. They've all been keen enough, in spite of the rain."

"You feel sorry for the dogs, I expect, Major, don't you?" asked Travers, the H.Q. subaltern. "I know I do."

"Frankly, yes," said Awdry. "I dislike the whole business of experiments on animals, unless there's some very good and altogether exceptional reason in a particular case. The thing that gets me is that it's not possible for the animals to understand why they're being called upon to suffer. They don't suffer for their own good or benefit at all, and I often wonder how far it's for anyone's. They're given no choice, and there's no central authority responsible for deciding whether what's done in this case or that is morally justifiable. These experimental animals are just sentient objects; they're useful because they're able to react; sometimes precisely because they're able to feel fear and pain. And they're used as if they were electric light bulbs or boots. What it comes to is that whereas there used to be human and animal slaves, now there are just animal slaves. They have no legal rights, and no choice in the matter."

"Well, of course, those are big questions, sir," said the R.S.M. "But these 'ere two dogs 'ave consumed a dead man's body and goodness knows what."

"They're animals and they were starving," said the Major, throwing his cigarette away and rising to his feet. "They can still suffer, can't they?"

"Well, we don't know how much, sir, do we?" said the R.S.M. comfortably.

"No, not really, but it just occurs to me that creatures living entirely in the immediate present, through their physical senses, may suffer more rather than less intensely than we do. Still, I suppose you may be right about the need to shoot them, sarnt-major—public concern and all that. What I don't like about this particular lark is what you might call the Spartacus set-up."

"That was a film, wasn't it, sir? About ancient Rome?"

"Well, the film was a lot of balls, really," said John Awdry. "The real Spartacus was a bloke who led a slave rising in ancient Italy and got away with it for a bit because there didn't happen to be an adequate Roman force in the country at the time. They had to bring an army back from Spain. But my point is that in the event these slaves, whose grouse was that most of them had been brought to Italy against their wills and made to exist entirely for other people's benefit and not their own, hadn't really got a chance. They were ignorant and disorganized. All that happened was that they went wandering about the country until they were smashed up, which is exactly what these dogs have done. Apparently one of them was being drowned in a tank of water every day, or something; so it didn't like it and acted accordingly. And now we're called in to shoot it at a public cost of thousands of pounds. I find that depressing. Still, you're right about one thing, Mr. Gibbs. It's bound to be over quite soon now. Where the hell have those R/T blokes got their feet under the table?"

"In the front dining-room, sir, by invitation of the good lady. She's laid on char and wads for them."

"Good for her. Well, let's go and see if they're in contact with B and C company signals yet. Look, here come the helicopters. Not long to go now. Let's hope it's over within the hour."

"They're going to kill us, Rowf. As soon as it's light enough for them to see us."

"How can you tell?"

"I don't know, but I'm quite sure they mean to kill us. They're watching us."

"How can they be? It's still dark."

"No, I mean the flies. The flies out of my head. They've grown huge—they're circling round and round over the hills. They can talk to the whitecoats. I dreamt it all."

"You're hungry and tired out. Why don't you go to sleep again?"

"No, I got nearly half the chicken in spite of you, old Rowf; I'm all right. I wish they hadn't taken the guts out, though. Not half as good as those ones we killed for ourselves, was it? Rowf, it's the last one we'll ever steal. I know that."

Rowf stood up and looked about him.

"No, they're not here yet, Rowf. But d'you remember the tobacco man had a little window he used to open and look in at us? They can watch us. They're going to kill us."

"They'll have their work cut out with me. Thought you said your master was out there?"

"He is, only he can't—oh, Rowf, I don't know what I meant when I said that. I was dreaming. Don't make it worse!"

"That's why it's bad for animals. We don't know anything, we don't understand anything. The men could do something for us if they wanted to, but they don't."

"There are men all round us. It's the mouse—the mouse told me."

Rowf was about to answer when Snitter threw up his head and howled—a long cry of anguish and fear. Two grouse got up and rocketed off into the darkness. Their rattling calls died away and the silence returned—a silence made up of wind in the ling and the rustling of the sedges covering half the surface of the little, lonely Eel Tarn on the edge of Burnmoor, five hundred feet above the Woolpack.

"Snitter, where *are* those men you talk about? They'll hear you—"

"I'm howling for my death—no, it's for yours, poor old Rowf; yours and tod's. I can't remember any more what it was he asked me to say to you. I do so wish I could."

" 'Gan on till the Dark.' Well, the tod's got no more to bother him now."

"I remember one thing he said. He said, 'It's not the Dark that frightens me, it's their riving teeth.' That's how I feel, too. I hope it won't hurt."

Snitter paused, nose in the wind. Suddenly he said, "We've finished being wild animals. That's all finished. So we'll go down now."

"But it's lonely here—safer."

"The flies would see us anyway, as soon as it's light. So we'll go down."

"I won't go back in the tank! I won't go back in the tank! Rowf! Rowf!"

The wind strengthened across the moor, driving the clouds eastward before it. Snitter began to move slowly away upwind, westward down the course of the little outfall from the Eel Tarn. Rowf followed reluctantly. Soon they came to the Brockshaw Beck, and thence to the big Whillan Beck pouring down off the moor to join the Esk below Boot. Stone walls and sheepfolds loomed up about them in the dark and a solitary light shone out from the village half a mile below. Snitter held on his way following the Whillan Beck down into the valley.

"Snitter, where on earth are we going?"

"There's a gully that leads into a drain under the floor. The mouse says we've got to find it. It's that or nothing now."

On they went, downward, down the course of the noisy beck in spate. Rowf could hear, somewhere beyond them in the dark waste, the rising, bubbling cry of the curlew and the whirring of a snipe disturbed from the bog.

"You say we aren't wild animals any more?"

"I don't think we were very good at it really, do you? Only when we had the poor tod."

"I know. If I were really a wild animal, I'd leave you now, Snitter. Wherever are you taking us?"

"We've got to be down the gully before daybreak."

"But, Snitter, *what* gully?"

"I don't know. Oh, look, Rowf, the stones are dancing! D'you remember the white stuff falling out of the sky?"

They clicked and pattered their way through Boot, watched only by the cats on the walls. Once, when a rat ran across the road Rowf, fearful and subdued, let it escape unchased between the stones of the wall. First light was coming into the east and the crinkled summit of Harter Fell showed plainly against the dawn. When they reached the road that leads down the valley, Snitter broke into a run and Rowf followed him, the wound in his neck throbbing as his pulse beat faster with fear.

"Snitter, this is a road, do you realize? Men, cars, lorries—"

"It's very close," muttered Snitter. "The gully's very

close now." As though following a scent, he laid his nose to the ground and ran on.

And now the terrified Rowf could hear plainly the sound of a car approaching behind them. As it grew closer he dashed across to the wall on the opposite side of the road.

"Quick, Snitter, over the wall!"

Snitter jumped the wall after him, his short legs scrabbling at the top before he cleared it and dropped down on the other side. The car drove past. Rowf, lying in a clump of withered goose-grass, docks and dead sorrel, looked about him.

A little way off, a broad strip of the ground was oddly black and granular, and along this some strange-looking metal lines went stretching away into the distance. On these was standing what looked like a row of small, painted carts—or at any rate, wheeled, wooden contraptions not unlike carts —some with roofs and others open to the sky. Beyond them, Rowf could make out a flat, concrete platform in front of what looked like sheds. But all was deserted. There were no men, there was no noise, no paper, no smell of tobacco: only, from somewhere in the distance, a hissing of steam and odour of coal-smoke.

Rowf looked back at Snitter and was appalled to see him curled up under the wall, conspicuous as a plover, apparently in the act of falling asleep. He reached him in one bound.

"Snitter, what in death's name d'you think you're doing? You can't stay there! Get up!"

"I'm tired, Rowf—very tired. The mouse says go to sleep now."

"To blazes with the mouse! Do you know where we are? We're in an open field, in full view—"

"I'm tired, Rowf. I wish you and the tod hadn't pulled me out of my head that day. I might have found out—"

Rowf bit him in the leg, and he stood up slowly and dazedly, as though roused not by pain but rather by hunger or some distant noise. Scarcely able to restrain himself from flight, Rowf urged and bullied him forward until, as they came up to the line of wooden carts—strange they seemed, on their metal wheels, like little rooms or pens, with benches inside—Snitter, of his own accord, made his way up on the concrete platform and there lay down once more. It was at this moment that Rowf heard the unmistakable sound, only a few yards away behind the sheds, of a man's boots on gravel, and caught a whiff of cigarette smoke.

"Snitter, there's a man coming! Come on, get in there, quick! Yes, there, under the bench, seat, whatever it is—right to the back!"

Agonizingly slowly, Snitter obeyed. Rowf, following, had just time to flatten his shaggy belly on the boards and crawl under the wooden seat as a man in blue overalls came round the corner of the shed and, with a scraping of nailed boots on the concrete, passed within three feet of them on his way up the platform.

"Driver *Orator*."

It was still dark. Digby Driver had a headache. He had not cleaned his teeth the night before, there was a foul taste in his mouth and he was busting for a pee.

"It's Ted Springer here, Kevin, of the *Meteor*. Aren't you blessing me, eh? I can hear you are! Listen, boy, I'm doing you a good turn, that's what. The dogs turned up late last night in Eskdale."

"Eskdale? Where the hell's that, Ted?"

"North-west of Dunnerdale. The Paras have moved in already. They're going to start combing the whole valley as soon as it's light this morning. Thought you'd like to know. Now aren't I a nice bloke? The things we do for England, eh? Don't forget me next time you run into something good, will you?"

"You're a pal, Ted. Thanks a lot. I'm on my way. See you down there."

Digby Driver crossed the landing and returned, rinsed out his mouth, put a Polo mint into it, huddled on his clothes and duffle-coat and made his way down into the hall. There was no one about. Thank Christ it wasn't freezing, anyway. As he was pulling on the muddy gum-boots which he had left in the umbrella-stand (wrought iron, circa 1890), the post came through the letter-box with a stuffing, a scuffling and a papery scraping, and flumped on the mat. From somewhere in the lower regions a warm, well-fed house-dog barked to hear it. Digby Driver had his hand on the Yale latch and was about to open the door when one of the letters caught his eye. It was addressed, in no hand-writing that he recognized, simply to *Digby Driver, London Orator Reporter in the Lake District.* He picked it up. The postmark was five days old. Someone had endorsed it *Try Dunnerdale* in violet ink, and below this someone else had written, in red ink, *Try Coniston.*

He shook it and bent it. It was thin, light and entirely pliant. It was evidently not a bomb.

Digby Driver sat down on the hall settle and split open the envelope.

"Well, here we are in Eskdale and it's perfectly possible—indeed, it's more than likely—that we're going to be in on the last act of this tremendous drama of the Plague Dogs, who've had the whole Lake District by the ears—yes, I said by the *ears,* ha ha—for several weeks past. I'm William Williamson of the B.B.C., of course, as I expect you know, and with me here is Major Aubrey, of the Paratroops—oh, sorry, Awdry, is it? Little Audrey laughed and laughed, no relation, eh, oh well, we're all disappointed, I'm sure. And Major Awdry is in command of this very necessary and exciting operation to find and shoot these dogs, who've been putting on a sort of wild west cattle-rustling act up and down these beautiful Lake District hills ever since they escaped from their Coniston Research Station six weeks ago. Now what's it feel like, Major, to be in command of a show like this?"

"Well, it's a job and it's got to be done."

"Do you feel like a bounty hunter after desperadoes in Arizona?"

"Not really, no. I feel sorry for the dogs. I like dogs."

"But not these dogs, eh? They're something that's just got to be dealt with at once, of course, before there are any more of these terrible tragedies. Well, that's very interesting, thank you, Major. Now Major Awdry's men are out on the fells and meadows of this beautiful Lakeland valley—rather wintry now, but in summer it's surely one of the great ice-cream carton resorts of England, ha ha—and as we move along the road you can see what a beautiful place it is—careful now, everybody, the dogs might be lurking just behind that shed there, let's have a look, no they're not and on we go. Well, here's the miniature railway station terminus at Dalegarth, just a little way below the charming, old-world village of Boot; and I don't know whether you're surprised, but I know I am, to see that one of the miniature trains is actually standing in the station and that apparently the engine's got steam up; because I thought this railway only ran during the summer, for the holiday visitors. Anyway, here's the driver coming along now, so I expect he'll tell us something about it. Good morning, sir, now let's see, you're called—er— Graham Withers, I believe, aren't you?"

"Well, just at present, yes."

"Ha ha. Justly celebrated local figure, eh? And you're going to drive that very smart little locomotive—I hope, viewers, you can all see the glossy paint and the brass shining, can you? It's obviously very well looked after indeed—and the whole train you're going to drive, down to—where, now?"

"Ravenglass."

"How far's that?"

" 'Bout seven or eight miles, as the line goes."

"Only I thought the train only ran in summer. Let's see, they call it Ratty, don't they?"

"Ratty, ay, that's right. Everyone oop here calls it Ratty."

"Why's it called that?"

"Well, Ah doan't just rightly know. But that's what everyone calls it, like."

"And how come you're up here at the far end of the line, with steam up, on a morning in late November?"

"Well, there's three locomotives, see—they're named River Esk, River Mite and River Irt—after the three rivers that flow into t'estuary at Ravenglass. We keep 'em in trim during t'winter—maintenance an' so on—and we'd just finished bit of an overhaul on this one, so I thought I'd just give it a run up to Dalegarth an' back, see how it were fixed. I came up Thursday, actually, but it were that wet and stormy yesterday I left takin' it back while today."

"Splendid. And of course *you* haven't seen anything of the Plague Dogs?"

"Nay."

"And what would you do if you did?"

"Happen give 'em a lift."

"Ha ha, very good. Well, there's an unexpected bonus for viewers—the Ratty's locomotive River Irt is just about to set out from Dalegarth for Ravenglass, with veteran driver Graham Withers in the cabin. Casey Jones got nothing on him, eh? Now we're going on down the Esk valley, as you can see, and here's the patrolling screen of paratroops—the Red Devils, as they're called—who are working their way up the valley to meet another lot of paratroops coming down. Up above, in the sky, you can see the Royal Naval helicopters who are patrolling the fells on each side, and I'm sure we all feel sure that this has really got to be the end of the Plague Dogs at last. If we're lucky you might even be able to see them shot. Now here's one of the paratroopers, and your name is—?"

"Private Lawes, sir."

"Well, how do you feel about this operation?"

"Well, I mean, like, yer on a job, I mean, aren't yer, and if yer on a job, I mean, well, yer sort of do the job, like, know what I mean? I mean, like, well, it's a job, ennit, know what I mean?"

"Yes, of course. And suppose you were to catch sight of the dogs under the bank of the river there? You'd shout tally-ho, would you?"

"Well, I mean, yer'd sort of see they was dogs, like, wooden yer, and you report to the section commander like, know what I mean, and the dogs, well, mean to say—"

"You know what the dogs look like?"

"Oh, yeah, well, I mean, the dogs, see, they're sort of like, well, dogs, know what I mean—"

"Now here's a very spendid-looking limousine coming along the road, and I believe this may be—yes, I'm right, it is—the Secretary of State himself, the Right Hon. William Harbottle. We'll just see if we can have a word with him. Good morning, Mr. Harbottle. William Williamson;

B.B.C. Television. I wonder whether you'd care to tell the viewers how you feel about this business?"

"Well, I'm very much concerned about it, naturally. I attach the greatest importance to finding and killing these dangerous dogs as soon as we possibly can. And that's what we're going to do. I believe my political—I mean, I believe public peace of mind positively requires—"

"Ah, there goes the train, puff puff puff, what a lovely sight! Everybody's childhood dream, eh? Thank you very much indeed, Secretary of State. Well, as you've seen, it would hardly be possible for a fly to get through this magnificent cordon of helicopters and paratroopers, so that probably by the time viewers see this programme the menace of the Plague Dogs will have been ended for good and all. At any rate we all hope so. And so, good hunting, the Red Devils! This is William Williamson returning you to the studio—"

Rattle and bump and clanking of wheels and puff puff puff from somewhere in front. Coal-smoke and steam blowing back through the sliding doors of the little wooden carriage. Chatter of water and hollow rumble over a bridge and peat-brown stream below.

Rowf lying tense, head on paws, peering out from beneath the seat at the tree-trunks dashing past and then at the long line of old mining cottages standing close to the track. Snitter, beside him in the far corner, curled up in the dust and grit, sleeping as though in a basket. The continual movement and fugitive shapes a few feet from his muzzle raise in Rowf an almost unendurable excitement; it's all he can do not to leap up and chase after these runaway plants and branches as they flick at him and disappear. A long, brown frond of bracken draws a line of peat-scented moisture along the threshold of the carriage before vanishing with a sodden slap and a spattering of drops against the woodwork. Rowf jumps up with a bark and Snitter wakes.

"Snitter! Where are we? What's happening? Why's everything got loose—where's it going? The wind—rowf, rowf!"

"Lie down, old Rowf! Let it alone! Be quiet!"

"Someone throwing sticks, rowf, rowf!"

"We're down the gully; the mouse's gully in the floor, remember? It's the only place left to hide, but you must keep still. There are men walking about just over your head."

"I do keep still, but everything else is moving."

"The tobacco man's washing the floor. Remember? It's only rubbish. He's brushing it all away."

Through Beckfoot Halt beside the road, labouring a little uphill now and a robin's sharp twitter here and gone among the trees. Scents of bog myrtle and soaking moss, and a distant shouting—men answering each other, high voice and low voice, whistles blowing down in the fields below Spout House and beyond the Esk.

"It's something the whitecoats are doing, isn't it? D'you remember, they put Zigger on some steps that kept on moving? He said he had to run until he dropped."

"Lie down, Rowf. We're all right here. You can tell—it doesn't hurt. They're just breaking up all the rocks and trees and heather they made, that's all."

"All those brown men, look—a whole line of them, red hats, going across the fields down there—"

"They're only breaking up the fields. Don't let them see you."

Curving down into the little station at Eskdale Green, watched by three children with their chins propped on the parapet of the bridge. Polished brasswork gleaming in the early morning sunshine and Graham Withers tooting on the whistle and giving them a wave. Slowly through the station, platform almost level with the floors of the carriages and an old paper bag blowing in, patting Rowf a wet sog on the nose, grab it quick splodge munch no good at all. A white gate and an old nanny goat grazing at the end of a long chain.

"The red hat men have gone now. What's coming when it's all gone?"

"The black milk will boil. Go to sleep, Rowf."

"You draggd me into this, Snitter, and now you say go to sleep."

Leaves and branches flying by; helicopter in the sky. Airborne soldiers on the lea, Plague Dogs riding to the sea. Redwings, fieldfares, cows and sheep; should we cheer, d'you think or weep? Plague Dogs all the way from A.R.S.E., riding down to Ravenglass. What's that car so black, sedate? That's the Secretary of State, him as sealed the Plague Dogs' fate. Wheel and piston, steam and tank, autumn oak-leaves in the bank, chuff chuff chuff and clank clank clank.

"You know, I was keen to be a good dog, Snitter. I really wanted to be a good dog. I'd have done anything for them; anything but the metal water."

"They weren't real masters, Rowf. They didn't particularly want you to be a good dog. They didn't care what sort of dog you were. I don't know what they did want. I don't believe they knew themselves."

And here's Irton Road station, and the little river Mite, all the way down from pretty Miterdale—least known and quietest of Lakeland valleys—formed from the becks of Tongue Moor, Illgill Head and the Wastdale Screes. Hail to thee, blithe Mite, and hurrah for Keyhow and the Bower House, and your wet green fields full of black-headed gulls! Whirling snipe, orange-legged sandpipers, gorse in bloom on a winter's morning. Meadow pipits flighting up and down, flying ahead of the train, flicker and shut, flicker and shut, tweet tweet.

"But surely, Snitter, dogs ought to be able to trust men, oughtn't they?"

"It doesn't matter any more, old Rowf."

"I know—I'm only saying these things to stop myself jumping up and barking at the things rushing past. I wasn't a good dog. Wish I had been."

"Whatever dogs were meant for, they weren't meant for the metal water. If you can't live by rotten rules you have to find some of your own."

"What other rules did *we* find?"

"The tod's."

"They weren't right for us. We couldn't live by them either."

"I know. The truth is I lost my home and you never had one. But it doesn't matter any more."

Now there rises on the left the hog's back of Muncaster Fell, its west face high above the line, throwing the little train into chilly shadow as it runs under the fellside and past Murthwaite, with only three miles to go.

"I remember a butterfly beating itself to bits against a window-pane. A whitecoat saw it and opened the window and put it out. He'd come to put me in the metal water. How'd you explain that?"

"The butterfly laid eggs that turned into the caterpillars you ate. Remember?"

Hooker Crag and Chapel Hill, and here's the Thornflatt watermill. A pitch forward-shot wheel, I rather think, splashing turning among its ferns and lichens and shining, green liverworts. Come on, wheel, sing up! *"War es also gemeint, mein rauschender Freund, dein Singen, dein Klingen."* Is that for poor Mr. Ephraim? Can you see our friend Rowf, peering out from under the seat and rattling by in bewilderment? *"Ach unten, da unten die kühle Ruh."* Well, you can't expect *him* to appreciate that, can you? Be reasonable, wheel.

On the slope behind, look, there are some rabbits who —yes, have the use of their eyes, really—sit up and watch the train a moment—then bolt for their holes—you can see the rufous patch at the backs of their necks. The rabbits get used to the trains in summer, but probably this lot weren't born when last summer's season ended with waving flags and paper bags and sticks of rock all round. A cock chaffinch, slate head and plum breast, flashes white wings and vanishes into the gorse. A magpie flickers in an elder tree and the Plague Dogs, the Plague Dogs are riding to the sea. Here are the pancakes of yellow tide-foam, and the Plague Dogs are riding to their salt sea home. Could you or I have contrived to disappear in Eskdale and turn up in Ravenglass, with two hundred soldiers looking for us under every stone? I trow not. Give them a cheer. There's nothing like a good loser, after all.

"Rowf, can you smell the salt?"

"I can hear gulls calling. How quickly they've changed it all, haven't they?—even the hills."

Along the estuary we go, black-and-white oyster-catchers flashing rapid, pointed wings and peeping off their alarm notes as they fly, and an old heron flapping slowly away by himself. Can that be the tod I see, with

Kiff, up on a cloud? No, I beg your pardon, must have got some hairspray in my eyes, but let's raise a cheer all the same. Never again, hide in a drain, ride in a train, died in the rain—it's not raining yet, anyway.

"Houses, Snitter! Look! Oh, Snitter, real, natural houses!"

As the River Irt came steaming into the Ratty terminus and depot, Snitter cocked his ears and looked cautiously out through the door. Seagulls he could certainly hear, and distant, breaking waves. Everything around seemed flat and open, smelt salty, stony. Sand and grass. Houses, smoke and dustbins.

"They've put the houses back, Rowf. I knew they'd have to, sooner or later."

"The trees and things have stopped flying past. All blown away, I suppose."

"I know. But there's the wall we jumped over, look—over there. I can recognize that all right. Well, obviously they'd want to keep that."

"What shall we do?"

"Stay here until everything's quiet. Then we'll run off among the houses."

"D'you think it might be a change for the better at last?"

"I don't know. It can hardly be a change for the worse."

"I'd like to be sure of that."

The letter was written in pencil and a shaky hand, and Digby Driver was obliged to take it over to the window.

21st November

Barrow-in-Furness

Dear Mr. Driver,

Although I do not know your address in the Lake District, I very much hope that you will receive this letter. I am seeking information on a matter of importance to me—though perhaps to no one else—and do not know from whom to obtain it if not from yourself.

I am at present in hospital, recovering—rather slowly, I'm afraid—from a traffic accident. My injuries were fairly serious and for the past few weeks, during which I have undergone three operations, I have read very little and have not been in touch with the news at all. Consequently it was only today that I saw, in the "Sunday Orator," an account by yourself of the dogs who apparently escaped some time ago from the Lawson Park Research Station, near Coniston. With the article were two photographs, taken, as you will know, by a motorist whose car was raided by the dogs somewhere near Dunmail Raise.

I am writing to say that I believe, on the evidence of the photographs, that one of these animals is, or used to be, my own dog. Indeed the markings, as they appear in one of the photographs, seem unmistakable. I should explain that I am a bachelor and live alone, so you may perhaps understand that I have been much attached to the dog, which I acquired as a puppy some three years ago and trained myself. I was told by my sister, after the accident, that the dog ran away from her house and that all efforts to find it had proved unsuccessful. This, while it greatly grieved me, came as no surprise, since the dog had known only one home and no other master.

I am hoping that you may be able to give me some help and information on this matter which, as you will now appreciate, is of considerable personal concern to me. If you could possibly spare the time to come and see me, Mr. Driver, however briefly, I would be most grateful. Is it possible that in some way or other the dog might be found and returned to me?

I'm not back to anything like fit yet and I am afraid that writing this letter has proved tiring. I only hope you can read it.
                                        Yours sincerely,
                                        Alan Wood

"Oh, boy!" cried Digby Driver, aloud. "*Now* he tells me! But what the hell to do about it?" He took out his car keys and swung them round and round his index finger. After a few moments they flew off and landed on the linoleum on the other side of the hall. Mr. Driver, retrieving them, suddenly addressed his reflection in the still-dark window-pane.

"The bloody cow!" he said aloud. "Good God! What did she——? Well, Christ, I'll see *her* for a start, anyway."

He turned up the collar of his duffle-coat, poked two of the toggles through the loops and pulled on his gloves.

"A line, a line, I gotta think of a line! 'The good journalist ignores no event that takes place, but turns all to his advantage.' Yes, but what the hell can I do with this?" He stamped his foot on the floor in frustration, and once again the dog barked in the basement. A female voice called soothingly, "Lie down, Honey. Wassa fuss-fuss, eh? There's a girl!"

"Darling doggies!" yelled Digby Driver, in inspiration and triumph. "Stares you in the face, dunnit? And with just a bit of luck it's got everything, Harbottle and all! O God, give me time, just time, that's all! What ho for the great British public!"

He dashed out into the winter dawn. Two minutes later the tyres of the green Toledo were sizzling down the wet road to Dalton-in-Furness.

Ravenglass, on the coast south-west of Muncaster Fell, has a railway station (other than Ratty), a pub, a post office, two to three hundred inhabitants and a single street two hundred yards long. All round it lie the sands and channels of the estuary of the Irt, Mite and Esk, and it is sheltered from the Irish Sea outside by the low, sandy peninsula of the Drigg nature reserve—two miles of dunes and marram grass—which covers the estuary as its flap a letter-box. As long ago as 1620 the place was noted for gulls' eggs and for the numbers of waders and sea-birds attracted to the feeding-grounds of these shallow, tidal waters. It is not a spot where strangers can expect to go unremarked for long—not in winter, not in the early morning, not if they happen to be plastered across the newspapers and wanted in three counties.

Was it Harold Tonge, perhaps, the landlord of the Pennington Arms, who first saw Snitter dancing in the street at sight of a real lamp-post? Or his trusty henchman Cec., having a look up and down the windy, gull-tumbled street, who recognized the grim shape of Rowf lifting his leg against a white wall below a fuchsia hedge? Or perhaps Mrs. Merlin, the postmistress, emptying a metal waste-paper basket *doing-doing* against the rim of a dustbin, caught sight of a black-and-white, cloven head looking perplexedly at the stony beach and seaweed-strewn pebbles below the houses? Before the outgoing tide had laid bare the sands of the estuary, conviction and consternation had flooded the village. Incredible as it might be, these were the Plague Dogs, walking the street in bewilderment and broad daylight. Fasten your gates, lock up the stores, bring all the cats and dogs indoors. Get on the *qui vive,* the telephone and the stick. Grimes is at his exercise. Those who despise us we'll destroy.

The instant Annie Mossity opened the front door, Digby Driver had his foot in it. At the look on his face she started back.

"Mr. Driver—what—what—you're very early—I—"

Digby Driver pushed past her, turned, slammed the door and stood facing her in the hall.

"Mr. Driver, what's the meaning of this intrusion? I can't talk to you now. I'm just going—"

Without a word, Digby Driver drew out the letter and held it up. For a moment she caught her breath and her eyes opened wide. The next, she had recovered herself. Her hand moved towards the Yale lock.

"Mr. Driver, will you please leave my house at—"

Driver put his two hands on her shoulders and spoke quietly.

"You can scream the bloody place down, you cruel, cold-hearted bitch! Now get this—I'm not going to be lied to and messed around any more, see, whatever you do to other people. I haven't got much time; and you're not dealing with a gentleman now, either, so just watch it, because I'm angry. If you try fainting or throwing hysterics, all that'll happen is you'll wish you hadn't, got it? Now, listen. Your brother knows that that's his dog, and he knows that it's alive. You didn't tell him you'd sold it, did you? You told him it ran away. Why did you let me think your brother was dead? Why? Come on, Mrs. Bloody Moss, you dirty, lying cow, tell me the truth or I'll break your neck, so help me Christ I will! I'm angry, see, and I might forget myself!"

"Mr. Driver, don't you dare to lay hands on me! You'll regret it—"

He stood back.

"Are you afraid of me?"

She nodded, staring.

"So you damn' well ought to be. Well, the remedy's in your own hands. Tell me the truth and I'll go. And mind it *is* the truth this time. Because if it's not, I'll make the whole blasted country loathe the name of Mrs. Moss, you see if I don't!"

When one rogue has been found out in the deception of another, the scene is seldom an edifying one. Mrs. Moss, sobbing, sank down on a hall chair, while Mr. Driver stood over her like Heathcliff getting to work on Isabella Linton.

"I—I—always ha-ated the dog! I hoped—hoped my brother would get married—he used to make use of the dog to tease me—I *know* he did—the house always so untidy and—and mud all over the floor—my brother didn't care! The dog caused the accident—people saw it— they told me—the dog ran on the crossing and my brother ran out after it. I *hated* the dog—why should I be expected to keep it—oh!—oh!—"

"Come on," said Driver. "What else?"

"I sold the dog to the research people. They promised me I'd never see it again! They said it would never leave the station alive."

"You took it up there yourself? And you took the money and spent it on yourself, didn't you? Keep talking."

"When you came to see me, I knew that if I told you my brother was—was alive you'd go and see him and he'd get to know what had happened. And then I realized you thought he was dead, so I let you go on thinking—why shouldn't I?—oh, hoo, hoo! I'm frightened, Mr. Driver, I'm frightened of you—"

"You needn't be, Mrs. Moss, you rotten, spiteful sow, because I'm leaving your shit-house now. You'll be delighted to know I'm on my way to see your brother in the hospital. And I can let myself out, thanks."

He left her drawing shuddering breaths where she sat on the chair, closed the front door behind him and strode swiftly down the path to the gate. He was surprised to realize that not all his indignation was for himself.

"It's not possible," said Major Awdry. "Ravenglass? There must be some mistake. Two other dogs. Fog of war and all that."

"How about asking one of the 'copters to go down, sir?" suggested the R.S.M. "He can be there in a few minutes and report to us on the R/T. Then if necessary we can call both companies straight in. If it really is our dogs at Ravenglass, they can't 'ardly run no further, and we could be down there by eleven-thirty at latest."

"Yes, good idea," said Awdry, putting down his tea-cup. "How far is it to Ravenglass by road, Mr. Gibbs?"

"About ten mile I make it, sir," answered the sergeant-major, consulting his map.

"Twenty-five minutes, then, once they're embussed. Sergeant Lockyer, can you call up Lieutenant-Commander Evans, please? I'd like to have a word with him myself."

"That was one of the flies out of my head, Rowf."

"Scared me stiff. I thought it was going to come down and crush us. The noise alone's enough to—"

"There's nowhere to hide—nowhere to go. What'll we do?"

"Snitter, it's coming back! Run, run!"

Bushes flattened in a tearing wind, all else blotted out by the smacking *blat-blat-blat* of the blades. Terrified, aware of nothing but fear, all senses—smell, sight, hearing—overwhelmed with fear like green grass and branches submerged in a flooding beck, Snitter and Rowf ran across the shifting stones and shingle, on to the pools and brown weed of the tideline and down to the bare ebb-tide sands.

"Over here, Snitter, quick!"

"No, not that way! This way—this way!"

"No—that way!" Rowf voiding his bowels with fear. "Away from the people! Look at them up there! They're watching us! I won't go back in the tank! I won't go back in the tank!"

From the shore of Ravenglass across to the Drigg peninsula is a quarter of a mile of water at high tide, but at low tide the Mite and Irt flow in a narrow channel down the centre of the sands and it is possible to cross almost dry-shod. As the helicopter turned and remained hovering a hundred yards away, Rowf, with Snitter hard on his tail, raced down the sands and plunged into the outfall, found a footing, lost it again, struggled, flung up his head, scrambled, clawed and dragged himself out on the further side.

Shaking the water out of his shaggy coat, he looked about him. The sodden body of a dead gull, evidently left by the tide, was lying a few yards away. He himself was bleeding from one hind paw. Snitter, carried down with the current, had fetched up against a rock and was clambering out. The helicopter had not moved. Ahead rose the smooth, sandy dunes, one behind another, tufts of marram grass blowing against the sky.

"No men up there, Snitter! Come on!"

Running again, wet sand cold between the claws, dry sand blowing into eyes and nostrils, sound of breaking waves beyond the hillocks; raucous cries of gulls.

"Rowf! Look!"

Rowf stopped dead in his tracks, hackles rising.

"It's the sea, Rowf—the sea the tod told me about that day, after I'd come out of my head! I remember what he said. He said, 'Salt and weeds. It's all water there.' I didn't understand how a place could be all water. Look —it's moving all the time."

"It's not alive, though. It's another of those damned tanks. They've turned the whole world out there into a tank! I wouldn't have believed it."

"The sand's nice and warm, all the same," said Snitter, lying down at the foot of a dune. "No men. Out of the wind."

He curled himself up as the song of the waves stole gently along the shore and through the whorls of his broken skull.

> "You have licked clean the bitter bowl
> And now need wander on no more.
> The charm's wound up and closed the scroll,
> For you have reached the furthest shore.
> Lie down and rest, poor dog, before
> Your great sea-change cerulean,

> *And sleeping, dream that we restore*
> *The lost dog to the vanished man."*

"I wish—I wish I could see my master just once again," murmured Snitter. "We were always so happy. That poor terrier—I'd have tried to help her if I hadn't been so frightened. I wonder what'll happen to them all now—the terrier and the lorry—the mouse and all the rest of them? I'm afraid they won't be able to manage without me. They'll disappear, I suppose. But I must go to sleep now —I'm so tired. Good old Rowf—I *must* try to remember —remember what the tod said—".

Rowf, too, had lain down in the sand and was sleeping as a dog sleeps who has wandered for two nights and a day. The tide was still ebbing and the sound of the waves receding, gentler and softer.

The helicopter remained where it was, poised above Ravenglass, for the dogs were in full view through binoculars and there was nothing to be gained by disturbing them as the soldiers drove up, got out of their buses and fell in outside the Pennington Arms.

Major Awdry, having located the dogs, was half of a mind simply to take a rifle and cross the estuary by himself. On second thoughts, however, it seemed best to send a platoon across in extended order, for the dogs had already shown themselves remarkably resourceful and even now might try to escape northward towards Drigg. No. 7 platoon, swearing at the prospect of more wet feet and wet boots, crunched down the shingle, deployed on the sands and began crossing the estuary. Awdry and the platoon commander carried loaded rifles.

It was too early for visitors at the hospital and Digby Driver, in the hall, was referred to a notice confirming the hours; however, as the reader will have no difficulty in believing, he knew a trick worth two of that. He spoke forcefully of urgent and pressing business, flashed his press card and offered, if desired, to bring Sir Ivor Stone in person to the telephone. The West Indian sister, an *Orator* reader, knew his name and found his check rather attractive. The hospital were not altogether unused to bending the rules for visitors on a Saturday and anyway the nurses felt sorry for the nice, gentlemanly Mr. Wood, who had suffered such dreadful injuries and had so few visitors. He was, Digby Driver learned, at present convalescent in a small post-operational ward of only two beds. The other bed was empty at the moment, the patient having been discharged on Friday. Putting out his cigarette and following the directions he had been given, Mr. Driver walked, breathing the familiar hospital smell, along numerous corridors, went up in a lift, and upon getting out found himself opposite the right door.

Mr. Wood, who had ceased to expect any reply to his letter, was surprised and gratified to find Digby Driver at his bedside. He looked wretchedly ill and explained that he still had a good deal of pain in his left leg, which had been broken in two places.

"It'll never be as good as it was, I'm told," he said. "Still, I shall be able to walk again—after a fashion—and drive a car; and I'll be able to get back to work, of course, which'll be everything. But Mr. Driver, kind of you as it is to come here, I'm sure you didn't make the journey simply to hear about my health. Can you tell me about the dog in the photograph? Is it my dog?"

"You tell me," answered Driver. "There are the originals." And he laid them on the sheet before Mr. Wood's eyes.

"Why, that *is* Snitter!" cried Mr. Wood. "There's not a doubt of it!" He looked up with his eyes full of tears. "Good God, what have they done to him? However could he have fallen into their hands? I can't bear to look at it. Mr. Driver, please tell me at once—where is the dog? Have they killed him or what?"

"Look," said Driver, "I'm terribly sorry, but I'm afraid the truth is that they may have. The two dogs were seen in Eskdale late last night and soldiers are searching the valley for them at this moment, with orders to shoot on sight. They certainly wouldn't listen to anything I could say, but if they'll let you out of here, I'll drive you up to Eskdale myself and give you all the help I can."

"Well, they can't legally stop me discharging myself.

You're most kind. But it's going to be a hell of a business. I can only walk with someone else's help. I can stand the pain, but I get very tired."

"I'm someone else, Mr. Wood."

"You really think there might be a chance of saving Snitter?"

"I think there's a sporting chance that we might be able to do something, though I'm damned if I can see what, just off the cuff. And I'm afraid it's more than likely that it may be too late. I can only repeat, I'll help to get you out and I'll drive you up there as fast as I can. This is one hell of a story, you see, and of course it's the story I'm after—I'll be frank about that. But I'm on your side, too, Mr. Wood—I genuinely am. Come on, where are your clothes—in that wardrobe? Right, here we go. Once we're in the car I'll tell you all about the whole thing."

To pilot Mr. Wood out of the hospital did indeed prove a task almost beyond the power of Digby Driver his very self. Only he could have pulled it off. Heracles would have owned the Alcestis operation a right doddle in comparison. Twice he almost came to actual grips with members of the staff. Telephone calls were made to consultants, but these Digby Driver ignored. The summoned house surgeon on duty, a pleasant enough young man, he invited to send for a policeman, sue the *London Orator* or jump into Wastwater, as preferred. The hall porter (Africa Star with 8th Army clasp) was told that if he laid a hand on the patient or his escort the *London Orator* would have his guts for garters. At the door, however, all resistance suddenly evaporated and the resolute, hobbling pair, watched with uncomprehending astonishment by the early visitors, festooned with dire warnings and leaving behind hands, both black and white, emphatically washed of them on all sides, reached the green Toledo and set off for Eskdale by way of Broughton and Ulpha.

The wind, veering round into the east, carried to the sleeping Rowf's unsleeping nostrils the smells of rifle oil, leather and web equipment. A moment more and his waking ears caught the sound of human voices. He stared in terror at the extended khaki line across the sands.

"Snitter! The red-hat men are here—they're coming!"

"Oh, Rowf, let me go to sleep—"

"If you do, you'll wake up on the whitecoats' glass table! Come on, run!"

"I know they're all after us—I know they're going to kill us, but I can't remember why."

"You remember what the sheep-dog said. He said his man believed we had a plague, a sickness or something. I only wish I had—I'd try biting a few of them."

In and out of the undulant dunes, the marram, gorse and sea holly, dead trails of bindweed and dry patches of clubrush. Down winding, sandy valleys doubling back on themselves, catching sight once more of the soldiers now horribly nearer; dashing through deep, yielding sand, over the top and down; and so once more to the sea—wet shore, long weeds, gleaming stones, flashes and pools; and beyond, the breaking waves.

"Snitter, I won't go back in the tank! I won't go back in the tank!"

Rowf ran a few yards into the waves and returned, a great, shaggy dog whining and trembling in the wind.

"What's out there, Snitter, in the water?"

"There's an island," said Snitter desperately. "Didn't you know? A wonderful island. The Star Dog runs it. They're all dogs there. They have great, warm houses with piles of meat and bones, and they have—they have splendid cat-chasing competitions. Men aren't allowed there unless the dogs like them and let them in."

"I never knew. Just out there, is it, really? What's it called?"

"Dog," said Snitter, after a moment's thought. "The Isle of Dog."

"I can't see it. More likely the Isle of Man, I should think, full of men—"

"No, it's not, Rowf. It's the Isle of Dog out there, honestly, only just out of sight. I tell you, we can swim there, come on—"

The soldiers appeared, topping the dunes, first one or two, here and there, then the whole line, red berets, brown clothes, pointing and calling to each other. A bullet struck the rock beside Rowf and ricocheted into the water with a whine.

Rowf turned a moment and flung up his head.

"It's not us!" barked Rowf. "It's not us that's got the plague!"

He turned and dashed into the waves. Before the next shot hit the sand he was beside Snitter and swimming resolutely out to sea.

"To *Ravenglass?*" said Digby Driver. "Are you sure? Can they really have got there since last night? It must be all of eight miles, even in a dead straight line."

"That's what the paratroop officer said, sir. Seems one of the helicopters actually saw the dogs on the beach. Anyway, that's where the soldiers went, and all the newspaper men have followed them; and the Secretary of State too, in his car. They're all down there."

"Good God!" said Digby Driver to Mr. Wood, who was half-lying on the back seat and biting his lip at each spurt of pain in his leg. "This seems incredible! Are you all right? D'you want to go on?"

"Yes, if that's where Snitter is, I can make it. It's very good of you, Mr. Driver—"

"Oh, bollocks!" said Digby Driver, letting in the clutch with a jerk that almost drew a cry from Mr. Wood. "I'm as big a darling doggies sucker as any old Kilburn landlady. On we go! We were left galloping, Jorrocks and I."

"Joris and I."

"Precious little the matter with you," said Digby Driver.

"Don't exhaust yourself, Snitter; don't struggle so hard! Just keep afloat."

"I can't seem—to manage it! Why have we gone such a long way already?"

"There's a current carrying us along the shore and away from it as well. Is it far to the island, Snitter?"

"Not very far, old Rowf."

"Bite on to my tail if you like. I learnt a lot about staying afloat in the tank, you know."

"Everything rocks up and down."

"Keep it up. We must get to the Isle of Dog!"

Splashing and struggling and choking mouthfuls of salt water. Tossing up and down, spray in the eyes. Bitterly cold now, and horribly lonely and a sudden screaming of gulls, fierce and angry, but nothing to be seen.

"Rowf? There's something terribly important I've got to tell you; about the tod; but I've hurt my head and I can't remember it."

"Never mind. Just stay afloat."

"Dammit!" said Digby Driver, pulling up. "This isn't right. I'm afraid I've been concentrating on driving at the expense of map-reading. This obviously can't be the road to Ravenglass. Have you any idea where we are?"

" 'Fraid not," replied Alan Wood. "I'm a bit done up, to tell you the truth—haven't been noticing much for a bit. I'll try and get myself together."

"That must have been Drigg we just came through," said Driver, looking at his map. "Yeah, and we've gone under the railway line, you see. I'd better turn round. Oh look, there's a chap just got out of that Volvo up there ahead. Let's go on up and ask him."

Jolting and swaying, and Mr. Wood clutching his plaster-of-paris leg and just succeeding in keeping quiet, with the sweat running down his white face.

"I say, excuse me, sir, we're looking for some soldiers —paratroopers—have you seen any? Can you tell us the way to Ravenglass?"

The burly, pleasant-looking, soldierly man in gum-boots and an anorak came up to the driving window.

"Looking for soldiers, are you? Well, as far as I can make out you've come to the right place—or rather, the wrong place from my point of view. Just got back here from Gosforth and find 'em prancing all over my nature reserve, restricted areas and all. Never so much as a word of warning, let alone a request for permission to enter. And there's a helicopter up there, terrifying every bird for miles. I've a damn good mind to ring up the War Office and ask them what the hell they think they're doing."

"I may be able to help," said Driver. "I'm a newspaperman. That's why I'm after the soldiers. And the soldiers are after the so-called Plague Dogs, if you know about them. D'you mind telling us where *you* fit in?"

"My name's Rose—Major Rose. I'm the warden of the Drigg nature reserve. That's all this peninsula, as far as it goes down—about two miles of dunes. Well, what the hell do the soldiers think they're doing, can you tell me? Fortunately it's a slack season now, very few migrants about, but dammit all, it's bad enough. My wife's told me she heard a couple of shots fired. I ask you! Shots!"

Mr. Wood could not suppress a cry of anguish.

As quickly as possible, Digby Driver explained the position. Major Rose listened with evident sympathy and understanding.

"Well, we might just be in time to do something yet. For one thing, no one can legally use a firearm in the nature reserve, and I don't care who the hell they are. Come on, let's get down there in the car—or as far as we can. I'm afraid the track doesn't go anything like as far down as Drigg Point, but it'll take us a good bit of the way and after that I expect we'll be able to manage something. Can I hop in beside you, Mr. Driver? Splendid. You all right, Mr. Wood? God, you've got some guts! Walked out of the hospital, did you, just like that? Good for you! Sure to be a blessing on that."

They had not gone far down the peninsula when they observed two red berets stumbling their way towards them over the undulant dunes. They could be seen pausing, looking out to sea through binoculars and pointing. Major Rose got out and went briskly to meet them, while Digby Driver helped Mr. Wood out of the car and gave him his shoulder to do the best he could to follow. It took them several minutes to reach the soldiers. When they finally did so, Major Rose seemed to have calmed down a little.

"Mr. Driver," he said, "this is Major Awdry, who tells me he's in charge of this dogs' exercise, and oddly enough we've both been in the same regiment—before he transferred and started jumping out of aeroplanes, that is. He tells me they haven't shot your dog, Mr. Wood, but I'm afraid it's a bad prospect for the poor beasts, all the same."

"What's happened?" cried Mr. Wood. "Where are they?"

"They're out there," said John Awdry grimly, pointing and handing over his binoculars. "I'm afraid you can hardly see them now. The tide's taken them out pretty far and there's a north-setting current that's sweeping them up the coast as well."

"They might come ashore on Barn Scar," said Major Rose. "That's a sandy shoal, you know, that stretches out quite a long way about a mile and a quarter north of here. Tide's on the turn, too. If only they can stay afloat," he added. "Your chaps won't be shooting any more, will they? Where are they, by the way?"

"I left them down by the point," replied Awdry, "while Mr. Gibbs here and I came up the shore to try and keep the dogs in sight. No one's authorized to fire except officers, and we won't, of course, so don't worry about that."

Mr. Wood, having been helped to sit down, remained staring out to sea through the binoculars without a word. There was, however, nothing now to be seen between the tossing waves and the grey, November sky.

"Can't—any more—Rowf."
"Bite on to me, Snitter. Bite!"
"Cold."
"The island, Snitter—the Isle of Dog! We must get there!"
"Cold. Tired."
No feeling in the legs. Cold. Cold. Longing to rest, longing to stop, losing two gasps in every three for a lungful of air. The stinging, muzzle-slapping water, rocking up and down. This isn't a dream. It's real, real. We're going to die.
"I'm sorry—Snitter, about—about the tod. All my fault."
"That's it! Remember—tod—tell you—reet mazer—"
"What?"
"Reet mazer—yows—"
Cold Sinking. Bitter, choking dark.

(HERE ENSUETH THE COLLOQUY BETWEEN THE AUTHOR AND HIS READER)

COLLOQUY

THE READER: *But are the Plague Dogs, then, to drown*
And nevermore come safe to land?

Without a fight, to be sucked down
Five fathom deep in tide-washed sand?
Brave Rowf, but give him where to stand—
He'd grapple with Leviathan!
What sort of end is this you've planned
For lost dogs and their vanished man?

THE AUTHOR: It's a bad world for—well, you know.
But after all, another slave—
It's easy come and easy go.
We've used them now, like Boycott. They've
Fulfilled their part. The story gave
Amusement. Now, as best I can,
I'll round it off, but cannot save
The lost dogs for the vanished man.

THE READER: Yet ours is not that monstrous world
Where Boycott ruled their destinies!
Let not poor Snitter's bones be hurled
Beyond the stormy Hebrides!
Look homeward now! Good author, please
Dredge those dark waters Stygian
And then, on some miraculous breeze,
Bring lost dogs home to vanished man!

THE AUTHOR: Reader, one spell there is may serve,
One fantasy I had forgot,
One saviour that all beasts deserve—
The wise and generous Peter Scott.
We'll bring him here—by boat or yacht!
He only might—he only can
Convert the Plague Dogs' desperate lot
And reconcile bird, beast and man.

CONDENSED EXTRACT FROM THE BRITISH WHO'S WHO

SCOTT, Sir Peter, Companion of the British Empire:
Distinguished Service Cross.

Chairman of the World Wildlife Fund. Director of the
Wildfowl Trust. Wildlife Painter. Ornithologist, naturalist and
international wildlife perservationist.

Born 1909, son of Captain Robert Falcon Scott [of the
Antarctic]. Exhibited paintings at the Royal Academy, London, since 1933. Specialist in painting birds and wildlife.

Many lectures and nature programmes on British television since World War 2.

Winner of the international 14-foot Dinghy Championship, 1937, 1938, 1946. Bronze medal, single-handed sailing, Olympic Games, 1936.

Royal Navy, Second World War. Awarded M.B.E., D.S.C. and bar. Three times mentioned in despatches while serving in destroyers in the Battle of the Atlantic.

President of the Society of Wildlife Artists.

President of the International Yacht-Racing Union, 1955–69.

President of the Inland Waterways Association.

President of the Camping Club of Great Britain.

Chairman of the Survival Service Commission.

Chairman of the International Union for the Conservation of Nature and Natural Resources.

Chairman of the Fauna Preservation Society.

Chairman of the Olympic Games at Melbourne, 1956; at Rome, 1960; and in Japan, 1964.

Member of the Council of the Winston Churchill Memorial trust.

Explored the unmapped Perry River area of the Canadian Arctic, 1949. Leader of expeditions to Australasia, the Galápagos Islands, the Seychelles Islands and the Antarctic.

Gliding: International Gold Badge, 1958. International Diamond Badge, 1963. British Gliding Champion, 1963. Chairman of the British Gliding Association, 1968–70.

Royal Geographical Society Medal, 1967.

Albert Medal, Royal Society of Arts, 1970.

Bernard Tucker Medal, B.O.U. 1970.

Arthur Allen Medal of Cornell University, 1971.

Icelandic Order of the Falcon, 1969.

Publications include: *Morning Flight, Wild Chorus, The Battle of the Narrow Seas, Key to the Wildfowl of the World, Wild Geese and Eskimos, A Thousand Geese, Wildfowl of the British Isles, Animals in Africa, The Swans* and *The Fishwatcher's Guide to West Atlantic Coral Reefs.*

Has illustrated (*inter alia*): *Adventures Among Birds* and *The Handbook of British Birds.*

ENVOY

Sir Peter Scott, despite his well-known ability as a sailor, did not very often put to sea in winter. There was always a great deal to do at Slimbridge, to say nothing of his passion for painting and the heavy load of correspondence, all over the world, with wildlife conservation groups and the like. The happy arrival, however, on a visit from New Zealand, of his old friend and fellow-naturalist Ronald Lockley had coincided with two letters asking for ornithological advice—one from Bob Haycock, warden of the Calf of Man nature reserve, and the second from none other than Major Jim Rose of the Drigg reserve at Ravenglass. The weather being mild for winter and his visitor entirely ready to fall in with the idea of a little sea adventure—the more so since, as it happened, he had never visited the Calf of Man—the distinguished pair had set out in the *Orielton,* a converted lifeboat which Sir Peter found extremely handy for coastal and island voyaging.

They had enjoyed unusually fine days during three hundred miles of seafaring north to Anglesey, putting in at several islands off the Welsh coast to visit old haunts of Lockley's and in particular staying a night each at the bird observatories on Skokholm and Bardsey, where they were welcomed with delight by the resident wardens. Once Anglesey was left behind they had a splendid following wind across the last sixty miles and finally anchored, one Wednesday evening, in the calm of Port Erin, where Alan Pickard, that best of booksellers, received them hospitably before their visit to the Calf on the following day.

The visit—though it is always pleasant and heart-warming to see the aerial games of choughs, to help to clear a mist-net, watch a qualified bird-ringer at work and read his records of snow buntings, purple sandpipers and yellow-browed warblers—had in one respect proved disappointing. Lockley, whose knowledge of sea-birds was unsurpassed and whose forte was the study of shearwaters worldwide, still entertained the hope that one day the Manx shearwater—and with any luck the puffin too—might be restored to the Isle of Man; or at any rate to the Calf, where it had first been discovered. There were, however, formidable obstacles, chief of which was the extreme difficulty of exterminating the rats which had made survival virtually impossible for both species by infesting their underground tunnels and devouring their eggs and young. Against such attacks these burrowing birds had no remedy. Bob Haycock had not felt able to be encouraging about the prospects, and Ronald Lockley and Peter Scott, despite their recollections of the success of various sanctuary projects they had founded (such as the Wildlife Trust at Slimbridge and more lately the establishment of New Zealand's first bird observatory on the shores of the Firth of Thames, near Auckland), were a trifle disposed, as the *Orielton* approached the end of the eighty miles between the Calf and Ravenglass, to give way to melancholy thoughts (or perhaps they were just plain hungry).

Ronald sat at the helm, cutting beef for sandwiches off the bone and reflecting on the frame of things disjointed.

"You know, ignorant sentimentality about animals and birds can be as bad as deliberate destruction," he remarked, wiping the spray off his glasses and turning the *Orielton*'s nose a point to starboard. "Well-intentioned amateurs like that chap Richard Adams—fond of the country—reasonably good observer—knows next to nothing about rabbits—hopelessly sentimental—everyone starts thinking rabbits are marvellous when what they really need is keeping down if they're not to become an absolute pest to the farmer—"

"But you said yourself in your book that humans are so rabbit," interrupted Peter Scott. "If that's not anthropomorphic—"

"Well, that's different," said Ronald firmly. "Anyway, humans need keeping down, too, come to that. But what *is* all wrong, for instance, is importing creatures like Greek tortoises, which are totally unsuited to a British climate, for sale as pets. The people who buy them usually know far too little about them; and anyway, for all practical purposes they start dying as soon as they get here. Sale of hens' chicks as pets is illegal now, but owing to some stupid loophole sale of duckling chicks isn't. Anyway *they* all die, too. I tell you, ignorant, uninstructed enthusiasm for birds and animals is worse than useless. We ought not to stir it up. Most small wild animals die if they become pets, simply through misplaced interference and disturbance."

"They always did, of course," replied Scott, opening a rip-off beer and taking a pull from the can, "from Lesbia's sparrow onwards."

"But it's the scale of the thing under modern conditions," pursued Lockley. "The demand for pets is so colossal now that it often comes close to exhausting the available supply and damn nearly brings the species on to the danger list."

"It can have the opposite effect too, you know," replied the undemonstrative and fair-minded Peter Scott (who had once, when asked by a television interviewer the reason for his defeat in a yacht race, given the refreshing reply, "The other chaps were better than we were"). "Look at budgerigars. Restricted to Australia until the early thirties. Now there are thousands all over the place, purely as a result of the demand for them as cage-birds. And they thrive, by and large."

"Then there are zoos," went on Lockley, ignoring Sir Peter's rejoinder. "I don't mind a good zoo, but too many will try to acquire rare and delicate animals which they ought to know they can't keep healthy and happy. Same story—in effect they start dying before or on arrival. But with a zoo, it isn't what you see, it's what you don't see. Animal collectors for zoos go into jungles, rain-forests and so on, and offer the natives big money to catch animals alive. So what happens? The natives go off, savagely trapping and injuring, killing nursing females to take the young and all that sort of thing. A few animals survive the journey back; and the collector's as happy as the public who buy his amusing book or go to his zoo and can't read between the lines."

"All the same," answered Peter Scott, "as far as goodwill and interest on the part of the public goes, zoos have played a fairly significant part. Altogether, in terms of educating people, we've gained a hell of a lot since the turn of the century—look at leopard-skin coats and stuffed humming-birds on ladies' hats—but the trouble is we've lost more, simply on account of the human population explosion. Too many people, animals getting crowded out of their habitats—"

"And an ignorantly sentimental attitude, as I'm saying," insisted Ronald, leaving the helm for a moment to rummage for a banana in the deck-locker. "People like Adams represent animals acting as if they were humans, when actually it'd be nearer the mark to consider them as automata controlled by the computer they inherit in their genetical make-up. I mean—in goes the stimulus and out comes the reaction. Very often the person who knows more than anyone else about looking after an animal is the man who hunts it—you used to, as a young man, so did I—simply because he's not sentimental. I say, Peter, is that the Ravenglass estuary over there on the starboard bow?"

"Yes, that's it. You're pretty well on course, Ronald. Just a shade to the south and take her down to the mouth of the estuary, can you? We'll have to hang around a bit for enough water to take us in. Not too long, though—I think we'll be able to get up to the moorings in time for a jar at the Pennington Arms. Wind's a bit fresher now, isn't it? I reckon the tide's only just turned."

A wave struck the *Orielton*'s bow and burst with a *slock* and a fountain of spray. Peter Scott turned up the collar of his anorak and reached for his binoculars.

"I must say though," he said, scanning the sea reflectively, "I think that for ordinary, non-specialist people, a certain amount of anthropomorphism's probably useful in helping them to arrive at feeling and sympathy for animals—that's to say, readiness to put the good of a species, or even just the welfare of an individual creature, above their own advantage or profit. We can't all have scientific minds. I imagine your poetess friend Ruth Pitter would agree with that. John Clare, too—excellent amateur naturalist, quite without sentimentality; yet there's a lot of anthropomorphism in his nature poetry. It expresses affection, really. But another thing—I'm sure the old notion of 'God made man in His own image' has a lot to answer for. And it isn't only western civilization, of course, or ignorant urban populations. Look at your New Zealand Maoris, killing the giant moa for a thousand years until there weren't any left. It's time people started thinking of Man as one of a number of species inhabiting the planet; and if he's the cleverest, that merely gives him more responsibility for seeing that the rest can lead proper, natural lives under minimum control."

"Certainly we're the most destructive species, but *are* we the cleverest?" replied Lockley. "That's a very debatable point, I should have thought. Consider a migrant bird. It's as real as you or I or the Secretary of State for the Environment, and it breathes air and lives with five senses on this globe. It knows nothing whatever about Monday or Tuesday or clocks or Christmas or the Iron Curtain or all the things which govern human patterns of thinking. It has a consciousness of life on the earth which is completely different from ours—we call it instinct but it's every bit as efficient—more, if anything—utilizing winds, temperatures, barometric pressures, navigation, thermal currents, adjusting its numbers to the food supply, its prey and predators, in a way we ignorant humans still can't compete with."

"God might just as logically be a dog or an albatross," said Peter Scott, smiling, "or a tiger. Probably is. Setting aside that we find many living creatures beautiful—and heaven knows we can't afford to lose any beauty we've got left—it comes down to a matter of dignity, really, doesn't it—real dignity, I mean—sort of a Platonic idea, don't you think? A tiger presumably ought to have a reasonable chance of being able to approximate to an ideal of tiger and a sparrow to an ideal of sparrow; rats too, no doubt," he added rather bitterly, "on the Isle of Man, you know. Surely our part in that lot is to do what we can to see that animals live in a world where they can fulfil their various functions, insofar as that's consistent with our own reasonable survival and happiness?"

"Yes," answered Ronald, "and of course in the total, real world we and our intellects are superficial. The birds and animals *are* the real world, actually, tens of thousands of years of instinctive living in the past; and in the future they'll outlive our artificial civilization. Our intellects are just the veneer, the crust over our base instincts, but just now they happen to have a good deal of power in the world to control its direction, rather like the rudder on this boat."

He broke off, putting up his binoculars and gazing to port.

"Are my old eyes deceiving me, or is that something swimming over there? It's a seal, isn't it, Peter? Black and fairly large, anyway. I wouldn't have thought these were seal waters—could be in passage, I s'pose."

"That's no seal, Ronald," said Peter Scott, also focusing. "Take her over that way a bit. I can see whatever it is you're on to, but there's something else as well—something white. Odd-looking—could be a gull sitting on the water, but somehow I don't think it is. Better investigate."

Lockley opened the throttle, turned the *Orielton's* bows to port and sent her bouncing and bucketing over a choppy tide-race.

"My God!" said Peter Scott suddenly, "d'you know what it is, Ronald?"

"What?"

"Two dogs, swimming."

"What? Out here? Nonsense! You might as well say it's your Loch Ness monster."

"That's what they are, all the same—two dogs. One of them's about all in, by the look of it. We'd better try and fish 'em out. Poor devils! How the hell did they get out here? Speed up a bit more, Ronald, and go a shade further to port."

A minute or two later Sir Peter Scott, having stripped off his anorak and rolled up his sleeves, engaged a boat-hook in its collar and hauled on board the limp, deadly cold body of a black-and-white fox terrier. He laid it at Ronald Lockley's feet in the stern.

"I'm afraid that one's a goner," he said, "but the other's still struggling away over there, look. Can you bring her round again?"

The larger dog, which had no collar, was hauled aboard by Peter Scott with both hands and a certain amount of difficulty. As the *Orielton* gained way and once more headed south for the mouth of the estuary he dragged it, shivering and growling, into the deck-cabin and laid it on the floor.

"I'm not sure this terrier *is* done for, you know," said Ronald from the stern, running his hands over it. "It's got a fearful head injury from somewhere—God knows what did that—and it's about drowned, but I can feel its heart ticking still. If you'll take the helm, Peter, I'll try some respiration."

"It's half-frozen," said Peter Scott, running a hand over it as he settled in the stern. "We'd better try and warm it up on the engine."

"Well, first we must get it breathing. I can't understand this head wound. Look, those are stitches. Ever heard of brain surgery on a dog? Anyway, how on earth did the two of them get out here, do you s'pose? Could some swine have pitched 'em overboard?"

Before Peter Scott could answer, the dog in the cabin began to bark as though for its life against all comers. Its furious, defiant voice rose above the sounds of engine, wind and sea as though to quail and shake the orb. Oddly articulate and distinct it sounded, each bark beginning in a low, savage growl—"R'r'r'r'r'r—" which rose to a fierce "Owf!" of desperation and rage, repeated again and again. "Rrrrr-owf! Rrrrr-owf! Rrrrr-owf—rowf!"

"Rowf, rowf, eh?" said Peter Scott. "Sounds like something's spoilt *his* temper all right, doesn't it? Or scared the daylights out of him; or both."

"This one might just possibly come out all right, I'm beginning to hope," said Lockley, continuing to press rhythmically. "The heart's stronger, anyway." He addressed the limp body. "Come on now, me poor little darling—"

Three minutes later the fox terrier opened its eyes.

"Peter, I know it sounds damn silly," said Ronald, "but d'you know what would come in handy now? A hot water bottle."

"Right, I'll heat up some water. I dare say we can put it into this empty bottle, or just soak a towel in it, as long as it's not too hot. Meanwhile, keep the poor little beast warm under your coat and hang on to the tiller."

As Sir Peter ducked his head to enter the cabin, the black dog leapt at him, barking like Cerberus at the damned; and then, still barking, cowered back under the folding table. Peter Scott, with an air of paying it no attention whatever, lit the Primus and put on the kettle (which was on gimbals) warming his hands as the water heated.

"How's the terrier doing, Ronald?" he called.

"Bit better, I think. It's not breathing too well, but it'll probably pick up as it gets warmer. I say, have you spotted those people on the sand dunes over there? Four or five of 'em—couple of soldiers and one or two others. They seem to be waving at us, for some reason."

Peter Scott put his binoculars outside and his head after them.

"One of them looks like Jim Rose," he said, "the Drigg warden. That's the nature reserve all along those dunes, you know. It's not like *him* to go waving at passing boats just for the hell of it. Take her in a bit nearer, Ronald, can you? We've got time on our hands anyway, until the tide really begins to make. We might as well find out what's exciting them. Come to that, you could take her gently in until she grounds. Tide'll soon float her off the sand. She's got such a shallow draught that we'll easily get close enough for a word with Jim."

Peter Scott took the terrier from Ronald Lockley,

wrapped it in a squeezed-out warm towel and laid it on the cabin floor. The bigger dog stopped barking and began first to sniff at it and then to lick its ears.

"Will you be wanting any more of that beef, Ronald?"

"No, thanks."

Peter Scott picked up a knife, cut the last of the meat off the bone and made himself a sandwich. Holding it in one hand, he allowed the closed fist of the other to drop towards the floor and hang still, close to the terrier's head. After a long and suspicious pause, the black dog began to sniff it over; paused again; and at last gave it a cautious lick. Peter Scott, looking up, met the amused glance of Ronald Lockley in the stern.

"D'you think it's got a name?" he asked.

As soon as he spoke the dog began to bark again, but ceased as neither of the two men made the slightest movement or sign of alarm.

"I should think it must be called 'Rowf-Rowf,'" answered Ronald. "It's said nothing else for the last twenty minutes."

"Hallo, Rowf," said Peter Scott, scratching the dog's ear. "Have a bone."

In the chilly, grey light of the November morning, Mr. Powell sat at the kitchen table, stirring his tea and watching the starlings running on the lawn.

"Why don't you turn the light on, Steve?" said his wife, coming in with a breakfast tray which she set down on the draining-board. "There's no need to make it gloomier than it is, after all. Oh, come on, now, cheer up," she went on, putting an arm round his shoulder. "It's not that bad."

"Feel I've let you down," muttered Mr. Powell wretchedly.

"Course you haven't! Now you listen—"

"I still don't understand why they've done it," said Mr. Powell. "I suppose I just can't have filled the bill for some reason or other. I was so keen at one time, too. Wanted to be a good bloke and all that. I just don't seem to have been able to manage it."

"Now look, don't upset yourself any more, dear. They're

not worth bothering about, those people, honestly they're not. I reckon they've treated you worse than a dog. Why not forget about it? It'll all come right, you see; and we don't have to move just yet."

"Is there anything left on that tray that I can give the monkey?" asked Mr. Powell, looking over his shoulder at the draining-board. "He seems a bit better this morning."

"The monkey, dear—that's the only thing that does worry me a bit," said Mrs. Powell. "I mean, they're not going to like it, are they, if they find out you took it away? Why not go in early on Monday and put it back? No one'd know, only that old Tyson, and then you could—"

"I *won't* put it back," said Mr. Powell, "and they can think what they like."

"But it's only one animal, dear, out of thousands. I mean, what's the good, and they've got to recommend you for a transfer—"

"I can't explain. It's not for the monkey's good, it's for my good. I *won't* put it back. I'm going to keep it."

"But it doesn't belong to us. It's their property."

"I know. Their property." Mr. Powell paused, drumming his fingers on the plastic table-top. "It's not—any more than I am. Sandra, love, I've been thinking. We don't want to leave here, do we? I mean, another move for Stephanie, maybe back to some big town, and she likes it here so much. It's done her good. The doctor was only saying—"

"But, Steve, wait a minute—"

"No, hang on, sweetheart." Among those who loved him and meant him well Mr. Powell could rise, on occasion, to a certain authority—even dignity. "This is what I want to tell you. I'm seriously considering looking for a different sort of job altogether, somewhere round here, so that we don't have to leave."

"You mean, not laboratory work at all?"

"That's it. It'll mean a financial drop, I know that, but all the same I'd like to give it a whirl. Could be teaching, might even be farming. I'm going to talk to Gerald Gray

at The Manor—he knows a hell of a lot about the neighbourhood—"

"It's a big step, Steve—"

"I know that all right. In jee-oppardy." She laughed.
"Just let me go on thinking about it, will you? I won't do
anything pree-cipitate, I promise," added Mr. Powell, as
though there might be some danger of his being deposited
at the bottom of a tank. "It's just—well, I don't know—
it's just that I feel, well, sort of that everyone's—well,
everyone's sort of entitled to their own lives, sort of—"
said Mr. Powell, frowning and stabbing with a wet fore-
finger at the crumbs on the table. "Anyway, not to worry."
He got up and kissed his wife affectionately. "How's
Stephanie this morning?"

"She seems a bit under the weather," said Sandra, still
in his arms. "She ate her breakfast all right, though."

"I'll go up and read to her," said Mr. Powell. "I'll just
see to the old monk—"

"You go on up, dear. I'll feed the poor little feller. No
honest," said Sandra, as Mr. Powell hesitated. "I'm going
to get really fond of it. Oh, Steve," and she put her arms
round his neck again. "I'll back you up, darling, honest
I will. I think you're terrific! Straight up, I do."

Mr. Powell, filled with the sustaining notion that he
was terrific and pondering on whether it would be feasible
to keep his establishment together while he took a teacher's
training course, went upstairs.

Stephanie, whose bed was by the window, was looking
out at the bird-table and the lake beyond. As her father
came into the room she put a finger to her lips and pointed
at the nut-bag hanging outside. Mr. Powell came to a stop,
craning his neck. Seeing nothing remarkable, he smiled
at her, shaking his head.

"Nuthatch, daddy, but he's gone. And a scobby."

"Scobby—what the dickens is that?"

She laughed. "It's what Jack Nicholson calls a chaffinch."

"Is it, now? Well, I never heard that before. How're you
doing, pet?" He sat down on the bed.

"Sort of—it does—sort of hurt a bit this morning.
I expect it'll be better later."

"Like one of your pills?"

"Yes, please."

He emptied the tumbler and fetched fresh water and the pill-bottle. She swallowed, grimacing, and then began to brush her long hair, first one side and then the other.

"Daddy, you know—" She paused, again looking out of the window.

"What, love?"

"I *am* going to get better, aren't I?"

"Course you are! Good grief—"

"It's only that—oh, daddy," and she suddenly looked up, flinging back her hair and putting down the brush. "I sometimes wonder whether they won't be too late for me. They won't find out in time."

"Yes, they will," answered Mr. Powell with laudable conviction.

"How d'you know?"

"They're finding out more and more every day." He took the dying child in his arms, laid his face against hers and rocked her to and fro. "They're doing masses of experiments all the time, they know more than they've *ever* known—"

"How do they find out with the experiments?"

"Well, one way they can find out a whole lot is to make an animal ill and then try different ways to make it better until they find one that works."

"But isn't that unkind to the animal?"

"Well, I suppose it is, sort of; but I mean, there isn't a dad anywhere would hesitate, is there, if he knew it was going to make you better? It's changed the whole world during the last hundred years, and that's no exaggeration. Steph, honest, love, do believe me, I *know* they're going to be able to put you right." He rumpled her hair affectionately.

"Oh, daddy, I've just *brushed* it!"

"Oops, sorry! Well, if you can complain you must be feeling better. Are you?"

She nodded. "Will you read to me now?"

"I surely will. *Dr. Dolittle's Zoo.*" He picked it up from the bedside table. "You know, there's only a bit of this left. We shall finish it this time. D'you want to go straight on with the next one, *Dr. Dolittle's Garden?*"

"Yes, please."

"O.K. Now, where had we got to?"

"Tommy Stubbins and the others had gone to talk to the Doctor about old Mr. Throgmorton's will."

"Oh, yes. Right, make yourself comfortable. This is Tommy Stubbins talking to the Doctor.

" ' "Now, don't you see, Doctor," I ended, showing him the scrap of parchment again, "it is practically certain that when this piece is joined to the rest that last line will read 'an Association for the Prevention of Cruelty to Animals,' or some such title. For that is the cause in which this man had already spent great sums of money while he was alive. And that is the cause which the wretched son, Sidney Throgmorton, has robbed of probably a large fortune. Doctor, it is the *animals* who have been cheated."

" 'We all watched the Doctor's face eagerly as he pondered for a silent moment over my somewhat dramatic harangue.' "

"What's a harangue?"

"Well, a harangue," said Mr. Powell, "it's sort of—well, if I make a very intense, excited sort of speech, about animals or something—"

Gripped by a searing cold which seemed to enclose him as a spider's web a fly, Snitter soared and circled slowly, wings outspread in a bitter, windy sunset. There was no stopping, no descending. Like a leaf spiralling above a drain he turned and turned, himself motionless yet borne on towards some terrible, still centre. And here, he now perceived, stood Mr. Ephraim, killer and victim, slapping his knee and calling to him without a sound in the freezing silence. Behind him, one on either side, stood Kiff and the tod; while far below, the pewter-coloured waves crept stealthily down the wind.

His eyes were filmed with ice and, now that he knew that he was dead, he peered through it, without fear of falling, at what lay beneath him in the twilight. The world, he now perceived, was in fact a great, flat wheel with a myriad spokes of water, trees and grass, for ever turning and turning beneath the sun and moon. At each spoke was an animal—all the animals and birds he had ever known—horses, dogs, chaffinches, mice, hedgehogs, rabbits, cows, sheep, rooks and many more which he did not recognize—a huge, striped cat, and a monstrous fish spurting water in a fountain to the sky. At the centre, on the axle itself, stood a man, who ceaselessly lashed and lashed the creatures with a whip to make them drive the wheel round. Some shrieked aloud as they bled and struggled, others silently toppled and were trodden down beneath their comrades' stumbling feet. And yet, as he himself could see, the man had misconceived his task, for in fact the wheel turned of itself and all he needed to do was to keep it balanced upon its delicate axle by adjusting, as might be necessary, the numbers of animals upon this side and that. The great fish poured blood as the man pierced it with a flying spear which exploded within its body. The striped cat melted, diminishing slowly to the size of a mouse; and a great, grey beast with a long trunk cried piteously as the man tore its white tusks out of its face. Still on towards the wheel he circled, and between him and the wheel Mr. Ephraim called him silently to fellowship with the dead.

Suddenly the whole vast scene began to crumble and gradually to disappear, like frost melting from a window-pane or autumn leaves blowing—some, others and more—from trees on the edge of a wood. Through the growing rents and gaps in the vision he could glimpse wooden planking and smell—for of course, it had been an olfactory as well as a visual apparition—oil, tar and human flesh. The appalling cold, too, was slowly breaking up, penetrated by needles of warmth as birdsong pierces twilight.

Whining with pain and the shock of return, Snitter struggled, fluttering eyes and nose to admit incomprehensible smells and images. Relapsing into darkness, he felt himself nevertheless once more drawn upward, as though out of a well. The pain, as feeling was restored to his numbed limbs, seemed unbearable. The wheel, the sky and the sunset were nearly gone now, faint as an almost-vanished rainbow, giving place to smells of canvas, rope and a salty wind that blew and blew. Someone was scratching his ear.

He raised his head and looked about him. The first thing he saw was Rowf, gnawing a large bone. He stretched out and gave it a cautious lick. It tasted of meat. Obviously they were both dead.

"Rowf, I'm terribly sorry. The island—"

"What about it?"

"The Isle of Dog. It wasn't true. I made it up to try and help you. It was made up."

"It wasn't. (*Runch, runch, crowk.*) We're going there now."

"What d'you mean? Where are we—oh, my legs! The bones are going to burst, I believe! Oh—oh, Rowf!—"

"This man isn't a whitecoat, that's what I mean. And he's not taking us back to the whitecoats, either."

"No, of course not. No more whitecoats now."

"He's a decent sort. I trust him. He pulled me out of the tank."

"Rowf, I saw—I saw a wheel— How do you know you can trust him?"

"He smells—well—safe. He's taking us to the Isle of Dog."

Outside the cubby-hole where they were lying, Rowf's man cupped his hands to his mouth and began shouting. Rowf, gripping the bone, got up and carried it as far as the man's rubber boots, where he lay down again. After a few moments Snitter followed, scrabbling off the warm cloth in which he had been wrapped. Everything was moving up and down in a most confusing way and the smell of oil lay over everything like a pungent blanket. Another man, talking gently to him, bent down to pat his head.

"My dam, these are real masters!" said Snitter. "I suppose *they* must be dead, too. I wonder why we're all rocking about like this? I shall have to get used to it. Everything's different here, except the wind and the sky. I hope that wheel's gone."

Rowf's man stopped shouting and was answered by another voice from some distance away. Rowf had put his front paws up and was looking out in the same direction as the man. Trying to join him, Snitter, still half-numbed, stumbled and fell back, but was at once picked up and held in his arms by the man with glasses who had patted his head.

There were the waves—white, sharp chips like broken plates—and beyond, not very far off, sand, blown dunes and the long spikes of marram grass blowing, blowing against the sky. There were men, too; a little group on the sand, and one of them down on the water-line, shouting to Rowf's man.

"Oh, Rowf, look, two of them have got brown clothes and red hats!"

"It doesn't matter any more. We're all right with this man. We're safe."

"I've never heard you say anything like that before."

"Well, you have now."

There was a gentle scraping, a slight lurch and then everything stopped rocking and became still. Rowf's man climbed over the side into the water and began splashing away towards the sand-dunes.

"Why's one of those men lying down on the sand like that?"

"Which one? Where? Oh!—"

Snitter stared and stared, waiting for the figure to disappear. It did not. Rowf's man, wading away, passed between them. When he had gone by, the recumbent figure was still there, and in that moment saw Snitter; and called him by name.

Snitter went over the side in a welter of waves and seadrift, Rowf barking, gulls swooping and the voice calling from beyond a white foam of rhododendrons all in bloom. And as the morning steals upon the night, melting the darkness, so his rising senses began to chase the ignorant fumes that had so long mantled his clearer reason. Water prickling in the ears, and long strands of brown, crinkled weed slippery under the paws. Snitter shook himself, ran up the beach like a streak of quicksilver and found himself clasped in the arms of his master.

Even Shakespeare, with all his marvellous achievements at his back, apparently felt unequal to depicting the reunion between Leontes and his Perdita, whom he had believed lost and mourned as dead. He showed better sense than his critics. So forgive me—I make a broken delivery of the business on the sand-dunes at Drigg. I never heard of such another encounter: a sight which was to be seen, but cannot be spoken of. They looked as they had heard of a world ransomed, or one destroyed. A notable passion of wonder appeared in them, but the wisest beholder could not say if the importance were joy or sorrow.

I have often thought (and this is me again now) that it is strange that no event or happening, however marvellous or splendid, can transcend the limits of time and space. They were hours and minutes that Leander spent with Hero, and certain musical notes necessarily comprised the song the sirens sang. The finest wine can be drunk only once; and the more words that are used to describe it, the sillier they sound. But perhaps, as Major Awdry would no doubt maintain, an animal living entirely in the immediate present (and believing himself dead) might feel the tide of joy even more intensely—if that were possible—than his master (who knew he was alive).

As Mr. Wood's tears began to fall upon Snitter's lifted face and slobbering tongue, Peter Scott, John Awdry and the others turned aside and strolled up the beach, looking out to sea and talking with careful detachment about the tide, the *Orielton*'s draft and the Ravenglass anchorage.

Now I saw in my dream that they had gone only a very little way when they were ware of a foul limousine coming to meet them across the lea. Bumping along the track, it made a slow course among the marram grass and came to a halt not far from where Mr. Wood was holding Snitter in his arms. In the back were seated the Right Hon. William Harbottle and the Under Secretary.

His companions turned to rejoin Mr. Wood and the Secretary of State got out of the car and also approached him.

"Good morning," he said, as Mr. Wood looked up. "You must be one of the splendid people who've helped to capture these dogs at last. I'm very grateful to you, and so will many other people be, I'm sure."

Mr. Wood gazed at him with a bewildered air, like a man interrupted in prayer or the contemplation of some splendid painting.

"Major," said Hot Bottle Bill, turning to John Awdry, "can we get this unpleasant business over at once? Shoot the dog as quickly as you can, will you, please?"

"This is the dog's lawful owner, sir," said Awdry. "In all the circumstances—"

"The dog's owner? This is very unexpected news!" said the Secretary of State. "I thought the Research Station—Well, I'm sorry, but I'm afraid it can't make any difference. Will you please carry on at once and shoot the dog?"

"With the greatest respect, sir," replied Awdry, "I am not responsible to you, but to my battalion commander. I don't intend to shoot the dog and I will tell my battalion commander my reasons at the first opportunity."

Hot Bottle Bill was drawing breath to reply when a second figure appeared beside Major Awdry.

"I beg your pardon, sir," said Major Rose, "but I happen to be the warden of this nature reserve. No animal may be killed here, by law, and to bring in a firearm is illegal. I feel compelled to point out also that motor-cars, apart from my own, are not allowed and that you have no authority to have brought one in. I must respectfully ask you to leave at once."

Still Hot Bottle Bill stood his ground.

"I don't think you understand—" he began, when suddenly there appeared beside the two majors a third figure, terrible indeed, shaggy-haired, duffle-coated and armed with a camera as Perseus with the Gorgon's head.

"In case you don't know *me,* Secretary of State, I'm Digby Driver of the *London Orator*. If it'll save any time, I may as well tell you that if you have that dog shot Sir Ivor Stone and I will make your name stink from here to Buckingham Palace and the House of Commons." He paused, and then added, "We can, you know."

Hot Bottle Bill was not a British Cabinet Minister for nothing. For one long moment he contemplated the dauntless three upon the strand. Then he retreated to the car and could be seen telling his higher civil servant to go and deal with the matter.

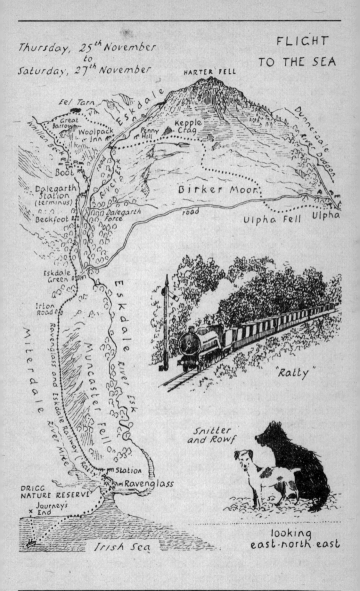

FLIGHT
TO THE SEA

Thursday, 25th November
to
Saturday, 27th November

HARTER FELL

Fel Tarn

Eskdale

Dunnerdale

River Duddon

Great
Barrow

Woolpack
Inn

Penny
Hill

Kepple
Crag

Whillan Beck

roads

Boot

River Esk

Dalegarth
Station
(terminus)

Dalegarth
Force

Birker Moor

road

Ulpha Fell

Ulpha

Beckfoot

Eskdale
Green

Irton
Road

Eskdale

River Esk

Miterdale

Ravenglass and Eskdale Railway ("Ratty")

Muncaster Fell

River Mite

"Ratty"

Snitter
and Rowf

Station

Ravenglass

DRIGG
NATURE RESERVE

Journey's
× End

looking
east·north·east

Irish Sea

The Under Secretary advanced with circumspection, evidently wondering whether it would be safer to tackle Titus Herminius or Spurius Lartius.

"Er," he began, "I—er—think—"

But we shall never know what the Under Secretary thought, for at that moment a white-fanged, snarling beast, black as a kodiak bear, hurled itself forward from behind Sir Peter Scott (even he jumped) and stood barking fit to defend the Bank of England.

"Rowf! Rowf-rowf! Grrrrrr-owf! Grrrrrr-owf! Rowf!"

The Under Secretary was not a senior civil servant for nothing. He hastened back to the limousine, which shortly reversed and went bumping away, with Rowf, still barking, in pursuit.

"Oh, boy!" shouted Digby Driver, literally dancing on the sand. "What a riot! And I've got two shots of Harbottle looking at the dog out of the window—panic all over his face—if only they come out!"

"I can't help feeling a bit worried," said Major Awdry. "I only hope to God we've done right. But to tell you the truth, I really felt so—"

"Don't worry about a thing!" cried Digby Driver, slapping him on the back. "Not a little thing! You were terrific, Major! What a fantastic turn-up for the book! Ever heard of the power of the press? Oh, brother, are you about to see it for real or are you? Sir Ivor'll give me the Japanese Order of Chastity, Class Five, for this, wanna bet? Old Harbottle, ho! ho!"

He capered among the *laminaria saccharina* as the tide came flowing in, but suddenly checked himself upon catching sight of the pale and sweating face of Mr. Wood, where he still sat at the foot of the dune.

"I say," he said, crossing quickly over to him, "how's it going? Are you O.K.?"

"Not too good, I'm afraid," gasped Mr. Wood, "but what's it matter? Oh, Snitter, Snitter, my dear old chap, there there, don't worry" (to be perfectly honest, Snitter did not look worried), "we're going home, boy, home! I'll look after you. We're just a couple of old crocks now, so you can look after me too. Who's this big, black fellow? This your mate, is he? Well, I dare say we can find a place for him as well. That's a good old chap, then! That's a good boy!" (Rowf stood like a dog in a dream as his ears were scratched by a second man within the hour.)

"I say!" called Ronald Lockley, who all this time had stuck by the *Orielton* and held her aground as the tide flowed, "I think it's time we were sailin' away. Are you fit, Peter?"

Sir Peter Scott, after a hurried exchange with Major Rose (in which the words "Pennington Arms" and "Saloon Bar" were clearly distinguishable), waded back on board, the screw went into reverse, the *Orielton* backed off the sand and the redoubtable two headed south for the mouth of the estuary. Major Awdry and the sergeant-major set off to rejoin their men, while Major Rose and Digby Driver helped Mr. Wood back to the Triumph Toledo.

"Er—I say," said Driver a little tentatively, as they hobbled along, with Snitter and Rowf following at their heels, "you know, you're going to need a bit of help when you get back to Barrow. I don't know whether you mean to go to the hospital or home or what, but—"

"Someone's got to look after these dogs," said Mr. Wood, resolutely planting one foot before the other. "I shall have to try to—"

"Someone's going to have to look after *you,* I reckon," said Driver, "or you'll wind up in the obituary column. I was thinking—I'll have to stay up here for a day or two yet. For one thing, I've got the story of all time to write —Sunday papers, too, I don't doubt. If you like, I'll move into your place and help you sort things out. That's if you don't mind a typewriter and a fair bit of telephoning— reverse charges, of course."

"I'd be deeply grateful," said Mr. Wood. "But are you sure?"

"Absolutely," said Driver. "To tell you the truth, I haven't felt so much on anyone's side for years. Not for years! As for that Secretary of State, well, he *will* be in a state by the time I've finished with him. He'll look sillier than that Boycott bloke, and that's saying something."

Mr. Wood resumed his place in the back of the car, Snitter on his lap and Rowf lying somewhat awkwardly

The Coniston Fells

at his feet. A silence of almost stupefied contentment fell, broken only by the mumblings and chucklings of Digby Driver at the wheel.

"Astounding Scene on Lakeland Beach," muttered Digby Driver. "Secretary of State Put to Headlong Flight. (Picture, exclusive.) But for the penetration and vigilance of the *London Orator,* a serious miscarriage of justice would have taken place yesterday on the sand-dunes of the Drigg Nature Reserve, where the so-called Plague Dogs, innocent four-footed victims of a bureaucratic witch-hunt launched from Whitehall—"

"Rowf?"

"What?"

"Did you want to stay with the man in the rubber boots?"

"Well—I don't know—well, I'd just as soon stay with you, Snitter. After all, you need looking after. He doesn't. And your man seems a decent sort too. I must admit I'd no idea there were so many. It's all different on the Isle of Dog, isn't it? Thank goodness we got there after all. I dare say I may be going to learn a few things."

"It's jolly being dead, isn't it?" said Snitter. "Who'd ever have thought it? Oh, Snit's a good dog! Come to that, Rowf's a good dog, too."

The beach is deserted now, save for a few gulls and a flutter of dunlins running in and out of the waterline. The breeze has fallen; the air is calm and on the level brine a single, sleek razorbill dives and reappears. The clustered blades of marram droop along the dunes, arc upon arc intersecting against the darkening eastern sky, still as their own roots in the drifted sand beneath. Farther off, where those roots have already changed the sand to a firmer, loamier soil, the marram has vanished, yielding place to denser, more compact grasses. The incoming tide, with a rhythmic whisper and seethe of bubbles, flows up the beach and back, across and back, smoothing and at length obliterating the prints of Snitter and Rowf, of Digby Driver and Sir Peter Scott, and finally even the indented troughs where the limousine reversed and went its way.

Before full-tide the gulls are gone, flying all together along the coast, gaining height as they turn inland above the estuary of the three rivers, soaring up on the thermals over Ravenglass, up over Muncaster Fell and the Ratty line winding away into Eskdale. From this remote height the sun is still setting, far out at sea beyond the Isle of Man, but below, in the early winter dusk, the mist has already thickened, blotting out the Crinkles and the lonely summit of Great Gable, the stony ridge of the Mickledore and the long, southern shoulder of Scafell; creeping lower, as night falls, to cover Hard Knott Pass, the Three Shire Stone and Cockley Beck between. Far off, to the east of Dow Crag and the Levers Hause, the lights of Coniston shine out in the darkness; and beyond, the lake glimmers, a mere streak of grey between invisible shores.